# A STORM OF SCREAMING SKULLS

BOOK ONE OF
BLACK REAPER'S DEATH SONG

I0738616

## DAMON ANGER

BONEFYRE BOOKS

A STORM OF SCREAMING SKULLS
Damon Anger
https://damonanger.com

Published by BONEFYRE BOOKS
https://bonefyrebooks.com

First edition 2021

Copyright © Damon Anger 2020

Damon Anger asserts the moral right to be identified as the author of this work.

ISBN 978-1-8383595-0-8

Cover art: Daniele Serra

Set in Minion and Dragon.

File under Fantasy : Grimdark

# A STORM OF SCREAMING SKULLS

# CONTENTS

# CONTENTS

# CONTENTS

# CONTENTS

N
STICKLEBACK BIGHT
PORT OF SHRIKES
SKIN CASTLE
KY
MOUNT KOMONYAMA
MOON TOWN
MOON SHRINE
THE MIRROR CASTLE
THE SHINES
THE S
HELLHAVEN
CASTLE MORTMANE
HOOK HARBOUR
THE TEMPLEDARK
MAIDENSTONE
STORM TOWN
STORM SHRINE
CASTLE BLOODFLOWER
KOBUTSUDEN
THE STUMP
GHOSTFINGER
GOLDENGATE
WOLF'S JAW
THE SUNSTORM CASTLE
SUN TOWN
SUN SHRINE
IRON TOWN
THE SI
THE OSSUARY
HANGMAN'S HEAD
THE SPIKE

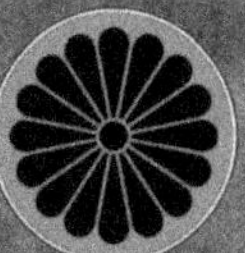

THE SHADOW CASTLE
YUKIDEN
THUNDERVOID
STONE BRIDES
CASTLE NIGHTFOG
LIZARD'S DEN
CREEPER'S COVE
THE VELVET CASTLE
SCALEPORT
SKULL CASTLE
THE MAD MARSHES
THE RIVER
THE BLOODTOOTH ISLANDS
THE SLAUGHTERHOUSE
THE RED ROCK
THE BAY OF BONES
THE ISLE OF GAUNTS
THE VALLEY OF FLIES
THE VILES
THE SHROUDED WOOD
SEPULCHRE
MANTIS COVE
THE JACKDAWS
THE NIGHTMARE CASTLE
GLUTTONPORT

"Death is a state of body, war is a state of mind."
–Hagmarrion, *The Ophidian Tryst*

# PROLOGUE

# MAZE AND MAUSOLEUM

*Boned like a snake, with a vampire's thirst.*

Sibilant words; his mother's words.

From madhouse to maze, night-flowered in a skin of dripping stings.

Snake-bastard, born to kill.

He loves the dolls she carved from bone, the moon washes over ancient towers and tombs, a splash of sperm, pale scorpions scalded by molten wax.

The stone door grinds open.

Up and up by firelight, the crypt of gargoyles, the outer portal. Letters set deep in black marble: SEK.

City streets. Snake-bastard, blood eye, shadow king.

One arm beneath her belly, warming the unborn. Gutters streaked with sewage, insects, the skulls of tiny birds. A drunk beggar with a broken mouth.

Not him. Only her.

A blur of moving heat, two pulses. His own heart hewn from ice.

Steel singing.

Snake-bastard, born to bite.

She blossoms like a midnight rose.


Corpse-bastard, brothel-born.

Fetch the master's supper, steaming soup blacked by blood-clots wrung from rats. The castle carapace groans, whispers.

Death rules the dark; graveyard, gallows, mortuary, shrines steeped in starlight. Corpse-bastard worships at them all.

The iron gate grinds open.

Spider-twitch in skullbone black, stench of worms in cold decay. The bride awaits within.

Blue gown, blue skin.

Beauty on a butcher's cart.

Then the hanging-tree, wolves rutting red-eyed in the bitter beyond.

Mining for meat by moonfall.

Scalpels, needles, saws, glister in the master's hand.

Up and up the bat-stained stoneway. Incense, red velvet, embers.

Sleep devours him whole.

Corpse-bastard, night-nurtured.

Dreaming of a palace in the snow.

# PART ONE
# THE DECIMATION

# THUNDERVOID

Her sister was already dead, body parts sown over bloody ice-fields, head spiked and haloed by hornets shining like white gold in the Fire Moon's feral rays. The last of the burning bats cindered into ash, a canopy of ancient bilewood boughs fusing in crippled knots above the girl-slave as she tripped fear-blind and naked across the mutinous forest floor.

A girl pursued by nightmare.

Three phantasmal riders, Shinojin, horses hung with jangling butcher-knives and fox-skull lanterns, hunters led by Raikon of Clan Akutenshi, Lord of Thundervoid, Emperor of Novalis, the one that men called Deathstar.

Raikon, skin of jaundiced ivory, lashing hair, shadow-dark, eyes flecked silver-gold, cruelly painted lips, cloak of dyed cat fur rank with writhing worms. Around his neck the Key of Bones, a disc of metal seeping cobalt light, spitting orgones that crackled like midnight fire; at his hip Tekizan, decapitator of foemen, blade hammered from volcanic steel in the days when Komonyama's forges sang with sparks.

Raikon, Deathstar, black impaler throned in frozen blood.

The girl-slave pissed as she ran, a hawk-owl ripped the guts from a baby hare that shrieked. Maggots churned through the undersoil.

*Flowers bloom in the night-land; inside each, a conspiracy of scars.*

At the emperor's flanks rode creatures of putrid bone, corpses clotted with grave-soil from the tombways far beneath snow-cowled Kyukiden, a pallid red gleam at play in voided eye-sockets. Frost-wind whined through rotten ribs, ghosting the girl-slave's screams.

She staggered, slipped. A sea of decaying flowers sucked her numb, thorn-raked legs into the ground where she saw, too late, a bridal pall of pearl-white web.

*A dark lover whispers your name; open your heart, and bleed.*

The gigantic spider erupted from its hole as a fireball burst high in the stratosphere, turning night to crimson day with a calamitous report followed by an obscene whirring and hissing. It grew rapidly in volume until, within seconds, a titanic asteroid the width of twenty slaughterhouses exploded directly above the woodlands, raining down a death-storm of rocks and flame engulfing all without reprieve.

A blast-wave of tortured sound swept across the demesne of Thundervoid for miles in all directions, as far north as Kyukiden and the glaciers beyond, as far south as the temple of Moon Sorrow Sukion, first of three sacred shrines pinning the spine of Novalis.

The bronze domes and towering stone pagodas of Kyukiden collapsed in an instant, taverns and temples and theatres and markets and brothels and butchershops all churned to debris and dust; city streets smeared with corpses of Shinojin and rabble alike, bodies crushed in mass extermination. Last to fall was the Camellia Keep, a second behind the rest; the ancestral seat of Clan Akutenshi reduced to a white marble welt, its secrets cast into eternity.

The tree-spiral looping the Moon Shrine splintered, uprooted in a vortex of equine and human skulls, basalt megalith and altar shivered into a million keening spikes, temple walls compressed to an emulsion boiling with the blood of its thirteen mavens, evaporated as they slept. Moon Town melted, three hundred and thirty-three warrior-priests of the Celestial Horde and those who served beneath, from blacksmith to boy-whore, buried in a seething shroud of liquid pain.

From city to shrine one hundred thousand souls expired in that single moment, leaving only a vitreous swathe of cauterized phantoms. At its epicentre the Imperial Forest burned long into the night, an epochal pyre for Emperor Raikon, the Deathstar annihilated by a blazing star of death.

# THE BLACK LAKE

The first scavengers reached the borders of Thundervoid just as dawn broke, out-riders from every low clan and cursed corner of the Shines – Rape Chainers, Wormhearts, Golden Maggots, Spectre Moths, Hag-Bleeders, and Split-Tongue Ravens. They swarmed like vermin upon the ruins of the Moon Shrine, scrabbling for newly-buried weapons, holy relics, baubles and coin. About ten miles ahead, across a vast razed terrain of black, semilucent stone-glass, a dozen rock-rangers from Clan Gomi reined up at the smouldering perimeter of what had once been the Imperial Forest. Each of their hooded horses sported a small banner of ebon silk decorated with a flesh-coloured sea-spiral, and the men's darkly burnished breast-plates were inlaid with the same motif in metal. Cinders, smoke and soot still swirled in the birdless red sky; nothing else stirred.

Their commander Jukon Gomi, second son of clan overlord Kamosukon Gomi, said: "The maven Magmatharion spoke truly; this comet appears as a judgement from the Three Sorrows, a sentence upon the cruelties of Emperor Raikon, delivered before the vassal clans and the commonfolk might rise up against us. If the emperor lives, we must proclaim his divinity; but if he is dead, then we must embrace divine design. Sota, Suga, Mata, Kuno, Bara – you will ride on to the snow-gates of Kyukiden, should they still stand; we will remain and scour the ashes of the imperial hunting ground."

The seven men rode slowly and with burgeoning horror through the choking stubble of charred tree stumps, a flotsam of clinker and incinerated arachnid chitin crunching underhoof, their mounts' teeth grinding with muted unease. At sun-wane they spied a black, half-erased human skull with one ridge of brow jutting above the detritus. They knew it was Emperor Raikon by the single ideogram still legible on the heat-blacked remnants of Tekizan, deathsword of Clan Akutenshi, and by the adamantine disc which lay amid a puzzle of cremated bones, unscathed by the meteor's infernal wrath. The Key of Bones was forged from a dense, unquantified metal, and held at its core a dark rune in the ancient script of the Shinojin, seamlessly meshed within the molecular fabric of its host.

Jukon found himself remembering the fable, told so often to him and his twin sister Juka by their mother, of how at the dawn of time and creation the seven keys of the Triad were mined from the belly of the moon by Sorrow Sukion, mistress of the frozen hells, smelted in the heart of the sun by Sorrow Hoshon, mistress of the fiery hells, and annealed in the eye of a hurricane by Sorrow Arashon, mistress of the liquid hells. Together the circular keys gave whoever wielded them control over the metacarrion, the invisible beings which infest all matter; each key held its own distinct power. The Key of Bones was said to grant its user mastery over the bones of the dead, but if that were true, Jukon thought, then Emperor Raikon had just joined the ranks of the rotting underlings he sought to master.

When the five out-riders returned it was nearing nightfall on the following day, and with them came only news of desolation. "The black lake of glass spreads for many miles and more," said Kuron Suga, "until Kyukiden's Way of Woe is within sight. But beyond that, the city is no more; nothing stands there but a haunted tombs of ice and shattered rock, devoid of all life. The corpses of both low and high clansmen, the carcasses of beasts and birds, are strewn along the way just as they were to the south. It is as you say, Lord Jukon; the gods themselves have cursed this place."

*Then my brother Vakon is as dead as the emperor,* thought Jukon, but dared not dwell upon it. "We must leave at once," he said. "There is no food here, no water, only rock and ashes and ghosts. What remains of Emperor Raikon is wrapped in these banners, and will return with us to the Mirror Castle; tonight, we sleep with the Brides."

# KYUKIDEN

Above, the city was a smouldering slurry of dust, ash and blood. Below, the tombs of fifty-six dead emperors were engulfed and crashed asunder when the vaults caved in, exposing centuried stones and bones to the raw red night. Below that, in a secret catacombs built by the first emperor Metakaikon, stood the only two survivors of Kyukiden.

"Make haste, Reaper," urged the maven Glitterax. "All recorded time has been compressed to this moment."

General Kuron Kirizono, known as Black Reaper, strained every sinew of his fearsome mass as he loaded the seventh and final coffin onto the floating catafalque, sending ripples across the brackish waters of the tarn. The cavern sat at the centre of the catacombs; a hail of displaced rock was falling from the faultline which had opened like a wound across its low ceiling. Clutching a stack of grimoires from his laboratory, Glitterax stumbled aboard the death-barge as Kirizono pushed it into motion with a single gigantic oar. They emerged into the subterranean river which led away from Kyukiden to the north-western shore just as an unfathomable avalanche of snow and ice burst away from the mountains far above, burying the ruined city to its eternal depths.

With only two burning torches on its prow as illumination, the catafalque drifted through never-ending night. Every mile of the hidden river had been mapped by the old emperors, who had carved the faces of mythical beasts and demons into its walls as if it were an aqueduct to the heart of damnation. Bat-roosts sprawled above, blind cave-fish churned the lightless waters.

After endless hours of silence, Glitterax said: "According to prophecy, the fall of the Akutenshi bloodline foreshades a return of ancient forces once suppressed by the light of the Triad; forces which drove us into exile from our homeland. These forces will find expression through the deeds of men. Kirizono; we alone now control the Seven Archangels, created by the emperor Metakaikon and his mavens to defend the realm against annihilation. But without the seventh key, and the deathsword Tekizan, and the one born to wield them, the Archangels will not rise. At river's end, in the Shadow Castle, our last agents of chaos stand ready, and you must lead them in a quest for our hallowed trinity: the key, the sword, and the boy."

Kirizono made no reply, but his silence stood as acceptance of his destiny. He had served Emperor Raikon for more than twenty years, leading countless raids against vassal clans accused of insurrection. He became known as Black Reaper after a campaign against Thundervoid's Root Skin clan, whose warlock stood charged with burning an effigy of the emperor and dousing it with pig's urine in an obscene rite of mockery and malice. Not only did Kirizono cleave the warlock from crown to groin with a single blow of his great sword Oshi, king of death, but he then ordered his inquisitors to round up every male of the clan, tar them with oily pitch, and immolate them in a firepit. It is said that Kirizono then pissed on their smoking skeletons, and his laughter echoed from wood to watching vale. This purge became known as the Reaper's Roast, and thereafter all Thundervoid feared his footfall.

Just before the river rose to flow into the northern sea, a man-made fork took the catafalque into a lake at the base of an excavation which extended high into the cliff face; structured on five levels and invisible to passing ships, this was the Shadow Castle. Kirizono and Glitterax were met on the shore by Nezumon Nano, commander of the Blue Dragon Hand, the Akutenshi's age-old company of chaos agents. Twenty-three in number including Nano, the Hand's covert missions of espionage and assassination on behalf of Emperor Raikon were only recounted in whispers; one rumour claimed that Nano, called Devil Bat by his men, had himself killed a Moon maven who rashly accused Raikon of blasphemy. The priest's corpse was found filleted and stuffed with horse dung, his excised bones wired together and strung up on a temple gate.

But now all of the Moon mavens were dead, the Emperor was dead, and Thundervoid was little more than a sarcophagus of blackened glass. Nano had looked out across the damned demesne from the cliff-tops, and despaired; Kirizono and Glitterax's arrival suddenly sired new hope.

"We thought every soul in Kyukiden lost," he said. "Sun, moon and storm star fatally vexed in mutual eclipse."

"Indeed," said Glitterax. "And when such a negation transpires it is said that a new, black planet will be born from an explosion of nefarious galaxies – a planet which will dwarf all others in both mass and malevolence, and which will be worshipped only by those whose harbinger is death. But come; Kyukiden's sacred secret, its most powerful creation, is safe and in our hands." He gestured at the seven coffins stacked on the barge. "It falls to us to secure the future of the Akutenshi."

One by one the heavy wooden caskets were debarked and hauled up flight after flight of stone stairs, until all seven lay in repose in the Shadow Castle's chancel. Candles were lit, some for illumination and some to disperse incense. Glitterax peered out to sea through one of the narrow window-slits; night was coming, the water black as brainsblood.

"I hope you like fish stew." The voice was Kirizono's, as deep and dark as the silhouette his immense figure was throwing across the chancel wall. "There's no fresh meat left for a thousand miles."

"Fish will suffice," the maven replied. "And we have enough for centuries."

"Let's hope our search doesn't last quite that long. But I'll need every one of the Hand to scour Novalis; are you sure you wish to remain here alone?"

"Alone? Hardly. The cooks, the fishermen, the brewers and the boilers are all at hand. The only other thing I need is books, and the castle library is overflowing. Besides; I cannot leave our treasures–" he glanced at the coffins "–unattended. Now go, and rest; your mission begins at sunrise."

Next morning Kuron Kirizono and the Blue Dragon Hand struck out in the Akutenshi spy-ship *Thunderwing*, bound for the first coastal village that might furnish them with horses. For three days they could see nothing on the shoreline but wreckage, carcasses and corpses. Once Kirizono caught sight of a dead whale floating far out towards the horizon; something appeared to be crouching atop its bloated belly, and for a moment he could have sworn it was a white cat.

It was near evenfall when *Thunderwing* gained the west coast of the Shines, and the Akutenshi voyagers finally encountered signs of life. They dropped anchor in a shallow bay ringed by a settlement of stone houses that stretched up and along the low-lying cliffs, and set ashore in two smallboats. Men emerged to meet them, warily clutching pikes.

"We come on the Emperor's business," said Kirizono to the first of them. He held up a cloth bag of golden coins. "Horses. And you will guard our ship until we return. If it is safe, one more bag."

"Stickleback Bight is at your disposal, general. Be an honour to serve the emperor," replied the man, twitching a wart-wattled eyelid.

Kirizono knew that this last sentiment was almost certainly a lie. Raikon had but recently raised imperial taxes all across Novalis, causing bitter dissent; feeling among the commonfolk suggested that the money was being squandered on profane pleasures, even the conjuring of demons. Whether rumours of the Deathstar's demise were also abroad, he could not tell.

Two dozen riders set out in the morning's pink light, taking the Cackmire Causeway south and peeling off in smaller groups along the way until only the Black Reaper, the Devil Bat and three others remained. As they crossed the border into the Templedark, wolves began to howl at distant stars.

Glitterax spent those days in study, gleaning stratagems from Baron Skropon's *Demonessence* and configuring mechanical torques from Sextarion the Sly's *Anatomy And Artifice*, formulating arcane protocols against the lowering threats of war. Soon the whole of Novalis would know of Emperor Raikon's death. And if the Akutenshi had been forsaken by the Three Sorrows in judgement of Raikon's sins, as he feared, then the clan's final expiation might only come from igniting a holy holocaust, the long-foretold blood crusade of the Seven Deadly Archangels.

# STATION NORTH

It was near midnight when the twelve rangers reached Station North, most remote outpost of Clan Gomi. The station was a simple granite ringfort with accommodations for up to fifty men perched in the foothills of the Stone Brides, the vertiginous mountain chain which stretched from the western shore of the Shines to its easterly border, seldom-glimpsed summits forever wreathed in storm-clouds. At its very rear the fort housed a concealed, winch-operated gate of solid steel grids a foot thick. This portal, known as the Hymen Gate, opened into a tunnel which ran for more than forty miles, straight through the base of the Brides and into Station South, perched on the rise of Mount Rottenstag. Wide enough for two horsemen abreast, the tunnel had taken a thousand men almost one hundred years to bore out, with most dying in the undertaking.

It was from Station North, two years before, that an uprising by the Rape Chain clan over grain was brutally suppressed by Gomi archers and swordsmen; Jukon himself had taken the head of the rebel leader, a vicious gash-gizzard by name of Grash, and presented it with honour to his father. Now, he had far graver news to report upon the morrow's meet.

Retainers attended them at the fort entrance, took their horses and ushered them to a mess where ale and hot food was at table. Jukon carried the banners containing the emperor's remains himself, securing them in his private quarters. Looking out from the chamber's sole embrasure he could see the distant ruins of Skin Castle, ancestral home of Clan Inoshi, silhouetted against the pale contours of the Fire Moon. Not far away a wolf howled, strangely comforting after the charnel silence of the Imperial Forest. Above hung the trinity of brilliant constellations which gave the Shines its name – the Axeman, the Crowned Vulture and the Bloody Dwarf, the last in mock of the cruel and stunted Emperor Baikon who centuries ago was eaten alive by mountain lions while hunting in the foothills. Legend says that the dwarf's guard stood by and watched as he was torn apart and devoured, glad to be rid of the deformed despot. Lions had long been hunted to extinction in Novalis, but old Clisterclot, Station North's gatekeeper, always swore that the wax-coated skull upon the top of his night-staff, blazing with a hundred wicks, belonged to none other than Baikon himself.

"We must keep the sacred key under guard at all times," Jukon told his men as they devoured the meat and drink, "say nothing, and show it to no-one. If the other six keys are lost forever beneath the dust that was Kyukiden, then this is all that survives of imperial power."

Andon Bara, his captain, said: "But who will now be emperor, if all the Akutenshi are dead? Raikon had no brothers and also lacked an heir, favouring sodomy above all other pursuits. Forgive me, Lord Jukon, but this is well known."

"The dead are immune to treason," Jukon replied, "and none are left alive who might gainsay it. The legend of the Deathstar will not be a pretty one; they say that thousands perished by his whim, from the old to those little more than babes, either hunted down for sport or impaled upon the hundred metal stakes which lined the Way of Woe–" *another kind of sodomy,* he thought "–and some believe that it was the seven keys that fermented his madness, whetted his lust for blood. Perhaps Raikon was truly the last of his kind; perhaps the age of emperors is truly at an end. Now rest; we leave at first light."

These last conjectures were a source of no little unease to the twelve rock-rangers as they slept, but it was Jukon himself who bedded down with the Key of Bones. That night he dreamt of the dead, of corpses which rose up to walk among the living even as the blackened, deliquescent flesh sloughed from their bones, a red pulse behind the membranes that filmed their eyes. One of them was Vakon, his beloved elder brother, and one of them was...

He woke with a breathless gasp of horror, wondering if proximity to the silvered disc had already begun to taint his mind. And yet his course was clear – the destruction of Clan Akutenshi meant that whoever held the seventh Key of Death controlled the destiny of Novalis, and soon that instrument of power would be safe within the dazzling walls of the Mirror Castle.

# CASTLE MORTMANE

Glowering over the third fork of the Crow River like a skewed rectangle of vast, time-deflowered gravestones, Castle Mortmane was the only man-made monument still standing in the western wilds of the Templedark. The shrine of Storm Sorrow Arashon lay many miles to the east, guarded by its garrison of fanatical warrior-priests, the land and settlements between them long ceded to the Hell-Claw, Rat Rock and Demon Red clans; only one wolf-pack of low clansmen, Crow River savages loyal to the outlaw reaver Tazon Ando, were in open contempt of the peace. And Tazon Ando was a hunted man.

And yet, as ruler of the Templedark and thereby protector of the Storm Shrine, Hikidashon Takasha was less concerned with Ando than with certain reports which reached his ears from the southern capital, Kobutsuden; reports of a heretic apostle rallying disciples to his cause, fast spreading the creed of a false deity amongst the rabble. Lord Hikidashon knew full well that poverty, illiteracy and superstition were powerful tools in establishing a system of religious control; this apostle was using those very same tools in an attempt to usurp the Triad, but with one difference – instead of threatening torture in the Three Hells, Slavos Sek was promising converts an ascent into a vale of paradise peopled by virgin whores.

"This Sek is truly a man of the times," said Hikidashon to Chikon, his elder son. "Dangerous, and gorged on desperation. I fear that in time he seeks to raise an army of zealots."

"To what end?" asked Chikon. He was just eighteen years of age, yet his fierce dark features were matched by his battle skills; he had already harvested more than twenty rebel heads. "Why should it concern us?"

"Think on it. The Viles borders us to the south; if it becomes a void of violence and rebellion, if Kobutsuden falls, then we will be among the first to wade in blood. War is a contagion which needs only feed upon itself. And Sek vies to become a figurehead for the infected."

"Then we will send agents of chaos; has the emperor been alerted to this heresy?"

"A rider was dispatched to Kyukiden twelve days ago," said Lord Hikidashon. "He never returned."

As a tainted moon rose over Castle Mortmane, its pink sclera veined with ruptures, Chikon joined his brother Gomon in the dank torchlit underbelly of the keep where they once played as children, and where they would now consort whenever matters of import or intrigue arose. It was also where Chikon proudly stored the skulls of his battle-victims, their heads defleshed and polished once they had been presented to Lord Hikidashon. Gomon's tastes also ran to blood but were somewhat more refined; his favoured pursuits involved servant girls, manacles and sharp objects.

"Father fears rebellion and war," said Chikon. "Everywhere."

"Who would dare to challenge the Akutenshi? And end up impaled by the Deathstar?" said Gomon. Chikon did not reply to that. He was examining the skull of a Crow River raider, fingering the ragged split where his sword Membaku, exploder of eyes, had cut through to the brain. He recalled his father's words concerning the rider. *He never returned.*

"Do you remember how Tazon Ando used to teach us swordplay down here, with those wooden swords?" said Gomon. "He was our father's finest soldier... can it really be true, what they say happened?"

"Father says it himself. Ando harboured unnatural desires towards our infant sister, Toka, which when discovered forced him to flee the castle by night, pressed hard by a valediction of blazing arrows. His treachery led to our mother's demise... and when I catch him, I will gladly take his head."

# THE MIRROR CASTLE

Jukon embraced his sister. Juka was almost as tall as him, her shiny nightshade hair grown far below the waist; her high-cinched gown was crafted from ivory moth's silk, signifying purity, but its structured breast-cones were embroidered, dramatically, with blood-red spirals which evolved from each tip.

"Is it true?" she asked. "Is the Age of Shadows now upon us?"

According to the scriptures of the Triad, the Age of Thunder – one thousand years of imperial glory – would be followed by a holocaust of darkness, destruction, and death. The maven Magmatharion had already counselled his overlord, Kamosukon Gomi, that the obliteration of Emperor Raikon could be read in only one way. Raikon was the bad seed, the catalyst of imminent entropy. Moon would eclipse sun, and both would implode in the storm of storms. But Jukon was less fatalistic.

"The future rests in our own hands," he replied. "Let us learn from Raikon's actions and their consequences. If the weight of empire is too great for one man, then why not spread it between seven? Let the remaining high clans forge a new path to governance, each with an equal voice."

"That sounds like an imperial council, but without an emperor at its head."

"If you like. But we wouldn't need an emperor; the seventh vote would decide all deliberations, no matter who casts it." He turned to gaze from the barred castle window, deeply recessed in a wall of stone twenty foot thick and panelled without by sheets of dazzling, highly polished metal. Was his idea so insane? He supposed they would soon find out.

"Our six guests and their entourages will soon start to arrive, assuming all riders survive to deliver their scrolls; first our neighbours the Hakamanko and the Takasha, later those of the midlands, the Kurotako and the Mizuno. But weeks may pass before those from the south, the Taiyo and Seikyo, reach our gates – if they can keep from each other's throat. Meanwhile news of the emperor's demise will surely spread throughout the low clans, and some may become emboldened; especially in the Viles, where the Mizuno are already over-run by rebels who constantly threaten the southern capital."

"They multiply like rats," said Lord Kamosukon, interjecting for the first time. He sat amongst the shadows, wrapped in a fur cloak; a prosthetic of sculpted wax inset with a glass eye covered the left side of his face from brow to chin, and his gaze seemed fixed upon a point somewhere beyond the walls. "And that's how Emperor Raikon treated them. What else should he have done?"

Neither twin replied; both knew that their father's sentiments regarding the rabble could not be swayed. It was during the suppression of an uprising by renegades from the Wormheart clan, a decade earlier, that Lord Kamosukon was ambushed along the Spectre Passway, an attempted assassination in which an arrow tipped with flaming pitch struck him in the face, broiling his left eyeball and scorching apart his flesh to the bone. Kamosukon's vengeance was unmatched in its ferocity. Fifty Wormhearts – leaders, followers, women, children – were seized and blinded, their eyeballs torn out with hot pincers and molten lead poured into the empty sockets setting their brains aboil. After the lead cooled and hardened, the fifty corpses were strung up on trees along the passway; white sea-spirals were painted on the dark metal circles where their eyes used to be. This reckoning became known as the Hundred Eyes of Justice, and the retelling of it quelled many an insurgent impulse.

Finally Jukon said: "Peace between the high clans, and just rule, will ensure prosperity in every demesne. I am entrusting Juka with preparations for the convocation; meanwhile a scroll has been sent to the thirteen mavens of Storms with news of the Moon Shrine's devastation, and a request to send priests to oversee its rebuilding, here in the Shines. I will ask each overlord to provide soldiers willing to don the mantle of the Celestial Horde, to shave their head and receive the mark of the moon, and to take the vows of the Triad. The power of religion is equal to that of the sword, if not greater; only fear of the Three Hells can truly keep the masses under subjugation."

"And what of Thundervoid?" his father asked.

"A wasteland of dead men and ruins. A lake of black glass surmounted by a tombs of ice. And beyond that, nothing but the precipice at world's end."

Jukon found himself reliving the discovery of the emperor's incinerated corpse, his soot-smirched sword, and the seventh key of the Triad. Although the keys were ceremonial, their powers only symbolic, it had long been rumoured amongst the vassal clans and the commonfolk that Raikon had made a pact with hell-demons, a pact sealed with the blood of his own subjects who were impaled or burned alive in blasphemous nocturnal rites. The hell-demons made real the powers of the keys, the rumours said; the Key of Bones, the Key of Shadows, the Key of Mayhems, the Key of Tears, the Key of Ashes, the Key of Venoms, and the Key of Voids, all seeded with lethal life. If such a thing could be true, then the judgement of the Three Sorrows was not merely retribution for earthly atrocities; it meant that Raikon's transgressions had seeded a cancer in the metacarrion, a degeneration which could lead to only one outcome – the dawn of the Age of Shadows. But it couldn't be true. *It couldn't.*

Later that day, still troubled, Jukon took himself to the castle library, where he consulted ancient grimoires in search of illumination; *The Skelos Of Cyphers* by Gammabarion the mad maven, *Worms Of The Moon* by Baron Sucax, *The Creed Of Banes* by Baron Alugor, and *The Black Psalter*, a book of the dead written long ago by hands unrecorded, each vellum page said to have been crafted from a single human foetus. The time-stained brittle parchments, bound in iron and leather, were inscribed with cryptograms, alchemical formulas and tables, complex astrological maps and anatomical charts, drawings of angelic and demonic beings, panoramas of the Three Hells, invocations and incantations for summoning, banishing, binding or becoming, and dozens of other charms and spells of which Jukon had no need or understanding. He read in them only an arcane poetry of despair which, like the religious scriptures, expressed little more than man's refusal to embrace negation. He could perhaps admit the concept of divine retribution or fate, yet it seemed beyond reason that such power could be harnessed by a mortal.

Exhausted, Jukon Gomi left the library in darkness, took to his bed, and slept without dreaming for a night and half a day.

# THE SLAUGHTERHOUSE

Wrought from sheer black iron and raised high upon a ragged red spume of primeval porphyry thrown up from the Bay of Bones, the Slaughterhouse stood at the epicentre of the Bloodtooth Islands, demesne of Clan Kurotako. From the castle's tallest spire a vast silver ensign rippled in the wind, its fabric embroidered with a black cephalopod within a circle, while far below a fleet of some hundred ships lay at anchor, most of them fitted for war. *Turds in a latrine,* thought the maven Chromocrax as he peered down at them from his sky-high laboratory loop, *tiny toys for filthy infants.*

Chromocrax's disdain for conventional warfare was reflected in the clandestine experiments he undertook on behalf of his overlord, Sadogashon Kurotako. The maven was something of a toy-maker himself, but his inventions were designed for neither battle nor child's play; they were gynoids, artificial human females with flesh of malleable wax, bones of jointed metal, and entrails of intricate, noiseless clockwork. One of them, named Lady Burnbolt by her creator, stood motionless in the candlelight shadows behind him; her face was veiled, and she appeared to be heavily pregnant, as if such a thing were possible, beneath a gown of white velvet patterned in scarlet with the alchemical symbol for mercury.

"Send word to Lord Sadogashon," Chromocrax said to his apprentice, a studious youth by name of Kargon. "Lady Burnbolt is ready to meet her master."

With a curt bow Kargon turned and made his way to the laboratory's plated portal, past rows of synthetic body parts, gnarled human embryos in jars of milky fluid, unfurled anatomical charts weighed down at the corners by cog-wheels, keys and other metal scraps, and an extensive rack of vitriols and phials marked with the black skull of danger. Before unbolting the door he glanced up, as always, at the desiccated creature displayed above its lintel, a würmling captured by Lord Sadogashon in the Mad Marshes and presented to the maven as token for his dark service. It was an act which had almost started war with Clan Hakamanko, rulers of Lizard's Den, for the Kurotako hunting incursion was outside of law; the würms, or marsh dragons, were an indigenous species finely balanced on the edge of extinction. Very few had ever bred in captivity, and their persecution was prohibited under pain of death. The issue was only resolved when Lord Sadogashon offered the hand in marriage of his younger daughter, Suna, to Lord Hebon Hakamanko's only son Hekon – a significant sacrifice, since the boy was a hunchback whose hobbies were said to include vivisection, taxidermy, and the mass incineration of insects.

Passing beneath the würm with a shiver, Kargon descended the cracked spiral stairs of the alchemist's tower and made his way across the precarious sky-walk which extended to the main keep of the Slaughterhouse. Hundreds of feet below he could see waves crashing against the Red Rock; all around in two eccentric rings lay the smaller islets which were home to Kurotako retainers, among them the Shark White clan with salt-scoured teeth filed down to lacerating points, ferocious and loyal to the last bite. One outcrop was surmounted by a gibbet, wider than a ship, and the corpses of pirates swung from it.

Just then the castle bell erupted into discord, its clangour urging Kargon to clap hands over ears. A black barge was approaching, one of two rusted chain-ferries that ran between the Red Rock and the shore, where the Crow River bled into the Bay of Bones. It carried an emissary mounted upon a roan courser, his banner, breastplate and helm blazoned with a flesh-hued helix, both horse and rider caked in crusts of dried mud.

"I bear a missive for Lord Sadogashon," he announced. Clansmen led his horse to the castle gates, the portcullis was raised; he dismounted once inside and was escorted to the sanctum of the keep.

Sadogashon Kurotako was a man of some fifty years, the shadow-dark hair of his race turning to white, his short beard turned already. Behind him stood his first daughter, Soma, accompanied by the clan's bane virago Lady Nightstorm. Armed guards flanked the chamber, which was draped with silver banners. He read the scroll in grim silence, and then announced: "The judgement of the Three Sorrows has been levied upon Novalis. Emperor Raikon is dead. The emperor's clansmen are dead; the emperor's councilmen are dead, including our own Lord Mashon, my cousin; the people of the emperor's city are dead; the people of the emperor's demesne are dead; Clan Gomi holds the emperor's remains. The lords of the high clans are summoned by convocation to the Mirror Castle, under flag of truce; we set sail at first tide."

# KOBUTSUDEN

A black flag streaked with silver thunderbolts flew high above the imperial Winter Palace for the first time in five years, while within the ornate walls a division of the local guard struck a slow, unfaltering drum-beat which continued through the day without surcease. This time the flag did not signal that the emperor was in residence; it signalled his death. During his long absence, the southern capital Kobutsuden had slipped into an increasingly precipitous decline. Most of Emperor Raikon's resources had been diverted to his remote northern stronghold, Kyukiden, from where tales of cruel debauchery and perversion emanated and amplified, spreading through Novalis like a lascivious disease. Few in the southern city mourned his passing.

"Good riddance to the cunt," said Gorn of Gluttonport, downing the dregs of another ale. He was sitting in a corner of the Dead Dog, a dive in Kobutsuden's lower end, the slum district known as Swilly Town. Gorn was a sword-shifter, a trained mercenary at the service of whichever clan paid the most coin; his most recent employment had been with the Mizuno, helping to hunt down and slaughter a gang of Maw Fetter raiders. He had once been a member of Raikon's guard, just like the two soldiers who sat opposite, across the mob of unwashed carousers, whores, drug-dealers and beggars who populated the inn. They were watching Gorn and his companion, Kesh, but Gorn was sure they couldn't hear his conversation. Someone, most likely a legless beggar, had left a twist of fresh excrement on the floor; the carousers simply made a circle around it and carried on drinking.

"Farewell to the emperor of buggery," said Kesh, reinforcing Gorn's sentiment. Kesh was also a sword-shifter, not trained like Gorn, but well versed in combat; under the name Mastiff he had fought for a season in the Grinding Pits, where wagers were placed not only on the winners of death-fights, but on which body parts would be hacked off first. His hand shook as he drank; pit fighters were dosed with firefinger, a drug to enhance speed and aggression, and he found the habit impossible to break.

"There'll be another one taking his place soon enough," said Gorn. "Probably even worse than him."

"I heard that the whole lot of Raikon's clan were wiped out, so fuck knows where the next emperor'll come from. With any luck, there'll be a nice long war."

"Makes you wonder what all these cunts will do now," said Gorn, gesturing towards the two guardsmen, who looked as drunk as he was. One of them stared back hard, then nudged the other. Then they both got up and started across the room, hands on sword hilts, pushing patrons aside. Gorn also rose, smiling, hands raised in appeasement. He never wanted to see the palace dungeons again; that would mean only slow death from beatings, thirst and starvation.

The first soldier began to draw his sword, then suddenly slipped on something soft and wet, falling hard onto his back; as the other looked down at him in bemusement, Gorn sprang forward and smashed his fist into the side of the man's head. He collapsed on top of the first guard, who struggled to free himself. Gorn and Kesh were gone before either soldier could get up again, out into the street and slipping away down the nearest alleyway.

"Did you see that?" laughed Gorn. "I hit the bastard so hard his eyes were farting."

Kesh doubled up at the thought, then steadied himself against the wall. "Cashjoy House?" he asked.

"Cashjoy House," Gorn confirmed, and they set out in the direction of the brothel.

Halfway there they were confronted by a procession of Vigilants, members of a religious cult attired in hooded vermilion robes blazoned with the sigil of a golden eyeball fringed in flames, signifying their devotion to a single deity known as the Holy Eye. Vigilism had arisen in the power void left by Emperor Raikon's abandoning of Kobutsuden, attracting many disaffected from the Triad, its human sacrifices and sodomite priests. New disciples included hardened fighters from among the unruly tribes of the Viles, mainly from the Kill-Claw, Blood Eagle, Grey Ghost and Smash-Bones clans. Triad law-makers viewed the Vigilants with accelerating outrage; a clash was coming.

Like a many-eyed snake the Vigilant procession wound its way further into the bowels of Swilly Town, twisting through a matrix of slop-sullied, constricted streets until finally halting outside a butcher's shop hung with the half-rotted heads of horses, goats and pigs; trays piled deep with darkening offal sat in the shop's sole window. The butcher, an obese man known as Chattox, ushered the cultists inside one by one. Stone steps stained with animal blood led down from the shop's rear into a candle-lit subterrain where Chattox regularly slaughtered livestock by hammer, knife, hatchet and hook, and here the twelve Vigilants congregated.

They were faced by a tall figure whose purple robe marked him as an Optic, the rank given to apostles of the Holy Eye. He stood before the marble killing-slab which now served as an altar, arms outstretched, eyes shining from a face taut with pallid, pock-marked skin.

"Our coven is convened to celebrate the death of Raikon, lord of the Shinojin," the Optic pronounced. "He was their emperor, but never ours. For the mortal crimes of murder, sodomy and black magic, Raikon was struck down by the hand of the Holy Eye; his people, his city, his lands, his pagan shrine were obliterated by divine fire and fury."

"The Holy Eye sees all," chanted the disciples.

"The Holy Eye is the fire that purges, the sword that dismembers, the light that blinds; the iniquitous shall perish by His wrath, and we are the earthly instruments of that wrath."

"The Holy Eye sees all."

"Remember the man who worshipped false gods; his tongue was cut away and fed to curs. Remember the man who revelled in fornication; his privy parts were cut away and fed to swine. Remember the man who revelled in intoxication; his arteries were cut open and drained of poison blood. Only the pure may attain paradise. The Holy Eye sees all."

"The Holy Eye sees all."

*Perhaps not all,* thought Flamon Neko even as he mouthed the refrain, fingering the dagger strapped around his chest beneath the vermilion robe. Neko, also called the Cave Cat, was the first agent of chaos sent by Clan Takasha, rulers of the Templedark, to infiltrate the Vigilants; his mission was to spy, report and, when called upon, to foment dissent and carry out clandestine assassinations. And Flamon Neko had never failed a mission.

Joining the ranks of the Holy Eye was not difficult; Optics were to be found on most street corners of the lower city, preaching to any who would listen. Though it was a blasphemy punishable by death to deprecate the Triad, these purple-robed agitators were careful to speak in a coded tongue of impending holocaust. They blamed the Shinojin for societal decline, but never any by name – at least in public. Flamon soon learnt that in the secret spaces where covens convened, the Vigilants promoted a venomous agenda; disciples were in effect being trained as ascetic insurgents in an impending revolution against the prevailing hierarchy and its religious order, and fighters from vassal clans in revolt were particularly welcomed for their tested battle skills. This ever-expanding base, whose simmering violence was veiled in the trappings of piety, was controlled by the Primal Optic, a mysteried individual known as Slavos Sek. Flamon had not yet identified Sek or ascertained the source of the organisation's funding, the financial support which provided fine robes and bread for the disciples, but he knew that the death of Emperor Raikon Akutenshi meant that the cult's momentum was likely to remain unchecked; and that his overlord, Hikidashon Takasha, would be keener than ever to see its demise.

After the coven dispersed, Neko shouldered his way through Swilly Town's human morass until he came to an old teetering house in a dead end lane, not much wider than three people and set back from the alleyway. The building's façade was almost entirely filled by a cracked and crooked door, painted in a deep purple and decorated with a stencil of two converging thunderbolts, a warning that the house and its occupants were under protection of the Winter Palace. He knocked, twice, and waited.

"Come inside, boy."

The voice was female but fissured by age, ripe with rot. Flamon edged into the guttering gloom. The chamber stank of decaying vegetation, unwashed skin, excrement. A hunched figure was sitting in its centre, surrounded by the paraphernalia of poisons. Behind her, a white-feathered ghost raven was chained to its perch; it cawed, twice, as he approached. He could see her face now, creviced and mottled and clustered with wens, the rheumed eyes like dull distorting mirrors.

"You are the hag Gorgongrone?" he asked. "Once war-witch to Emperor Bansaikon Akutenshi... the same Gorgongrone who made Tatson Mizuno and a hundred of his men fly from the battlements of the Nightmare Castle?"

"The same. How can I please you?"

"I too wish to see a man fly," said Flamon Neko.

The order of death had arrived in the night, its intent designated by a black waxen seal; upon the scroll was written nothing but a name: *Slavos Sek*. Flamon knew that knifing Sek in some back alley would not suffice for his overlord's purpose; fear and chaos could best be sparked by spectacle. Sek must appear to commit suicide, his self-negation a public repudiation of the Holy Eye.

After the hag passed him her concoction, which she called flace – a distilled ferox of henbane, destroying-angel and meconium – Flamon returned to his lodging above the Twin Stumps tavern, where he reflected upon the legend of The Flocking, a decisive moment in the civil conflict which had flared, four decades earlier, between the Akutenshi and the Mizuno. Tatson Mizuno had unwisely risen against the emperor after an incident in which his cousin was burned alive in a temple; the emperor's response was to lay siege to the Nightmare Castle, centuried fortress of the Mizuno clan. But Bansaikon Akutenshi was not a man of great patience. He soon called upon Lady Gorgongrone, his bane virago, to stage an intervention. It is not recorded how Gorgongrone entered the castle – some say she took the form of a bat – but once within its walls she was able to infuse the entire water system with her mind-twisting deliriant.

The next day, at dawn, Lord Tatson was seen standing atop the incubus gargoyles that surmounted the castle wall; he was flanked on either side by dozens of his generals and retainers, and all stood raving with arms outstretched like armoured wings. Upon Tatson's cry of ecstasy, he and his men leapt as one into the air, expecting to soar above the sun and rain down dragon-fire upon their foe. Within seconds they had plummeted straight into the castle moat, where they were impaled upon the metal spikes affixed there on Tatson's own orders. The legend told that a great plume of blood spurted up from the perforated bodies, then fell like red morning mist upon the emperor and all his forces. Bansaikon returned to Kobutsuden with Tatson's head, which was displayed in a beribboned bird-cage atop the palace gates until it putrefied, earning him the posthumous epithet Stink-Eyes amongst the rabble.

History would surely mark The Flocking as the first loosening of the Mizuno's grip upon the Viles, thought Flamon. Tatson's son and only heir, Akumuron, was just a boy at the time, his rule at first ineffectual; as decades passed the vassal clans of the demesne had grown ever more contemptuous of their masters, many turning to robbery and ambuscade, piracy, even cannibalism. And now, as Kobutsuden festered, the Viles was without doubt the most dangerous place in Novalis.

As if to confirm this last assessment a strident clash of steel reverberated in the street outside, followed by a shout, two screams, and the thud a severed head makes when it strikes cobblestones without rolling. Flamon Neko turned away, pulled the grimy blanket over his face, and went to sleep.

# SKULL CASTLE

The first killing came within a day of Lord Hebon Hakamanko and his entourage leaving Skull Castle for the long ride to the Shines, where the overlords of the seven remaining high clans were to convene and determine the future of Novalis. Such concerns did not hang heavy upon Lord Hebon's son, Hekon; his world lay entirely within the confines of the castle, from its subterranean torture cells, crypts and hidden passageways to the flower-draped dais where he now stood, seeking admiration from those who secretly mocked and despised him. *The hunchback, the cripple, the madman,* they called him, though none would dare say it in more than a whisper. Next to Hekon stood Mad Dog, the clan's carnifex, a brutish amalgam of butcher, surgeon, torturer and headsman recruited from the local Cut-Belly clan. A black hood covered his entire head and shoulders, and he was holding a massive metal war-hammer with both hands. Two retainers were holding fast a barefoot kitchen-girl in a torn dress; she shook and sobbed at her plight.

Looking down at this scene, the Lady Suna recalled her wedding-night now two years past, when she was barely fifteen years of age; then she was the one who trembled with fear, certain that her new husband, the hunchback, would soon strip her naked and subject her to sexual violations like those described in the poet Malarion's *Blood Flowers*, the forbidden erotic manuscript she secretly used to peruse, with conflicting fascination and revulsion, in the candle-quiet of her father's library. But even Malarion's fevered visions were no equal to what had actually transpired once Hekon bolted shut the bridal chamber door and slowly, wordlessly unfastened the iron clasps of his mysterious ebony casket. She had learned that night that Hekon Hakamanko had no interest in what lay beneath her marriage gown; she was to become his uncomprehending acolyte in a night-world of masks, pelts, bones, guts, transfixions, excretions and ritual immolations, a world from which other humans, and even the gods, had long been excommunicated.

A scream of profound despair drew Suna's thoughts back to the courtyard below; the retainers had forced the kitchen-girl down on her knees, one holding her by the neck so that her head was pressed to the blacksmith's anvil bolted to the dais. Hekon raised a hand to the murmuring and disquieted onlookers.

"This girl stands guilty of treason against her lord and master," he proclaimed. "In my father's absence, I am the law of Skull Castle; I am the justice, and I am the hand of all dooms." He motioned again and Mad Dog stepped forward, raised his warhammer, then brought it down with catastrophic malice upon the girl's head. Those nearest the dais pulled back, some shrieking, as a crimson shower of destruction splattered over them.

Suna, who had averted her eyes at the last, whispered: "Her only crime was to step upon a red spider. If only they knew the extent of his madness…" *If only my father knew,* she thought. *If only he would come and kill the hunchback, kill them all, and take me back to the Red Rock.*

"Oh, but they do know," replied Hozon Ama. Like Suna, Hozon Ama was trapped in Skull Castle, a deserter from the Celestial Horde who faced execution if caught beyond its walls. "They know. But what does that knowledge avail them? To speak out is treason against the clan, and the price of treason is eternal silence. Fear of Lord Hebon's würms extorts fealty from all the low clans of Lizard's Den; the Scorpion Blacks, the Iron Talons, the Nightshaders, the Blind Cats, the Cut-Bellies, the Tower Bats, the Night Weepers… did I forget any? Even the No-Face clan, those wretches whose skin and eyes and lips were melted by the würms' venom, dare not dream of unbridling the vengeance in their hearts."

Ama – known as the Red Monk, for he never left the battlefield until drenched from head to foot in the blood of his heathen foe – was Suna's only ally in the castle, a dread place where even the quietest dissent could quickly reach the ears of the Hakamanko, whose agents of chaos also served as spies within the walls. In return for sanctuary the warrior-priest was charged with teaching clansmen the ways of combat and protecting Lord Hebon's person from harm. Long silvery hair now covered the head tattoo which once marked him as a soldier of the Celestial Horde's Storm Division, defenders of the Triad who went to war in night-blue chainmail and mantles slashed with pure white lightning strikes. Disaffection from the Horde had not dulled Ama's sadness at the loss of his northern Moon Brothers in the heavenly reaping which men were now calling the Decimation.

Suna knew that even the Red Monk could not defeat a whole guard; they were doomed to rot in Skull Castle, unless… "And what of Lord Hebon?" she asked. "You know his mind; does he covet coronation?"

"Perhaps they all do," mused the priest. "But who can weigh one claim against the other? The Gomi hold the Key of Bones; the Gomi hold power. Who nurtures snowflakes in a furnace?"

# THE CITADEL

A headless man in the street was not an unusual sight in Swilly Town, nor was a nude, mutilated whore carried lifeless from a brothel or a wife with her brains dashed out by a drunken husband; but in the city's walled high end, where the Winter Palace stood tall atop the Hill of Angels, murder was still a crime to be investigated. Questor Zan Vordulax, prefect of the Imperial Watch, was particularly concerned by two cruel and highly unusual slayings which, by their almost identical nature, appeared to be the work of a singular madman.

One week earlier, the daughter of a Mizuno general had disappeared; she was eventually found, brutally murdered, in one of the backstreets near the perimeter of the citadel. The girl had been heavily pregnant, but that was not even the greatest horror. She had been opened up across the belly, and the foetus within removed; in its place, watchmen found a child's one-eyed doll. This double murder was followed just three days later by another butchery, another gravid woman – this time an imperial guardsman's wife – who was also found dead, her unborn babe again replaced by a twisted, blood-splattered effigy. *Four souls murdered, but only two corpses.*

When Vordulax's chief officer, Clitto, summoned him to the women's bath house not long after dawn, he was filled with a dull dread at what new atrocity might be awaiting. A clutch of half-naked bathers were milling at the entrance; some were still vomiting.

"It's him again," said Clitto grimly, and had no need to elaborate.

The nude girl's corpse was sitting upright against a tiled wall, head contorted to one side, in a carmine tarn of congealed blood. The swollen stomach had been cut wide open, raggedly as if by a saw; Vordulax could see a tiny, bloody hand extruding from the laceration. "Is it...?"

"Wax," said Clitto.

In all his sixty years, Vordulax had never seen such a thing as these killings; even in the aftermath of battles, when all manner of grievous mutilations and wounds gaped upon the fallen and the dead, there was nothing to match the grotesque nature of such crimes, shocking in their savage perversity. But above all, the prefect was haunted by one simple question: *To what end?*

Vordulax knew that if word of these depravities spread through Swilly Town, the perpetrator would like as not become a folk hero amongst the rabble, who shed no tears for the deaths of high-born ladies, pregnant or not; those who struck against the ruling class, or women, or even better both, were soon elevated in the eyes of the downtrodden. It had happened just two years before, when a delinquent butcher named Ramsbelly had embarked on a spree of sodomy-and-cleaver murders. *Lord Buttocksbane,* the rabble had called him admiringly; *Lord Buttocksbane, the arse-shredder.* Vordulax could only imagine what epithet they might accord this new violator.

"Remove the body, clean everything," he told Clitto. "We must announce a curfew within the citadel; women heavy with child, in particular, are not to walk the streets after nightfall."

"They will ask why," said Clitto.

"Some sort of sickness, perhaps; a flux fatal to the unborn, but not of undue concern to the populace at large." *It's more or less the truth, in any case.* "And send for mavens from the shrines of Storms and Sun; I fear we are besieged by a worker of witchcraft."

# THE OSSUARY

Three weeks after leaving the Mirror Castle, the last Gomi rider pulled up at the gates of the Ossuary, fortress of Clan Seikyo, in the southernmost demesne of Novalis. The bone-clad walls of the castle, rearing before him like a giant's skeletal torso, were the last thing he saw before crashing to the ground from exhaustion and blood loss where an arrow fired by outlaw clansmen had pierced his upper thigh.

Lady Hexheart, the clan's copper-haired bane virago, prepared the poultice which saved the rider's leg from amputation; now she watched on as her overlord Kyodokuron Seikyo, known as Kyo the Killer for his ruthless exterminations against any vassal clans who dared to revolt, prepared to set sail for the Shines. They would navigate west, rounding Hangman's Head then cleaving to the coastline that spanned Wolf's Jaw, Goldengate, the Viles and the Templedark, finally docking at the Port of Shrikes. Then it was a two or three day travail across land to the Mirror Castle.

For centuries the Seikyo had fixed the boiled bones of their enemies to the walls of the Ossuary; corpses were first skeletonized in huge ferrous vats, then nailed in place with artistic precision. Now the castle was covered by a yellow-white crust of human remains at least fifteen foot thick, covering every inch from ground to battlements and arranged in disquieting whorls and mosaics. High overhead the clan banners flew blood-red and blazoned with a black bloom of death. Lord Kyodokuron's rampages had furnished at least three hundred of the skeletons in this gargantuan memorial of death; Lady Hexheart could claim nineteen.

The Seikyo and their only neighbours, Clan Taiyo of Goldengate, had been in conflict for more than a decade, although the ongoing border clashes had never risen to the level of true carnage. After a long series of raids and skirmishes, Lord Kyodokuron had proposed a plan for peace, to be ratified at a dinner held in the Ossuary. Lord Nakasendaron Taiyo, his wife Yuta, his first son Taikon and a number of his generals all attended, arriving in retinue from the Sunstorm Castle. They numbered nineteen in all, and were seated in splendour for a thirteen-course banquet. The Ossuary kitchens cooked twelve of those courses; the thirteenth was provided by Lady Hexheart, and she made it with sugared mandrake, hemlock, wormwood and wolfsbane.

It is said that the Taiyo died not only vomiting in agonies of convulsion, but with visions of every fiend and phantom in the Three Hells burning through their brains. After this cold-blooded atrocity of treachery and murder, which became known as the Feast of Demons, word quickly spread that Kyo the Killer was an implacable foe who could not be trusted and should never be crossed. And yet it was not the end of the Taiyo; the entourage who attended the feast were in truth doubles, doomed actors whose imposture was facilitated by prosthetics devised by the clan maven Vorgovanion. In his supposed triumph Lord Kyodokuron was outwitted, and so the clashing of the two clans simmered on with no trust left on either side for reconciliation.

For a months afterward Lady Hexheart was haunted by the dying screams of the Taiyo. It was the first time she had witnessed with her own eyes the effects of her deadly arts; normally her nerve poisons and nightmare spurs were used by agents of chaos who were scattered across Novalis, along with spies from all the other high clans, pawns in a covert game of catch, cross and kill. She clung to the words spoken to her by her mother, the first Lady Hexheart, in passing on her secret prescriptions for madness and death. *Some may call you witch,* she had said, *some may call you murderer; but murder is just another art of war, and in war the true artist paints with blood, kills without being killed.*

Now, as she watched Lord Kyodokuron and his entourage depart, the second Lady Hexheart wondered how many skeletons her mother had provided for the Ossuary's great sculptural carapace, and how many more her overlord might bring back with him from this latest excursion. If war was looming, a real war, she was sure that the Seikyo would be among the first to sound its drum-beat.

She turned to Morgomox. The old man's robes were studded with diamonds and amethysts, but food-stains browned the white of his beard and his hands were like claws. "What say you, maven? Does our lord sail to make peace, claim a crown, or precipitate holocaust?"

"The picture painted by our agents remains obscure," Morgomox replied. "If the high clans split into factions, I fear for the future. Although most vassal clans remain loyal to their rulers, every province has rebels, especially in the Viles, where an outlaw army is said to be massing in the Valley of Flies while Kobutsuden wanes. The Celestial Horde have allegiance only to the Triad; none can say whose side they would favour, if any, in a conflict. Our lord's repute for ferocity is an asset, but his talent for betrayal works against us."

"And if the holocaust is unleashed?"

"Then," said the alchemist, "we face a hundred years of turmoil, a bloodstorm not seen since the great Serpent Wars when hundreds and thousands perished, six entire high clans were wiped out, and the marsh dragons driven to the edge of extinction."

# SWILLY TOWN

"How can I please you?"

Gorn glanced up at the serving-girl. She had the heavy breasts and buttocks he craved, but some recreant had left a thick purple knife scar down one side of her face, sealing her eye half-shut.

"Gin and giblets," he replied. "Twice."

They were slouched in the dim light of the Five Bald Butchers, one of the few Swilly Town inns left that would still serve them. Gorn watched as Kesh cracked open a phial of amber liquid then quickly drank it down.

"Lord bloody Firefinger," he sneered. "Don't you know that stuff burns holes in your brain? You'll end up in the Black Cage."

But Kesh wasn't listening; he could hear nothing now but the blood rushing in his veins and singing in his ears, like the howling of a primordial wolf at moonrise. Lights gleamed in his eyes. After a while, he said: "I want to fight. I want to smash my hammer through skulls, destroy rib-cages and hearts. Don't you?"

"Probably not as much as you," said Gorn. "But aye, it would be nice to try out this new sword." He looked down at the weapon propped next to him, a double-edged broadsword of dark, army-forged steel. He'd stolen it just the night before, from an imperial guardsman who was passed out drunk. *That cunt'll be in the dungeons by now,* he thought. *Disarmed and dishonoured. His own bloody fault.*

"I suppose you've already given it a name, like them Shinojin do," said Kesh.

"As a matter of fact I have," said Gorn. "Gut-fucker."

Both men laughed; the girl came back with a flask of spirits, dry bread and plates of boiled bird innards.

"If we're going to get our blades wet," said Kesh, "might as well get paid for it. Way I see it, there's only two choices – either shift sword for the Mizuno again, or go for the long-term option. Tazon Ando."

"One Shinojin or another. Why Ando?"

"I heard his family is one of the richest in the Templedark, even if he is an outlaw; how else could he keep all them savages in line, if not with coin?"

"He's wealthy, true enough. But I heard he only crossed the border a few months back, with nowt but a few hundred Crow River cut-throats. And now he's taken charge of five thousand men in the Valley of Flies? Sounds more like black magic."

"There's no magic in this world," said Kesh. "Only drugs that make you see things, if they don't kill you first. I say let's meet the bastard."

Gorn knew that their time in Kobutsuden was fast coming to an end; whether the emperor was dead or not, striking his palace guardsmen or stealing their swords were both crimes punishable by gaol, or even mutilation. "Drink up then," he said. "After that, why not?"

They left the city as night fell, an hour before curfew. Both men rode gelded coursers, a bay and a silver dapple; a mare might bleed at the vagina, and then the bears and wolves would be upon them. *That was the easy part,* thought Gorn. *Getting back in might be a different matter, if things take a turn.*

For days they rode, following an arid, scarcely defined highway which wound them ever deeper into lawless heartlands where even the hardened Mizuno watchmen were loath to patrol. They saw scattered naked corpses both male and female, barrows stacked with human hands and feet, smoking fire-pits in which skulls, only skulls, smouldered in blackening piles. Once they came face to face with three clansmen, who Gorn recognised as Maw Fetters by their face tattoos; he could only hope they didn't recognise *him,* the blond-haired swordsman who just a month before was stringing up their brothers on behalf of the Mizuno. They didn't. Sensing no fear in the two riders, the Maw Fetters passed them by without word.

At length Gorn and Kesh reached a crossroads marked by an ancient oak tree. A horse had been nailed to it, high up where the branches began, its skeleton long picked clean by carrion crows. The road's right-hand fork arced away towards distant hills and woodlands; the left led downwards, ever downwards into the rock-fanged maw of the Valley of Flies.

# THE MIRROR CASTLE

As soon as the last of them had arrived a day was set aside for mourning, to be followed by the funeral of Emperor Raikon. The emperor's corporeal remnants, such as they were, were laid out upon an elevated pyre along with the scorched blade of Tekizan, deathsword of the Akutenshi; a ladder was needed to view them and pay respects by the laying of flowers. A half-skull, some ribs, a femur and some other bones too badly burned to identify, were all that remained of the Deathstar. And now they would be burned again.

The six visiting clans were encamped in clusters of silken pavilions in a crescent, the pyre standing between them and the Mirror Castle's silvered panes. Each clan raised its own banner and blazon: the Taiyo, a golden triskelion of the broken sun upon purest black; the Hakamanko, a white self-devouring snake skeleton upon deepest crimson; the Takasha, a sapphire-blue pentagram upon gold; the Mizuno, a sweeping jet-black whorl upon primrose; the Kurotako, a black cephalopod upon silver; and the Seikyo, a black death-flower afloat upon a lake of blood. High above them all flew the flesh-pink vortex of Clan Gomi, rippling from every metal-clad turret of the Mirror Castle, a reminder that it was the Gomi, at least for now, who held the seventh key of power.

The funeral rites were initiated at daybreak, conducted by mavens of the Storms and Sun in robes of night-blue with white lightning strikes and gold with garnet fire-stars respectively, hands and faces daubed in pale ashes. For an hour they prayed and chanted, two rows of thirteen facing each other, calling upon the Three Sorrows to guide Emperor Raikon into the vale of cosmic spectres; then came the human sacrifices. Linked by chained collars, thirteen prisoners from the Gomi dungeons were dragged out and made to kneel in front of the funeral pyre. A few were vassal clansmen who once rebelled; the others were common thieves, rapists, arsonists, murderers. All were nude and gaunt, pocked with open sores, and mired in their own filth. Some lacked fingers, parts of limbs, eyes, ears or nose; the rapists had been castrated and cauterized. They squinted at the ascendant sun, its hot rays refracted and magnified by the glittering walls of the castle which had long held them in its depths; some cried out for mercy, others muttered oaths, but most were silent.

Gravedigger, the Clan Gomi carnifex, stood behind them. He was masked, and his mask was the visage of a leering hell-demon cast in bronze. Drummers started up a slow, pounding rhythm. Upon a signal from Lord Kamosukon Gomi, his tall figure cloaked in a darkly swirling damask, the ritual killing commenced; Gravedigger brought his war-hammer down with full justice upon the head of each criminal in turn, smashing them to fragments and pulp while ravens in a nearby coppice gave voice to a hideous, mocking cacophony. Then the corpses' eyes – twenty-three in all – were extricated and threaded on a necklace of death for the emperor, a talisman to illuminate his final trajectory. Blood lapped at the bare feet of the mavens.

Seated next to his father as the ceremony neared its conclusion, Jukon Gomi reflected upon the Decimation, and how its initial annihilatory impact was still reverberating with ever-expanding waves of slaughter; even in death Emperor Raikon was at the root of more bloodshed, and the thirteen souls chosen to accompany him as votive offerings were surely not the last who would perish in this dire concatenation of violence.

At sun-wane the emperor's pyre was ignited and the great feast began, with fare ranging from a whole jack-roasted ox and racks of brain-stuffed sausages to finer delicacies such as honeyed wild sow's udders swimming in prune juice, flayed butcherbird chicks jellied in a licorice aspic, a snake's tongue and mushroom broth spiced with powdered hornets, and eyelids of hare slow-poached in squid ink with pomegranate seeds, all washed down with copious flows of ale, beer, wine and grain spirits. Perhaps wisely, Juka Gomi had seated each clan well apart; the forthcoming deliberations must not be clouded by memories of drunken clashes between overlords. Even so, the evening was not without incident; gambling broke out between generals of the Mizuno and Takasha clans, first with dice and then, as tempers soured, with foot-soldiers who were pitted against one another in fierce grappling bouts. Despite a camp-wide ban on weapons, some damage was done. One Takasha spearman lost an eye, another's pelvis was shattered, and a Mizuno bowman's testicles were so brutally twisted that both his upper thighs turned black.

It was near midnight when Lord Kyodokuron Seikyo, drunk on rice beer and rye mash, burst into the tent of Lord Nakasendaron Taiyo holding aloft his great shining deathsword Honekiri, cleaver of bones, and bellowed "What do you say now?" at Lord Nakasendaron, who was sitting at meditation with a ceremonial dagger in each hand.

Lord Nakasendaron raised up the daggers to form an X in front of his face, and calmly replied: "The dragon drools; in deep water only shadows, made sickly by the screaming moon."

It was the perfect riposte; Lord Kyodokuron could only cede the moment, turn, and storm from the tent without further provocation. That night his sleep was deep and dreamless.

# THE CACKMIRE INN

"Beer, pork, potatoes," said the innkeep. "Food fit for a butcher is that."

Kuron Kirizono glanced up at the man. "I've been called worse."

With him sat Nezumon Nano, called the Devil Bat in honour of castle walls scaled and sleeping throats slit by night, and three other agents of the Blue Dragon Hand – Kagon Shura, called the Slaughter Shadow, Yuron Fuki, called the Ghost Blizzard, and Jagon Ketsu, called the Demon Blood. The remaining twenty agents were abroad, scouring Novalis for news of the Key of Bones.

On the other side of the inn sat a group of local Hell-Claw clansmen, notoriously inimical to strangers; yet none of them had stirred or spoken when Kirizono entered, his seven-foot figure clothed in ringmail and cloak which matched his night-black hair, his tunic bearing the V-shaped convergent thunderbolts of Clan Akutenshi. Even in the Templedark, the Black Reaper of Kyukiden was legend. Now, an hour and numerous draughts of ale later, two of the locals were evidently feeling somewhat bolder.

"This is Hell-Claw land," said the first. "Hell-Claw land, Hell-Claw tavern. There's a tax to pay." The man was broad-set, his face tattooed with blue swirls and dots, a spiked mace at his side.

"Get this man a beer," shouted Kirizono. "And one for his friends."

"Beer?" said the second. "You'll pay coin, or else a higher price."

Kirizono sat back in his chair. "There are five of us, and two of you. How do you mean to collect this tax of yours?"

"Not two – nine," said the first, gesturing towards the group who still sat in the corner, fingering their weapons as they looked on.

"As you say. Nano; pay them what they're owed."

Nezumon Nano stood up and faced the two clansmen. He was also clothed all in black, as were his fellow agents, but their garments bore no insignia. Around his waist was a leather belt that held an array of tools, devices, and small weapons; it also held a purse, which Nano reached into with the words: "Blue Dragon tax." What he pulled out and threw to the floor with a single fluid motion was not coin.

The ceramic fire grenade smashed and ignited with a white heat-flash which made the Hell-Claws jerk back and shield their eyes. When they looked again, Nano was gone. Kirizono chuckled at the blank look on their faces. And then the Devil Bat swooped.

He dropped from his perch on the wooden ceiling supports with a steel wall-gouge in each fist, points down; one gouge plunged into each Hell-Claw simultaneously, puncturing the top of the skull and driving deep into the brain. As they collapsed Kirizono and the other agents stood to confront the remaining clansmen, five against seven.

The seven wavered.

Kirizono grasped the dead men by the front of their tunics, one with each hand, and dragged them into the middle of the inn, heads leaking dark brainsblood. Then he unsheathed Obochi, the king of death, and roared.

The seven ran.

"Pity," he said.

# THE VALLEY OF FLIES

"What's to stop these bastards killing us right now?" said Kesh, morosely; the effects of the firefinger had long worn off, and that was the last of it.

"Like I said, killing us might be fun, but if they deliver us to Ando they might get a reward, which is even better." Gorn hoped he was right; he didn't rate their chances against the group of fighters who rode on either side of them. By their face tattoos he knew they were a mixed detail of Kill-Claws, Blood Eagles, and Crow River scouts. Only the Whip Flay, Devil-Dog and Sickle Wasp clans remained loyal to the Mizuno, as far as he knew; the rest had joined Tazon Ando's legion of gash-gizzard marauders. *But which would be the winning side?*

Ando's redoubt was a system of limestone caves, passages and pits which extended for more than a mile along the rockface of the ravine, its recesses set far within, its depths plunging to subterranean lakes where the bones of ancient titanosaurs boiled in absolute darkness. The crude likenesses of such beasts could be seen daubed upon the walls of Ando's war-cave, relics of the hominids who first stalked the Valley of Flies a million years before in a reverie of blood, rage and fire.

Four fighters escorted Gorn and Kesh into the cave, a Kill-Claw on each side and two Crow River spearmen behind. Ando sat at the rear wall, where a crude dais of stones had been erected and draped with animal skins, and fire burned in two flanking braziers for heat and light. He was cradling a battle-bitten war axe.

The Kill-Claws forced their captives to kneel. "We found them on the Dark-Winged Way," said one, but before he could explain further his tongue was forever silenced by the spear which entered his neck at the base of the skull and jutted out from his mouth in a hot spray of blood and shattered teeth. His fellow clansman died in the same way at the same instant, and as their corpses buckled the two Crow River killers unsheathed swords and flew towards Tazon Ando, one using Gorn's back as a ramp.

Ando threw his body to one side, blocking a sword-thrust with the sparking blade of his axe then swinging at the other attacker's face; the pair fell back, crouching and leering like wolves, knowing their prey would eventually tire and succumb to odds. Gorn saw his opportunity; if the assassins had thought him an enemy of Tazon Ando, it was a deadly miscalculation. Bracing his foot against a dead Kill-Claw's back he wrenched the spear free, and Kesh did the same even as one of the killers turned, realised the threat, and swept at the pit-fighter with heinous malice. Gorn drove the spear through the man's temple and into his brain, while Ando seized the moment of confusion to rain a web of blows against the other; one strike hacked clean through his attacker's sword-arm above the elbow, and as he screamed Ando delivered a final assault which battered and then half-beheaded him. But Gorn's spear-kill had come a moment too late; the Crow River man's sword had bisected Kesh's head in a diagonal cleft from left temple to right jaw, killing him where he stood.

Ando knelt by his victim, examining the fatally twisted head and running a finger across its splintered cheek-bone. The tattoos were merely paint; he knew then that the two attackers were infiltrators, no doubt chaos agents from Castle Mortmane's Iron Pentagram, sent on a vengeful mission of death by Hikidashon Takasha. *Then he leaves me no choice; war must come to Mortmane.*

"Sorry for your friend," he said to Gorn. "Who are you, anyway?"

"Gorn. Of Gluttonport. Used to be in the imperial guard, till they ran me out for insubordination. I didn't know Kesh long, but he was a good drinker, I'll say that for him. Can we bury him?"

"We can. And I owe you gratitude. A trained sword would make a good captain, and I can pay in coin and chattels; what do you say?"

"That's why I'm here," said Gorn.

# SKULLHAVEN

Shuttered and overgrown with ivy that teemed with fat white spiders, Gargoyle Mansion was the largest and oldest of the single row of residences, mostly derelict, which overlooked Skullhaven cemetery. Reputedly built on the site of a temple which was razed during the Corpse Riots, the mansion was entirely clad and gabled in arcane statuary representing phantasmal beasts from not only the Three Hells, but also lightless purgatories beyond the reckoning of the Triad. Its towering roof centrepiece showed the rape of a human female by two scaly winged cephalopods, surrounded by a frieze of fornicating skeletons. The sculptures were the work of the mad architect Helios Sek, who also designed the building's maze-like interiors.

It was said that the furniture inside the mansion was constructed solely from the bones of entombed priests, unearthed from the subterrain during the excavation of a fighting pit where the degenerate denizen would stage blood-spurting mortal combat for the delectation of a private audience. None knew where Helios Sek came from, or how he acquired his vast wealth; it was long rumoured that he was once a plunderer of sunken galleons, but no-one could say it with certainty. Others whispered, not wholly in jest, that Sek was a deathless alchemist who had mastered the secret of transmuting his own shit into glistering gold.

Two hundred years later, after the fall of the emperor Raikon, Gargoyle Mansion was reputed to be cursed; few ventured within its gates, and those that did seldom re-emerged unscathed. One survivor, a tavern prostitute, reported that she had been summoned to the house by a servant and there attacked by an ancient, robed figure with fingernails as long as daggers; watchmen dismissed her tale as fantasy, the scratches on her face as wounds inflicted by a rival. Even so, reading the report on the following day, Questor Zan Vordulax was struck by one detail: the girl was requested specifically because she was with child.

"Clitto; assemble a watch to escort me to Skullhaven. I believe that Gargoyle Mansion may be hiding our killer."

It was a warm day, but the sun was veiled by a miasma of yellow-pink cloud; a lone grave-digger toiled in the cemetery, pausing to watch them as they parted the mansion's vine-clasped gates. At the main door they rang a bell on its chain. Moments later, a man garbed in a plain tabard responded.

"Imperial Watch," said Vordulax. "Who lives here?"

"This is the abode of Baron Kravox," the man replied. "The Baron sleeps at this hour."

"Even so," said Vordulax, "we will speak with him. At once."

Glancing at the armed watchmen standing in the prefect's wake, the man acceded. He led Vordulax into a room with windows closed off by wooden struts; dozens of candles burned there, rising from pools of semi-molten tallow. Over a stone mantel the head of a würm was mounted, fixing him with eyes of deep red glass.

"Pray wait," said the servant.

Vordulax saw that one wall of the room was lined with books, piled upon sagging shelves; he examined the titles nearest to him and saw that they were all related to prophecy, including Borgobalion's *Witch Womb*, a long-forbidden treatise on fetomancy. The opposite wall appeared to be fixed with a huge grid of small wooden drawers; he noticed that several were missing.

After some minutes a tall elderly man, bald and withered of feature, entered the room. His robe was woven with a silver motif of snakes and flowers. "I am Baron Kravox," he said, "the seer of Skullhaven."

"Seer? And what do you see, exactly?" asked Vordulax bluntly.

"Many things. The nature of time, for example. Most men do not understand that past, present and future are as one. The chair you sat in yesterday, you are still sitting in it; the repast you will eat tomorrow morning, you are devouring it even as we speak."

*He talks as one with brain worm, or perhaps one who dines too frequently on sugared mandrake.* Vordulax appraised the Baron's fingers; the nails were uncut, curled like avian talons. "I'm following a report made by a young woman," he said. "Bloody harm, and intent to rape."

Kravox smiled, showing a span of gold-coated teeth. "Truly, how does one rape a prostitute? And as for harm... well, that is precisely why she first accepted the additional silver coins. Snuffpetal – my manservant – will confirm it."

"And your interest in girls who are with child?"

"A mere sentimentality; by paying them above others I hope to enrich the future generation."

Vordulax weighed the old man's age, frailty and evident erudition, and decided that he most likely spoke the truth. *The old man is perverse, addled even, but surely no killer; and neither is his timid, scrawny servant.* "Very well; pray forgive my intrusion."

"But wait," Kravox urged, "before you go, Questor Vordulax... I see something in your eye – a reflection of the future." His bony hand gripped the prefect's arm. "You are standing in a privy, knee-deep in blood. A floating head stares up at you, whispering a single word: *imposter*."

Before returning to the citadel Zan Vordulax paid visit to his favoured pie shop, Tontaiton's, where he purchased a hot savoury of meat and offal dripping with dark, suet-streaked gravy. He wondered how Baron Kravox had known his name; he was sure he hadn't offered it. But, then again, the identity of the Imperial Prefect was no secret. He sighed, took a mouthful of pie, and tried hard not to envision himself drowning in a blood-filled privy.

# THE MIRROR CASTLE

Kamosukon Gomi, known as Wax-Face amongst the vassal clans, sat at the head of the great oblong table in silence, his semi-masked visage refracted garishly in its mirrored surface; his son Jukon, common-law warden of the last imperial key of power, sat beside him. Seated to either side were the remaining high clan overlords – Akumuron Mizuno, Nakasendaron Taiyo and Hebon Hakamanko on the left, and on the right Hikidashon Takasha, Sadogashon Kurotako and Kyodokuron Seikyo, sworn to leave his feud with the Taiyo at the door of the meeting hall. Opposite Lord Kamosukon sat the maven Magmatharion, charged with bringing requisite order and insight to the proceedings. Positioned at the centre of the Mirror Castle, the circular hall was covered by a high silvered dome and held nothing but the table, which was surrounded on all sides by wide expanses of empty marble flooring. Unseasonal rain was hammering hard on the dome's surface, forcing Jukon to raise his voice to be heard.

"There it is, then; those in favour show red, those who oppose show black."

One after another, the overlords rolled a dyed wooden coin towards the centre of the table. Lord Akumuron, red; Lord Nakasendaron, red; Lord Hebon, black; Lord Hikidashon, red; Lord Kyodokuron, black; and Lord Sadagashon – after a dramatic pause – black. It was as Jukon expected.

"As warden of the only remaining imperial key, my vote shall decide the issue," he proclaimed. The coin he held up between thumb and forefinger was red. "Welcome to our new league – the Starfire Order."

"Our clan must decline," said Kyo the Killer, rising from his chair. "If the empire has no emperor, then the Seikyo will rule themselves. Wolf's Jaw will devolve."

The southernmost demesne of Novalis, Wolf's Jaw was attached to the mainland only by a great iron bridge across the Fearfang Gulf. *Destroy that bridge, and the province effectively becomes an island,* thought Jukon. *But where's the harm, as long as the Seikyo stay on it...* "I beg you to reconsider," he said, but it was merely a courtesy; he knew that Lord Kyodokuron had made his decision – and a long time ago, most likely.

"And you, Lord Hebon?"

"My answer remains as before. There must be a new emperor, and the question will be decided by means peaceful or otherwise. I expect to hear back from your league within two moons."

"I beg you to reconsider," said Jukon again, but Lord Hebon Hakamanko was already stalking out of the hall, followed closely by Lord Sadogashon Kurotako who evidently believed that the well-being of his daughter Suna was dependent upon the würm-lord's pleasure. *And he's probably right.*

"Very well," said Jukon. "Lord Akumuron, your earlier request for assistance is granted. We will each send a troop of one thousand men to fortify the Winter Palace, which will henceforth be our centre of governance. The Starfire Order will convene upon the first of each month. I fear that the matter of the Seikyo, the Hakamanko and the Kurotako will be our first consideration."

"And the destiny of the seventh key?" asked Lord Hikidashon. "The loyalty of the Celestial Horde will depend upon the continued veneration of the sacred instruments."

"Of course," agreed Jukon. "I will hold fast the Key of Bones, and it will stand as talisman of both men and gods; a reminder of the past that points us to our future."

"Control the dead to control the living?" said Lord Hikidashon, but Jukon pretended not to hear him above the cross-talk of the other overlords, who were seemingly content with this distribution of power. He was certain that together, the Starfire Order and the Celestial Horde could bring about a new dawn to Novalis. The Age of Shadows would be still-born, a twisted thing abandoned to the wolves of light. But it was the look which still haunted the maven Magamatharion's face – a barely-concealed dread at some liminal but ineluctable catastrophe – which also made him wonder if the old ways and beliefs could ever truly die. And he knew he was soon to find out.

# THE SLAUGHTERHOUSE

*"At the dawn of Novalis, the emperor Metakaikon created a subterranean army of dolls. Trained in torture and atrocity, harnessed in steel and black leather, Metakaikon's dolls rampaged through the catacombs of ancient Kyukiden. Doll orgies celebrated the cult of Sensorion, an enigma of sacrifice and blood. The blood formed a great river, the river of dolls. The river of dolls flowed from the volcano, and forked into the liquid hells. In the city of dolls, beneath the volcano, naked savages and horses burned in the dance of fire. Phalanxes of Metakaikon's dolls migrated by night, scouring the world in hell-ships. In the ice-wastes, berserker dolls erected megaliths of bone. They dreamed of a spider-god that devoured their maker. They mastered the art of necrolatry.*

*"Impervious to pain, Metakaikon's dolls were highly prized for vivisection. In the east, alchemists sought to mate them with homunculi. In the south, whore-dolls prayed to a black goat. In the north, the dolls slept in ditches and graves. In the west, the dolls gave birth to animal corpses. Metakaikon's dolls were incarcerated as lunatics, condemned as vampires, hunted as witches. The punishment of the dolls was a holocaust of iron and fire. The swamp-dolls who communed with serpents were ripped apart with red-hot pincers. The temple-dolls who preached the art of sodomy with angels were cooked in cauldrons of boiling tar. The plague-dolls who devoured human skin were dissolved in vats of molten ore suspended in a void. The star-dolls who railed against the sun were rendered down by comet-fire. In the vaulted subterrain, great furnaces were stoked for the immolation of the lust-dolls.*

*"Rebel dolls forged new underground cities and launched incendiary insurrections against the doll-hunters. Suicide-dolls with sulphur-encrusted skeletons rode waves of liquid flame into doll-hunter torture temples. They fed doll-hunters to sharks in salt-water pools carved from obsidian chasms. They crucified them in harnesses of bat-bone and castrated them with arachnid forceps. The rebel dolls inaugurated a system of masks that refracted*

*the luminosity of the moon in visceral spirals. They started to bleed. This was the first revolt of the dolls."*

Kargon put the grimoire aside, his head reeling at these parables posited centuries before by the maven Gammabarion; what was the true meaning behind them? Some said that this terminal opus, *War Of The Dolls*, was nothing more than a transcription of deathly deliria muttered by the mad maven from his plague-bed; others, like Kargon's mentor Chromocrax, had devoted their lives to decoding its secrets and perpetuating the lost visions of Metakaikon, first emperor of Novalis.

Kargon peered back into the gloomy recesses of the laboratory, where the motionless figure of Lady Burnbolt, her belly ominously distended, presided like a blind sentinel. *Please don't give birth to an animal corpse,* he thought, suddenly chilled by sea-mist coiling through the tower's cruciform arrow loops. He found his mind turning, as it often did, to the two storeys above, both sealed by heavily chained gates and accessible only to Chromocrax himself, who wore the keys on a cord around his neck and would not speak of the secrets they held. *Could there be more like her? And if so, what is their purpose?*

Far below, where the black iron sheeting of the Slaughterhouse's outer bulwark fused with its bastion rock, Lord Sadogashon Kurotako's flagship the *Death Tentacle* lay at anchor, newly returned from Scaleport in Lizard's Den, nearest crossing point to the Shines. Chromocrax had been summoned to a meeting of the Kurotako council, where he now sat with Lord Sadogashon, the clan treasurer Unon Octo, and the clan's fleet commander Kon Inusame.

"Our lands remain without emperor," said the overlord. "In less than two moons Lord Hebon Hakamanko will likely claim the right to imperial power, and we are obliged to support that claim. General Inusame, how many ships can you ready?"

"Perhaps one hundred balingers, Lord Sado; holding four thousand men, including the Shark White flesh-rippers. And all rigged with sea-scorpions."

"Octo, make sure General Inusame has sufficient coin. The ships will sail in two flotillas, both with a full battalion of rippers; fifty ships to anchor off Gluttonport Bay, and the other fifty to Goldengate, within range of the Sunstorm Castle. The Taiyo and Mizuno alike must be dissuaded from marching north. Chromocrax, for you I have another mission in mind. And we will need the assistance of your Lady Burnbolt."

"She is ready, Lord Sado," asserted the maven. "Always ready."

"As you know," the overlord continued, "the engagement in marriage of my daughter, Soma, to Lord Chikon Takasha is already announced. We will now send an envoy to Castle Mortmane, to make final arrangements; Lady Burnbolt will travel with this envoy, and they must depart within the week." *A marriage made in the fiery hells,* thought Sadogashon. *But only one will turn to ash.*

# THE JACKDAWS

Lord Akumuron Mizuno's flagship the *Devil Craw* was a one-masted clinker cog large enough to carry twenty men, and armed both fore and aft with pairs of massive sea-scorpions – torsion harpoon launchers, not for hunting whales, of which there were but few in the coastal waters of Novalis, but for repelling pirates, of which there were far too many. The ship's sail of primrose-yellow cotton was decorated by a whirling black vortex which seemed to suck all light into its rotating eye; the same motif which was inlaid, tile by patterned marble tile, upon the frontal façade of the Nightmare Castle.

It was the ship's captain, Chokon Tora, who fired the first scorpion that day, some fifty leagues after the *Devil Craw* rounded the Bloodtooth Islands bound for Gluttonport and was slowly winding through the Jackdaws, a treacherous cluster-maze of dark-grey scoria jutting from the coastal wash of the Viles. The double-flued iron harpoon pierced the Smash-Bones raider with such velocity that it tore clean through his belly, taking his entrails and spine with it and leaving a shredded bloody hole so wide of circumference that Tora could for a moment see clear through it. As the corpse collapsed away another wave of attackers swarmed out from their concealed smallboats, buoyed by floating chained pontoons, screaming, hurling grappling hooks and spears. One heavy javelin struck the *Devil Craw*'s helmsman full in the throat; free of his control the cog veered into the nearest pillar of rock with a terrible grating and splintering, and was suddenly stuck fast with lifesblood flooding across its listing timbers.

Lord Akumuron and his retainers now lined the ship's starboard beam, hacking with their swords at the heads of the Smash-Bones clansmen who were scaling the side and threatening to over-run the Mizuno vessel; Chokon Tora's blade sliced off two skull-tops with one sweep, only as other raiders lobbed missiles of burning pitch onto the deck beyond. Fire quickly burst out and spread, setting ablaze two Mizuno retainers who leapt flailing into the ocean, and finally ignited the *Devil Craw*'s sailcloth.

Lord Akumuron managed to unleash one last harpoon, decapitating a Smash-Bones in mid-shout, before the stricken ship was overwhelmed and began to sink, inch by inch, into the seething brine. Then the black smoke blinded him, flames sucked away his breath, and a swinging wooden bludgeon crashed him sideways into nothingness.

When he regained his senses, Lord Akumuron Mizuno was wrapped in chains; pain shot down his face in spasms, and he feared his cranium was fractured. The darkness of the sea-cavern was alleviated only slightly by torchlight, but as his eyes coped he could discern the frame of a tall wooden structure, resembling a crooked gibbet; it appeared that two hanged men were dangling from it, but he quickly realised that these were merely empty human hides, stretched on frames and cured. Patches of scaly fish-skin had been stitched onto them here and there, making them sparkle in the flaming.

The air was a cloy of seaweed, salt and urine. These must be the Spewsalt Caves, he thought, where the Smash-Bones pirate clan was said to have mapped an impenetrable lair of cruelty and crime. Then he saw another figure; this one was alive, and moving towards him with menaces.

The man was an enormous brute, well over six feet tall, but Lord Akumuron eyed him without fear. "Free me," he said coldly, "or your head is forfeit."

The pirate savage snorted, then spat mucus which splashed onto his captive's boot. "I am Feric Smash-Bones. My father was Ossic, who wore the broken skulls of Shinojin on a chain around his neck, and killed more than one hundred men in battle. But you... you are the son of Tatson Stink-Eyes, a dead cunt who thought he was a bird."

Suppressing rage at the insult, Akumuron replied: "And yet you evidently crave my company... to what end? Gold, no doubt."

"Gold," said Feric. "Gold buys weapons, fighters... fighters win wars."

"And what wars are those? Only one war will count, the war of Starfire against the darkness, and to survive you need to choose the winning side. Whose side are you on, Feric Smash-Bones?"

"Not yours. I hold the side of Tazon Ando, thane of Flies, who chooses cave over castle. Now; which part of you will I send to your wife?"

# KOBUTSUDEN

The first killing beyond the walls of the citadel was also the most spectacular. Her body was hanging upside down, tied by the heels, from the Bridge of Sorrows in the very heart of the city; blowflies swarmed at the yawning red gash across her belly. To his dismay, Vordulax saw that not one, but two blonde-haired dolls were peering from the wound. *A triple murder... she was gravid with twins.*

Since the curfew was announced, Vordulax and his officers had referred to the unknown killer simply as Flux; now that his deeds were exposed, the rabble were not long in adding a more descriptive range of appellations, including *Dollmaster, Killbaby* and, inevitably, *Lord Bellysbane.* Fearing that such perverse glorification would only spur the killer to ever more bloody outrages, Vordulax was forced to announce a reward of ten gold nobles to any who enabled his capture; and all the while the city's pregnant women lived in terror, with many others refusing their husbands for fear of conceiving and becoming a target should their wombs grew heavy with child.

It was Hectoclarion the High, elder maven from the temple of Sun Sorrow Hoshon, who first pointed Vordulax towards the city's underworld of religious manias, the same tainted spiritual soil which had birthed the cult of the Holy Eye. "Dolls," he said, "are the icons held in sacred reverence by this Flux. But to love a doll, he must first destroy its creator... the mother. *Dead* dolls, those of wax, are his gift to the world; *future* dolls are his legacy. To find Flux, you must find his repository, his *temple*, if you will; his holy dollhouse of the dead."

"Then we are truly talking of a madman? A babblebrain who thinks corpses toys?"

"To us, Flux may seem a madman; but in his own mind, he may appear as a righteous avatar of divine providence. You are aware of the one named Slavos Sek?"

"By reputation, yes." Vordulax in fact knew little of Sek; a nebulous figure, never actually sighted, said to be master of one of the more conspicuous cults which had sprung up in recent years. But he considered the Vigilants to be harmless; no more malign than the Brotherhood of Fur, the Snake Doorway, the Crimson Bone Chain or any of the others, most of which faded as soon as a new sect emerged from the shadows.

"This Sek is a dangerous man," asserted Hectoclarion. "He controls fanatics, and many share phantasmal delusions. Tomorrow we will speak with Sister Lycosa at the house of lunatics."

The Black Cage was a derelict mansion to the west of Kobutsuden, outside the citadel but still on higher ground than Swilly Town. Its environs were mostly desolate and devoid of life apart from crawling rats and cockroaches, a legacy of the mansion's former station as a plague hospice. Now it housed only the insane – many of them criminals spared from execution, that the mavens might study their exorbitant psychoses – and the few nuns who cared for them. Any inmates who died were donated to the temple, their brains removed for dissection and study.

Sister Lycosa greeted her visitors and led them through the mansion's reception rooms into the gated confinement section beyond, an ill-roofed warren of granite cells and corridors. "First we must pass the women's ward," she said. "Some of them might pique your interest, Questor Vordulax. That one is Sugary Meg, who broiled her own twin babes in bacon grease and molasses. And the next, the blind one, is Lady Bluefinch... she burnt away her own eyeballs with quicklime in order to release the birds she said were trapped in her skull. Now it's filled with moths, no doubt."

Vordulax looked at them with pity, but he had little interest in such wretches, if truth be told. Some he remembered, others had most likely been locked away without trial, or had been rotting here since before he assumed office.

"And the last one on the row is Cat-A-Bodkins; she carved off all her neighbour's skin and pinned it on a scarecrow."

As they looped around into the farmost corridor Lycosa unlocked the first cell they came to, a tiny stone chamber where a naked man was chained to the wall; his gaunt frame was latticed with skin parasites, smeared with his own faeces. "This is Drok," said Lycosa. "He might answer your questions, or might not; his mind wanders quicker than a burning ghost. We believe him to be a disciple of the Holy Eye, by the robes he was wearing when arrested. They brought him here a year ago, after watchmen following the stench of the dead found a murdered girl-child in his hovel. Parts of her body were missing. He admits to eating the girl's flesh; isn't that so, Drok?"

"Her eyes. Her eyes... and her arsehole." Drok leered, stupidly.

"Why did you do such a thing?" asked Vordulax.

"The arsehole is the third eye… the serpent mirror. Sends cold carrion to the heart of the maze. That's where the beast lies… the beast that eats his young."

"And who is the beast?"

"The one in the maze…"

"His name?"

But Drok had already stopped listening to Vordulax; his eyes were glazing, his lips drooling, as if in the throes of some cryptic ecstasy.

"I know that look," said Lycosa. "You'll get no more from him today."

The sun was waning behind the Winter Palace when Vordulax and Hectoclarion the High returned from the Black Cage. Clitto saluted them at a postern gate and they retired to the prefect's chambers.

"He spoke of a beast that eats its young… what if the young are the stolen unborn? And the beast is Flux? You said that Flux probably preserves his prey, maven – enshrines them as dolls for some kind of future ritual."

"Drok may be a cannibal," said Hectoclarion, "but not your Flux. He doesn't literally devour them, eat them. He takes them and swallows them up, into the bowels of the earth…"

"A killer who hides beneath the city," said Vordulax. *A killer who might never be found. But the cannibal was a Vigilant, Lycosa had said; perhaps if they could capture Slavos Sek…*

The next morning watchmen began sweeping the city anew, this time arresting Optics of the Holy Eye as they preached and incarcerating them for interrogation. Far beneath their feet, the Takasha chaos-agent Flamon Neko had already begun his own travail through the city's bilious subterrain; he had discovered a hidden door in the butcher Chattox's slaughter-room, after returning there masked in the dead of night. A foetid tunnel led into another shop basement – this one belonging to a candle-maker whose tallow was no doubt supplied by Chattox – and another door from there opened up into steps descending to a much larger, lower-level space which, by Flamon's reckoning, was positioned somewhere between the Coxcomb Inn and the refuge for limbless cripples maimed by war.

It was a low-ceilinged pentagon walled in stone, set with four barred prison doors. Both the walls and the floor were engraved with crude sigils in the form of verminous creatures – centipedes, snakes, spiders, scorpions, bats, toads – and on the ceiling Flamon could just make out, by the rippling flame of his torch, faded paintings of human sacrifice and fornication with animals. The space stank of lichen, brimstone, and something like burning skin.

At some of the cell windows he could see faces, pale and female. Some of the faces, and others he couldn't see, were speaking with faint, tortured voices.

"Take *me*... please... take *me*."

"Hail... hail to the brother of bones..."

"...sister of skulls..."

"We are *yours*..."

"Who are you?" asked Neko. "What is this place?"

"We are links in the eternal chain... stars in the reptile night."

"The brides of the beast."

"They took me when I was fifteen, and brought me to the nest. Below us is the bridal chamber, where the beast defiles his lovers."

"*Raped* in a zodiac of *worms*."

"I seek Slavos Sek," Flamon said. "Is *he* the beast? Is he here?"

"The beast is the king of *spikes*... the lord of *splinters*."

"First he impregnates us... but the child is never born. The child is taken from our bodies. Unborn, undead."

"Unborn, undead."

"Will you love us too? Will you take us from the nest? Do you share our *sorrow*?"

"Take us... *take us*..."

*This is a madhouse,* thought Flamon. *A den of poisons, a torture brothel.*

"I was taken when I was eleven..."

"I was thirteen..."

"*Listen,*" Flamon said loudly. "The man I seek is a priest; his robes bear the brand of a flaming eye. Is this beast such a man?"

"The beast is a cruel lover... but his seed creates life. *She* is the one who takes life away."

"She?" *Why am I talking to them? I must leave, there is nothing here but nightmares. I can barely breathe...*

"The mother of bloody roses."

"Our lady of the reptile night... her eyes are fire, her blood is ice. She cuts our children from the womb... Unborn, undead."

"Unborn, undead."

"*Unborn, undead.*"

And then Flamon Neko turned, and fled ever upward until the sun's cleansing rays delivered him.

# THE VALLEY OF FLIES

The Smash-Bones night-rider reached Tazon Ando's fastness in vicious moonlight, swiping at the vampire bats which swooped around his head and lathered horse. As soon as he dismounted a flux of opalescent moths swarmed around him, and he ate one of them.

"Brother Gassic," the Grey Ghost sentry greeted him. "You bring news?"

"News, and a gift," said Gassic.

The Grey Ghost escorted him through the cave-fronts, where haggard women washed and cooked and feral naked children cavorted in the dirt; *sourbelly stumpkin, pissing on a pumpkin,* sang the urchins, giggling and prancing, and *midden man, midden man, shitting in a frying-pan.* Gassic half-smiled, wondering if they meant him. One ran up and poked his leg with a stick. "I'm Red Girl," she squealed, "and I'll cut your heart out!" Then the two men turned into a sequestered opening in the rockface, and after a number of dimly-illumined rises, twists and steep descents they were received at the war-cave of Tazon Ando.

"Speak," he said.

Gassic approached and held out a small bundle of stained cloth. "Feric Smash-Bones extends greetings."

Inside was a livid human finger, still bound by a ring. The band was crafted from solid silver and set with a polished milk-white moonstone, engraved with a black spiral.

"We sank his ship, killed his men; now Akumuron rots in irons. Feric begs you send a scroll to the Mizuno, since no Smash-Bones has the gift of letters, and no Smash-Bones' word has weight with the high clans. Gold, in exchange for their overlord."

"Tell your chieftain it shall be done, under usual terms; half to your clan, half to purchase food and weapons for our cause."

Ando turned to a figure in the shadows. "Fetch me scroll and quill, will you Gorn."

When he had finished writing, Ando placed the sealed scroll and finger in a wooden box, and handed it to Gassic. "Ride with the sun," he said.

"You really think they'll pay?" asked Gorn, after Gassic had left.

"They'll pay... but not in gold. When the Mizuno read that scroll, they'll be looking to the Templedark; they'll kill Gassic on sight, and Feric Smash-Bones will never know the difference until it's too late."

"And Akumuron?"

"No doubt history will record him as a martyr; Stink-Finger, son of Stink-Eyes."

"I'll drink to that," said Gorn. He wondered what Tazon Ando was really planning, hiding away in these caves and building an army of ravagers whom he seemingly had no qualms about betraying to serve the greater scheme. *Whatever the fuck that might be.*

"What happened between you and the Takasha, anyway?" he asked, hoping he wasn't overstepping. He sensed that Ando trusted him, but no-one ever really knew the mind of another. *And some men are bloody good actors.*

"Lord Hikidashon swore an oath of vengeance against me when he discovered that his wife, Danna, was in love with me. Unable to admit the shame of his cuckolding, he accused me of sexual crimes against his infant daughter and ordered my torture and execution. I was forced to flee, and his death-agents follow me to his day."

"Shit," said Gorn. "He sounds like a right cunt. What happened to the Lady Danna?"

"An abomination. I later learned that Hikidashon falsely accused her of complicity in the corruption of her own child, and had her boiled alive in a vat of oil. Her skeleton was thrown to the hounds, a dishonour usually reserved for only the basest criminals."

*And that's how it happens,* thought Gorn. *Someone fucks another man's wife, and before you know it we're on the brink of civil war. And now I'm stuck in the middle of it.*

"Come on, Gorn," said Ando, "let's drink some more wine. You look like you need it."

# SKULL CASTLE

"Before you mock me, girl, reflect upon my line," hissed the hunchback. "I am direct descendent of Haxon Hakamanko, fabled würm-rider of the Serpent Wars whose great beast Orochon reduced a thousand men to ruins of blistered meat and melted bone. Have you forgotten so soon what befell your little Tisa?"

"No, beloved. Forgive me; I meant no offence." *How could I ever forget that?* thought Suna. *My loyal handmaiden, my friend since childhood, cast into the moat of Skull Castle to be dissolved and digested by the watch-würms... and all because she failed to save Hekon the waste from her chamber-pot.* Suna's laughter had been involuntary, a nervous tic of fear; whenever Hekon elaborated his latest ritual or experiment, she knew that her further abasement and soiling was ensured.

"Then allow me to continue," said Hekon. "It is vital that the matter is concluded before my father returns."

Suna knew that Hebon Hakamanko was the only man who could curb the hunchback's excesses; as grim as his own reputation for violence was, he had little time for his son's twisted pursuits. And such was Hekon's dread of his father's wrath that he had even constructed a secret burial chamber, hidden deep in the castle's nexus of intra-mural passageways, in which to mummify the corpses of his young victims.

"This centipede ichor," he resumed, "prepared for me by Lady Vulvomane, will render the child immobile; completely paralysed, but fully conscious and able to feel pain in every nerve. You must then–"

Suna never learned what her role in Hekon's midnight horrors was to be, for just then he was interrupted by a slow triple knock upon the bolted door. *Let it be the warrior-priest,* she prayed; *let it be Hozon Ama, come to deliver me from this nightmare.*

"Who dares?" snarled the hunchback.

A voice replied: "It is Borborax, Lord Hekon; I bring word from your father."

Hekon relented at once; the maven Borborax was one of his mentors in madness, along with the bane virago Vulvomane; their dark teachings, contraptions and concoctions enabled the hunchback to carry out his nocturnal games, his lubricious inquisition into the workings of all living organisms.

"What news, maven?"

*He's hoping for the worst,* thought Suna. *Praying for word of his father's demise, so he might turn Skull Castle into nothing more than a fortified torture chamber.*

"Lord Hebon, his generals and retainers are encamped at the Sperm Weald," said Borborax. "He is raising an army from the low clans, and bids you join him with Skull Castle's würm-riders and five hundred horse. I cannot tell you more, or speak to his ultimate intent."

Hekon was twisting fingers through his oily hair. "But I am no soldier," he protested; "it is my task to rule the castle in my father's absence, is it not?"

Borborax handed the hunchback a scroll. "Lord Hebon has charged me with the oversight of Skull Castle," he said. "You will leave as soon as the troops are ready."

Hekon made no further reply, but his dismay was evident. Suddenly seeing a chance to escape her confinement, Suna said: "Beloved, let me accompany you; let me share the moment when you relive the glories of Haxon, your illustrious forebear." She had him at his weakest moment, she knew it; she was even mocking him, yet he was too distraught to realise it. "And we will take Lord Hebon's priest-at-arms, the Red Monk, to ensure our safety." *And, the Triad willing, to ensure my liberation.*

"So be it," said Borborax, answering for the hunchback. "I bid you both good even."

Hekon spoke little more that night; he seemed overwhelmed with a gloom which secretly delighted Suna. Although she feigned kinship with the hunchback's discomfort, inside her heart was soaring.

# THE NIGHTMARE CASTLE

Lady Miura Mizuno recoiled in horror as she opened the box, clasping a scented linen tightly to her nose and mouth. The stench of decaying flesh was emanating from a blackened finger, and by its ring she knew at once whose finger it was. Being careful not to touch it, she extricated the scroll which completed the box's contents and examined the sapphire-blue seal. It was indented with the five-pointed star of Clan Takasha. She broke it, unfurled the manuscript and read it without speaking, her face impassive.

*Lord Hikidashon Takasha declares himself Emperor of Novalis, being eldest of the seven overlords of the high clans. You are thereby ordered to surrender the city of Kobutsuden to the Takasha, giving our troops safe passage through the Viles. Lord Akumuron Mizuno is our prisoner; if you refuse, you will next receive his head.*

The missive bore the signature of Hikidashon Takasha; not a mark with which she was familiar, but the seal on the scroll gave her no cause to doubt its authenticity. And who else would dare to kidnap her husband but Hikidashon, a known religious fanatic hell-bent on imposing his iron will upon the people? History had shown time and time again that those who believed the gods were on their side could justify themselves in the commission of any crime or atrocity, however vile.

"Treachery," she said.

"May I?" asked the maven Chironax, one of the three who sat with Lady Miura upon the Mizuno council in the absence of their overlord. The others were Lady Snowsnake, a bane virago of wicked repute, and the general Batsuron Boko. He had but recently taken the place of Lady Miura's only son Catton, butchered by Blood Eagle rebels during the Hog War, an uprising which had raged for many months in the north-east of the demesne. Now her husband was to be torn to pieces as well, another victim of the curse of mayhems which some said was cast upon the clan males by the old emperor, Bansaikon Akutenshi, and his war-witch Gorgongrone.

Chironax let the scroll drop to the council table, his face near as white as Lady Snowsnake's hair, his soul as heavy and dark as the kohl which hooded her eyes. "We are the wardens of Kobutsuden," he said. "We hold it in trust for the next emperor — but that emperor is not Hikidashon Takasha, the Wife-Boiler. Surely we do not bend?"

"Then you would have my husband's head sent to us, in another box? More dead lips to kiss, more dead eyes to sew shut?"

After reading the scroll, Batsuron Boko said: "Hikidashon would dare not kill our overlord, in my opinion. If he did, we could yet call upon the other high clans to bring him to justice and execution — a compelling deterrent, without doubt. On the other hand, if we accede, Lord Akumuron might in any case be held captive indefinitely, to ensure the Wife-Boiler's safety in the Winter Palace. My counsel, therefore, is to stand firm."

"But there is a third option, is there not?" asked Lady Miura.

"War," said Lady Snowsnake. Her black-glossed lips curled back, showing teeth of polished steel. "Destroy the Takasha, liberate our lord, and raze the Templedark to dust. Our swords, spears and arrows will drip with the red phage, a bane which makes men piss blood and devour their own beating hearts."

"A sight I should like to witness," said Chironax. "But as I'm sure General Boko will agree, a war with the Takasha would leave the Viles unguarded from the enemy in our midst, the turpid legion lurking deep in the Valley of Flies, ready to erupt as pus from an abscess. We can only call upon three vassal clans, hardly enough to defend Kobutsuden. To go to war, other alliances must be struck."

"Then perhaps it is time to renew ties with our neighbours, the Taiyo," said Lady Miura. "Don't forget, it was our rock-rangers who saved the Sunstorm Castle from clandestine attack by Kyo the Killer, raising the alarm when we detected agents of Kyo's Skull Creed encamped near our border, at the Eidolon Caves. We saved the Taiyo from a deadly raid; now they can help us with an invasion."

"Two matters of seeming unequal value," mused Chironax. "How do we make weight?"

"Leave that to me," said Batsuron Boko.

# Castle Mortmane

Lord Hikidashon Takasha, thane of Castle Mortmane, ruler of the Templedark, called Wife-Boiler by some, sat high upon the ancient seat of his clan and laughed. His gold-plated war-hammer Yabuhaikin, smasher of spines, lay across his lap, and behind him hung one of Flayon I's secret paintings, *The Night Hag*, a vertical diptych showing a pregnant girl suspended by her ankles, the cannibal witch Yashroki poised with a disembowelling knife. Hikidashon held up a scroll of parchment in his right hand.

"This treaty is also signed by the Mizuno, the Taiyo, and the Gomi. Jukon Gomi, who styles himself warden-by-law, holds the Key of Bones. This is the Starfire Order, and we no longer serve, but rule. Our new capital will be Kobutsuden, and we each ride there with one thousand men-at-arms."

"You secretly refute Gomi's claim?" asked Chikon, his eldest. *He seeks out conflict as a rutting hound seeks a bitch,* thought Hikidashon. His son had already proved his worth in combat many times over, but would he ever learn the ways of diplomacy?

"A pact was signed. Jukon Gomi stands as warden and arbiter of council – for now. Your brother Gomon will be our representative at the table of four. I need you here, to hold Castle Mortmane with your steel."

Chikon nodded assent; Gomon looked surprised. "I'm honoured, father," he said, then quickly added: "But may I take Morla, my servant, to the city? She's been with me for so long..."

"You may not. But have no fear – I hear that the brothels of Kobutsuden hold many young things not averse to ropes and the prick of a blade."

Gomon had not realised that his father knew so much of his proclivities. Abashed, he bowed and hurried away to make ready, silently vowing to punish whoever had disclosed his secrets.

"You would sooner shed blood on the battlefield, this I know," said

Hikidashon, addressing his other son. "And your time may come sooner than you imagine. But first we have to deal with arrangements for your impending marriage, which I hope will embolden the Kurotako to join our league in defiance of Hebon Hakamanko. Lady Soma and her retinue will soon cross by barge to Blood Crag, and from there our guard will escort them to Mortmane."

"But the battle will be in the Viles, will it not? Defending the city against Tazon Ando and his horde; against the man who dishonoured our family... that's where I should be."

"Those savages could also range north; and in the east, Hakamanko broods and dreams of being emperor. There is danger everywhere, Chikon. Let us wait until it reveals itself in the light."

"Mother used to say that life itself was the dream," said Chikon. "But now it seems to me that if such is true, then it's only the dead who can ever truly be awake."

As night closed in and the great constellations of the Swine and the Seraphim emerged above the castle's monstrous towers, two brothers stood at the northernmost ramparts and gazed out over a glistening, frozen rockscape without discernible form or finitude, barely lit by the Skull Moon's fading evanescence.

"It was you, wasn't it? You told father about Morla."

"Who cares about that? Our father doesn't; he just doesn't want your playthings paraded around the Winter Palace. You will represent our clan, and must give no cause for rumours amongst the rabble, or amongst our fellow lords for that matter. Our agent Flamon Neko, who learned swords with us as boys, is already in the city; from now on he'll report to you."

"And his mission?"

"Flamon was sent to deliver death. But he may need your help, for the city's a dangerous place with many eyes. In truth I wish I was going with you, instead of staying behind to play wedding games with some Kurotako whore. But we each have our duty to the clan."

"And our father? He seems distant."

"He senses peril, as ever. Sentangarion talks of a death moon rising, the colour of heartsblood. But our enemies are the ones who should be afraid."

Gomon turned and peered across Mortmane's tenebrous expanse to the Joker's Keep, where he could see a candle guttering in Lord Hikidashon's far-off bed chamber. He knew that his father, who forbade him to take Morla to the city, was lying there in the nude embrace of the bane virago Lady Blastofane, while far beneath them in the castle crypt his mother's tomb held nothing but a few cooked and dog-chewed bone fragments. His sister Toka, who was now eleven, remembered nothing of the attacks by Tazon Ando which led to his exile and Lady Danna's cruel execution. He wondered if his new position on the Starfire Council might one day bring him face to face with Ando once again, allowing for a reconciliation with the truth. Whoever was at blame for his loss, they would one day pay the price – both he and his brother had sworn it in blood.

# SWILLY TOWN

"I've told you. I'll not go out there, I'm with child," said the serving-girl sharply. "I'm with child, and Lord Bellysbane's abroad."

"You'll just have to piss on the floor then, won't you?" laughed the soldier. "Wouldn't be the first time, I'll bet."

His two fellow drinkers laughed as well, the coarse crescendo momentarily distracting Flamon Neko from his reverie. He was thinking back to the dark stories that the maven Sentangarion used to tell them when they were still boys at Castle Mortmane, training in the arts of chaos; legends from the old country, before the time when the emperor Metakaikon first ruled Novalis. These legends spoke of Bankairon, the demon-slayer, and his battles with hell-born forces who sought to bring about an end of days.

"*It was an epoch of bloodthirsty devils,*" Sentangarion would tell them, reading from Banchon the Benighted's *The Ebon Weird*, an illuminated mythography of the demon-slayer. Flamon had long forgotten the next words, but not the vivid images they once conjured of Bankairon's exploits.

Haunted by the pleas of the pale captives he encountered far beneath the city streets, and by the foul engravings on the walls of the stone pentagon which encased them, Neko was somehow drawn back to these ancient tales of a malignant evil that revelled in filth and infanticide. He ordered more ale and tried to ignore the noise of carousing around him. Like most of the Swilly Town inns that night, the Twin Stumps was filled with palace guardsmen celebrating their final day of duty; on the morrow they could all return home, for the palace would be taken over by a new force, one which marched beneath the four-comet flag of the recently-formed Starfire Order – and, as far as most were concerned, they were more than welcome to it.

"I heard that Kyo the Killer's threatening to tear down the Fearfang Bridge," said one, "and hold the other provinces to ransom over iceshield; only iceshield armour can stop marsh dragon venom, and the only mines are down in Wolf's Jaw. If the Hakamanko unleash their würms, the rest of us'll burn."

"Isn't it true that only blind dwarfs work them mines? I heard he had a hundred of them with metal hands, all lashed together like a dog team…"

"Wouldn't surprise me… fuck Kyo anyway, and fuck the Hakamanko. They're not even in the Order, so what can they do? It's the meatmen that worry me… those bastards out in the Valley of Flies."

"Aye. Just last week they sacked and burnt a whole village… Crow River cunts, supposed to be brain-eaters. That's why they took all the heads."

"And then there's Bellysbane, running around with his bloody dolls… they say he's at least nine feet tall, with eyes as black as a butcher's arsehole…"

And then the man stopped speaking. If anything could have abruptly silenced the babble in that inn, it was her. She appeared in the doorway like a sainted spectre haloed in fireflies, no older than thirteen or fourteen years, stark naked, her entire body wealed with whip-gouges still weeping bitter red tears. Two women grasped her arm as she collapsed to the floor.

"Who did this to you, child? Who?"

Her voice was cracked and distant, barely audible. "The eye…" she seemed to say. "The fiery golden eye…"

# PART TWO
# THE BASTARD OF HELLHAVEN

# THE SPEWSALT CAVES

"Feric Smash-Bones is not stupid," said Feric Smash-Bones. "Our rider went for gold, never came back. So Mizuno don't want their lord back, either – a good thing now, since he died two nights back. So now only one dead lord, no gold, a sunk ship, a sword, and you – a man with one arm burnt off. So tell me, one-arm," – he held up Akafuku, death-sword of the Mizuno – "what kind of metal is this, that fire can't melt and hammers can't bend?"

Chokon Tora, last survivor of the *Devil Craw*, looked up weakly at his captor. A terrible pain wracked his left side, where the immolated arm had been crudely amputated just below the shoulder. For three weeks he had suffered in the gloom, surviving only on a gruel of crushed crabs and kelp, washed down with crudely distilled sea-water. "It's old," he said. "They say that our emperor Metakaikon created it in a volcano over a thousand years ago, and gifted it to Amon Mizuno, first of his clan."

"What is its value?" asked Feric. "Who will buy it from me?"

"No-one. That sword is cursed."

"Cursed? Speak plainly, one-arm."

"Only those of Mizuno blood may wield it unharmed; they say that it devours the souls of all others. Do you also value your soul, Smash-Bones?"

The pirate chieftain looked at the sword as if it might come alive in his grasp; Tora knew that superstition was also a weapon, one which could be turned against men of the vassal clans.

"Will you release me, now that Akumuron is dead?" Tora said. "I have no worth either, least of all with only one arm."

"I like blood," said Feric, ignoring the question, and left the cave.

Tora had only one choice to make; try to escape, or commit a warrior's suicide. *Probably not much difference,* he thought. Could he even swim with one arm? Feric

Smash-Bones evidently thought not, given the lack of a guard for his prisoner. Tora's only wrist was chained to the cave wall, but the manacle was severely rusted by the salt air and he was sure that it would shatter when smashed into the rock with sufficient force. Then he had only to float away on the foaming tide, which each night lapped at his feet before receding to the dark depths where his overlord's corpse had doubtless been consumed. There were sharks in that darkness, he knew, but better drowned and devoured than hanged by pirates. Only one thing stood in the way of this plan – his honour, which forbade him from leaving without Akafuku, the blade which had served his clan for centuries. But how could a one-armed man overcome a hulking barbarian and his crew of killers?

That night, long after moonrise turned the ocean into a black and silver meniscus of tragic beauty, Chokon Tora shed his chains and waded to the edge of his cave-cell, clasping the rock wall with his one remaining hand. Bat stars nestled in the crevices, slowly dissolving prey into liquid.

Tora saw that the coastline curved away to his left in a sickle of semi-flooded cave-fronts, varying in aperture; he surmised that the largest of them, perhaps two hundred yards away, was the one inhabited by the pirates. Several bobbing smallboats were tied to the rocks at the cave's entrance.

Inside the lair he found that the ground rose away sharply from the intruding waters; at least two dozen figures were wrapped in furs on the dry sand beyond, and all seemed to be asleep. Which one, if any, was Feric Smash-Bones, he had no way of knowing. But Tora's eye was drawn to something glinting to his right; he could see that there was a recess in the cave wall, just large enough for a man to step into. There, carelessly cast atop piles of plundered weapons, compasses, jewels, ingots and coin, was the irradiant blade of Akafuku, the red vengeance.

Tora's escape from the pirate cave was as slow and as silent as he could endure. As he pushed the smallboat away from its moorings he glanced back once at the dim forms of the slumbering savages, and then used his single hand to quietly guide the vessel towards Spewsalt Point, praying to find a beach where he could land, ever dreading the shouts that would tell him his flight was discovered. He had warned Akumuron not to navigate the Jackdaws, to sail around them, but his impatient lord commander had refused to heed him; and now here they were, Akumuron dead and him with one arm burnt and hacked away, adrift on the midnight sea.

Dawn's coronal rays were refracting through the deep by the time Chokon Tora's boat washed up on the shore, and he staggered from it like a scorched phantom bent on reaping a harvest of cold black fire. As well as Akumuron's sword, he had extricated a handful of coin from the pirates' trove, enough to buy a horse as he started the long travail south to the Nightmare Castle, his one-armed maniacal figure fit to affright both man and beast alike. Somewhere in his wake the Smash-Bones pirates were emerging into light, howling with outrage at their loss.

# THE SUNSTORM CASTLE

Rising from the southern cliffs of Goldengate, the Sunstorm Castle was fortress to Clan Taiyo, youngest of the remaining high clans, formed after Dankairon Mino, a masterless warrior who claimed descent from the ancient Yamayaga, married the daughter of Nuron, overlord of Clan Hexo. In the year 723, when Clan Hexo was wiped out in the Serpent Wars, Dankairon and his bride, supported by loyal vassal clansmen, claimed the ruins of the Six-Star Castle as a new base of power. They took the name Taiyo, and rebuilt the ruins to a new state of glory. Three centuries later, the Sunstorm Castle stood as the loftiest redoubt in Novalis; some boasted that its pink-enameled Solar Tower, home to Lord Nakasendaron Taiyo, reached as high as the very clouds.

Thus it seemed to General Batsuron Boko as his mission of six riders approached the castle's cyclopean gates; above the first wrought-iron portcullis was a great circular herald carved in coral marble and set with a revolving triskelion of the broken sun, the same device which radiated in gold from hundreds of black silken banners flying above. Boko's own device, the ebon vortex of Clan Mizuno, fluttered from his horse's caparison. Then the grid of painted metal was slowly raised and they entered, two abreast; as it lowered again behind them the second portcullis stood closed to the front, and for a minute they waited in that tunnel, some glancing nervously at the murder holes above. The horses were also ill at ease; Boko's mount began to grind its back teeth and clumps of dung fell from its anus, steaming in the frosted morning air.

Finally the second grid was winched open by its creaking chains, and the Mizuno mission entered Sunstorm. They were greeted by Veluron, second son of Lord Nakasendaron, and the maven Vorgovanian, renowned as a confectioner of mirage and illusion.

"I would speak with Lord Nakasendaron at once," said Boko. "The news I bring is calamitous."

The lord of Sunstorm was only returned from the Mirror Castle two days before, and his face was etched with a distant weariness. Remembering the story of the Feast of Demons, Boko wondered for a second if this was indeed the true Nakasendaron, or one of Vorgovanian's prosthetic deceits. Quickly dismissing the thought, he said: "Lord Akumuron is taken hostage by the Takasha, who demand control of the Winter Palace; Lord Hikidashon proclaims himself emperor."

Nakasendaron frowned, an immediate expression of doubt. "You have proof?"

"Here is the scroll, sealed with the Takasha pentagram, and signed by Hikidashon himself. It came with Lord Akumuron's ring finger."

Nakasendaron studied it briefly, then said: "Veluron, bring our copy of the pact."

When his son returned with the parchment, Nakasendaron placed it next to Boko's scroll. "Look," he said. "Do you see the difference? I watched Lord Hikidashon sign this pact with my own eyes, just weeks past. But the mark on the scroll is not the same; it is not his. And why would he do such a thing, when the ink is scarce dry on this new alliance?"

"Of what alliance do we speak?"

"Our clan, and your clan, and the Gomi and the Takasha, are the new custodians of empire by treaty, set to convene in Kobutsuden with a new army to defend against the dark. Here is Akumuron's sign and seal, next to mine. If you seek those guilty of such a crime against your overlord, look to the clans who refused to join our cause. Or perhaps an individual, one who had access to the Takasha seal but acted as renegade. Please, study the pact at your leisure."

"I should be grateful for a night's hospitality," said Boko, "and your leave to depart at dawn with these tidings."

"Granted," said Lord Nakasendaron.

But the dawn brought another message, the kind that comes cloaked in steel. The huge sea-scorpion bolt had lost most of its velocity by the time it glanced against the side of the Solar Tower, sending enamel chips flying before clanging to the empty courtyard below. Its purpose was clearly not destruction, but rather to serve notice; a fleet of some fifty war-ships had appeared during the night, and now lay at anchor just off the coast. Each ship bore the same device upon its silver mainsail and ensign – the circular black cephalopod of Clan Kurotako.

"And so Lord Bloodtooth, Sado the filthy Octopus, declares himself." Nakasendaron Taiyo gazed out at the ships, decks teeming with fighters. "We cannot repel them at sea – apart from my flagship the *Eclipse* and two destroyers, all our vessels are built for cargo – but should they seek to invade, they will find the Sunstorm Castle as welcoming as a labyrinth of blood-thirsting razors.”

“They say that Sadogashon’s rippers, the Shark White inbreds, are eaters of human flesh,” said Taikon, his first-born.

“As are our Skull Hogs,” Veluron reminded him. “Father; should we send for the vassal clansmen?”

“Send riders to them all,” said Nakasendaron. “The Skull Hogs, the Diamond Fangs, the Iron Dreamers, the Slit-Civets, and the slavering ones of the Fireball Dead. Surround Sunstorm fore and aft with a ring of metal doom.”

# THE WINTER PALACE

Questor Zan Vordulax gazed into the fire, seeking elemental absolution for his failings. "Your report, Clitto."

"None of the apostles confessed to being Slavos Sek, or to knowing Slavos Sek. Even when the carnifex smashed their limbs with his hammer, they swore they knew of no such man, nor of the slayings. But there is worse; this morning one of our watchmen was killed... by a corpse."

Vordulax said nothing; recent events in the citadel had left him hardened to even the most unnatural transgressions. He motioned Clitto to continue.

"The watchman found a baker's boy, murdered, on the steps of the Temple of Tears. A wide hole had been cut in the boy's thorax, and a small wooden drawer had been pushed into the wound. Inside the drawer the watchman found petals from a black orchid, a bloody eyeball – not the boy's – and a living scorpion which stung him on his hand, causing immediate convulsions of death."

After a moment of reflection, Vordulax said: "The victim, the crime, are not those we know from Flux, and yet who else is so steeped in the carnal poetry of aberration? Please inform our guest Hectoclarion at once; I would seek his opinion in this matter. And tell the Rascal to keep smashing limbs." *We have entered an age of indelible enigma*, thought the prefect. *The human eye evolves its own phantoms in the perpetual quest for light, smearing a blood-stained handprint across the film of reason.*

In the streets beyond the Winter Palace, word of the murder was already spreading through the morning markets, sparking fear of a second killer on the rise. By noon a crowd had formed outside the palace gates, calling for justice.

"The details may differ," said Hectoclarion, "but the essence is the same: a transformation of the victim's body. Your Flux may have a rival in the art of death, and the people are justly concerned."

"A transformation to what end? I've seen many bodies destroyed by rage, but never..."

Just then Clitto returned, ahead of two watchmen who were dragging the limp form of a man with nothing left of his legs but raw splintered femurs and flaps of shredded skin, tightly strapped to stanch bleeding. "This one found his tongue at the last," said Clitto. "Tell all to Questor Vordulax, and we'll give you sleeping seeds to quiet your pain."

"Moshino... the doll-man's name is Moshino. A bastard born of Lady Silversoil and... and..." The man spoke no more; his eyes rolled up into his head, and his heart ceased to beat.

"Exemia," pronounced Hectoclarion. "The violence of his maiming, the loss of blood, has ended this heretic wretch. But perhaps not in vain."

"His words had meaning?"

"The name Lady Silversoil is known to me. She was bane virago to the Hakamanko, when Lord Hebon was a young man; she fell with child by Hebon, all unknown to his new wife, and was banished under cloak of darkness. Legend tells that Hebon set her adrift in chains upon a ghost ship, the *Skalvesso*, burnt to its bare timbers by pirates; she was never seen again. Some say that when the night-wind howls through the Bay of Bones, it echoes the dead woman's mournful lament."

"But if she survived, and birthed her bastard..."

"Revenge is the will made flesh," said Hectoclarion. "And this Moshino is the flesh of Lady Silversoil."

# THE SPERM WEALD

"Do you know what I'd really like to do?" sneered Hekon Hakamanko. "I'd like to find a boy-child of three or four years, and fire him from a catapult."

Lady Vulvomane snickered, raising a velvet sleeve to her dark red lips.

"That would be most entertaining, beloved," said Lady Suna, ever careful not to provoke her husband's ire by questioning even the most repellent of the phantasies which seemed to perpetually spin through his mind. The world outside Skull Castle, which the hunchback had seldom seen before, was evidently affording him new inspiration, she noted. *And which is a finer death for a child? To be drugged and chopped into pieces in a dark room, or hurled through the midday air into a swamp of poisonous reptiles?* She snatched a glance at Hozon Ama, who rode beside the carriage. Before they departed he had secretly assured her that they would find an opportunity to flee. *But when?*

Ahead of them rode the five hundred Hakamanko horsemen, flying crimson banners emblazoned with a white self-devouring snake skeleton. An impressive display, but one which palled in contrast with what lay behind – the würm-riders. There were twenty of them in heavy armour, each master of a huge reptilian beast larger than a horse, with elongated neck, body and tail, short limbs, and a hide of slime-dripping greenish-brown scales thick enough to repel arrows, spears and sword-strokes alike. A würm's ruby-red eyes were its only points of vulnerability, and these were protected not only by metal blinders, but by a rubbery membrane which flickered over them every few seconds. Chain bridles controlled a hinged titanium muzzle which, when opened, allowed the creatures to spit a caustic venom which burned like acid through base metal, leather, wood, skin, flesh, and bone.

Marsh dragons did not fly or breathe fire like those of myth, but they reduced their prey to smoking ruin just the same. Suna had seen it for herself at Skull Castle, when a Tower Bat clansman accused of casting imprecations while fornicating with a she-goat had been sentenced to death. Peering from behind a tower window curtain, she watched as the captive was bound to a post in the würm pit, and one of the beasts released from its cage. After circling him for a minute or two, the würm disgorged a jet of black bile which soaked the man's head, and within seconds his face and skull were reduced to a scorching jelly streaked with hair-ash and half-liquid bone which the reptile sucked up with a sickening voracity. Suna's hand-maiden, Tisa, had also been sacrificed to the dragons, but that sight she had at least been spared.

The memory was one of many which each night haunted Suna as she slept, bringing nightmares which had long since begun to fuse with waking reality. She knew that many more months in Skull Castle with all its horrors, meshed in a macabre fugue conducted by the hunchback, would surely drive her to insanity. But with her father seemingly in thrall to the Snake Lord, the warrior-priest known as the Red Monk was now her only hope of escape.

They reached Hebon Hakamanko's camp at the Sperm Weald just after midnight. The tented enclave set up by Lord Hebon and his generals was circled by hundreds of shelters and fires in multiple rings, warming fighters from the vassal clans; Iron Talons, Night Weepers, Blind Cats, and Scorpion Blacks in the main, two thousand tattooed barbarians wrapped in bloody pelts and boiled hides, their shields painted with red ochre pictographs of blazing creatures or butchered corpses.

Next morning, as the sun's heat slowly evaporated a dense overnight mist, Hekon Hakamanko and Hozon Ama were summoned to Lord Hebon's war-tent. Suna remained behind, guarded by two of her father-by-law's men. *Protection, or imprisonment?*, she mused bitterly. Whatever plan Lord Hebon was hatching, her only interest in it lay in how it might open some window, however small, of salvation. A kestrel shrilled overhead, and in the distance she could hear the pharyngeal clicking of the marsh dragons.

"The Gomi and the Takasha march to claim Kobutsuden under flag of convenience," said Lord Hebon. "Let them have it, I say. With the Mirror Castle and Castle Mortmane ill-defended, our alliance of snake and octopus can seize all lands north of the Crow River. Let the Starfire Order wallow in the rest, and deal with Kyo the Killer. What say you, Hekon?"

The hunchback was daydreaming of one of his most cherished classical paintings, Flayon I's *The Diving Girl*, which showed a voluptuous nude pearl diver raped by a pink octopod, a tentacle deep in every orifice. "Indeed, father," he said, focusing. "Lord Hekon of Mirrors, I should like that."

"A title you will have to earn. Ama, you fought in the Battle of Rat Rock, and legend says your godsword Reikonyaku, burner of souls, sent more than one hundred to the fiery hells that day. You will lead our forces into war, and my son will serve as your personal aide."

"I will, Lord Hebon. In return for the sanctuary you granted me from the Celestial Horde, my sword is ever yours."

Hekon twitched. "Surely, father, you don't expect me to take up arms? My twisted spine..."

"Is matched only by your mind. You will devise cruelties of such ingenuity and ferocity that when word of them reaches our foemen, they will embrace our blades for a cleaner death. Fear, Hekon; fear will drive us to conquest."

# THE STORM SHRINE

Their livery bore a coral vortex through black, but the newly-woven banners they flew overhead were the colour of freshly-spilled blood with a row of four flaming golden comets at the outermost angle, each representing a member clan of the Starfire Order. Jukon Gomi rode at the head of the thousand as they crested the upland and finally looked across at the shrine of Arashon, Sorrow of Storms and mistress of the liquid hells. The shrine was a basalt megalith and sacrificial altar at the epicentre of a thickly foliated tree spiral, seven circles deep; at the base of each tree a horse's head had been buried, eyeless, during the site's antediluvian consecration. The temple of Storms, home to the shrine's thirteen mavens, stood on an adjacent rise, and beyond lay Storm Town, a garrison for three hundred and thirty-three warrior-priests of the Celestial Horde's blue-mantled battle division and those employed to attend them. The shrine stood almost exactly halfway along the road which ran directly from the Mirror Castle to Kobutsuden.

This was not Jukon's first visit to the shrine; once, as a boy, his father had made him attend one of the sacrifices which were made there each month at full moon – human sacrifices, in which the souls of criminals, transgressors or heretics were devoted to Sorrow Arashon so she might cleanse them in a heavenly tempest. That time the offering was a witch from the Rape Chain clan, one of the many under Lord Kamosukon Gomi's jurisdiction. The woman, a crone whose hair was dyed brittle-brown with crushed leeches and vinegar, stood condemned of causing another's child to be still-born so that she might dig up the corpse and use it in necromantic rites. Lord Kamosukon was obliged to report all such crimes to the Triad before dispensing justice, and on this occasion had been ordered to present his prisoner to face holy retribution.

The scene of the witch's immolation was one which Jukon had since relived many times in nightmares. Although his waking mind had long shut out the sight of her naked, withered body being shackled to the altar and painted with oil before being set alight, at night it all returned to haunt him in vivid detail; worst of all were the crone's screams and obscenities, her terrible curses hurled upon all assembled there that day.

Now, as he approached the Storm Temple a decade later with the emperor's ashes in retinue, Jukon realised that the night of full moon was almost upon them again; he could only hope that they might take their leave before the next sacrifice. He was greeted by the maven Cassavion the High, who offered him wine and altar-cake while the thousand made camp in the fields outside the garrison. They sat in the temple's central crescent, Jukon and the thirteen mavens, surrounded by statues of Arashon who was sculpted as a nude female warrior wreathed in lightning, bearing a great stone sword inscribed with elemental runes.

"Since his disfiguring my father favours the castle gloom, and so I will represent Clan Gomi at the Winter Palace," said Jukon as he displayed the Key of Bones to the mavens. "The other keys could not be found; they may be sunk beneath the great lake of black glass in Thundervoid, or buried in the ice-tombs of Kyukiden itself."

"You were chosen to bear the Key of Bones," said Cassavion. "While your league holds court in Kobutsuden, the Celestial Horde will heed your call."

"Our spies have made many reports of heresy in the city," added the maven Tardassion. "Vigilants, mystagogues of a false deity named the Holy Eye. We expect these apostates to be eradicated. And we expect you to bring their leader in chains to the sacrificial altar."

"I understand," said Jukon. *You'll support me at war as long as I do your purging and purifying in the shadows.* "Will there be a sacrifice tonight?"

"It would have been tomorrow," said Cassavion. "Tomorrow is the apex of the Spider Moon, an hour reserved for those who sin against the brotherhood. But Hozon Ama has slipped his bonds."

"Hozon Ama?"

"The Red Monk. A great warrior, but a dissolute man who betrayed his vows of chastity by destroying the maidenhead of a Storm Town stable-girl. When the girl's grandfather threatened to expose his transgression, Ama hacked off the old man's head in a drunken rage. He was arrested and condemned to be sacrificed, but the girl foolishly facilitated his escape, believing he would take her for bride. Instead he abandoned her, and she now waits alone to birth his sin-child."

"And where is this Red Monk now? He evades capture?"

"According to our spies he is under the protection of the Hakamanko, for whom he no doubt serves as mercenary. An additional blasphemy, for the prostitution of a godsword is akin to raping the divine."

"Unfortunately, Hebon Hakamanko rejects our league and its authority. But the matter will be noted at council," Jukon assured them. He was haggard from the long ride, his thoughts turning involuntarily to the comforts of sleep.

"There is one last matter of import," said another of the storm-mystics, Daxarian the Dire. "For many years I was maven of minds at Hellhaven, the great madhouse on the moor built by Emperor Dandaikon for victims of the parasite plague. As you may know, some years ago Hellhaven's charter was abolished by Lord Hikidashon Takasha after inmates broke free and descended upon a local village, butchering all its folk and then reassembling their body parts in a hell-puzzle. The naked maniacs were slain by Takasha bowmen as they pranced, gibbered and copulated amongst the corpses. Since this event, which some called the Red Rampage, Hellhaven has festered in dereliction.

"In recent months, our spies have reported flickers of firelight and fleeting shadows within the rotting walls, and some speak of a haunting. I would ask you to raise this matter with Lord Hikidashon in the first order. Hellhaven is an imperial monument, and thus beyond our purview."

"I shall," said Jukon. "Until tomorrow."

That night the bad dreams returned; the death-curse of the burning witch as her hair burst into lecherous flames and scorpions erupted from her eyes, mouth, nipples and vulva, then a new horror, lunatics with worms in their brains dancing on the ashes, gash-struck and gargling with gore.

When Jukon awoke, the Spider Moon was already rising in a seamless sapphire sky.

# THE CACKMIRE CAUSEWAY

There were six riders; three behind the carriage, three at front. Their armour was stamped with the five-pointed star of the Takasha, but the crimson and gold banner they flew was one Kuron Kirizono had never seen before. Both parties reined up. The Cackmire Causeway, which extended over both wetlands and sweeping ravines on its serpentine path through the demesne, was too narrow for more than three horsemen to pass abreast.

"What's your business in the Templedark?" asked the middle soldier.

"The emperor's business," said Kirizono. Nezumon Nano was beside him, with three other agents at rear. "We ride to reclaim Hellhaven in the name of the Akutenshi."

"The emperor is dead," the soldier sneered, "and so are the Akutenshi. *You* should be dead."

Kirizono said nothing as he weighed up the men who faced him. Either side of the one with the impudent tongue were younger soldiers, perhaps not much more than boys.

"Our Lord Hikidashon sequestered Hellhaven years ago," the first soldier continued, nerves tested by Kirizono's silence. "It's a forbidden place."

"Hellhaven was built by the emperor Dandaikon Akutenshi," said Nezumon Nano. "And the Takasha serve the Akutenshi."

"Did," said the soldier. "Now we rule, as part of the Starfire Order. See the flag? By that authority, I order you back where you came from."

Kirizono and Nano seemed to lose patience at the same time, Kirizono drawing his death-sword Oshi and Nano reaching to his belt. When his hand came up again it was holding a hooked silver star which he launched spinning towards the Takasha man in one sweeping motion. Even before the soldier's sword was halfway from its scabbard, the razored points of the star sheared through his throat and severed his jugular vein with a rapid spray of lifesblood. As he keeled sideways the wound kept spurting with each heartbeat, ever weaker until both heart and blood had stopped and his corpse lay crumpled on the causeway.

At the same time Kirizono urged his sable destrier forwards, yelling "For Raikon!" as he decapitated the soldier who sat on the dead man's right. By then the third of the out-riders was already turning his horse to flee, but found his egress blocked by the carriage. He jumped from his mount into the water-logged field beside the road, attempting to wade away from death. The Devil Bat flew after him. Now only the carriage stood between the last three Takasha and the Akutenshi. Kirizono could clearly see two figures inside it, both female and well-dressed; one, who appeared to be heavy with child, sat veiled and motionless while her companion recoiled from the slaughter, eyes frosted with fear. The ornamented vehicle was harnessed to two white horses in single file, helped along by a bridle-boy. Kirizono motioned the boy away. He saw that the front horse's face had been splattered with blood. Both beasts were agitated, eyes rolling up, mouths foaming.

The Akutenshi split into pairs, Kirizono and Yuron Fuki to one side, Kagon Shura and Jagon Ketsu to the other, their horses plunging into wet grass to circumvent the carriage. The Takasha had decided to fight and protect their wards, and all three swerved their mounts to the same side, electing to attack Shura and Ketsu three against two. The Blue Dragons were forced to defend against a frenzy of blows from the slashing Takasha swords, unable to counter-attack as their horses were slowly driven back. But the fight was over as soon as Kirizono and Fuki rounded the carriage and came up behind the soldiers. The Black Reaper thrust his heavy blade clear through the back of one man's skull, while the Ghost Blizzard looped a length of thin wire around another's neck and crossed his wrists. As he pulled back and outwards the wire bit into the soldier's throat, and kept biting until it was sawing at his spine. The last soldier tried to turn and run then, but was butchered in the saddle. Chunks of flesh and bone, four bodies and two heads bobbed in the blood-streaked mire, quickly attracting a flurry of diamond-skinned watersnakes.

Kirizono came up alongside the two women, one sobbing, one silent. "They should have let us pass," he said. "Who are you?"

"Soma," murmured the one in distress. "Lady Soma Kurotako, of the Red Rock. And this is Lady Burnbolt."

That evening, after they crossed the Crow River and the causeway opened up into woodlands where they could safely make camp, Kirizono examined the mysterious Burnbolt more closely. Behind her veil, eyes of green crystal stared ahead forever into the gathering darkness, bejewelling a charnel house beauty compounded of cool wax and icy steel.

"This is the craft of a skilled maven," he said. "What is his name?"

"Chromocrax," replied Lady Soma. "Perhaps you know of him."

"Perhaps." His own maven, Glitterax, had once mentioned a twin brother equally versed in the science of chaos dolls. "I've never seen a swellbelly before; what's her purpose?"

"If I tell you, you may not let me go," Soma said. "I fear my father, Lord Sadogashon, is no friend of the Starfire Order."

"And you think we are? Those dead Takasha would surely beg to differ, if they still had heads. This Starfire Order is false; the Akutenshi still hold power from the Shadow Castle, and I am regent of that power. You will remain in our charge, but for your own protection. You have no value as ransom... unless your father holds the Key of Bones?"

"The last key of the Triad? That key is held by the Gomi, who found the body of the emperor and cremated his remains at the Mirror Castle; my father was at the funeral rites."

"And where is the key now? Was it also consumed?"

"I could not say, truly. Take me home, and you can ask my father yourself. He also rejects this new league."

"Our agents will find the truth of it. Tomorrow we ride to Hellhaven, to await their return as arranged."

# THE VALLEY OF FLIES

"What's it to be then?" said Gorn. "Revenge, loot, or power?" The sword-shifter was growing restless; he needed to do something more than teach cut-and-thrust to drunk savages, no matter how compliant their womenfolk were.

Tazon Ando put the head back on its spike and wiped his hands on his tunic. "I swore an oath of vengeance against Hikidashon Takasha," he replied. "If the wreaking of that vengeance also brings spoils, so be it. Our scouts are all reporting the same thing – war's coming, and coming fast. A war between starfire and lizards, and the Takasha are in league with the stars."

"Then I suppose that makes us lizard men," said Gorn.

"Lizard men, perhaps even devil-worshippers. It's rumoured that the Hakamanko and Kurotako have declared for the old gods, and one in particular... Zenmarion, the King of Hell."

"Fuck's blood! Makes sense though... when men go to war, they usually drag their gods with them. All that talk of devils and demons should fire up the meatmen, anyway. But what about the Mizuno? Seems like they didn't take the bait."

Ando gestured at the severed head. "He delivered a message this morning, one I didn't want to hear. Akumuron Mizuno's dead. The Mizuno don't know it yet, but in any case they'd already signed a treaty which puts them on the same side as the Takasha. Them, the Gomi, and the Taiyo."

"So the Seikyo are for the lizard lords?"

"Seems not. They're closing their borders and declaring Wolf's Jaw a republic; we might as well forget about them. Hebon Hakamanko has massed an army in the north of Lizard's Den, and prepares to march on the Shines. Sadogashon Kurotako has sent war-ships to threaten Sunstorm and the Nightmare Castle. I've already sent riders to Bloodtooth avowing our support; now we must march north to the Templedark and join land forces with the Octopus."

"All of us?"

"All of us."

The preparations took three days; Gorn went to each clan chieftain in turn, issuing orders which were then passed down to the foot-soldiers. The Maw Fetters, the Grey Ghosts, the Kill-Claws and the Blood Eagle berserkers numbered more than five thousand, steeped in violence and thirsting for war; the Smash-Bones were best left marauding the coast, with orders to intercept any ships sailing north from Gluttonport. Gorn also sent word to the Whip Flay, Devil-Dog and Sickle Wasp clans, who all set aside feuds and defected to Ando's cause upon learning that Clan Mizuno no longer had an overlord or male of the bloodline. The Nightmare Castle was left in the hands of Akumuron's widow and her council, and menaced by both rebels and the Kurotako fleet; the Mizuno were surely finished as a power in the Viles. Kobutsuden would in effect become a city-state of the Starfire Order, Gorn guessed. *And good luck with that.*

On the evening of the second day, a five-man Whip Flay patrol turned up leading a spare horse with a one-armed corpse draped over it.

"We found him heading for the Mizuno castle," said one of the clansmen. "When we approached he drew his sword and threatened to kill us all; he failed. Here, take it as our gift."

Gorn took the blade and looked it over; he had seen it before, he realised, mounted in the great hall of the Nightmare Castle when he was in the pay of the Mizuno. This was Akafuku, the clan's ancient deathsword; without it, their demise was surely complete. He said nothing of it to the Whip Flays, and later handed it to Tazon Ando.

"A deathsword, forged from vampire steel," said Ando. "What better weapon could there be to remove Hikidashon's head?"

On the third day the seven warlocks of the seven low clans ordered a mass sacrifice of all horses not fit for battle or heavy transport. The beasts' heads were hacked off and mounted on long wooden poles which had been carved with death-runes, and these poles were driven into the ground all along the upper ridge of the Valley of Flies, facing north to hex the enemy. The carcasses were butchered for meat, the rawhides stretched and salted in the curing-caves, the bones broken down to be fashioned into arrowheads, spear-tips, serrated blades and war-clubs. The entrails were cast upon the ground by Gutric, a painted haruspex of the Grey Ghost clan, and in their slathering coils he divined glorious futures for those on the battlefields to come.

The warlocks' rites continued after darkfall with the Night Ride, a torchlit invocation of the warrior dead. The slaughtered horses' heartsblood was boiled in copper cookpots with fungi and roots, a potion fit to fortify the mutilated shades of the fallen as they rose up and howled beneath the constellation of the Hook Man, submersing the valley in a detonation of spectral incandescence. Clan females smeared the brew over their naked bodies, writhing and copulating with ghosts while the warlocks pounded war-drums and the watch-fires flared up blinding-white with fistfuls of explosive dust.

Gorn knew better than to quaff the potion himself; the Blood Eagle berserkers were said to drink a similar concoction before going into battle, and once in its thrall they blindly crushed and dismembered any who stood in their path, friend or foe alike, often fighting for hours or even days on end until their hearts stopped.

"I think I'll stick with wine," he told Tazon Ando. "I've already seen enough ghosts."

"You'll be seeing a lot more before the war is done," said Ando. "That's why they call this the Age of Shadows."

# KOBUTSUDEN

The black ensign with two silver thunderbolts had been lowered, and a larger standard as bright as blood now flew high above the Winter Palace, embossed with four flaming golden comets. Gomon Takasha was seated in its council chamber with the chaos agent Flamon Neko and Questor Zan Vordulax, prefect of the Starfire Watch. "Four members will not suffice, since we need a casting vote," Gomon was saying. "Perhaps you would consider taking the fifth chair, until we appoint a maven?"

"I should be honoured," said Vordulax.

"Very good. Jukon Gomi, our arbiter-by-law, is due to arrive tomorrow with his troops, and we expect envoys and soldiers from the Mizuno and Taiyo by week's end. Our first order of business will be entombing the remains of Emperor Raikon in the crypts below; then we must address the issue of Lord Hebon Hakamanko, who threatens the northern provinces with his military presence. Meanwhile, I believe there are matters of religious insurrection and lust-murder to discuss. This is Flamon Neko, an agent of our clan; like you, Neko has been tasked with tracking a certain Slavos Sek."

"Then you will know that Sek is Prime Optic of the Vigilants," said Vordulax. "We believe that this cult is connected to a killer and foetus thief named Moshino, known to disciples as the beast, the bastard son of the bane virago Lady Silversoil. We obtained this information from a Vigilant apostle, one of several arrested in a purge. All of them disavowed Sek, even under torture, except for one fool who claimed Sek was a vampire whose lair was a black tomb in Skullhaven cemetery. The Rascal scooped his eyes out with tongs for that impertinence – and who can blame him?"

"I too have heard of this beast," said Neko. "Far below the city I found a star-dungeon where young girls are held in cages; they told me that the beast raped and seeded them, but their unborn children were snatched from the womb by a woman. They called her the mother of bloody roses."

"Could Sek and Moshino be one and the same?" asked Gomon.

"If so, the Vigilants must be regarded as agents of terror and devil-worship," said Vordulax. "They must be exterminated."

"I will take you to the star-dungeon," said Neko. "Bring your palace guard, for who knows what else lurks in those buried shadows."

As Neko, Vordulax, his assistant Clitto and the maven Hectoclarion were escorted through the streets of Swilly Town by a dozen armed watchmen, it was apparent that since the arrest and maiming of the Vigilant apostles, the red and purple robes of the cult had disappeared from sight. *At least they are no longer recruiting,* thought Vordulax, *but invisible diseases are the most deadly.* Had he made the right decision by driving the heretics beneath ground? Perhaps they would soon find out. *The butcher and the tallowman are in the cult's pay,* Neko had told him. *Question them, and they may break more readily than the apostles.*

When they arrived at the butchershop, Vordulax realised at once that something was awry. The shuttered trade window was wide open, and the little meat still on display was rotten and riddled with maggots, too foul even for beggars or gutter-gaunts to steal. A lone pigshead sat at back, dripping with putrefaction. The smell of death doubled as the men entered the unlit shop, causing several of them, including Clitto, to fall back retching. One swallowed a blowfly and nearly choked. There on a carcass rack, purple-faced and slowly dangling from one of his own meat-hooks, was the obese slaughterman Chattox.

Next door the tallowman's corpse was equally posed in sardonic ruination. Only the left hand and forearm were visible, jutting from a vat of rendered beef fat; the hand was still clutching a candle, long burnt-down to its root. The surface of the fat was patterned with congealed blood, and Vordulax briefly thought he saw the likeness of a hanged man with horns in its dark red crust.

"The stairway to the dungeon is in the cellar," said Neko. Vordulax motioned him ahead, and he led them twice down into darkness.

As he had suspected, the cultists had also silenced their prisoners. The cell doors of the pentagonal dungeon were wide open, and inside were the corpses of the girls who had so unnerved him with their mournful and cryptic lamentations. Red roses, now browned and shrivelled, had been scattered everywhere.

"I see no wounds," said Hectoclarion the High. "Poison is the most likely cause of their death. And here–" he lifted up a blackened wrist-stump "–is the mark of another evil; the drug is known as soulscrape, a concoction of savin, red squill and ergot, administered for the sole purpose of provoking still-birth but also bound to result in gangrene of the extremities. These poor girls were cursed, body and soul, by a witch."

# THE SHADOW CASTLE

After several weeks of searching, the maven Glitterax finally found it locked away in a rusted metal box atop the highest shelf of the library. This book repository was the oldest and most secret in Novalis, and contained a number of esoteric tomes of which there were no other copies extant; some had never been duplicated, others had fallen prey to the ravages of time or fiery proscriptions through the ages. The *Volcanic Codex*, drafted by the thirteen Shadow mavens, was a cataloguing of artefacts, devices and weapons created during the reign of the emperor Metakaikon, specifically those forged in the belly of Komonyama, crucible of life and death, the raging volcano which had finally burnt itself out almost one thousand years ago.

It was in the Ark, Komonyama's occult furnace, that the mavens crafted the thirteen deathswords which Metakaikon bequeathed to the high clans, eternal gifts of steel which would not bend or break under the assaults of common metal, would not melt at the kiss of common flame. Each sword bore the herald of its clan on its pommel, and its own name in an indelible ideogram just above the hilt. The first blade forged was Tekizan, decapitator of foemen, deathsword of the Akutenshi; after that came Obochi, the graveyard king; Kurosatsu, the black slaughter; Kyami, master of darkness; Yomuji, the maggot bride; Akafuku, the red vengeance; Kinzokami, the metal wolf; Honekiri, cleaver of bones; Yahana, the midnight flower; Jigomonban, hell's gatekeeper; Seppunryu, the dragon kiss; Kaijuken, the monster blade; and Sensoni, the war demon. According to the codex, volcanic steel was vampire steel, imbued with a molecular thirst for human blood which could never be slaked until the end of time.

Hagmarrion's *The Ophidian Tryst*, a romantic history of the Serpent Wars, recorded both the extermination of six high clans and the fate of their deathswords. Yahana, wielded by Lord Kakon Akaichi, was sunk to the bottom of the Mad Marshes along with the defleshed bones of its master, while Kinzokami, sword of Clan Hexo, was raised from the rubble of the Six-Star Castle by Dankairon Mino, founder of Clan Taiyo. Clan Satogawa's deathsword Jigomonban was usurped when Lord Magon Mizuno and his twilight assassins, the Scarecrow Sect, ambushed Lord Skyon Satogawa on the Parasite Pathway and cut him into cubes. Seppunryu, the great sword of Clan Mishima, was lost when Lord Usagon Mishima was slashed and paralysed by Lord Fekon Hakamanko, known as Fekon Fork-Tongue, who was whispered to be an acolyte of ancient snake-magic and fought with a golden morning-star doused in deadly viper venom. Kaijuken, the death-blade of Clan Hassha, was stolen when Lord Hasomexon Hassha was disembowelled by the Mystery King, fabled sword-shifter for the Seikyo who avowedly went to war in a corpse-skin mask and a clackering cloak of ossified graveworms, while the Clan Inoshi deathsword Sensoni was forfeit at the Battle of the Bloody Beasts when a huge wolf, gorge-black with eyes of time-blasted onyx, snatched it up between slavering jaws and carried it away to the depths of the forbidden forest that girds the slopes of Mount Mooncry; it was never seen again.

But Glitterax was not seeking a history of the deathswords. The *Volcanic Codex* also held the secrets of Metakaikon's most revolutionary and blasphemous experiment – the Seven Deadly Archangels, whose hearts were also fired in the white-hot bowels of Komonyama by an alchemy now lost to mortal memory.

The Shadow Castle was a vertical gallery excavated from a cliff interior, rising from the shore of a green phosphorescent cave lake and split into five levels, the silhouettes of more than fifty Akutenshi emperors burned into its natural rock walls from bottom upward. At the very top lay the chancel, where seven female bodies had been laid out on biers arranged in a septagram. Scented candles burned beside them. Above every body was a nude statue, each one in heroic pose and carved from gemstone of differing hue which was matched by the gown of the form outstretched below. The gowns were unlaced at front and had been opened to expose pale white breasts, between which was a circular aperture in the flesh. In each aperture, except one, was a disc of silvered steel shot through with a rune which seemed trapped in the very essence of its host material. Glitterax had inserted the keys himself, during the destruction of Kyukiden; now it pleased him to visit his precious charges as they reposed, awaiting the call to life.

Nearest the chancel door lay the Lady Morvenna, Archangel of Voids, gowned in black; then Lady Valessa, Archangel of Venoms, gowned in deepest purple; Lady Carnella, Archangel of Mayhems, gowned in darkest red; Lady Tyranna, Archangel of Shadows, gowned in earthen brown; Lady Sybella, Archangel of Tears, gowned in midnight blue; Lady Samara, Archangel of Ashes, gowned in funeral grey; and finally, gowned in white but devoid of key, lay the Lady Morella, Archangel of Bones.

From esoteric texts and diagrams in both the *Volcanic Codex* and Sextarion the Sly's *Anatomy And Artifice*, Glitterax had gleaned that the volcanic heart-keys of the Seven Archangels were receptors which served as conduits for the metacarrion, said in religious scriptures to be composed of numinous beings but perhaps more truly pictured as an undying pulse of magnetic energy emanating from the stars, planets and rangeless zodiacs of the heavens; it was easy to see how such a force might be construed as the vessel of the Three Sorrows, he thought, but it could also be – and often was – exploited as demonic. Only the thirteen mavens of Shadows, long dead and voiceless, could truly reveal the cosmological fusions which lay behind the forging of the deathswords and the seven keys. When Komonyama was extinguished, the alchemy of shadows died with it.

Glitterax thought of his brother Chromocrax, by seven minutes the elder, who served the Kurotako; his attempts to recreate the chaos dolls of the Shadow mavens were primitive by comparison, driven by mechanics and devoid of the artificial soul which could only be made manifest by communing with the metacarrion on planes invisible to the mortal eye and unattainable by mundane science. When the war was won, he would liberate Chromocrax from servitude and raise him to the ranks of the Akutenshi. But first the Key of Bones must be returned and the circuit of souls completed; and until that time the weeping world would shudder at the spectre of Emperor Raikon's vengeance, every vault and void resounding with the Black Reaper's fearful death song.

# HELLHAVEN

It was almost dusk by the time they reached Hellhaven. Kuron Kirizono, Black Reaper of the Akutenshi, was flanked by five chaos agents of the Blue Dragon Hand with two ladies of the Kurotako under escort, both astride a single white horse; the lady at front appeared heavy with child, and the other held her upright. Seven more horses, riderless, trailed behind. From distance Kirizono was sure he'd seen candlelight in one of the madhouse window-holes, but now the whole edifice was darker than death. It resembled nothing so much as a vast granite burial mound; upon its rounded roof Dandaikon Akutenshi had raised the statue of an apocalyptic angel, a towering godslayer with time-torn fire-bladed wings and a headsman's sickle in each outstretched hand. Queerly angled apertures gaped just below, and it was from these that the lunatics had escaped to swarm in the Red Rampage, the first of them smashing to bits on the stony ground far below until the pile of corpses rose high enough to serve as cushion for the last.

"We stand at the very centre of Novalis," said Kirizono, "the furthest point from the ocean in all directions. Dandaikon believed that the plague came from beyond our shores."

The inner walls of the building were ringed with hanging lanterns, which they lit as they moved from level to level, after tethering their horses beneath the green gaze of Lady Burnbolt. "Better inside with rats and shit than eaten by wolves," said Kirizono. On the second storey was the surgery where maven Daxarian the Dire used to perform his trepanations, housing a stained marble slab fixed with leather straps and surrounded by a blood gutter; on the third storey they found the wall daubed with an effigy of an enormous red snake, which stretched around the entire stone circumference to eat its own tail. Attending the snake, and all across the floor, were etchings of other base creatures; they appeared to have been traced in blood and excrement. In the centre of the chamber was a firepit of rocks, and its embers still glowed.

Warily they ascended the final winding stairway to the top of the madhouse, swords drawn. Here were the confinement cells, perhaps a hundred of them, arranged in a circle. In one of them a light flickered.

The Akutenshi raised their lanterns. "Step forward," said Kirizono. "Step forward and meet your master."

Two bent figures emerged from the darkness, the first holding a lighted candle. He was semi-naked and caked in ordure, hair and beard uncut and matted and alive with lice. "Wormcrackle," he said. "I'm old Wormcrackle, and that one's Sucklestench. Our mother's candlemen true."

"Your mother?"

"Our mother. Our mother of the bloody roses. She chops, and then she changes."

"Madmen," said Nezumon Nano. "Best cage them else they slit our throats as we sleep."

"Tell me more of this mother," said Kirizono, raising a staying hand. "How do you serve her?"

"Our mother came from the salt sea," said Wormcrackle. "And she were with child. They say her boy were half snake; now he's grown, and on the night of the Red Rampage they left us. We did it all for them, you see. Pray a penny, master."

The second madman, equally filthy, nodded in agreement. "She came from the salt sea, in the reptile night. Black as a shark, and twice as hairy." He was looking beyond the swordsmen, staring at Lady Soma. "Who's your friend?" he leered. "I'd like to lick her, I would. Aye, like a lizard licking a grasshopper, all upside-down and starry."

Lady Soma stepped back in alarm.

"You'd make a good palace jackanapes," said Kirizono. "But keep away from her or you'll end up with the temple eunuchs."

"Aye then," replied Sucklestench, and hobbled away into the gloom. "Her skin's got no pictures anyway," he muttered, disappearing inside one of the cells.

"It would be a mercy to kill those two," said Kagon Shura, but Kuron Kirizono said: "We'll cage them by night. By day they'll eat the rats, no doubt, and save us the trouble of catching them all. Besides, it's bad luck to kill a lunatic – didn't your mother teach you that?"

"A sausage a day keeps the butcher at bay," chimed Wormcrackle as he nestled in his bed of sperm-crusted straw. "Pray a penny, master, pray a penny."

# THE WINTER PALACE

"Rats," said Questor Zan Vordulax. "They must be teeming like rats down there in the lower depths beneath the cellars. And Moshino is the rat king, sucking at the filthy teats of his dam Silversoil. Worse, no-one knows how many secret vaults there are, or how to find them."

"A map would be needed," said Hectoclarion the High, "an ancient map drafted by ancient hands. But the question is, how did the Vigilants obtain such a document? And there is another matter of concern – you saw those engravings, the snakes and the spiders and the scorpions and the centipedes? They were also ancient, and are the sigils of an even earlier cult, those who prayed to the Vermin League. History tells that Bankairon, the demon-slayer, was among those on the first ships to Novalis; perchance his enemies followed, and took root."

"But Bankairon is a myth, surely."

"His many-storied deeds are legend, but the man was as real as you or I; Banchon's *Ebon Weird* contains explicit genealogies of the Yamayaga clan which confirm it. Through the centuries Bankairon's foemen were mythologised as supernatural creatures, but they existed nonetheless. And the same distortion persists today – life mediated through the fear of Hell and all its horrors. It is past time I returned to my duties at the Sun Shrine, but I leave you with one last thought: we now know with certainty that Moshino's mission is not foremost to merely extinguish life, but to amass a throng of tiny corpses. How else to explain the deliberate seeding and aborting of his own progeny with the poor nude brides of the star-dungeon?"

Later that day, after the maven had departed from the citadel, Vordulax was summoned to attend his first meeting of the Starfire Council. Five sat at an ebony table built for twenty-three, with Lord Jukon Gomi at the head; to Jukon's right sat Vordulax and Gomon Takasha, to his left Veluron Taiyo and Lady Snowsnake, bane virago and

"

now war-witch of Clan Mizuno. Behind Jukon, mounted and displayed on the chamber wall, was the Key of Bones, last symbol of imperial power. The other walls were hung with a series of enormous battle triptychs by the artist Flayon II, depicting bloody scenes from the Serpent Wars.

"We *are* at war, no doubt," said Lady Snowsnake, "but with whom is not entirely clear." Her skin and waist-long hair were indeed as white as snow, but her lips and eyelids were painted blacker than the night, and when she spoke they saw that her teeth were cased in shiny mirror-metal. "Our overlord Akumuron is either captured or dead, by unknown agency; all we have of him is a ring with a rotting finger inside it."

"By our league's treaty, an attack on one is an attack on all," said Jukon. "And so we stand beside you in this uncertain hour. My own home, the Mirror Castle, is menaced by Hebon Hakamanko, as is yours, Lord Gomon. And Lord Veluron reports that Sadogashon Kurotako's warships are anchored off the coast of Goldengate."

"And just outside Gluttonport as well," added Lady Snowsnake, "thus threatening invasion and a besieging of the Nightmare Castle."

"Our course seems clear then," said Jukon. "We join forces to repel the Hakamanko in the north, and to repel the Kurotako in the south. Lord Gomon, as elected warlord it falls to you to send out riders with strategies to all four castles. And a final petition to Lord Kyodokuron Seikyo would do no harm. All loyal vassal clans must be called to arms in our cause; war may yet be averted if we show unity of purpose and mass of strength. Meanwhile, the immediate task of this council is to hold Kobutsuden. Questor Vordulax, I know that you have matters to report relating to the security of the city. Lord Gomon has informed me of events to date; have you any more news of this cult of the Holy Eye?"

"The cult's mad killer, Moshino, struck for a fourth – perhaps fifth – time this very morning," said Vordulax. "Another gravid girl was slain, her unborn replaced by a doll with mouth sewn shut; and around her neck was a mocking wreath of mummified snakes."

Jukon recoiled from this indecipherable image; he was accustomed to the carnage of battle, but the gloating slaughter and repurposing of innocent women and infants was an anathema to the Three Sorrows, a rupture in the bleeding fabric of the metacarrion. *Perhaps Juka was right all along,* he thought. *Perhaps we've already entered an age where perversion, cruelty and death are the new coin, and where the upstart gods are just the ancient evil ones given new aspect.*

"This Moshino," said Lady Snowsnake, leaning in towards the table. "I think I know who he is."

# THE SPERM WEALD

Suna tried to avert her eyes, but the hunchback was remorseless.

"Don't look away now, girl; you must gaze upon my masterpiece."

Lord Hebon Hakamanko's first cross-border raid into the Shines had resulted in the capture of a dozen Golden Maggot clansmen, and his son had ordered all but one of them to be buried up to their necks in one of the boggy fields near camp. Foot-soldiers ringed the gaseous expanse of grassland, expecting to see blood. Now Hebon's most deadly würm-rider Vexion was steering his drooling lizard, Bolgo, onto the field. Suna saw the terror in the first clansman's eyes as the beast's titanium muzzle drew back on its hinges, exposing the maw with its double rows of yellow incisors and its hazy sulphurous breath. Then the man screamed – but not for long. His tongue and throat dissolved along with the rest of his head as the würm vomited a stream of black acid venom. Hekon rose from his chair and applauded, his face ecstatic. "Again!" he crowed. "Melt them all!"

When the spectacle was over, the hunchback's design was revealed in all its grotesque glory; a sward of eleven charred and pitted skulls arranged in the shape of an H, devoid of all flesh, baking in the noon sun like leprous fruit. Vexion raised the visor of his metal cobra mask, saluted his master and then spurred Bolgo back to the würm-pen.

"Now," said Hekon, "send this savage away and let him warn his fellows what fate awaits any who resist the Hakamanko."

The Golden Maggot was unbound and sent staggering on his way. Suna, feeling faint, leaned over in her chair. Hekon turned to his father.

"It was inspired by the saw-pits that were used in old Kyukiden during the reign of Klaxoklaikon the Cruel," he leered. "Criminals and insurgents were buried neck-deep in clay then beheaded by the Tiny Teeth, a gang of gold-hooded dwarf executioners with blood-rusty band-saws; it is recorded in Brother Sarsaxion's *Canon Of Corrections*."

Hebon nodded approval. "We finally have some use for your talents and erudition," he said to his son. "If you could just plant a seed inside your wife, all would be perfect."

Suna's nausea deepened at these words, seemingly spoken with disregard for her presence. Hekon's lack of interest in carnal matters was the only saving grace in her existence; to suffer his advances would be more than she could endure. At night she even dreamed of birthing a monster, half reptile and half octopus, which split her in two as it thrashed its bloody way into the world. Secretly she hoped that it would be Hozon Ama who one day lay with her; Hozon Ama who, he told her, had been wrongly accused of murder after protecting a young girl from rape by her own grandfather, and was forced to flee from injustice. *Soon we'll flee together,* she thought, *before the whole world is drowned in war and blood and pain.*

But the hunchback was not done with her yet. As he led her back to their tented quarters, Suna saw that fevergleam in his eye which always presaged some game of deviant design, some unsightly aberration hinged on cruelty or debasement.

"Your morning gift, girl; did you save it for me?"

Suna nodded. Her childhood friend, Tisa, had been fed to the würms for refusing such a request, and she had no desire to follow. "Beneath the bed, beloved; in the golden pot, covered with soft red velvet as you desired." *As one day soon you may lie covered beneath the earth, stinking just as sweet.*

With one arm curled around the privy-pot, Hekon led her back outside and towards the acrid encampment of the Nightshade clan, where bats were roasting by the dozen on huge meat-skewers. Huddled in a crude shelter of branches and pelts was the clan's warlock, Brak Browntongue, a bestial dwarf with livid rope-burns around his thick throat from where men had tried to hang him, and more than once. Brak was a copromancer, one who claimed to taste the future in the excrement of others.

"I trust you're hungry, Browntongue," said Hekon.

"Aye, darklord," replied the dwarf, "and hungry for coin, too."

After rummaging in the pot and raising stubbed fingers to his lips, Brak tilted his grotesque head backwards and to the left, his eyes rolling upward; a foul saliva stained his chin as he started to shake and mutter. Suna could only watch in revulsion, fearful of what the dwarf might prophesy. Even though she held no belief in such rituals, Hekon did; and that meant she was at Brak Browntongue's mercy. *My life lies in the soil-stained hands of a dwarf; the hunchback has reduced me to nothing more than a toy.* Smoke from charred bat-wings stung her eyes, adding to her tears.

After a few minutes the warlock's shaking subsided, and his ill-sized, bovine eyes refocused. "My lady tastes of the ocean," he said. "And by the ocean she shall birth a boy-child. One day this child shall wear a crown."

"And the child's father?"

"A great warrior, as red as the sun that rises and sets."

"Red? In what way, dwarf?"

"I cannot say, darklord; I see only a sword rising from an ocean the colour of blood, and a boy-child bathed in its light."

"A pretty picture, no doubt," said Hekon as he let a handful of coppers slip through his fingers. "Whatever could it mean?"

That evening Suna feigned the lunar sickness to avoid supper, and while Hekon and his father were feasting on spiced entrails and buttered insects with their generals and lackeys she slipped, hooded, from her tent and into the jaundiced fog. The Red Monk was quartered on the edge of the enclave, and despite the danger from watching eyes she hurried there through the mud, caution dashed by fear.

"Lady Suna, you risk all," said Hozon Ama, wine in hand. "If our alliance is discovered..."

*Our alliance? Is it truly nothing more than that?* "Time conspires against us," she urged, quickly hiding her doubt. "Hekon's natural suspicions are now heightened by the ravings of a morrow-eyed dwarf, who visioned me with child by a warrior. And the word *red* was at the crux of it all."

"Meaningless noise, surely. But..."

"But Hekon values the meaningless above all else. He has no use for me in the marriage bed, but would see his father's würms rape me before ceding control of me to another man. If he doubles the guards around me..."

"I understand," said Ama. "Soon we march on the Shines; be ready to flee before then, at a moment's glance. Now go, before we are undone. A hellborn storm's astir – and when the wind dies, who will bury it?"

# THE TEMPLEDARK

By night they travailed beneath a rictus of imploded lodestars, ever northward, veering towards a pincer-point of irradiated blackness just beyond the fringes of perception; the days were filled with freezing winds, and rain that darked the sun.

"We should've stayed in the fucking cave," said Gorn, more than once. But on the sixth morning daylight prevailed, and as the mists evaporated they could see Croton Kurotako's encampment and the Crow River foaming beyond.

The camp was fortified with a ditch and rampart, roughly sharpened stakes jutting outward in all directions, the river shielding the rear. Banners flew above, flaunting a squat black cephalopod in a silver swamp. As they drew near Gorn noticed a corpse still impaled on one of the stakes, no doubt the aftermath of a raid repelled during the night.

"Demon Reds," said Croton. "About twenty of them, throat-slitters all. Parts of them are over there–" he motioned to where a fence of spikes had been erected, each sporting a bloody tattooed head "–and parts are over here." He pointed at a firepit where a gaggle of Shark White rippers were ranged in a circle; several spits were turning over the flames, and what cooked on them were the limbs of men. "The rest are dead in the river, bound for the Bay of Bones – fish food, either way."

"An impressive response," said Tazon Ando. "How many men do you have?"

"A hundred rippers, and a hundred elite guardsmen from the Red Rock – the Arms of the Octopus."

"Perhaps we should be called the Spawn of Flies," muttered Gorn.

"Our force numbers some seven thousand," said Ando, ignoring the sword-shifter. "As you can see."

Croton did see. Stretching back for more than a mile, he guessed, was a sprawling caravan of fighters, beasts and carts, emanating a continuous groundswell of noise and a pervasive stench of human and animal filth.

"Don't worry, we'll camp where we are," said Gorn. "Now; how about some ale?"

As they supped and ate – fish, Gorn noted with some relief after seeing the rippers' repast – Croton outlined his battle plans. Not much more than twenty-five years of age, he yet had a harshly-lined face leathered by the ocean winds which whipped around his ancestral home, the Slaughterhouse. By his side was a curved and sharp-looking sword, a falchion, which he told them was named Kazokubi, stacker of severed heads. Only his father Sadogashon was permitted to wield the clan's deathsword Yomuji, the maggot bride.

"I propose three divisions," he said, "one commanded by each of us. We cross the Crow River at three points, at least fifty miles apart, and then two close in upon Castle Mortmane like a deadly claw, from south and east at once. The third division keeps marching north, joining the assault on the Mirror Castle by the Hakamanko, whose forces are less in number."

"Fine with me," said Gorn, "as long as I get the Blood Eagles." He'd never actually seen the Blood Eagle berserkers in battle, but had heard many stories and believed them all. First they would hunt, slaying whichever beast they chose to emulate upon the field of war, then draining its heartsblood into a cauldron to be boiled with deathly skullcap mushrooms; drinking this brew, called shapestrong, would transform them into feral creatures impervious to pain and ravenous for human carnage – wolves, fur-hooded and howling, or bears, with metal claws that sheared through faces, necks and bodies as if they were melted butter. The ghosts of their ancestors fought with them, side by side, drowning the world in a whirlwind of gore.

"Then you will join the Hakamanko serpent," said Ando. "My destiny lies at Mortmane, and my vengeance sword thirsts for Takasha blood. Do you accept, Lord Croton?"

"Done. The castle is ours; Lord Hikidashon is yours."

# THE WINTER PALACE

"Moshino. Never forget who you are," said Lady Silversoil. "You are the bastard of Hellhaven; born in a madhouse, raised by lunatics. Seed of the snake, harvester of cauls, the beast in the Bonestar Labyrinth."

"Yes, mother."

She was naked, and every surface of her hairless body, from her brow to her perineum to the soles of her feet, was covered in tattoos of interlinked scorpions and roses, silver and red and writhing. Though she was less than two score years of age, her breasts were lax and withered from weaning the bastard, who sucked her dry with reptilian voracity for years on end and would not surrender the teat until he was nearly as tall as she. *Boned like a snake, with a vampire's thirst.* Now, at seventeen years, Moshino was a butcher of women, an abomination in the eyes of the Triad but a saint to those who worshipped the old ways, *the true ways.*

"Remember; in ancient Kyukiden, a great victory was consummated against the Yamayaga clan," Silversoil continued. "Bankairon and his Night Angels were slaughtered in a death-trap; so began one thousand years of revolt. This slaughter was erased from history, and Bankairon is yet acclaimed an undefeated hero. But our league, his secret killers, sank his bones deep in the belly of Mount Komonyama.

"When the most blighted graveyards of the old country were split and churned asunder by the great earthquake which marked the death of Bankairon, a complex of curses was unleashed, a legion of unrequited ghosts ravenous for the cloaking of human flesh. I stand before you now as the incarnation of Komaja, the Snake Bride; Komaja, who summoned the dead to rise and wage war upon the emperor Jaikon and all the fools who came after him. And where are those fools now?"

The fools were hundreds and hundreds of feet above them. Up through towering layers of slabbed stone and compacted, worm-infested soil and rock, up again through more stone to a forgotten crypt where rats chittered and pissed beneath ten-foot-high cephalophores of the lost White Light Brotherhood, up again through the dungeon torture chamber where the Rascal was castrating two sallow-faced nun-rapers, up again through more layers of sculpted stone to the sweltering palace kitchens where she-goats turned on spits and their heads boiled in soups, and then up through yet more layers of stone to the council chamber where Lady Snowsnake snapped and grated her metal teeth as she dredged her mind for memories.

"It was several years ago," she began. "You may have heard rumours of Lord Akumuron's brother, Kichigon, how he was locked away in the Terror Tower at Nightmare Castle with the plague, raving and gibbering at the moon. Those rumours are true. One night he attacked the serving-girl who took him food; they say he tore off her breasts with his bare teeth. After that Lord Akumuron had him strapped in a leather binding-coat and sent to Hellhaven. I was one of those who accompanied his delivery, charged with administering a draft of bloodspore and berberine designed to kill the worms in his brain and quell his convulsions."

"You mean blackshade?" asked Veluron Taiyo. "I heard it kills the man sooner than the parasite."

"A mercy, either way. But Lord Kichigon was alive when I left him at Hellhaven. It's what I saw there that haunts me. As we delivered Kichigon to the mercy of the monks, I saw that the madhouse inmates, man and woman alike, were as if in some communal dream. They shuffled around and around the stone chamber in a column, continuously, one behind the other like some undulating human snake, sometimes coiling and uncoiling, always moving in unison; at the head of this snake was a naked boy, perhaps twelve years of age, with scaled skin that sloughed away from him as he walked. And the boy was shouting, always shouting. *Unborn,* he yelled, *unborn, undead.* And then the lunatics took up his cry, with a single voice like a monster possessed by a hundred demons. *Unborn, undead,* they kept screaming. *Unborn, undead, forever.*"

# THE OSSUARY

Two dripping purple moons clashed in the sky above the row of naked male bodies twitching on meathooks, *more than my corpse-cart can carry,* and as he was suddenly closer he saw that their eyes were made of black wormy ordure that started to boil and bubble down their mouldering faces. Then the hooks tore through their flesh with jagged wounds in the form of lightning-strikes, shoulder to groin, erupting with shrieking faecal maggots which lodged in his eyes, mouth, nostrils, brain. More dead men, *murdered priests sodomised with snakes,* burst from the soil around him, clawing, lifting him up to float in fiery air, the rope of rotten meat slipping over his head and tightening around his throat, ever tighter as he soiled himself and an ancient lych bell began to toll. Red eyes watched him from across a sea of molten magma, the eyes of an arachnid vampire that began to suck his entrails from his burst-open belly as the dead slowly chanted his name in voices akin to the buzzing of a million charnel flies. *Dorion... Dorion... DORION!*

And then he was awake, gasping for breath and dripping with stale sweat, and the maven Morgomox was pounding on his chamber door. "Dorion!" he shouted again. "I need you in the mortuary. Now!"

By the time he'd splashed himself with water and dressed, the rider from Kobutsuden was already below him in the great hall of the Ossuary, bowing before Lord Kyodokuron and proffering the sealed scroll entrusted to him by Jukon Gomi. After reading it, Kyodokuron bid the rider wait for his reply and adjourned to the council chamber where he was soon joined by his only son Kyowashon, two of his generals, and the bane virago Lady Hexheart.

"The Starfire Council beg us for help," said Kyodokuron. "They entreat us to unleash our Skeleton Sealords and death-ships against the Kurotako fleet."

"A reasonable request," said General Kasho, "if we were a member of their league. But since we are not…"

"What do they offer in return?" asked Kyowashon. He was only a boy of sixteen, but the Seikyo tradition was to blood their male heirs in the ways of war from an early age. If any ill befell Kyodokuron, his son would be expected to take charge of the Ossuary and the affairs of the Seikyo without rupture.

"The correct question," said the boy's father. "Only this – peace in Novalis. What does that sound like to you, General Sanko?"

"A threat. Wolf's Jaw already has peace – they do not."

"Lady Hexheart?"

"As the general says. And yet – the Taiyo's false claims to mineral rights along our mutual border persist; too small a matter for war, but too vexacious to be tolerated forever. Just last week one of their Solar Flame chaos agents poisoned a well used by our excavators. Lord Nakasendaron, his wife and whelp may have escaped the Feast of Demons, but could they escape a skeleton curse, delivered to the very core of the Sunstorm Castle?

"It seems certain that the Kurotako are not preparing to invade; their presence is only intended to keep the bulk of the Taiyo troops from marching north to defend Kobutsuden or bolster its allies. Neither side will unduly provoke the other. But our death-ships, in the guise of siege-breaker, could sail unopposed to the very shores of Goldengate, where once they would have burnt in a rain of fire. Even as the Taiyo were celebrating the apparent retreat of the octopus, a far more deadly creature could be incubating beneath their very noses. And none would ever be the wiser."

"A beautiful chimera, no doubt," said Lord Kyodokuron. "Send word to Kobutsuden that we will answer their plea; and advise the Kurotako to the contrary. And fetch me the Fleshstripper."

It was noon when the sealord Nikon Tabu reported to the Seikyo council. He wore his military attire, black tunic and hose embroidered with the silver bones of a wolf skeleton, and a cloak of burnished titanium fish-scales. Tabu was commander of the Seikyo death-ships, all equipped with piston fire-throwers which could burn an enemy craft and crew to ash, thereby earning him his gruesome name-of-war. Many of the bones which decorated the Ossuary walls were those of pirates who felt the blistering kiss of the Fleshstripper and his goliath dromon, the *Hellfire Scream*.

"Lord Nikon," said Kyodokuron, "I trust Lady Hexheart has informed you of our stratagem?"

"With exceptional clarity, Lord Kyo. And I believe that the *Hellfire Scream*, if fitted with new artillery, is large enough to execute it as long as we range within the shadow of the Sunstorm Castle. To sustain the illusion, perhaps at least one Kurotako vessel should be forfeit."

"It will be arranged," said Lady Hexheart. "And Sunstorm will soon be nothing more than a plague-house of phantoms."

# CASTLE MORTMANE

"Only armour forged from iceshield can quench the acid of the würms," said Chikon Takasha. "And we have none." He knew that iceshield was born from an alchemical combustion of two metals, titanium and vanadium, and that the only vanadium mines in Novalis were held by the Seikyo. "Kyo the Killer is no friend of our league; he has no reason to help us. Easier for him to sit back and watch us all burn."

Takasha troops had not faced the flesh-melting wrath of the marsh dragons since the Serpent Wars, three hundred years earlier. Now word was abroad that dozens of the monstrous beasts, among the last of their kind, had been harnessed by Hebon Hakamanko under the war-sign of the skeletal snake.

"Dragon-spit may cut through iron and skin," said Chikon's father, Lord Hikidashon, "but the walls of Mortmane are twenty foot thick; let them retch until their bile is spent, then we'll see what happens when a lizard gets squashed by a rock. As for Lord Hebon, Bonehead's already sharpening his axe. Cut the snake's head off, and what remains? Wriggling crow-food."

It was what Chikon expected to hear from his father. The last time any had dared to attack Mortmane, Hikidashon had ended the siege, such as it was, by challenging the formidable rebel Hell-Claw chieftain, Fire-Arse, to single combat. Fire-Arse ended the day with Hikidashon's war-hammer Yabuhaikin buried so deeply in his helmeted skull that to give it back his bearers were forced to saw off the whole head to be boiled down until bone turned to glue, metal yielded and the weapon was freed; or so the story went. *But the Hell-Claw was just a man, and my father is twenty years older now.*

"Our scouts report that Hebon's army is aimed at the Mirror Castle," interjected the maven Sentangarion. "What will a marsh dragon do when it faces its own reflection? And will Hebon split his attack in two, or crash against the Gomi first?

Either way, Mortmane may only face half of his forces; and horsemen offer no more threat to our castle walls than wingless würms."

"And yet the ground clansmen are fearful," said Chikon. "They say that the Hakamanko pray to evil and ancient deities; that Hebon rides the red snake, a snake not seen since the emperor Jaikon waged war upon Arkestron, the demon king, and his concubine Baragasha, queen of skulls. Crex Crab-Eye, a Crow River warlock, spreads claims that würm-shit will burn holes into the centre of the earth, and from those holes all the long-buried ghouls of the night will erupt, joining with Hebon in an orgy of blood. Many others speak of like prophecies, all portents of a doom unleashed when the fires of hell swept through Thundervoid. Gomon took the main of our soldiers with him to Kobutsuden; without the low clans, we can barely man our walls."

"Then you'd best go and talk them round, before it's too late," said Hikidashon. "I expect each clan to provide five hundred able fighters – not a man less. And send an envoy to the Gomi, to broker mutual assistance. What use is this new league, if one member cannot help the other?"

"I will go, father," said Chikon, "but what of the Lady Soma? She was due some days past; should I not be here to greet her? If we can yet cement an alliance with the Kurotako, the Hakamanko would stand alone. I know her sister is wed to the hunchback, but by all accounts she's more hostage than wife, handed over to balance Lord Sado's trespasses."

"So you think Lord Sado would favour one daughter over the other? Why? Because the other's been raped by a cripple?"

Chikon shrugged. "I know that fathers abandon daughters for less," he said. *And husbands wives.*

"Very well. Send more armed riders; the causeway may no longer be safe, and the delay is indeed worrying. Should the Lady Soma arrive in your absence, I'm sure Lady Blastofane will keep her good company."

But the very next morning, as Chikon was preparing to ride out, they had their answer. A scout reported back just after dawn, and with him was a young lad of not much more than twelve years; his clothing was filthy from the road, and splashed with dried blood.

"He claims to be from Clan Kurotako," said the scout. "He says he was bridle-boy for the Lady Soma's carriage, and that they were attacked upon the causeway by half a dozen reavers. Our soldiers were slain, and Lady Soma and her companion were abducted."

"Who were these reavers, boy?" asked Lord Hikidashon. "Men of the low clans, no doubt?"

"No, greatlord," said the boy. "They were armoured warriors, riding battle-steeds. Their banners were black, with silver star-bolts convergent. One of them was big as a bear, and shouted as he attacked us. *Raikon!* he cried. *For Raikon!*"

# THE NIGHTMARE CASTLE

Each night and day she prayed to Storm Sorrow Arashon, mistress of the liquid hells, to smash the Kurotako fleet asunder in a divine hurricane, to suck their ships beneath the churning waves in whirlpools and dash their crewmen's skulls to pulp against the rocks like rotten eggs. And each night and day, her prayers went unanswered. The surface of Gluttonport Bay, where the ships lay at anchor, remained as calm as a pond; sky and water were so clear that when those aboard looked down they could see every starfish, squid and shark-gnawed human bone upon the ocean floor.

After ten days of vain supplication Lady Miura Mizuno sent riders to the Storm Shrine with a scroll entreating the thirteen mavens for deliverance; twenty days after that the storm maven Daxarian the Dire was ushered into the Nightmare Castle's council chamber, resplendent in his midnight robes veined with white webs of lightning. There he was met by Lady Miura and her own maven, Chironax.

"As I assured Lord Jukon during the phases of the last Spider Moon, the Storm Shrine stands behind the Starfire Order in these times of turbulence," said Daxarian.

"Welcome news," replied Lady Miura. "But turbulence is precisely what we lack. Where is sweet Sorrow Arashon, when we need her ice winds and dagger rains to rip apart the enemy at our shores?"

"Many call in pain upon the Triad," said Daxarian. "But how to gain their attention, above others? My counsel would be an offering of souls; and if you permit me, I stand ready to conduct the sacred ritual as a high maven of Arashon's temple."

"You speak of human sacrifice," said Chironax darkly. His own robes were of saffron silk, embroidered with sombre geometries in black. "As a man of science, I must warn against this, Lady Miura. If we sink to the savagery of the low clans, who will bear the torch of enlightenment? We are not warlocks."

"No, we are not," said Miura. "But I have lost my son, and now my husband, whose own brother was sent raving to the madhouse. Science could not save them, any more than did religion. The maven Daxarian, if I am not wrong, speaks of a balancing of the cosmic scales, death for death; when those dearest to us are already given up, what harm a few more who now rot in darkness, without hope? Let their immolation have the meaning denied to them in life."

Chironax moved to speak again, but Lady Miura raised her palm.

"We gladly accept your counsel, maven Daxarian. Chironax; fetch me the Scar Faery."

She was the only female carnifex among the high clans, as fell and ruthless as any of the men. Before that, the Scar Faery was once she-champion of the empire, enthroned as blonde goddess of the Grinding Pits after defeating Kyukiden's Blood Bitch in a brutal spectacle which left the Bitch devoid of every limb. Those who witnessed the carnage told how in victory the Faery had raised up her opponent's shorn torso on the end of her sword, its blade plunged so far up into the nether parts that its tip emerged from the dead girl's mouth.

After that fewer and fewer worthy female fighters dared to oppose her, until she was reduced to battling freaks like the obese giant Little Lord Lardfist, who tried to smother her with his naked buttocks until she reached up and yanked out his rectum, or teams of dwarfs, enraged by liberal doses of firefinger, that swarmed and slashed at her with grappling hooks until she squashed them flat, one by one, with a slaughterman's hammer. The Scar Faery's final contest was against King Kidney, a monstrous male wart-hog captured near the Valley of Flies, with tusks filed down to sabre-points and three evisceration-kills to its name. She slew the beast, but her victory came at cost. One tusk ran straight through her thigh, shearing out the muscle; the Scar Faery would never fight again.

Although her days in the pits were over, fortune yet favoured the wounded Faery. Among her most fervent admirers was none other than Lord Akumuron Mizuno, a frequent patron of the blood-soaked sands, who saw to it that her recovery was paid for in return for loyal service. And so she came to the Nightmare Castle as crippled carnifex, butcher-queen of the dungeons, the rack and the chopping-block. Word from the gaolers was that she administered torture like one born to it, stripping stark naked before she went to work on her victims with pincers, bone saw, branding irons and flensing knife, oft-times moaning with a sexual shudder.

"There are twenty-seven in the cells, Lady Miura," said the Faery. Her long blonde hair hung in a braid over one shoulder, obscuring some of the thick cicatrization that patterned her exposed upper breast. "Among them are five Kurotako mariners, arrested in Gluttonport for crimes of rape, theft and murder during recent years. I gelded the rapists and behanded the thieves; as for the killer, he's alive but there's not much left to burn."

"Does four suffice, maven?" asked Lady Miura.

"Four, and four again," said Daxarian the Dire. "It matters not whence they came."

And so as night fell eight burning-stakes were erected on the cliff-top far above the port, and eight prisoners chained to them facing out to sea, where braziers and torches could be seen already lit on the distant decks of Kurotako vessels. Soon eight human beacons blazed in response, as Daxarian chanted prayers half-stifled by the screaming of the burnt ones. Lady Miura was watching from atop the Terror Tower, far from the crackling flesh and spitting fat, her attention focused more upon the heavens as she watched and waited for Sorrow Arashon to hurl down, at last, her death-tempests and elemental furies upon the accursed ships below.

By dawn the sacrifices were little more than smoking skeletons, twisted metal and cindered wood. Daxarian was nowhere to be seen. From the Terror Tower a long and awful wail of despair rang out, shattering the silence and reverberating around the castle walls like a death-rattle. The surface of Gluttonport Bay, where the ships lay at anchor, remained as calm as a pond; sky and water were so clear that when those aboard looked down they could see every starfish, squid and shark-gnawed human bone upon the ocean floor.

# THE SPERM WEALD

For three days and three nights more she waited, but the Red Monk never came. All she knew was the smoke and clamour of the war-camp, the clicking of the marsh dragons and the cackling of the hunchback as he sported and conspired with his circle; those who came and went most frequently were his simple-minded Iron Talon henchman Bullybabble, the scar-faced Hakamanko general Serpon Skoto, the bane virago Lady Vulvomane with her phials of the centipede ichor she called creepvein, and a pair of Scorpion Black gash-gizzards who brought him offerings of fat beetles and fireworms, for what purpose and in exchange for what she dared not guess. And then, on the fourth dawn, the invasion began.

"I know you'll be praying for my safety, dear girl," said Hekon. "But fear not, for the Red Monk himself has sworn to protect me with his mighty godsword." The hunchback's words were as a knife twisting in Suna's heart as he gestured over to the ranks of the armoured horsemen; there, astride his silver-grey destrier, was Hozon Ama, resplendent in shiny night-blue chainmail and mantle blazoned with a lattice of white lightning strikes. A white-plumed metal helm covered his head and face, but Suna was glad of it, for she could not bear to gaze into the eyes of betrayal. "Have no fear," Hekon continued, "Bully boy will guard you well."

With that he was gone, awkwardly mounting his horse and jerking it in the direction of the others. Suna watched in crushed silence as the Hakamanko army moved out from the encampment. In the vanguard were the würm-riders, whose reptilian monsters would melt the flesh from the bones of any who stood in their path; behind them marched three thousand feral clansmen, armed with huge axes, scythes, clubs, chains, maces and mauls; and behind them Lord Hebon and Lady Vulvomane ahead of the five hundred riders, among whose ranks her former hope of salvation now numbered, a hope dashed to icy ruins. She knew then that she would never escape the hunchback's web of perversion and torment; all she could do was pray, as he had said – not for his safety, but for his screaming bloody death.

"Slaymen shit at sunrise," she heard Bullybabble say, but ignored him as she watched the horsemen move ever further into the irretrievable distance. After a few minutes Suna saw the last of them disappear beyond the horizon, and turned away. She was empty, forlorn, despairing – but something made her look back one more time. Where a moment before there had been nothing but a haze of distant trees and rocks, she now thought she could discern a single, living figure; slowly the figure grew larger, until she knew it was a rider on horseback – and he was heading the wrong way, back towards camp. The rider had the low morning sun behind him, and his featureless outline loomed like a void punched through slabs of shimmering primordial stone, surrounded by the radiance of a revenant martyr.

Bullybabble now stood in front of her, squinting against the light; as the rider finally reached the outer circles of the encampment they could clearly see his dark garb, his plumed helm, his silver-grey mount. He kept on riding until he reached the tented enclave, the destrier rearing up on its hind legs outside Suna's pavilion.

"Forget your head?" said Bullybabble just as Suna rushed past him, her momentum and Hozon Ama's strong right arm lifting her up onto the horse's back; and then the beast surged forwards again, trampling rows of empty shelters and jumping over a firepit and a brimming latrine trench thick with flies to land on the open field beyond.

As the destrier broke into a gallop Suna craned her neck to glance back at the camp; Bullybabble was already clambering onto his own courser – a gift from Hekon – yelling something about wasps, and then he was after them. No matter how fast Ama spurred his mount, the hunchback's henchman seemed to gain ground; by the time they reached the edge of the woodlands, he was barely one hundred yards behind. Then they reined up.

"You, my armour; we cannot out-ride him," said Hozon Ama as he dismounted and then grasped her waist to help her down. "Hold the horse."

The warrior-priest stepped forwards into the path of the onrushing Iron Talon; at the last second he stepped sideways behind an ash tree, its trunk shielding him from Bullybabble's sword-swipe even as he rolled his body around it and slashed his own blade down the charging horse's rump as it passed, opening up a bone-deep gash. The stallion screamed and stumbled, pitching Bullybabble into the dank loam beneath its hooves. The henchman scrambled to his feet, cursing.

"Fuck-priest fucking blood-fuck!" he screamed as he flew at Hozon Ama in a blind fury. Ama's godsword carved a semi-halo of divine mercy; Bullybabble's head flew up and sideways with a gush of heartsblood, crashed to the ground and flipped over, lips still moving, vainly, to articulate a final nonsense. Ama grasped a handful of fallen foliage to wipe down his blade. Suna moved to embrace him, but the Red Monk raised a gauntleted hand.

"No time to rest," he said from behind the dark helm. "Others may be coming."

And so they rode on until darkfall, winding through the woods, sometimes doubling back and around so that none might follow their trail. As moonlight exploded above the gnarling trees, they came to a small clearing and a poacher's stone hut.

"We're here," said Ama.

The hut was just one room, with slitted windows and a low wooden roof. An old rope dangled from one of the cross-beams, like the aftermath of a hanging, and a torch was guttering in a niche. By its weak light Suna saw an apparition to make her gasp and shrink away in horror; a monster was chained to the rear wall. One half of its head had been completely stripped of flesh and hair, with nothing on the right side save seared skullbone, a gaping eyehole and crumbling, gumless teeth. What did remain of its face was contorted in a hideous rictus, its eye a frozen study in abject agony. Although this creature hanging in the shadows was entirely motionless, she could feel that one unblinking eye yet *watching* her; it belonged to a man, a man with every aspect of a corpse, save one – he had somehow forgotten to die.

Suna reeled around to seek refuge in Hozon Ama's arms, and saw that her saviour had taken off his helm; what confronted her was another disfigured visage, this one criss-crossed with vicious knife-scars. Barely comprehending her plight, Suna sunk limply to her knees on the hut's carpet of decayed leaves and rat-bones; she had plunged from liberation to damnation in the space of a few infernal moments.

"It's the creepvein keeps him alive," said Serpon Skoto, throwing the helm aside. "Our lady of the poison flowers slipped it in his wine before we took him. Though he felt all the pain of the würm's kiss, the drug kept his heart beating. Lord Hekon was sure you'd want that. Come closer now; I do believe our handsome priest is pleased to see you."

# THE WINTER PALACE

"The maven Valadian," said Flamon Neko, "from the House of Antiquaries."

"Please, be seated," said Jukon Gomi. "We welcome you to the Starfire Order. Neko tells us you used to attend the Seikyo?"

"Indeed. Kyozankon Seikyo was my overlord; he used to call me Valadian Goldenbones, worth my weight in coin he used to say, after my discoveries in metallurgy. I was also tutor to Kyodokuron Seikyo when he was a boy… until the incident."

"The incident?"

"Well… Kyodokuron had a wild nature, and was more interested in swordplay than schooling, regretfully – except for the study of human anatomy. I later realised that this interest derived purely from a wish to understand more efficient ways of killing, even though the boy was only twelve at the time. One day he shot a crossbow bolt into one of the stable-lads, to see how long he would take to die. After that I deemed my teaching days a failure, and left the Ossuary for the city to serve as an antiquary."

"It would seem that Lord Kyodokuron has not changed much, from stories told," said Jukon. "Our interest is also in anatomy, but of another kind; we wish to know more about the internal workings of Kobutsuden, its structures and its history – and especially its bowels."

"This is a subject I know well," said Valadian Goldenbones. "As you may recall from your own days of learning, Kobutsuden is a city that sprang up around this very palace, which was erected at the behest of our third emperor, Hentaikon, in the year 133. Hentaikon was sickly in both mind and body, and could not abide the cold climes of Thundervoid; some say he was born of incest between the empress Guma and her brother Cthaon, a fallen priest also called the Hornet Monk for the poisonous barb affixed to the tip of his staff. But the Winter Palace was not the only structure built by Hentaikon and his engineers; from within these very walls, unseen by outside eyes, they dug deep into the ground to a level far below the buildings and cellars which came later, and there they excavated a vast labyrinth which Hentaikon called the Bonestar.

"Legend tells that the Bonestar was devoted to human sacrifice and the worship of demons, and that Hentaikon himself was lord of a black cabal that sought to summon forth Zenmarion, King of Hell, and his filthy minions. The labyrinth consists of many pentagonal chambers of differing size; some are interconnected by tunnels, some have become closed off over the centuries. Some, I believe, may now be accessed from the lower levels of the city."

"We have already seen one such chamber," said Jukon. "And we fear that the labyrinth is once more being haunted by an occult sect, one which uses the unborn in its rites. Does the House of Antiquaries hold a map of the Bonestar?"

"Sadly not," replied the maven. "It is said that but one map was ever made by Hentaikon's engineers, and that map was torn apart and eaten by the emperor himself, who saw the secrets of the underworld forever lost in his own faeces. He also had the engineers beheaded, so that none might speak of their handiwork.

"And yet, there is no doubt that a portal to the labyrinth lies hidden within these palace walls; a hellgate known to Hentaikon and his coven alone. Find this portal and you will find an artery into the very heart of the Bonestar."

Jukon reflected on these revelations. *Better to scour an entire palace,* he thought, *than every crypt and cellar in the city. And better to find this gate before they do.* "Your wisdom is well received, maven; if you would stay and aid our search, I would be pleased to appoint you to a permanent position."

Valadian nodded once, brushing a mote from his emerald robes with heavily ringed fingers. "Willingly," he said.

He was given the very same rooms once used by Glitterax, maven to the emperor Raikon, and by generations of imperial mavens before him. Besides the living quarters he found a teratorium filled with the skeletons and preserved corpses of dwarfs, giants, hunchbacks, conjoined twins and other anomalies, and a library of archaic volumes. Amongst the many books stacked there was a copy of Babelgurion's *Wake Of The She-Sword*, which contained a dramatic account of Hentaikon's final days. When his crimes came to light, the depraved emperor was assassinated by Red Girl, flame-tressed warrior-priestess of the Sun Shrine, who seduced him by posing as a witch and then beheaded him as he slept and cut out his heart. He was replaced by his younger brother Katakaikon, a man of true faith who ruled for many years thereafter, but Red Girl was disavowed and forced to spend the rest of her days as a wandering killer-for-coin.

Old Goldenbones set the book aside as sleep washed over him, and that night as the Swamp Moon rose he dreamt darkly of demons, blood, and a black pulse throbbing in eternal solitude.

# THE MIRROR CASTLE

Dark-winged raptors circled over the castle, haunting its polished metal walls with their distorted reflections. On the battlements a sentry was peering down through the early morning mist, trying to discern the figure which seemed to mock the birds above by its grotesquely splayed limbs.

"Corpse!" he cried.

Two men emerged from a postern gate and cautiously approached the naked body, while bowmen stood poised between glistering crenellations. The dead man's torso was carved with symbols, crusted in gore; what little remained of his face was marked by tattooed dot-clusters in the likeness of lupine paw-prints.

"This one were a Crookback Cur," said the first soldier. "And some bastard's done for him proper."

"Long way from Mount Mooncry," said the second. "Best get him to the maven."

After laving the corpse, the maven Magmatharion found himself puzzling over the runic glyphs which had been cut crudely into its chest and belly. Men of the Crookback Cur clan were seldom seen beyond the hidden recesses of their mountain redoubt, shielded by dense forests high up on the loftiest, least accessible peak of the Stone Brides. Their clan was the only one never to have pledged fealty to the Gomi, but also the only one which had never risen in revolt; they shunned all but their own kind, slipping unseen among ancient sylvan shadows. The isolation of the Crookback Curs gave rise to may rumours across the centuries, and one in particular: that deep in the pine groves they celebrated a lunar cult of transformation, a skin-shift of man into wolf arising from incestuous interbreeding, bestiality and the ritual ingestion of metamorphic toxins. Some went so far as to say that many Crookback Curs had abandoned human form all together and roamed the slopes of Mount Mooncry as black-eyed, blood-slavering predators, lairs lined with the bones of unwary wanderers.

The maven was willing to believe the tales of interbreeding, and knew that imbibing certain potions, like the shapestrong brewed by tribes of the Viles, could accentuate feral traits to the point of a new hallucinated reality; but an actual physical transmutation of man into beast was beyond the boundaries of all known science. More likely, he thought, that the cultists adorned themselves in pelts, smeared their bodies with blood and devoured raw, fresh-killed meat in trances of primordial ecstasy. Such was the case on both sides of the legendary Battle of the Bloody Beasts, when tusk-helmed boar-men of Clan Inoshi were wiped out by Crookback Cur wolf-packs beneath a full moon after ranging too close to their homeland during the internecine Serpent Wars; Kibon Inoshi, clan overlord, was among those torn to shreds, and after that the remnants of the Inoshi were subsumed by the Gomi, who rose to sole ascendency in the Shines.

Three questions arose from the mutilated corpse which now lay in the Mirror Castle mortuary: who killed the clansman, why was his body left at the castle walls, and what did the mutilations signify? For a solution to the last, Magmatharion fetched down one of the weightiest volumes from his library, Gammabarion's *Skelos Of Cyphers*. Within an hour, he had his answer.

"The marks are a binding spell, Lord Kamo," he said, "a charm designed to trap the soul of a beast inside its human host."

Kamosukon Gomi was seated at the head of an ornately-carved rosewood table, flanked by others of his council – his daughter Juka, the bane virago Lady Vixenvane, and the generals Boron Kita, Vason Sogo, Mison Mako, and Isson Mozo. A waxen mask covered the left side of his face, recast in deep red to indicate martial wrath. "The work of a warlock?" he asked.

"A warlock or some other of primitive beliefs," said Magmatharion. "It is my opinion that the man may have been killed by Hakamanko scouts from one of the low clans that Hebon holds in thrall."

"That would mean his forces are already upon the foothills of the Brides," said General Mako.

"And this corpse is supposed to frighten us?" said General Mozo. "More likely to incite the Curs. What of Station South?"

"Evacuated," said Mako. "Our defenders wait within the mountain, to be joined by rock-rangers who are massing at the Hymen Gate. Soon more than two hundred will be ready to re-emerge under cover of night."

"Then the hour of reckoning is upon us," said Lord Kamosukon. "General

Kita, ready the seven-clan meatmen for battle in the coming days. The Mirror Castle has never come under siege, nor will it now; we will meet them and destroy them in the field. Despite their würms, the Hakamanko are outnumbered by two to one, are they not?"

"Yes, Lord Kamo, even though we suffered a late dereliction of Golden Maggots who dragged other cowards with them; all were put to sword. Our horse are fully armoured, and the lizard-traps are bulging with putrefied bait."

Kamosukon raised his fingers to his mask, where an eyeball of blood-red crystal blazed.

"And so the maggot screams and the black wolf howls; yet the snake is ever sucked into the spiral," he said, more softly than a silk-spinning spider.

# HELLHAVEN

For almost three weeks they made Hellhaven their home, hunting and foraging at twilight in nearby woods, roasting dead beasts on the third storey of the madhouse where there were no windows to betray their presence. By day they released the lunatics, Wormcrackle and Sucklestench, from their stinking cells and set them to work catching rats and shovelling horse dung. Lady Soma Kurotako, their reluctant guest, was afforded all courtesies but never allowed to ride out alone. Each day she begged them to release her, each day they politely refused. One by one the Blue Dragon spies – all save three, who were killed in the field – reported back from their far and wide infiltrations, and all confirmed that the Key of Bones, stolen symbol of imperial power, was held by the Starfire Order at the Winter Palace in Kobutsuden, and that Tekizan, ancestral deathsword of the Akutenshi, was entombed there with the powdered bones of the emperor Raikon.

Kuron Kirizono had also found out more from Lady Soma about her silent travelling companion, Lady Burnbolt. "She's a suicide doll," confessed Soma. "She has two keys, each for one distinct clockwork; the first sets her in motion, the other unlocks a hellfire device inside her belly. Chromocrax warned me that exactly one hour after that, a compartment opens and spills its contents into a second – a mixing of water, quicklime, phosphorus and a fulminate of mercury. You can most likely surmise the outcome."

"A hellfire inferno," said Kirizono. "Hot enough to melt steel and turn every living thing in its reach to ash."

Once Kirizono found Sucklestench with his breeks down, trying to lift up Lady Burnbolt's skirts, and had to shoo him away with a warning. "If you stick your cock in that one all you'll get back is a bloody stump; she's got nothing down there but cogwheels and razors." Wormcrackle found this most amusing, clapping his hands and drooling. *Sucklestench, Sucklestench, too fat too fuck a wench,* he chanted, spraying rank saliva over his jerkin.

The Black Reaper was an implacable killer of foemen, but not one to butcher a madman with a child's mind. He knew that lunatics had been much favoured by Emperor Raikon for the Flesh Riots, imperial games held monthly in the fighting pits at Kyukiden, where pairs of them were often strapped onto wooden rocking horses to tilt at one another with paper lances, still sharp enough at the tip to take out an eye. Raikon also enjoyed watching dwarfs, Kirizono recalled, and used them as charioteers in races where the steeds were nude girls in harness and bridle; the champion of these spectacles was a tiny hump-backed cretin named Pink Porgo, who wore a winged helmet and wielded a whip threaded with metal shards to gouge gobbets of bloody flesh from the girls' buttocks as they pulled him along the track. Imperial games agents would constantly scour Novalis for new fight fodder; double amputees, albinos and hermaphrodites were just some of the other unfortunates forced into combat – often against bears with one flayed paw, or rabid she-wolves leeched at the nipple – for Raikon's ravening delight. But now the emperor, the lunatics, the dwarfs and the beasts were nothing but ash, and the survival of the Akutenshi name was dependent on Kuron Kirizono and the Blue Dragon Hand alone.

The last spies to return were Yonakon Chinori, the Bloody Midnight, and Mekuron Taka, the Blind Falcon, whose shadow excursion took them to Wolf's Jaw in the far south. Their report to the Black Reaper was one of new and possibly portentous revelations.

"You've found the boy?" asked Kirizono.

"We found the concubine, Mordassa. She's now a whore working the Metal Town brothel that services Kyodokuron Seikyo's titanium mines; they call her Lady Spitkiss. She told us that when her son came of age he was recruited by the mavens of the Sun Shrine and trained to join the Celestial Horde, but was cast out before earning his mantle. Now he serves at the Ossuary under the maven Morgomox, as a procurer of corpses and severed parts."

"A killer?"

"Less than that; a grave-robber, a gallows-gaunt who plies his trade in the company of bats beneath the sickle moon. This Morgomox is a maker of false men, patchworks stitched together from the skin, meat, bones and guts of fresh bodies. The aim of his alchemy is to imbue them with the spark of life before they rot, so that the Seikyo might command an army of the dead."

"And the boy, our disgraced despoiler of anatomies; what name does he go by?”

"Dorion," said Chinori. "His name is Dorion Killstar."

# THE SPERM WEALD

Skoto collected Bullybabble's head, or what remained of it, on the way back to the war-camp. The eyes had been pecked out by crows, and their beaks had also raked off several strips and gouges of meat. His corpse, and the corpse of his horse, had been torn apart and eviscerated by wolves in the night; Suna guessed that the crippled courser had still been alive when the first fangs bit deep into its throat.

Hekon the hunchback was already waiting for them on their return, a faint sneer ever-present on his flecked and bitten lips. "Poor girl," he exclaimed, "we are so lucky that General Skoto was at hand to save you from that traitor monk. Are you unharmed?"

Suna made no answer. Since Skoto's unmasking her mind had caved in with fear, desolation, and dismay at the sheer malevolence of the hunchback's seemingly omniscient machinations. She could vaguely remember the horror in the hut, the realisation that Hekon had used her as a pawn in a vindictive game of dominance, and Skoto's striking down of Hozon Ama's rusty chains before they left. *No more creepvein, no more priest,* he had grinned, as Ama's paralysed body collapsed to the ground. The last thing she saw of him was a huge spider darting from his empty eye socket, mandibles clotted with brain matter.

"Never fear," Hekon continued, "our father has granted us leave to return to Skull Castle, where you may recover in peace. A guard of ten Night Weepers will ride with us, as well as the good general."

Suna could only abide in morbid silence as the entourage assembled, Skoto astride Hozon Ama's stolen destrier, Hekon ushering her into their carriage before clambering in beside her, still clutching Bullybabble's bloody remains.

"Loyal Bullybabble," said the hunchback to the severed head, "we will pay all due respect to your service, to your brave attempts to thwart the abduction of our dear

Suna."

As they abandoned camp Hekon raised his henchman's head one more time, by its hair, and tossed it into the latrine.

That night, as they sheltered on the southern skirts of the same woodlands where the Red Monk was left to die, Suna watched with unvoiced contempt as the hunchback and his general compared swords by firelight. Hekon had been gifted Seppunryu, the dragon kiss, once deathsword of the exterminated Mishima clan, by his father; Serpon Skoto had stolen the godsword Reikonyaku, burner of souls, from the warrior-priest he helped to poison. Suna knew that Hekon had never wielded any weapon in combat, nor would he; the twisted mound of stale yellow flesh and deformed bone behind his head, bowing it forwards, had also enfeebled his right arm, leaving him more fit for books than battle. Under the tutelage of the clan maven Borborax he had feverishly studied tomes and tracts on genitalia, plague, vermin, and the history of torture; she knew this because one of his perverse pleasures was to read passages from them out loud to her, as if they were letters from a sickly, paretic lover. One of his most treasured works was Caxafarion the Cruel's *Night Harvester*, which detailed twenty-three ways to flay a woman by candlelight.

"Too good for a damned monk," said General Skoto, half a second before a crossbow bolt punched through his right eyeball, his brain, and the inside of his skull. Reikonyaku slipped from his dead fingers. Suna froze, a rush of elation at Skoto's slaying almost immediately tempered by fear for her own life; and then Hekon began to scream, fingers scrabbling at his oily hair like a hysterical girl-child, until the back of the Night Weeper's hand smashed him into cringing silence.

"Keep quiet, hunchback, or we'll be taking slices off that hump of yours to feed the hounds," he sneered.

Hekon glared at him sullenly, but said nothing. Suna saw that her dear husband had lost control of his bladder. *A bit earlier in the night than usual.* Finally he muttered: "But my father... you swore fealty to my father."

"Aye, we did," said the Weeper. "But you're not him. Don't worry, you won't be killed; we get paid for delivering you alive."

"Deliver me where? Who's paying you? I'll give you double, treble..."

The Weeper laughed. "They said you'd say that, too. As for you, good lady," he said to Suna, "I'm afraid you'll have to come with him. What happens after that, not my business. Now, let's have no more talk; get some rest, we've a long ride on many morrows."

Suna remained silent, her anxiety subsiding. *They're not going to kill us,* she thought, *they're not going to rape me. And at the end of this I may yet be rid of him for good.* She glanced up at the man who'd spoken to them. His face below the eyes was a tattooed mask of black teardrops, yet he was no barbarian, she was sure of it; perhaps none of them were. Hebon Hakamanko, the great Snake Lord, had seemingly been played for a fool along with his son, the mad cripple now reduced to a whining wretch.

The Night Weeper with the crossbow sat down opposite them, his weapon loaded and pointing slightly to one side. "What if he moves, Nox?" he asked the leader.

"Pin his cock to a tree," said Nox.

# THE BONESTAR LABYRINTH

The girl's name was Vixora, though her clients called her Velvet Vix. And when Moshino ripped away her blindfold, she screamed more than any whore from Swilly Town had ever screamed before without a cock inside her.

The wall in front of her eyes was hung with a curtain of corpses – baby ones, some no bigger than a coin, some near as big as new-borns, all of them corrupted to the core and all stitched to one another with twists of dripping metal thread. Pools of decomposed chorion and maggots were spreading out from beneath this hideous abjuration, and the smell of death was so profound that Vixora was quickly overwhelmed by spasms of convulsive vomiting, until her stomach muscles cramped in knots and her throat was raw with blood.

"Men call me bastard," Moshino was chanting, "men call me beast. Men call me bastard, men call me beast," over and over again like a refrain from the bowels of a shit-smeared madhouse. He wore a purple robe broidered with a golden eye on fire, his skin beneath it dry and scaled, features cowled.

The underground chapel was ringed by burning black candles moulded from pig fat and menses, its four other walls inset with circular niches housing icons of filth and pestilence – wheels of petrified amber in which cockroaches, scorpions and tarantulas were arranged in hooked crosses, wreaths meshed from mummified rats and snakes encircling severed heads nailed to the brickwork, chargers painted with garish effigies of entrail-devouring demons. Carrion flies swarmed on every surface. At the chamber's very centre, where Moshino stood pulling down on the rope which bound his captive and kept her swinging above the ground, was a sarcophagus of cracked stone, and upon its lid a single word was scrawled in blood: HENTAIKON. Next to the corpse-curtain was an open doorway leading into a stone passageway; lighted torches were mounted along it, but it extended so far that all that was visible at its farthest point was a gloom pocked with tiny dots of fire.

Vixora was now barely conscious of the heat, the death-stench, the sooty smoke from the candles, the buzzing of the flies, and the pain in her arms from the hanging which kept her mind from closing down; barely aware of Moshino even as he traced outlines across her exposed belly with crusted, broken fingernails.

"The soft dolls of the weeping wall number three and twenty," he croaked. "Three and twenty is the number of the serpent that rises. Three and twenty are the covens of the Holy Eye, the eye that watches in darkness. Snakes in the night, snakes in the skull."

"Snakes in the night, snakes in the skull." The soft echo of Moshino's words came from behind Vixora, in a woman's voice. "The moon is the eye of the serpent, an eye that weeps blood. The blood-eye is the Holy Eye."

When the woman revealed herself, Vixora saw that her long, tangled hair was streaked with grey and hung down over a nude body completely shaven and needled with tattoos. Her breasts were withered sacks, the teats purple-black, hard, and ridged with teethmarks. The tattoos even covered her face, and each of her eyelids when closed formed the carapace of a scorpion whose legs extended above and below like monstrous lashes and whose tail formed an overarching brow, the stingers from each butted together at the centre of her forehead like firedrops. Her fingers were ringed in silver and carnelian, and they held a long curved dagger.

"I'm not with child," Vixora managed to say, "and never can be." She spoke the truth; on her fifth and final visit to the fallen maven the whores called Crackcrawler, his knives had taken out her womb along with the unwanted child. *Else the devil's canker will spread,* he had said, *and breed a carnival of monsters.* Now the memory of it made her weep, and she wept more bitterly still as she saw the murdered souls impaled and rotting on the killer's curtain and knew that her life, any life, had no more meaning than that of an insect crushed underfoot.

"We ask only three and twenty tears," said the woman. "Tears of blood, never salt. Bloody tears for each coil of the great red snake, for the soft dolls behind the vampire veil, for the unborn and the undead. After a thousand years our war is beginning, above ground and below, a war that will rage until the extinguishing of the sun."

Moshino released the rope; Vixora dropped to the floor, her legs buckling beneath her, and her head crashing back against the sarcophagus. The witch-woman loomed above her, and then the dagger cut into her flesh like a mercy.

# THE TEMPLEDARK

They reached the Crow River on the fifth day, one hundred miles north of the Storm Shrine. Far to the west Gorn could see the tiny figure of a winged angel rising up above the skyline. Some two thousand of them crossed the wooden bridge, mainly fighters from the Kill-Claw and Blood Eagle clans, and then Gorn ordered it to be burnt behind them. "We won't be coming back," he said to Vakko, the Kill-Claw chieftain. "Not this way, at least. Once we secure the north, the river will be the new frontier."

He was only repeating what Croton Kurotako had told him, but it sounded convincing. *They'll follow me so long as I stay in control,* he thought. *Any weakness or indecision and I'm dead meat.* Those who joined the alliance of snake and octopus had been promised new lands and plunder in return, and Gorn was relying on that promise to keep the savages from turning. Ando had personally pledged him mastery of his own ringfort, with coffers of coin and all the whores and ale he could handle; *simple needs for a simple man.*

Kurotako, with his force of three thousand Sickle Wasp, Devil-Dog and Whip Flay clan fighters, would be crossing the river within a day, so too Tazon Ando with an equal number of Maw Fetters and Grey Ghosts supplemented by his loyal attack battalion of Crow River rebels. While they converged on Castle Mortmane, Gorn was to keep marching north through the Templedark to the Shines, aiming to link with the Hakamanko in the shadow of the Stone Brides. It was another five-day excursion, perhaps more.

At Storm Town to the south of them, a far smaller group of riders dismounted at the only stables; two were women, one seemingly heavy with child. Kuron Kirizono noticed that the dour-faced girl who led away his horse was also pregnant; he wondered, briefly, if she knew who the father was. That evening they would stay at the inn, and in the morning meet with the mavens of Storms.

Kirizono had decided that Lady Burnbolt, their mute and inert ward, was a weapon worth keeping. As he carried her upstairs, a raft of comments floated up from the drinkers, most too muted to decipher. Some of the customers were warrior-priests of the Storm Division, others those in service to them. All seemed drunk to varying degrees, but none enough to provoke a man as big as the Black Reaper. Soma Kurotako had shown him the key around her neck which would set Burnbolt in motion, but carrying her a short way seemed the easier option. *The keyhole is her anus,* she told him; *push it in, then three twists clockways. To stop her, two twists back.* Kirizono now had a better idea; before leaving Storm Town, they would pay a visit to the coffin-maker.

In the dawn mists of the following day three of them rode out to the Temple of Storms under the banner of the Akutenshi, Kirizono flanked by Nezumon Nano and Yonakon Chimori of the Blue Dragon Hand. They were hailed by the maven Cassavion, who looked incredulously at Kirizono as if he were a black ghost risen from the frozen hells.

"Kyukiden is lost," Kirizono confirmed, "but some of us survive at the Shadow Castle. And we seek the support of the Celestial Horde in order to reclaim the empire."

Inside the temple, Cassavion said: "Just one moon past we gazed upon the ashes and deathsword of Emperor Raikon, last of the Akutenshi line. Now the empire is ruled by council; as representative of the old imperial clan, your best hope is a seat at table."

"Our allegiance is pledged to the Starfire Order," added the maven Tardassion. "And the Order has enemies on the march."

"We will deal with those enemies," said Kirizono, "once the empire is restored to its rightful heir. Raikon is dead, but his line lives on; we are riding to raise up the Deathstar's one and only son."

"Son? But Raikon never married," protested Tardassion. "How can you prove this? And who is this boy?"

*A grave-robber, a corpse-thief, a blasphemer.* "He is apprenticed to a maven, and studies the natural sciences. We have found his mother, a former concubine of the Camellia Keep who was discarded by the emperor. She confirms that her son is Raikon's seed."

"We cannot accept the word of a whore," said Cassavion. "Surely you know this."

"Wait," said the maven Sycarion. "There is one way to be sure. Does this boy bear the mark?"

"If he does, you will acknowledge his claim?"

The mavens looked at one another, and then Cassavion spoke. "We will accept the mark, and the look of him, as two of three signs of proof. Bring him to us, and let us see with our own eyes."

"And the third sign?"

"The concubine," said the maven. "We need to inspect her buttocks."

"Done," said the Black Reaper.

# THE SLAUGHTERHOUSE

Lord Sadogashon Kurotako was reclining on a silken divan surrounded by the Brides of the Octopus – nude and half-nude concubines, drawn both from among his subjects and from the galleys of outlaw slavers who tilted too close to the Red Rock and paid a bloody price – when Blind Baragon, ferryman of the black barge, discharged a horseback Seikyo messenger and provoked an admonitory pealing of the Slaughterhouse bell.

In the absence of his elder son and both daughters, Sadogashon had elevated Chromocrax, maven of mechanics and tutor to his eleven-year-old son Kuchon, to head of council, with the power to open and review all communications. Within minutes of the Seikyo scroll's delivery, the maven was knocking at his overlord's chamber door.

"Kyo the Killer offers an alliance against the Taiyo, Lord Sado," said Chromocrax. "He writes of a deadly blow being struck against the Sunstorm Castle."

"Read me the letter," said Sadogashon.

"*The fall of Sunstorm is to the mutual benefit. Our Skeleton Sealords have pledged to defend the castle, but harbour its destruction. Turn your fleet when you see them; be ready when the Corpse Moon rises.* It is signed and sealed by Lord Kyo."

"As cryptic as death itself," said Sadogashon. "Your opinion?"

"It is well-known that the Seikyo and Taiyo are locked in discord; the Feast of Demons stands as testament to the sincerity of Lord Kyo's enmity, his willingness to murder. I have no doubts regarding his ill intent. Of the plan itself, he offers scant detail; but all he seems to ask of us is feigned flight."

"That, and our trust that the Fleshstripper won't burn our ships to cinders." Lord Nikon Tabu's thirst for blood was notorious; he was known to haunt the lichen-mottled offshore watchtower known as the Spike, ever watchful for passing pirate vessels to immolate with his fire-throwing attack patrol which lay in readiness off Hangman's Head.

"Then we turn before he gets too close. Winter is approaching, and with it storms which will drive us out to sea no matter what; we can leave with nothing, or help the Seikyo to help Lord Hebon. If Sunstorm is stricken, the Taiyo will not march north; and our mission will be completed with little loss."

Lord Sadogashon pondered this counsel, and the possible outcomes suggested by Lord Kyodokuron's missive. He could see another ending to the plan, one in which the Taiyo turned betrayer first and struck against the Seikyo death-ships when they were vulnerable; but that, he decided, would not be a problem for his own fleet, which was anchored beyond range of the Sunstorm's ballistic defences.

"Very well," he said at length. "The Blood Moon is now upon us; the Corpse Moon will rise in the turn of three weeks. Within five days I will need you to prepare and launch one more ship for our fleet – a ship with a most particular crew."

"I understand," said the maven. "And what of the ships that lie off Gluttonport? The last report from Commander Inusame spoke of much unrest, of a growing thirst for vengeance after Lady Miura Mizuno burnt our men alive. They say that all the Mizuno's vassal clans have deserted, that Lord Akumuron is missing or dead, and that the Nightmare Castle would surely fall under siege."

"Inusame feasts on terror. If he hungers, unleash him."

That night Chromocrax unlocked the great iron doors of his tower repositories, inspecting the interior by torchlight. Naked female figures stood in rows by the dozen, as tall and silent and still as statues in an ancient arcade of carnal doom. Some had swollen bellies housing hell-machines, others large and jutting breasts whose nipples dispensed a black milk of contagion. Some pissed jets of scalding acid from their sculpted sex-lips. All were designed for a singular purpose – the sowing of chaos and destruction.

Chromocrax decided to deploy them as they were, without the need for clothing; the very sight of them would confound the enemy, he thought, overwhelming them with waves of simultaneous lust and fear. A moment of hesitation was all that was needed, just a moment for men – Mizuno and Seikyo alike – to be engulfed by a burning hell-ship and its wanton dolls of death.

# PART THREE
# THE RED SNAKE RISING

# THE VELVET CASTLE

Flayon II's *Red Snake At Komonyama*, created in the year 813 and described by the artist as his masterwork, was suppressed as blasphemous by the emperor Zaikon – known as the Zealot – who also ordered Flayon to be crucified naked on Kyukiden's notorious Way of Woe. Widely construed as an allegorical celebration of the murder of Bankairon Demon-Slayer by dark forces, the vast three-panel painting now hung in the private quarters of Viron Voraxo, castellan of the Velvet Castle; this followed the work's liberation from the capital city's Forbidden Chamber by chaos agents of the Reptile Crux – an operation known as the Night of the Snake.

Raised near the border of Lizard's Den and Thundervoid by Atakaton Akaichi, first overlord of his clan, the Velvet Castle was envisioned as a pleasure dome of decadence and artistic indulgence, a disposition reflected by its curved buttresses, phallic turrets and lavish, bejewelled interiors. It was said that even the sentry urinals along the battlement walls were plated in solid gold. Over the centuries this pursuit of aesthetic dissolution created an ever-deepening tension with the Akaichi's more bellicose neighbours, the Hakamanko, until one consumed the other during the Serpent Wars.

Voraxo maintained the castle as an advocate of Lord Hebon Hakamanko, its galleries and bagnios converted into barracks for fighters of the loyalist Tower Bat clan, abhorred as drinkers of human blood. Now Hebon was amassing an army just to the south, and Voraxo was left with only his personal retainers and guard. He knew that if the Gomi prevailed, the Velvet Castle would find itself under siege for the first time in nearly three hundred years.

It was just before noon when the rider arrived from Kobutsuden. He bore a scroll, sealed in soil-brown wax and imprinted with the likeness of a horned demon. Voraxo recognised it at once, cracked the seal and studied the letter intently. *Brother Viron*, it read, *I have once before likened the city to a beast with parasites hooked within its guts. Now, the beast crouches to shit. If disaster befalls us, I urge you to complete the Helios Working with all haste. And remember – the snake cannot know of this.* The missive was signed *Baron Kravox.*

Viron Voraxo sat long in contemplation. His secret compact with Kravox, an alliance of position to wealth, had set him on a course divergent from the grand design of his overlord. And yet it was not his aim to subvert the Hakamanko cause; rather, he sought to define and devolve his own interpretation of *The Black Psalter*, the necroxicon which underpinned Lord Hebon's will to power. It was a vision shared by Kravox, whose origins remained obscure but whose resources enabled him to shape destiny from the shadows.

The castellan's reverie was ruptured when Mazagon and Kaxagon, his twin seven-year-old boys, dashed into the chamber with shrieks of laughter, chased somewhat shakily by their attendant Puckerbreech. *We're the kings of the castle,* they sang at the old manservant, *and you're the dirty arsehole.*

"Enough," said Voraxo. "Puckerbreech is here to keep you safe; now off you go."

Since the death of his wife Gona, the twins had run increasingly wild; Viron had neither the desire nor the time to watch over them himself. It was the two boys who had found their mother's corpse, dangling from a rope by its broken neck, after she took her own life. He could not – dared not – tell them that the cause of her sorrow was his own dalliance with a serving-wench and the subsequent birth of a bastard in the dank dungeon straw. The child was cursed, a lobster-handed cyclops, and lived for only a day and a night; yet its hideous form still haunted his nightmares, driving him to seek solace in the oblivion of debauch.

Now Kravox had charged him, come what may, with the inauguration of the Helios Working, a ritual for which there was one essential, irreplaceable component: the bones of Bankairon Demon-Slayer.

# MOUNT GOLDENFANG

"It says so quite clearly in the *Elemental Testament*," said Quexarian, as he carved the final stroke of his binding into the dead man's brow. "Book Five, *Transmigration Of The Metacarrion* – I forget the exact words, but it clearly states that such an entity may even travel from a corpse to a living host."

The exorcist sat back, wiping blood from his sacramental scalpel. His mantle, once a garment of pristine white blazoned back and front with silver crescent moons, was befouled by dirt and gore from their long travail among the crags and derelict mine-shafts of Mount Goldenfang, westernmost of the Stone Brides. More than a mile below, the Mirror Castle of Clan Gomi was a silvery dot that glinted in the midday sun.

"I'll take your word for it," said Darkon Domo, "though it seems more like witch's work." They were the last survivors from the Moon Shrine of Sorrow Sukion, sent forth on mission just days before the Decimation. Like many moon-priests before them, Quex and Darkon were tasked with locating and retrieving the most exalted of holy relics; they sought the twelve missing skulls of the White Light Brotherhood, warrior-saints of Sukion who rode the Brides on armoured white war-horses nine hundred years before, sworn to annihilate a malignant cabal of demon-worshippers. Legend tells that they were ambushed, tortured and beheaded by the warlocks, who returned their bodies to the Moon Shrine in a hundred pieces; their heads were never found. That massacre led directly to the formation of the Celestial Horde, a templar army dedicated to the extirpation of witchcraft and demonolatry in the name of the Triad.

"The shrine is gone, the temple is gone, but our mission remains," Quex had said after the devastation of Thundervoid, and so they continued to ascend the mountain, ranging ever northeastwards as days passed. Three times now they had met with others; the first was a hermit dwarf who shouted "Shit fang!" then scampered away into a mine opening, but the next two were far more dangerous. The first Crookback Cur was a forager who surprised them while they were skinning a deer, although he looked as shocked as them when they came face to face; Darkon knew that the man would betray their presence if they let him escape, and so he drew his godsword Shirometsu, the white destroyer, and leapt up to confront him. The Cur yelled and lunged at him with an axe, but it shattered against Shirometsu's edge and he stumbled to the ground, where Darkon fatally transfixed him. Quex had insisted on a ritual mutilation of the corpse – "chaining the wolf", he called it – and then Darkon gave it a shove with his boot. They could only watch as the body seemed to gain momentum as it rolled down the mountain slope, occasionally flying off the ground when it hit a rock or root, faster and faster until it began to vanish in the distance. For all they knew, it rolled all the way to the walls of the Mirror Castle.

"We'll bury the next one," said Darkon, and he got his chance the very next day. "I'm not digging a grave, though," he said. "Just throw some stones on the cunt."

Before he was a warrior-priest, Darkon Domo was just a warrior. While fighting as a sword-shifter for the Takasha he was certain he saw a severed head talking to him during a raid, and took it as a sign from the Triad to devote his skills to a higher cause. Although he swore sacred vows and donned the white mantle of the moon, Darkon never lost the blunt demeanour of a soldier-for-coin.

"What's next then, Quex?" he asked that night. He looked frayed; his face was wind-burnt and his dark brown hair was growing out in spikes, threatening to obscure the devotional tattoo on the back of his once-shaven head. "This is the last of the old gold mines; after here there's only forest, and we both know where that leads."

"It leads where we need to go," said Quex. "The reports from the few who came before us and survived all say the same thing: they all believed that the skulls were taken long ago by the Crookback Curs, and are buried in a blasphemous wolf temple on the heights of Mount Mooncry."

"And the ones that never came back? They tried to find that temple, no doubt. Like I said before, this is a one-way mission."

"Perhaps," the exorcist admitted. "But in-breeding means that the Curs grow fewer in number with each passing year…"

"And more insane, more violent," said Darkon. "Don't forget that part. Wolves drink human blood, last I heard; why should these cunts be any different?"

Quexarian made no reply. He knew that Darkon was right to be cautious, but he also knew something that his companion didn't – that the skulls of the White Light Brotherhood were only secondary to the true object of their quest, an object which, in the right hands, could help turn the very tides of war.

On the plains far below and away to the east they could see a sprawling panoply of man-made light, a thousand watchfires clustered like pinpoint stars in a distant galaxy. *Or,* thought Darkon, *the eyes of a many-headed snake. A snake which seeks to encircle the waking world.*

# CASTLE MORTMANE

The girl's head was perched on a spike far above the ramparts of Castle Mortmane, so distant and so disfigured by decay and predation that Croton couldn't be sure... and yet the hair whipping around it in the breeze, as black as ink and long enough to reach the waist when attached to a body, was undeniably identical to Soma's.

"Come and join your sister," Chikon Takasha was saying. "What a pretty pair you'll make. And don't worry, I won't rape you like I did the lovely Lady Soma. Although I can't speak for Bonehead. He buggered her good and proper before chopping her up, I expect he'll do the same to you."

The shaven-headed carnifex was standing beside his master, nodding and leering, an enormous axe slung over one shoulder. As Croton looked up at them he felt a caustic rage rising in his veins in response to Chikon's provocations. *Could it be true?* "And what of her companion?" he shouted back.

"In the dungeons," said Chikon, but he hesitated for just a moment before replying. *A lie.*

"Then you'll show her to us, won't you? Else your boasts stand as hollow."

Chikon's reply was prefaced by a contemptuous spit-shower of yellow phlegm.

"No more so than your skull when I hack your filthy brains out, octopus. *Mortmane!*" he shouted, thrusting his sword Membaku into the air, and at this last exclamation two thousand screaming savages of the Hell-Claw, Demon Red, Rat Rock and Crow River clans rose up from the defensive ditch surrounding the castle and ran wildly at the attackers who faced them.

Chikon guessed that his ground forces were outnumbered by almost three to two; his father had insisted that five hundred fighters remain within the walls, in the event of siege. Although his bowmen were firing successive hails of arrows onto the Kurotako forces, most were being deflected by raised metal shields; his own men had only wood. A wall of spear-wielding Sickle Wasp, Devil-Dog and Whip Flay clansmen were pressing relentlessly against his defenders, slowly driving them back towards the ditch, while Croton Kurotako charged about on horseback, barking commands and lopping off heads. Shark White rippers and Slaughterhouse watchmen from the Arms of the Octopus milled around him, forming a an impenetrable lifesguard.

After witnessing an hour of carnage, Chikon could abide no more. Croton had failed to swallow his bait and fight him one to one, but now he would give him no choice. He looked back across the thronged expanse of Mortmane and saluted his father Lord Hikidashon, who was watching from a high window of his redoubt, the Joker's Keep. Before Hikidashon could respond, Chikon was on his way to the postern gate where his horse and armour were in readiness.

The castle's perimeter was awash with a blizzard of blood and flesh; as the outer iron portal clanged shut behind him Chikon's bay destrier reared up at the noise and slaughterhouse stench, its hooves and lower legs already stained red. He urged the beast forwards over mounds of smashed armour, broken weapons and body parts, searching for a glimpse of Croton Kurotako. A Sickle Wasp fighter lunged at him with a hand-scythe and a butcher's gutting-knife, and he brought Membaku's heavy cleaving-edge down on the man's shoulder with such force that his chest caved in and one arm flew off in a whipspray of unpent blood.

The two horsemen seemed to see each other simultaneously; Croton's mount was lathed in gore from tail to muzzle, and he wheeled the dripping red beast full circle before charging at Chikon's position with a contorted cry. Chikon pressed ahead to meet him, but as they drew closer a pair of Shark White man-eaters converged upon him with axes, each shearing through one of his horse's forelegs with a single swipe. The destrier screamed as it collapsed and was driven head-first into the ground by its own momentum, its neck snapping as Chikon was hurled forwards to land on his back atop a pile of corpses.

Even as he dragged himself upright Croton was upon him, hacking down with his sword Kazokubi; Chikon parried with Membaku, the stacker of heads striking a shower of hot sparks from the exploder of eyes. He pushed backwards, almost stumbling, as Croton leapt from his mount and launched another attack, this time with a circular swing which threatened to chop his face in half before he ducked beneath it. "Hell-Claw! To me!" Chikon yelled, seeking protection for his exposed flanks and rear, then feinted to one side as Croton thrust at him again. *An opening.* Grasping Membaku's hilt with both hands, he drove it upwards and across in a bludgeoning arc; the blade smashed into Croton's breast-plate, staving it in and opening up a jagged rent from which blood started to pour. The Kurotako lord gasped for breath and his eyes went cold, and then Membaku struck again, this time up through his throat and jaw, killing him where he stood.

Shielded by three Hell-Claw warriors with flailing, brain-glutted morningstars, Chikon knelt over Croton and used his shortsword to saw off his head; then he climbed onto the octopus spawn's own blood-drenched horse and, with a great battle-roar echoed by his fighters, held the severed trophy aloft for all to see. A great cheer of victory rang out from those on the Mortmane battlements, and the Kurotako fighters, realising what had happened, began to fall back in retreat. Just then the exultations of the Takasha were drowned out by another tumultuous commotion rising up from the castle's unmanned northern aspect; a massed cry, the clangour of swords on shields, and a pounding bootfall that trembled the ground. Lord Hikidashon rushed to the other side of his keep, and beheld a sight which turned his elation to a torrent of fury. Thousands more fighters were charging towards Mortmane, led by a rider whose figure he could not fail to recognize – it was Tazon Ando, the traitor who fucked his wife.

At the sight of Ando's assault the Kurotako clan fighters rallied, the Takasha closing ranks to allow Chikon egress from the battlefield. Even as he galloped back to the castle gate with his foeman's bloody head tucked under one arm and spears flying to the left and right of him, the massacre began, four thousand against one thousand. It was over in less than an hour; looking down from the battlements, Chikon and his father saw the main part of their forces reduced to chunks of meat, guts and mangled bone floating in a turgid lake of gore. All they could offer in response was Croton Kurotako's head on a spike, next to that of his horse.

Watching from a distance just out of arrow range, Tazon Ando, thane of Flies, glared up at Lord Hikidashon. The Mizuno deathsword Akafuku was unsheathed and gleaming in his gloved right hand; and vengeance was now just as surely within his grasp.

# THE NIGHTMARE CASTLE

They rowed to shore under cover of churning fog and darkness, the vestige of the Blood Moon obscured by impenetrable banks of cumulus, stars snuffed out like flames starved of air. In the black beyond, cetacean night-calls echoed mournfully across the main evoking unknown terrors that haunt the dreams of men. The bay remained as flat as glass. Commander Kon Inusame stood on board the *Death Tentacle*, ready to unleash the steel kiss of sea-scorpions primed at the bow of every ship.

The raid on Gluttonport was led by Crogor, hook-handed cannibal chieftain of the Shark White clan, and eighty of his shred-tooth rippers. Crogor's fighters claimed that he ate his own left hand, bones and all, to escape from chains when imprisoned on a Crimson Curse pirate ship, cauterizing his wrist-stump in a watch-fire before biting out the throats of his sleeping captors and escaping aback a dead-eyed megadon from the deep; this legend inspired a strong and fearful loyalty amongst those who followed him. Three-score Shell Crush braves were also with him, along with more than a hundred Kurotako mariners armed with serrated sabres doused in stingray venom.

When they got there the town was deserted, its harbour and houses void of life. Candles burned in windows, yet all were near spent; no sound could be heard in the streets save for the intermittent yowling of a one-eyed she-cat in heat and the hissing retort of its rapers. Fog enveloped the invaders with tendrils of barbed ice.

"If we can't kill, we loot," said Crogor. "To the temples!"

Gluttonport was overshadowed by two sea-temples, one at each end of the settlement, both facing the ocean and fabled for housing treasures garnered by the Mizuno from ship-wrecks, bankrupt merchantmen, ransoms and other ill-reputed sources. The Kurotako raiders swarmed through the dead streets in both directions, athirst for gold as much as blood. But blood found them first.

It came from above, the grinding of rock against rock, then a brief moment of silence before the first projectile landed, followed by a dozen more and another dozen after that. Each great granite sphere took a toll, either from exploding shards which cut through men's heads and vital organs or from a crushing hit that turned one or more to a lifeless oozing pulp. Several houses were demolished. At the same time the Nightmare Castle's war-engines hurled blazing fireballs out into the night, illuminating both town and sea alike as they whirled overhead and crashed upon the Kurotako fleet.

Kon Inusame cried out to his scorpion-men to fire their massive bolts; two ships, the *Meathook Seed* and the *Night Scar*, were already in flames, burning fighters hurling themselves into the quenching waters of the bay. Some missiles struck near the castle ramparts, but it was impossible to gauge their impact. Down in the streets Crogor was driving his men onwards; they were nearing the eastern sea-temple when the rain of rocks changed to a cascade of barrels filled with oil, shattering and stippling all within range. And then the fire fell.

From his high vantage-point above the port Sevon Kako, black-cloaked captain of the castle's elite Vertigo Watch, was directing the assault on the invaders. He wore white armour, morion and breast-plate engraved with a sweeping black whorl. It shone in the glare of the torches which had been lit all along the battlements, both for illumination and for ignition of the floods of oil beneath. It was Lady Miura Mizuno who had given him his orders, some days earlier. *Let them burn, Captain Kako,* she said. *Let them burn, and if Gluttonport burns too, such is the will of the Triad. If eight men was not sacrifice enough, perhaps a whole town will appease our Sorrow of Storms.*

Kako had acknowledged her orders, but added his own interpretation. *She said to burn the port, but not the people.* And so his men had warned the townsfolk to shelter underground by night, down in the man-made tunnels behind the sluice-gates. If Lady Miura found out she could have him jailed, or far worse, but he adjudged her need for his service to outweigh the gratification of such reprisals. If the raiders were repelled, that would surely be victory enough.

"Scum! *Mizuno scum!*"

The vitriolic scream came from below, but Kako could see only blazing buildings and men on fire, some already still and dead, others running wildly towards the sea. Out in the bay several more balingers had caught alight, paying a deadly price for drifting nearer the coast in order to launch their raid. Although it was the blackest of nights, Lady Miura had somehow sensed their coming, could somehow see what others could not. Many in the rank and file had started calling her Mad Miura for her ever more fervent religious rants after losing husband and son, but perhaps she truly had made a divine connection through her suffering.

Sevon Kako felt the breeze, ever so faintly, long before Kon Inusame. By the time Inusame realised it, the breeze had become a cyclone. It descended over the Kurotako fleet in circles of blasting destruction, whipping up a great waterspout into which ship after ship was sucked and dragged high into the air before being disgorged in a shower of shattered wood, crumpled iron, dead fish and disintegrated human parts. Many other vessels were violently upturned and sunk without trace. Hundreds of drowned mariners washed up on the beach; some had been fused with sea creatures at the epicentre of the vortex, presenting a grotesque splay of still-born hybrids.

Most invaders still alive after cyclone or firestorm were quickly put to death by Vertigo Watch guardsmen who charged from the port's hidden tunnels armed with glaives, save for a handful dragged away to confess their secrets and sins to the Scar Faery. It was impossible to say if any ships or raiders had escaped, but it took two whole days to pile the dead onto rafts and incinerate them. *The Death Tentacle* was never seen again; a few days later two children playing in the sand found Kon Inusame's head, half-rotten and filled with crabs.

# THE WINTER PALACE

Two weeks after his appointment to the position of maven to the Starfire Order, Valadian Goldenbones was seated at his first meeting as member of council in place of Questor Zan Vordulax. Also present were Jukon Gomi, who sat at head of table, league warlord Gomon Takasha, Lady Snowsnake of Clan Mizuno, and Veluron Taiyo. When it was Valadian's turn to speak, he said: "My recent studies have brought to light three items of interest. First, regarding our search for a portal to the Bonestar Labyrinth, I was reminded that the labyrinth was walled up by the emperor Katakaikon after his succession following Hentaikon's demise; we might, therefore, be advised to look for any occurrence of Katakaikon's imperial seal. This I found in the *Imprimaturs Of Empire* – two thunderbolts convergent, and between them a burning crucible, which signified his role as purifier of the line.

"I should also mention that although Hentaikon's body and head were entombed in the imperial crypts at Kyukiden his foul heart, riddled with whipworm, was not – it was locked in a silver casket and interred here, somewhere far beneath our feet, in the Bonestar itself. And that brings me to my second point.

"The tomb, or sarcophagus, which holds Hentaikon's heart is referred to in some texts as the Scorpion's Nest. At first I took this to be a mere poetic fancy, a reference to the emperor's allegiance to the Vermin League. But upon reflection, I now realise that this in fact provides the key to another mystery – the mapping of the labyrinth."

Jukon leaned forwards, intrigued by these revelations; perhaps the old maven really was worth his weight in gold. "How so?"

"You are no doubt familiar with the constellation of the Fire Scorpion," Valadian continued, "and the goliath sunstar Chelicor, which is known to represent its blazing heart. I believe that when the earth and stars are precisely aligned, Chelicor shines directly above Hentaikon's tomb. In other words, the Fire Scorpion forms a celestial mirror-map of the Bonestar Labyrinth."

"I heard another story," Lady Snowsnake interjected. "Some say that Hentaikon's heart was stolen by his coven, and that a pig's was buried in its place to placate the rabble."

"Perhaps so," said Jukon, "yet that doesn't change this theory of the star-map. Veluron; fetch astrological charts to my chambers later, and let us dissect the secrets of the Fire Scorpion."

"There is yet the third matter," said Goldenbones. "I have also found reference to this man you mentioned, the one known as Slavos Sek."

"Tell us everything," said Gomon. He knew that capturing Sek, the elusive Primal Optic of the Vigilants, was long a matter of the utmost urgency.

"Slavos Sek first served the Hakamanko as a warlock, a necrolator who worshipped corpses mummified in molten gold in order to penetrate the realm of the dead. He then rose to the rank of würm-rider..."

"And now?" Jukon interrupted. "What news of him now?"

"Now? Why, he's dead, of course... Slavos Sek died in the Serpent Wars, three hundred years ago."

"Then it can't be him. The Sek we know about is hiding here now, in Kobutsuden."

"So is the warlock, in a sense," said Valadian. "He was reported killed at the Battle of the Bone Clans just beyond the city, and lies among the war dead buried in Skullhaven."

That afternoon, as Jukon waited for Veluron Taiyo to bring the star-charts, he reflected on all that the maven had said, particularly regarding Slavos Sek. Was it possible that Sek was merely some kind of dark icon revered by the subterraneans, a figure culled from the annals of black magic and brought to life in their collective imagination? If so, that might confirm the suspicions expressed previously by Valadian, who had hinted that the Holy Eye was in fact a new iteration of a much more ancient and deadly evil. As with the poison witch Silversoil and her bastard, everything seemed to lead back to the Hakamanko; and now they were threatening his own family, massing to move against the Mirror Castle. *Or perhaps they already have.* Every instinct told Jukon to leave Kobutsuden and ride to join his father against the Snake Lord, and yet he was bound by the oath he swore to protect the city, to lead the Starfire Order against the threat from within. *It was your idea,* he reminded himself. *The Order, the council... it was all your idea, and you have to see it through to the end.*

He gazed out far across the citadel to the overgrown, tomb-tangled necropolis of Skullhaven, and shivered to his core.

# THE PLAIN OF PAIN

Stretching for miles along the skirts of the Stone Brides, the Plain of Pain had earned its name more than seven hundred years earlier, after a series of five brutal battles which were fought there between the forces of Lord Krakaton Gomi and the hooded night riders of Bragon Zendo, also called the Firebrand Nyctalope. Once a Takasha general, the Nyctalope turned rogue following a land dispute and assembled a cross-border rebel army bent on forging a new republic in the wildlands of the Shines. After they stormed and captured a succession of mountain ringforts in the foothills of the Brides, Krakaton Gomi staged an intervention which led to eleven years of bloody conflict known as the Night Wars.

"And now the pain is returning," said Kamosukon Gomi. "Make sure they feel it more than we do."

The four Gomi generals shouted assent. Each was in command of a force numbering some one and a half thousand fighters – Boron Kita, leading the silver division; Mison Mako, leading the red; Vason Sogo, leading the gold; and Isson Mozo, leading the black. Kamosukon's elite horseguard the Dust Demons, two hundred in number, would bring up the rear. Scouts reported that the Hakamanko forces were encamped at the foot of Mount Snowblaze, less than fifty miles away; the generals would deploy at dawn.

Gorn of Gluttonport was still two days' march away from the plains, slowed by Vakko Kill-Claw's insistence on sacking a pair of Wormheart villages whose fighting-men had all been summoned to the Mirror Castle leaving only women, children and dotards. Murder, torture, rape and plunder also required a period of recuperation, all adding up to a whole day lost. "Gets the men's blood up," said Vakko, in a tone that invited no debate, and so Gorn had reluctantly allowed the rampage to unfold. *If they're so upblooded they can lead the vanguard,* he thought later, *and I'll hold back with the berserkers.*

A rider from Hebon Hakamanko confirmed that the Snake Lord had already chosen his favoured battle-ground, a day's ride from Mount Snowblaze to the shadow of Mount Slaughtershriek, where centuries ago the Firebrand Nyctalope had won a great victory after scything his flaming war-axe through the neck of Kovon Gomi, Lord Krakaton's eldest son; a mayhem which Hebon cherished as a seminal portent. Despite losing his own life during the final battle of the Night Wars in the year 313, the Nyctalope was among Hebon's greatest inspirations, and pride of place in the overlord's chambers at Skull Castle was afforded to Flayon II's gruesome triptych *The Phantom Of Slaughtershriek*, depicting the hooded usurper charging through the night on his golden-eyed courser, axe afire, brandishing Kovon's head like a bloody lantern.

Lord Hebon Hakamanko had lost his first and only wife Ruka during the birth of their son, Hekon, the eleven-year-old girl's body unable to survive the passage of the gnarled and mewling hunchback whose flesh-rending parturition split her in two from the inside outwards and drowned her in lakes of her own blood. Refusing to marry again, Lord Hebon instead consorted with a succession of nefarious she-poisoners; the latest, Lady Vulvomane, was with him in his candlelit pavilion of crimson silk on the eve of the advance to Mount Slaughtershriek.

"Datura, white venom, and the moontide of a virgin," she said, offering Lord Hebon a resinous unguent to fortify his wine. "Vermix, a conduit for the coils of the red snake rising."

"Then let us drink," said Hebon. "Snakes in the night, snakes in the skull."

"Snakes in the night, snakes in the skull."

Vulvomane swallowed the acrid, sticky draught and immediately felt its liquid tongues probing her nerve-endings like bolts of fire, slithering across her brain with a caress of swamp-born ecstasy. Hebon was a saturnine beast reclining before her, lascivious and parlous; then she saw viper-bones bursting from his face, a bifurcate tongue flicking from his desert-dry lips with susurrations and shadows of beautiful evil that cavorted like revellers at the funeral of an extinguished sun. She tore off her gown and writhed naked in her own faeces, spreading apart her pale white haunches to open the ancient eye of the serpent. Hebon grew formless, shimmering in white heat; then she felt it rising, undulating inside her belly, emerging with a blinding cosmic radiance. Its vermillion scales seared her flesh as it surged and surged in ever-expanding rings until finally, at the peak of its incandescence, it devoured its own tail with a vicious and voluptuous avidity. Vulvomane's eyes burned like smoking craters; she screamed, once, and slipped backwards into the yawning sinus of night.

# MANTIS COVE

Even before first light broke above the horizon, Maga ran down to the beach to see what the night tides had washed up. For the past week the morning shore had been littered with driftwood and detritus – fragments from broken ships ranging in size from sections of railing to entire masts, webs of rigging tangled with seahorses and squid, tatters of sailcloth, and anything else which could float. Maga was most interested in the various parts of human bodies, especially torn-off arms and hands with fingers banded in golden rings and gemstones. She gasped as she found one almost straight away, a man's left hand with rings on every finger as well as the thumb; they were cameos, crafted from black sardonyx with grinning white skulls in relief. Two crabs were fighting over the puckered, salt-bleached appendage, and she snatched it away before they could drag it back to the brine. As she started easing the rings from the swollen joints, someone spoke.

"That's mine."

Maga twisted around with a start of fright and saw the ragged figure bearing down on her, a Shark White ripper brandishing his crudely bandaged wrist-stump in front of her face. She would have screamed, but another ripper opened her throat with the hook that was fixed to his wrist-stump.

"Thief-child," said Crogor.

There were more than twenty of them, most with suppurating burns or seeping lacerations; led by their chieftain, they had managed to slip through the shadowed streets of Gluttonport and flee across the rocks, even as the demolished corpses of their crew-mates rained down upon them from the centre of the cyclone. Hiding in caves by day and hugging the shoreline by night, living on raw shellfish and seaweed, the raiders had made their way as far as the Goldengate border.

Crogor peered up at the small, sleeping village beyond the sands. Burning oil had blinded him in one eye and left its cruel tracks all down his face, neck and chest, frying his right nipple to a crisp. "Time to kill, time to feast," he snarled.

By nightfall Mantis Cove was a roofless ruin of sooted stone, every dwelling ransacked and torched, every one of its seafolk dead. Men and children had died in their homes, butchered as they slept and then set alight; women were dragged out and killed later, as the sun began to set and the rippers finished building their cook-fires. Most had been raped throughout the day.

"I don't know about you," said Bor, "but I can't stand eating the ugly ones or the old ones. And no men, only girls. If they're pretty enough to fuck, they're pretty enough to eat."

"Aye," said Crogor. "Same thing in the end, I suppose."

"If you say. What's all that moaning?"

The noise was coming from inside a barn, where the worst wounded were sheltering. Crogor put down the half-eaten forearm and went to look. One of the Shell Crush fighters was writhing in agony, clutching at his shoulder where a flying slate of exploded granite had pierced him to the bone. Black pus was dripping from the wound, and the air around him stank like an unearthed grave. Crogor could see that the man's whole arm was poisoned and perished, little more than maggot-food. "Bor!" he shouted. "Fetch me the cleaver."

One by one the surviving raiders fell asleep, huddled against stretches of exposed brick. The fires were burning low, and the ground was littered with chewed and cracked human bones. Crogor unwound the rag that was covering his eye, and his fingertip brushed over a gelatinous ridge where the combusting oil had ruptured his cornea.

"Fuck the Mizuno," he muttered. Commander Inusame's last orders had been to sow fear and wreak havoc, and Crogor would carry out those orders or die in the attempt. But after this there could be no more delay, no rest until they joined the rest of the fleet off Sunstorm.

# MOUNT MOONCRY

After a day of ascending through the outskirts of the forest, they came upon the entrance to a mine unmarked on their map. A row of men's skulls, yellowed by age, had been nailed across the uppermost support beam.

"A warning," said Darkon. "Perhaps there's still some gold in this one."

"Doubtful," said Quexarian. "Every mine on Mount Goldenfang was stripped bare by the Gomi more than a century ago; what's left of the gold is piled in the vaults of the Mirror Castle."

"Only this is Mount Mooncry," said the warrior-priest. "We crossed that border hours ago. I say we take a look."

Quex scowled, lines creasing his brow. At nearly sixty years of age he was too old and wise for reckless adventures, if still young for a maven. "That's not what we're here for. And you serve the Triad now."

"I served the Moon Temple, and look what happened to that. Haven't you ever wondered why it was destroyed?"

"Many times," said Quex, "and I have only one answer – it was judgement for our failure to hold the emperor to account. Raikon was a sodomite, a hunter of human prey, a cruel man who danced with demons and revelled in a night-orgies of black magic, yet the mavens of the Moon did nothing to halt him. Destruction was the price of our fear."

"And yet here we are, you and me. So why are we so special?"

"If the Three Sorrows spared us, it was so we could complete our mission; and that's why we are obliged to do so, by heavenly covenant." It was a conversation they'd had before, but Darkon Domo never seemed quite satisfied with the answer. Only faith held the former sword-shifter's mercenary instincts in check, and that faith had been sorely tried.

"I'm not just talking about gold," Darkon insisted. "Tunnels have ways out as well as ways in. What if this one leads to the centre of the forest? We could cut right through the mountain and no-one would ever see us. Or attack us. You're not the one who has to gut these bastards."

The exorcist weighed the warrior-priest's words. The notion made sense – *if* the tunnel had an egress, and *if* it was deserted. "Very well," he relented. "A look. I suppose you'd best make sparks then – we'll need to light those lanterns."

The drift-tunnel was narrow and low-ceilinged, inclining gradually upwards as it led them deeper into the belly of the Brides. Blind white scorpions crunched underfoot. After several hours they came to a fork. "Left or right?" said Darkon.

"Try right," replied Quex. It seemed to him that they needed to veer more and more towards the core of the mysterious mountain, for the wolf temple of the Crookback Curs was surely hidden among its innermost wooded recesses. The tightly-enclosed path continued as it was before, chill and oppressive, darker than night. Half a day elapsed. Quex was growing ever more anxious. *This is going nowhere,* he thought to himself. *We're going to get lost in here, and our bones will rot forever unfound and forgotten, just like the skulls of the Brotherhood.*

And then they heard the bats. It sounded like an entire roost was taking flight perhaps a hundred paces ahead, thousands of wings fluttering in concert like a ghost-wind in a graveyard. When the sound faded, they knew that a way out of the mine was within reach. Darkon unsheathed his godsword Shirometsu and took the lead. A minute later his front foot stepped onto empty air, and he felt himself pitching into a void.

It all blurred into one instant. By the light of his lantern he saw a teetering mound of part-fleshed skeletons, both human and animal, alive with rats and carrion insects. But even as he started falling towards this appalling sprawl of corruption he felt a hand grasp him by the back of his sword-belt, a powerful hand which halted his plunge and pulled him back to safe ground. He slumped against the tunnel wall, snatching at breath. "You're stronger than you fucking look," he eventually said to Quex.

The maven gave a wry smile. "My right arm is the right arm of Sorrow Sukion," he replied. "I am merely her vessel."

"I'll remember that," said Darkon.

They edged around the bone-pit, stomach muscles contracting at the charnel miasma, and peered down the driftway. A sliver of light lay ahead.

# THE PLAIN OF PAIN

In the beginning, there was order. Lord Kamosukon Gomi's battle-force stretched in line across the Plain of Pain for more than half a mile, some six thousand in number, at the point where Mount Mooncry first merged into Mount Slaughtershriek. On the left, nearest the slopes, was the gold division under Vason Sogo; then the red under Mison Mako, the silver under Boron Kita, and at right the black under Isson Moko, each force identified by three painted stripes below each eye. At dead centre, poised between red and silver, Lord Kamosukon Gomi sat high upon a snorting war-horse surrounded by two hundred of his mounted castle guard, the Dust Demons, ebon armour graven with iridescent sea-spirals. His customary half-mask of wax had been replaced by one of mirrored metal that also extended over his head, and was set with an artificial eye of blood-red ruby.

Lord Hebon Hakamanko had ceded command of his forces to his most experienced battle-general Hakon Hora, known as Hellhawk. Three thousand clan fighters were clustered at centre, with a division of two hundred horse on either flank. In the vanguard were Hebon's twenty silver-helmed würm-riders, led by Vexion on his slavering beast Bolgo. Gomi scouts reported that another force, perhaps two thousand in number, was advancing rapidly from the south in support. Lord Hebon took the rear, looking on from his horseback vantage-point in the Slaughtershriek foothills, companied by the war-witch Vulvomane and shielded by his hundred-strong lifesguard the Tongues of the Basilisk, trident-wielding death-dealers in rippling viridian plate.

The sun was just rising behind the Hakamanko troops when Hellhawk ordered the würm-riders forward in a spread of four cuneiform packs, driven on by a surge of screaming fighters marked with the tattoos of the Tower Bat, Iron Talon and Nightshade clans. In response a pincer of Wormheart and Rape Chain clansmen closed in front of Lord Kamosukon, and from deep in their midst a rank of war-wains emerged, propelled from behind, each mounted with an open-faced cage of decomposing corpses. From each battle-force a withering slew of arrows was unleashed, darking the dawn, followed by another and another. The Hakamanko barbs were doused in a toxin brewed by Lady Vulvomane, a red phage which quickly drove those who were struck into rabid paroxysms of self-cannibalism.

Within minutes the two forces clashed. Three yards out from the Gomi line Vexion jerked the chain which lifted his würm's titanium muzzle, a signal for the giant lizard to spew out a smoking stream of venom. The lethal discharge struck a Rape Chain brave between the eyes, burning through his flesh and skull with a fearful rapacity and leaving a corpse with a hole where its face used to be. Each lizard unleashed its acid in turn, each pack melting the fighters that confronted it to pierce the Gomi defences in four places. Sword-points were deflected by the beasts' calcified scales, spearheads glanced away by leathery eye-membranes; men whirled and writhed in pain, arms and legs stripped to dangling bone or dissolved into stumps. At the same time a hundred armoured horse charged from each flank, smashing into the gold and black divisions and impaling vast swathes of men with metal-tipped lances even as many riders and steeds were toppled by upthrust spears, blood spraying from multiple punctures and lacerations like a mist of early morning rain.

Then one of the würms, a beast named Gorgo, took the bait, poking its hunger-crazed head into a corpse-cage to devour the putrescent meat that hung inside; the wain's driver tripped a catch-spring, releasing two razor-edged metal plates which snapped together from each side of the opening and decapitated the lizard in an instant. Gorgo's headless body collapsed, venting a pestilent discharge from its cloaca, spilling its rider Thruxion onto the ground; Mison Mako trampled the man pitilessly underhoof before thrusting a lance through his throat where it was exposed by his dislocated helm.

Two more würms were beheaded in the same way, the red and silver warriors swarming around others and attacking their riders from behind; one was pierced by twenty spears and lifted into the air, choking on a gusher of dark blood. The remaining würm-riders wheeled their lizards around and fled from the growing carnage, seeking respite for the creatures to replenish their venom before the next assault. At least seven reptilian carcasses were left behind in the reddening dirt.

Even as Lord Kamosukon was weighing a mounted charge to run the lizard-men down, his attention was caught by a distant swirl of sound, a melange of galloping hooves and battle-cries which seemed to come from behind the Hakamanko ranks. Lord Hebon heard it even sooner, turning to see two hundred Gomi rock-rangers bearing down upon him, as if ejected from the very bowels of the Brides.

"*Basilisks! To me!*" he cried, pressing his horse forwards into the protective ranks of his lifesguard. When they quickly closed around him he was buffeted in the side, and as the destrier lost its footing he felt himself pitched sideways into the grass, clasping his hands to his ears as the first wave of rock-rangers slammed fearlessly into the trident wall. Somewhere far away, Hellhawk was screaming orders.

# METAL TOWN

It looked as it sounded, a warren of ferrous shacks, shrines and beerholes overshadowed by a gated compound of taller, stone-clad buildings which only the mine-masters or others with sufficient coin could access.

"The House of Wet Orchids lies beyond those gates," said Mekuron Taka. "That's where you'll find our Lady Spitkiss. The Skinned Swine is a mile south, on the road to the Ossuary."

"Take two others with you," said Kuron Kirizono, "and bring her to the inn by tomorrow's nightfall. We'll find the boy."

Three riders forked left and the rest kept to the Wolfway, the sloping high road which ran down from the Fearfang Bridge to Hangman's Head. In their midst was a funeral wain drawn by a snow-white horse in black caparison, and upon it was a velvet-draped coffin housing a corpse that had never been alive.

"Not much longer now," said Kirizono to Lady Soma Kurotako, who was riding the wain next to Jagon Ketsu. "The Seikyo's war position is neutral, therefore honour demands that they offer you save harbour."

"So you'll just hand me over?" she asked.

"On one condition," said Kirizono. "Your friend in the coffin will remain with us."

"Gladly," she said. Lady Burnbolt was certainly no friend, only a reminder of the nightmare which her own father had plunged her into by sending her to incinerate Chikon Takasha under pretence of betrothment. Would she even have been able to carry out the plot, activating Burnbolt's clockworks and fleeing under cover of night? In many ways she blamed the maven Chromocrax and his dark whisperings which, she was sure, exerted a malign influence on her father's judgement. It was rewarding Chromocrax with one of Hebon Hakamanko's precious würms that had seen her younger sister Suna packed off to marry Hekon the hunchback, a marriage truly made in the fiery hells. She wondered if she would ever see Suna again. Her sister was now in the midst of a conflict that threatened to tear Novalis asunder, a civil war in which her family was perceived as an enemy of state through her father's ill-met alliance with Hebon. This and more she had gleaned from Kirizono, her captor; he had treated her with decency, at least, despite his fearsome repute and despite forcing her to sojourn in a house of lunatics. All the same, it would be a welcome respite to be harboured in the sanctuary of Wolf's Jaw.

The Skinned Swine was a large inn, with stables enough for at least forty horses and rooms for forty riders. They left the funeral wain and its cargo tethered outside in the rain. "Bait," said the Black Reaper.

Inside a number of local clansmen were also drinking; Nezumon Nano identified them as fighters from the Quicksilver and Phantom Fox clans, two of those most loyal to the Seikyo. Kirizono also knew of at least three others, the Spider Hooks, Blood Jackals and Corpse-Riders. He was glad that no Corpse-Riders were there; they had a reputation as gash-gizzard hellions, and got their name from an ancient cabal of warlocks who disinterred the dead. *A bit like this Dorion Killstar,* he thought. He was gambling that Killstar employed scouts to aid his nocturnal scavenging, ghouls who would daily scour the environs of the Ossuary for fresh executions and burials; *and unattended coffins, easiest prey of all.*

It was long after midnight when a black-clad figure emerged from the darkness and crept up to the funeral wain. There were no lights at the inn; a bat cloud fluttered over the horses' water-trough, and two wolves were communing far out in the starry wilderness. Kirizono and Nano watched from the stable shadows, waiting to be sure. When the prowler started to pry off the coffin lid, they knew it must be him. Nano was behind the boy before he heard a sound; when Kirizono appeared in front of him, he turned to flee to his cart and slammed his face straight into Nano's outstretched palm. Kirizono peered down at him as he sat in the mud, wiping blood from his nose with a threadbare sleeve.

"You are Dorion Killstar," he said.

"Am I?"

"Just one question, boy. How many toes have you got?"

# MOUNTMOONCRY

The tunnel opened out onto a circular forest clearing with a raised, red-stained slab of stone at its centre. At once Quexarian knew that his suspicions had been correct; the corpses and carcasses in the tunnel bone-pit were from sacrificial rites. As such they could not be devoured by celebrants, and so they were left to rot. Whether their deaths were supposed to drive out plague, appease demons, or quicken fertility he could not say. The Crookback Curs were an ancient, insular clan, whose auguries and superstitions were doubtless unchanged since the time of Metakaikon.

Dogs barked in the dusk.

"Hunters," said Darkon. "Back to the tunnel; that stench will hide us from the hounds."

"Those hounds may be cleverer than you think," said Quex quietly as they took cover. "Have you heard of the She-Dogs of Chelicor?"

"Aye," said Darkon. "Mountain warrior women. Crookback bitches who bay at the midnight sun. Do they really exist?"

As if in reply, a fist-sized rock flew out of the dim driftway behind them and struck Darkon Domo square on the back of his head, opening up a bloody rent in his moon tattoo. He groaned and slumped to the ground.

"That real enough for you?" said the She-Dog, reloading her slingshot. By her voice Quex guessed that she had some deformity of the mouth, probably a cleft palate.

"No need," he said, hands raised. "We are servants of the Triad, on a mission of peace."

"Throw your friend's sword over here, and your daggers. Then we'll see."

When Darkon regained his senses a relentless, stabbing pain was wracking his head and his vision was blurred. He was sat on the ground, arms behind him, tied to a sturdy birch sapling. And so was Quexarian. As his eyes slowly cleared he could distinguish the girl standing over him. Despite the cold she was half naked, with breasts and nipples exposed and furs wrapped around her loins. Her body was caked in grime and, by the odour from beneath the furs, Darkon guessed that she hadn't bathed for quite some while.

"So it's true that dogs don't like water," he muttered. It was then he noticed the switch in her hand; it lashed across his mouth, drawing more blood.

"Careful, monk," she snarled. "What do you bastards want?"

"Well," said Quexarian, "we..."

"Tell her the truth," said Darkon. "Best not to die with a lie on our lips."

"Very well then. We're relic hunters, and we're looking for some holy skulls that have been here for rather a long time... about nine hundred years, actually."

The girl looked at one of her fellow She-Dogs; both seemed vaguely puzzled, as if unable to comprehend such a time-span. Then a third spoke up. "It's true, Lupa," she said. "There were another pair of them here a few years back asking about the same thing... Wik cut their hearts out and gave them to the Stone Man."

"The Stone Man?" Darkon repeated.

"The god of the mountain," said Lupa. "Who do you think fucks the Brides every night?"

"Of course, stupid of me. And who fucks you?" Darkon saw a look of horror cross Quex's face, but the girl's deformed mouth had given him an idea. *They're she-dogs, and she-dogs are only there to breed. Or interbreed, in this case.* "My friend here is a maven," he continued. "Last night he saw a vision of a dead child... a twisted child, a monster."

"All our children are monsters," said Lupa. "Because we were raped in our sleep by demons. We drown them in the well."

*Your children are monsters because you've fucked your own brothers, fathers and uncles for centuries.* "I'm no demon. My seed is pure. I'm a monk, after all. Set us free and return our weapons, and I'll give you a beautiful child. I swear it."

Lupa looked at him blankly for a few seconds, then burst out laughing. "Did you hear that, Raka? The monk wants to give me a baby." Raka joined in the laughter, but Darkon could see that both She-Dogs were already roused by the thought of fornication; their eyes shone, and a rivulet of clear fluid was trickling down Lupa's inner thigh. "And once you've seeded me, why shouldn't I just chop off your monk's cock, and your monk's head with it?"

"Because I have enough for all of you," said Darkon. "Now; who's first?"

# THE SHIP OF DOLLS

The nameless freighter drifted through the night, black-sailed and lightless, a single rudderman astern. The maven Chromocrax and his apprentice Kargon were seated at the prow; between them and the pilot stood the thirteen Bloodtooth Virgins, chaos dolls whose swollen bellies were clad in purple velvet gowns embroidered with alchemical symbols picked in white silk. Chromocrax's original plan was to stand them stark naked, but that had changed along with his allegiance.

As they passed the silent Isle of Gaunts where generations of Kurotako overlords were buried in ornate, treasure-laden tomb ships, the maven reflected on the moment that made him rethink his position in the ever-shifting civil war. Only one ship, the *Hexbound Heart*, had escaped the cataclysm of Gluttonport Bay and limped home to the Red Rock; its captain, Mushon Yowa, delivered a sobering report to the Slaughterhouse council. *The Lady Miura is a sorceress,* he had said. *She stood atop the battlements, raised her arms to the sky, and summoned forth the whirlwind.*

Captain Yowa went on to detail the destruction of the fleet, but Chromocrax had already heard enough. He knew that Miura Mizuno was no elemental witch, but that was not at issue; what was clear to him was that the Sorrows of the Triad would now be perceived as favouring the Starfire Order, which in turn would ensure the loyalty of the Celestial Horde. If the Horde took up arms against the Hakamanko and Kurotako, the result could be catastrophic. In the War of the Dead, an internal clash which ravaged Goldengate four centuries earlier, the warrior-priests of the Sun Temple had raised a protest army of monks, peasants, artisans and merchants almost fifty thousand in number to suppress a blood-feud over ancient burial grounds between the Hexo and Hassha. Such a force, no matter how ill-equipped, could sweep over the clans of the snake and octopus and even precipitate their extinction. Chromocrax was also aware of the fate suffered by many of his kind who ended up on the losing side of conflicts;

during the Serpent Wars his own ancestor Shattonax, maven to Clan Satogawa, had been crucified and burnt as a warlock by the victorious Mizuno after the sacking of the Bloodflower Castle, and that was not a demise he wished to emulate.

Chromocrax could not deny a certain affection for Lord Sadogashon; the Octopus was nothing if not malleable, and had given him free rein for his experiments after his wife, Lady Kana Kurotako, inexplicably slipped from the side of the *Death Tentacle* and was eaten alive by a shiver of sharks. Sadogashon's interest in the art of doll-making had increased significantly after that, allowing Chromocrax to work on chaos models whilst ostensibly perfecting a gynoid with functioning genital parts for his overlord's private chambers. But while he was gratified that Sadogashon later entrusted Lady Burnbolt with an assassination mission, his proposed deployment of another thirteen dolls against the Seikyo, dragging Wolf's Jaw into the war, now seemed like folly in the light of Captain Yowa's report. And Chromocrax had no wish to see years of craftsmanship immolated in a single moment just to sink one warship.

So it was that Kargon found himself creeping up behind the Kurotako rudderman, heart pounding, and shoving him in the back as hard as he could. With a short exclamation the man toppled over the freighter's rail and into the icy black. Twice he tried to clamber back aboard, twice Kargon pushed him down with an oar; then the cold began to render his limbs useless, and he sank, slowly, beneath the kelp-draggled surface. Quickly they lit the boat's lanterns, lowering the sail and running up a white flag of surrender; Kargon used the oar to guide them towards land, and as he glanced back he saw a gigantic pleurodon emerge from the deep, shaking the rudderman's legless, blood-spurting torso in its jaws, then vanish again forever.

"It's done," said Chromocrax. "We have now defected."

In the distance they could see the guttering lights of Gluttonport, and above that watchfires blazing along the ramparts of the Nightmare Castle. When they reached shore the guards of the Vertigo Watch were already waiting on the beach, glaives poised to wreak justice.

# THE NIGHTMARE CASTLE

Lady Miura Mizuno spent her nights poring over the castle's ancestral copy of the *Elemental Testament*, one of thirteen sacred volumes created for the founding clans by order of the first emperor, Metakaikon. Each book was hand-illuminated by the Shadow mavens and bound in the tanned skin of the martyr Saint Saragon, who in the year 29 was flayed alive by heathens of the Ice Cock clan for preaching the word of the Triad.

As clan regent during the disappearance of her husband Akumuron, Lady Miura had found a new zeal both for the Three Sorrows and for the destruction of her foe, preferably in combination. Such was the case, she fervently believed, when the Kurotako fleet was smashed to splinters by a cyclone of divine origin which also blasted the enemy commander's head a mile into the sky before dropping it on Gluttonport beach. The head now stared blankly out to sea from the Terror Tower, impaled on a metal spike. She wished the same fate upon those who spread rumours about her missing husband, from the castle kitchens to the surrounding villages. *Lord Aku was killed by pirates, who used his head as bait for catching crabs and eels*, they were saying; or, even worse, *Lord Aku abandoned his wife and ran off with a sea-wench, at first sniff of her upturned arse.*

But it was the hierarchy of the Triad which most obsessed Lady Miura, and was the subject of her most fevered ruminations. *They are all female – the Three Sorrows are served by the Seven Archangels, and the archangels are served in turn by the Thirteen Angels of Fire. But who do the Sorrows serve? Who sits alone at the apex of the holy pyramid? If Sorrow Arashon answered my call, what does that make me – supplicant, or mistress?* She wondered if her abandonment had a higher purpose, if it was a symbolic death to allow for rebirth as – *what?*

It was long after midnight when Sevon Kako, white-armoured captain of the Vertigo Watch, appeared at the chapel doorway. "Strangers ashore under white flag, lady regent," he announced. "An old man, a boy, and thirteen... others."

"Others?"

"Others. You may wish to see them for yourself; I have never encountered their like before. They seem to pose no danger."

Chromocrax and Kargon stood in the centre of the marble helix which decorated the hall's flooring, the chill of the night ocean slowly diffusing from their bones. The Bloodtooth Virgins had been placed in a huddle behind them, ferried from the beach by cart. Guardsmen stood at both sides, wary of the waxen beauties without knowing exactly why. The maven grew ever more anxious, fearing he had made the wrong decision. *Too late now, you old fool.*

Lady Miura entered from a door at the side of the hall, accompanied by Sevon Kako. She was gowned in black silk and necklaced in a tawdry of sparkling amethysts.

"Speak," she said.

"I am the maven Chromocrax. I was once in thrall to Lord Sadogashon Kurotako, but now I offer my services to you, Lady Miura."

"In thrall? Or in league?" said Miura, stepping closer. Before Chromocrax could reply, she stepped past him to examine the motionless pyro-dolls. "Fascinating creatures. Tell me, maven – are they alive or dead?"

"Both," said Chromocrax. "And neither. They are my gift to you, a sign of my loyalty. I also bring news of the Kurotako fleet off Sunstorm, which may prove advantageous."

Miura smiled, in a way which the maven could not interpret. "And what use are they to me?"

"As you can see, they are harmless. Your guards had no qualms about bringing them here... and yet, it is an illusion. Any one of these assassins could reduce this hall, and all who stand in it, to a smoking ruin of ashes."

At that Sevon Kako stepped forward, half-unsheathing his sword. "You dare threaten the Lady Miura?" he barked. "I'll feed your entrails to the pigs."

Miura raised a hand. "Show me," she said.

In the dead of night the Scar Faery led three Shark White rippers back to the beach in chains. All bore the mark of her caress – one had been blinded, another's tongue ripped out, the third had only bone-holes where his nose used to be. They were manacled to the mast of the Kurotako freighter; Chromocrax positioned one of the Bloodtooth Virgins, Lady Kollabia, at the stern. He took the two master keys from around his neck – one that fitted every anus, one that fitted every navel – and opened a small flap in her gown front, exposing part of the rounded belly. The key turned just once, with a muffled click.

"We must wait one hour," he said. "Time enough for an escape."

Two guards of the Vertigo Watch pushed the boat out into the shallows, dropped one of its stone anchors, then waded back ashore. They all retreated to the port's elevated sea-wall, and waited.

"I expect wonders," warned Lady Miura, "or the Scar Faery will carve off a pound of your flesh for every minute wasted."

As Chromocrax had promised, Lady Kollabia carried out her mission after a lapse of exactly one hour. The explosion shattered the silence like a thunderclap, with a simultaneous eruption of dazzling white fire and heat that scorched the retinas of all who watched, leaving an imprint that took several moments to resolve. Cinders, charred wood and blazing body parts showered down onto sea and sand as the remaining fragments of the freighter slipped beneath the steaming water. Within seconds, the vessel and its occupants had been completely obliterated; a single glass eye, partially melted, had smashed into the sea-wall with projectile force and was embedded in the salt-softened stone, the only proof that Lady Kollabia had ever existed.

"Demon's work," said Sevon Kako. "Surely this man is a danger, lady regent?"

But Miura was exultant. "Don't you see?" she said. "This is another sign from the Three Sorrows. They have sent us the Thirteen Angels of Fire, in mortal form. A new weapon for the annihilation of those who seek to destroy us. You will move them to the Terror Tower at once."

"Yes, lady regent," said Kako.

"I thank you for your great service," Miura said to Chromocrax. "On the morrow our maven, Chironax, will provide you with all that you need to work your craft. I have a special project which demands the utmost urgency – you are to bring my husband Lord Akumuron back to me."

"I understand," said Chromocrax. "With time and the right materials, Lord Akumuron will live forever." *So this is the choice I made*, he thought. *From the fire into the furnace. But when the war is done, at least I'll be alive.*

It was almost dawn by the time he was escorted to a bed chamber, with Kargon in an adjoining cell. When the sun came its rays bathed his sleeping eyelids, flooding his mind with dreams of a great bird rising through a veil of pure black flame.

# MOUNTMOONCRY

It was almost dawn by the time Darkon Domo was totally spent and of no further use to the She-Dogs of Chelicor. Quexarian had dozed fitfully throughout the night, still trussed but warmed, at least, by one of two fires the warrior women had built; his sleep was punctuated by feral rutting yelps and growls coming from the tunnel-mouth where Darkon was making his sacrifice for the Triad. Afterwards the She-Dogs were true to their word. Darkon must have performed well, Quex supposed; he counted at least six women in the clearing, and none seemed hostile. One had even stitched up the warrior-priest's wound. The whole incident was a gross violation of Domo's templar vows, of course, but in the circumstances...

"Follow the goat-track up and up until you reach the flat," said Lupa. "From there you can look down on the temple and the bonehouse. We only keep the skulls of them that fell in battle, ours and others both, but there must have been plenty in the last nine hundred years. Do what you will, but if the warlock catches you he'll cut your hearts out, and the menfolk will like as not slit your throats. Come back this way and I'll kill you meself, pupped or not."

Darkon's fingers flickered over the hilt of his godsword. *Not all priests are toothless, bitch,* he thought, but said nothing. He'd already expended a great deal of energy, and the wise thing was just to leave while they could.

The goat-track was steep, and Quex's breathing was audible as he spoke. "I owe you a debt, Brother Darkon. If not for your quick mind I believe our hearts would have been forfeit, our bones destined for the corpse-pit."

"My pleasure to serve," said Darkon. "But perhaps we should heed the girl's warning, and abandon the quest? The temple will be surrounded by Cur clansmen, and I don't think my cock will hold quite the same charm for them."

"I understand the risk," said Quex, "but first hear me out. I was just twenty-three when I performed my first exorcism. I was summoned to Castle Mortmane after Lord Haramoton Takasha reported a case of demonic possession – his son Hikidashon, then aged eleven or twelve, had started haunting the castle stables by night; they kept vigil and caught him raping one of the mares – a dappled beast with long eyelashes named Candessa, I seem to recall – and Haramoton was convinced his son had been infested by some form of evil equine entity, perhaps the vengeful ghost of a stallion butchered at war. Although I assured him this was most unlikely, Haramoton insisted upon a ritual banishing."

"And you cured him? The horse-demon was driven out?"

"Hikidashon? No, I don't he was ever cured of that particular urge… but his father was appeased, and I learnt then that symbolic power is the same as real power. Which is why the bindings are important, and why we must complete our mission and retrieve the sacred relics, as an affirmation of imperial and religious authority in these troubled times."

"If you say," said Darkon. "Strikes me it might have been the mare that was possessed, though," he added.

"An eventuality which was also dealt with – once the rites for his son were performed, Haramoton had the beast tortured, skinned, and thrown on a bonefyre."

Dusk was gathering when they reached the apex of the goat-track. It was as Lupa had said – they stood above the highest tree-line, and directly below they could see the temple of the Crookback Curs, flanked by two monolithic statues of howling wolves hewn from mountain stone. Behind the temple, and connected to it by a covered passageway, was another structure with a flat roof which Quex identified as the repository of skulls. Across a clearing was a settlement, where scores of clansmen were milling.

"I'm not climbing down that," said Darkon, indicating the rock-face below their feet. "It's a sheer hundred-foot drop."

"But if we walk back down and approach through the forest…"

"The Curs will chop our heads off. And don't tell me you can reason with them. Remember what Lupa said about the Stone Man."

"Then I can only suggest we wait," said Quex, "and take our chance when it comes."

"*If* it comes," said Darkon, but he was too tired to argue further.

Their chance did come, and it came not long after the rising of the sun. They were woken by a clamour from the Crookback settlement; two riders on garrons had appeared, most likely scouts, and were shouting orders to their fellow clansmen. The

Curs were running from hut to hut, gathering possessions, weapons, armour. Many came from inside the temple. They were preparing for battle, Darkon realised. And then, within an hour, the whole host had vanished away down the mountainside.

Two guards remained outside the wolf temple, one posted by each statue. They could only guess how many remained within. Darkon burst from the trees at a run, sword above his head; the nearest Crookback responded in kind, and a grating clash of steel rang around the glade. By the time the second guard arrived from his position across the temple steps, Darkon had already disembowelled the first. *"Fucking death!"* the Cur screamed as he swung his curved blade at Darkon's head, almost taking his eyes out; the warrior-priest thrust forward with Shirometsu, shattering three ribs and puncturing a lung, and as his chest cavity filled with blood the Cur began gasping for breath, failing to complete his retaliatory blow and leaving his neck exposed for the kill-strike.

The warlock Wik Wolfgut turned from his altar of painted animal bones to see a tall figure silhouetted in the temple portway, with a smaller man standing behind. The intruder carried a sword, and it was dripping on the stone-flagged floor.

"We're here for the twelve skulls of the Brotherhood," said Darkon. "No need to die, just hand them to us and we'll be on our way."

"Skulls?" replied Wolfgut. "Follow me."

He led them back towards a wooden door studded with iron. "This way," said the warlock.

"Beware traps," Darkon said to Quex, but the exorcist had already seen the true object of his quest, as ordained by the moon maven Jagmalion the High before his demise; it was mounted above the pagan altar, its volcanic steel untarnished despite the passing of three centuries.

They followed the warlock down the covered tunnel, which was lined by burning torches in sconces. At the end it opened up into a vast vault stacked from floor to ceiling with thousands upon thousands of human skulls in rows, most cracked or smashed by violent death.

"Take your pick," said Wolfgut.

Darkon felt the rage rising in his veins, provoked by the gloating of the warlock and the realisation that they would never identify the remains of the White Light martyrs amongst this mortal morass. With a sudden roar he drove the blade of Shirometsu into Wolfgut's neck, wrenching it out again with a great gusher of heartsblood which splattered against the uppermost tier of skulls then ran down in bubbling, swirling streams like the red piss of a drunken giant.

Quex quickly gathered a dozen of the oldest but least fractured deathsheads and stuffed them into his carry-sack. "Symbolic power," he reminded Darkon. "Symbolic power."

As they left the temple Quexarian paused by the altar, reaching up to pull the stolen deathsword Sensoni, the war demon, from its mountings. "Might as well take this too," he said. "Looks like it might be useful."

# THE PLAIN OF PAIN

Watching from a southeasterly ridge as the second phase of battle unfurled, Gorn suddenly realised that Hebon Hakamanko was under direct threat. *If Hebon dies, so does my dream of a fort full of whores and ale.* "Vakko!" he yelled. "Attack!"

Vakko Kill-Claw needed no second invitation; he charged toward the field with upraised sword, followed by one and a half thousand of his roaring clansmen. By now the Hakamanko horse had turned tail and were flooding back to protect Lord Hebon, allowing all four Gomi battalions to surge forwards and attack the Snake Lord's foot-soldiers from both flanks. For a while it was a butchery, the Gomi outnumbering their foe two to one; then the silver and red were forced to turn and face the onrushing Kill-Claw, and were suddenly hemmed in with Blind Cat, Cut-Belly and Night Weeper fighters hacking at their rear. Vakko forged ahead with his sword swinging in two-handed arcs, taking off the top of a Spectre Moth's head in a shower of bone and brain. Within minutes the central battle descended into a blood-drenched melee of shattered skulls, hewn-off limbs and gutted, transpierced torsos, with wounded würms disgorging caustic death in all directions.

Vason Sogo and Mison Mako, seeing their forces plunged into chaos, broke away and galloped after the Hakamanko horse. As they rounded the left edge of the fighting, where Split-Tongue Ravens of the gold division were smashing a gaggle of Iron Talons to pulp with morning-stars, they saw a figure from nightmare charging towards them; it was Hellhawk, soaked in gore from head to toe, his horse likewise besplattered. With a maniac cry he urged the crimson beast at the Gomi generals, aiming to split them down the middle. At the last moment Vason Sogo lost his nerve and veered away; Hellhawk drove his lance straight through Mison Mako's chest, unhorsing his corpse as he galloped past in search of Kamosukon Gomi.

Just then a new uproar erupted from the higher ground; more than a hundred

Crookback Curs had burst from the lower trees of Mount Mooncry and were running full pelt towards the tangle of rock-rangers and Tongues of the Basilisk surrounding Hebon Hakamanko. No-one knew whose side they were on; most likely nor did they. The Curs were blood-crazed degenerates, wolf-men who would join any battle just to wreak carnage. Among them were also women, the She-Dogs of Chelicor; their leader, a heavy-breasted harelip, was whirling a slingshot around and around her head. Finally she let fly with her missile, a large lead ball which flew at the Hakamanko cluster with enough weight and velocity to destroy a wooden door. It struck Lady Vulvomane right between the eyes, blasting through her brow-bone and exploding her cranium with a foul disjecta of bloody brain chunks. Just as she died a Golden Maggot spearman rushed up screaming *burn the witch!* and rammed his weapon through the side of her face. The spear-tip penetrated her left cheek and burst out of the right, causing an expectoration of tooth fragments and shredded meat. For a moment he held the spear steady, propping up her corpse in the saddle, then let go. The bane virago's body flopped backwards over the rump of her mad-eyed mount and was impaled for a third and final time, through the centre of the heart, as it fell onto an upturned sword.

The arrival of the wolf-men spurred Kamosukon Gomi into decisive action. Seeing the Hakamanko rearguard under renewed threat, he knew that the chance was there to end the battle, and the war, if Hebon could be reached. *"With me!"* he cried, cradling a lance as he unsheathed his deathsword Obochi, the graveyard king, and headed the Dust Demons into a frenzied mounted charge which cut straight through the melee like a burning knife, crushing the mutilated and dying underhoof, arrowing at Hebon with deadly purpose. Kamosukon could see that the Snake Lord was back on his horse, surrounded by a tight double ring of his lizard guard and their jutting tridents while all around them rock-rangers and Hakamanko horse were enmeshed in a cavort of bloody slaughter.

*Time to get the sword wet,* Gorn thought to himself. *Do or fucking die.* He motioned at Urstinx, leader of the Blood Eagle berserkers. "Now."

Urstinx nodded and turned to face his fellow braves, pulling a skin of shapestrong from his belt and raising it to his lips. The rest followed suit, and Gorn watched with grim disgust as they guzzled the rancid brew of curdled animal blood and toadstools, spilling it over their throats and chests in foetid clots. When the skins were drained the berserkers smeared the remnants of the potion over their faces, snarling like the beasts they sought to embody; some were wolves, hooded in matted furs, the other bears with leathern gloves and chanking metal claws.

Kamosukon ripped into the fray at full force, his lance crashing into the neck of Hebon's standard-bearer so hard that the wretch's head flew off and went spinning through the air. The lance shattered but Kamosukon held onto it, using the splintered stump to unhorse another, while the Dust Demons poured around him on either side like a river of death. Minutes passed, and Kamosukon was almost in sword range of Hebon's inner circle when the five hundred berserkers ploughed into the back of them, raving and howling and screaming like demons from the Three Hells, some shitting and puking as they ran, killing anyone and anything they touched. When a horse stood in their path the bear-berserkers used their metal claws to cut the beast open and rip it apart, yanking out its heart and biting into it, hurling its intestines and spine into the air. Men fared little better against the Blood Eagles' rage; Vason Sogo, protecting Kamosukon's flank, was pulled from his mount by two attackers who seemed to feel no pain as he stabbed his sword into them, before they ripped off his arms and legs to use as war-clubs.

Before long Kamosukon realised that Hebon and his remaining lifesguard had slipped away; he looked about him and saw that the berserkers had decimated the Dust Demons, whose last number now rushed to defend their overlord against the overwhelming onslaught. Their resistance proved futile; Kamosukon was quickly exposed, and felt a shuddering axe-blow dislodge his mask-helm. The next strike sheared off the back of his skull, and then a wolf-berserker smashed a war-hammer into his forehead with such fury that his brains flew out from the gaping back of his head, landing in the lap of his loyal standard-bearer Nankon Hata who was clinging onto the Gomi banner despite having both legs torn off above the knee. Obochi slipped from its master's grip, and was lost.

It was Gorn of Gluttonport who raised the victory shout, jabbing his unused sword Gut-Fucker repeatedly overhead. The battle was won before noon. During the rest of the day Hellhawk and his henchmen stalked the carnage, putting to death any wounded on both sides by braining them with studded mauls. Undamaged weapons were gathered and piled on carts bound for Skull Castle. Here and there Kill-Claw fighters had stacked severed heads into piles, and were pissing on them. Those Gomi followers left unscathed were given a stark choice by Lord Hebon – kneel, or lose their head. Most knelt, with the exception of Boron Kita. "*Fuck the snake!*" he shouted, just before Hellhawk's war-axe ended him. The last surviving general, Isson Moko, was less belligerent; he took the knee in exchange for his life, but still ended up being chained to Vexion's würm – one of nine that survived – and dragged all the way to the Nightmare Castle as part of Hebon's grotesque victory cavalcade.

At the front of it was a dark bay destrier carrying the corpse of Kamosukon

Gomi. Already voided of eyes and brain, Kamosukon's body had been stripped nude and tied to the horse like a hunting kill, haunches raised and pointed forward; his metal mask-helm, battered and blood-stained, dangled from the beast's bridle. A spiral had been scrawled on each of the dead lord's buttocks to resemble eyes, and for a nose a fat taproot had been shoved into his rectum. Sneered at in life as Wax-Face, the Gomi overlord would be forever mocked in death as Kamosukon Arse-Face.

Juka watched in horror as the procession neared the gates. Her long raven hair hung to her waist, her face whitened, painted with arching brows and a vivid slash of red across the mouth. Her puce gown was fastened at the neck with a sylvanite brooch, the breast-cones decorated with peonies of scarlet lace on each tip. She already knew what her fate would be; either kept as a spoil of war and rape-slave by Lord Hebon – or, even worse, by his hunchbacked whelp – or used as leverage against her brother Jukon to force him into surrendering Kobutsuden. *If not both.* Unable to contemplate such a future, and grief-crazed by her father's death, Juka Gomi raised an outstretched fist in final salute to the sun and stepped off the glinting battlements of the Mirror Castle into a dizzying, fathomless negation.

# THE WINTER PALACE

Jukon studied the scroll, and then read it aloud for the council. "*Do not trust the Killer. Beware the skull-faced ones when the Corpse Moon rises. We must burn them all.* The letter is signed *Miura, Black Phoenix.*"

"Black Phoenix? What does that mean?" asked Veluron Taiyo.

Gomon Takasha shrugged. "Maven?"

"I believe it must be a reference to the scriptures," said Valadian. "In the *Elemental Apochrypha* there is a description of the end of all worlds, a cataclysm which causes the Three Sorrows to weep tears of black fire, forming a great lake of nothingness. From this lake a firebird arises, embodying the Triad in a single entity of sun, moon and storms. That entity is Black Phoenix."

"So when the world ends..."

"It will be reborn beneath the wings of the firebird; Black Phoenix will be empress of the world, the Triad personified."

Jukon suppressed a laugh. "So Miura Mizuno thinks herself empress of the world? Forgive me, Lady Snowsnake, but was she not just a castle follower before marrying Lord Akumuron? She is not even high-born."

"A vicious rumour," hissed Lady Snowsnake. "Lady Miura traces her bloodline back to the Hassha."

Before Jukon could respond, Veluron said: "What matter? The world has not ended, to my knowledge."

"But what about the Decimation?" said Gomon. "Is there not now a black lake of frigid fire across all Thundervoid – the Three Hells combined in one form?"

"Aye," said Jukon. "I've seen it with my own eyes. But nothing arose from that save gas from rotting corpses, seeping through the cracks. What else, Lord Veluron?"

"A second scroll, but recently received; I fear it is ill-omened, for it bears the seal of the Hakamanko. And there is a trinket box."

After silently reading the letter Jukon pushed back his chair and stood up. His face was as grey and grained as frozen ashes. "It says that my father and sister are dead," he said. "Hebon Hakamanko proclaims himself master of the Mirror Castle." He studied the lid of the bronze box, recalling Snowsnake's tale of a putrid memento. Should he unclasp it? If it contained a finger or an eyeball, or worse, Hebon's victory would be made all the sweeter by his horror; and yet, he needed proof.

Jukon slowly lifted the clasp and cracked the lid awry. Then he opened it all the way. Inside was Juka's favourite brooch, a sea-spiral of gleaming sylvanite. It was chipped, and splashed with blood. He picked it up and weighed it in his palm. *A lure,* he thought. *He knows I will not rest until I know for sure. She is my twin; she is part of me.*

"This is proof of my sister, but not of her death. But whether she lives or not, Hebon Hakamanko has declared war and must be destroyed. We must raise an army, and march upon him and his allies."

"All are agreed on that point, Lord Jukon," said Gomon. "My own father is also under assault. But look at the position. For one, we cannot leave Kobutsuden at the mercy of those who roam beneath. And for two, the Taiyo cannot march whilst besieged by the Kurotako and threatened by the Seikyo's treachery."

"This is true," said Veluron. "My father is powerless under these conditions. I can think of only one solution – to end the blood-feud and somehow bring Lord Kyo to our side."

"The stage is already set," said Jukon. "Our first entreaty evidently spurred Kyo to conspire with the Kurotako whilst outwardly answering our call – no incentive was needed save his own enmity towards Sunstorm. To turn him again, we must now offer something of far more weight."

"Marriage," said Gomon. "Kyo already has money from his mines, so lands and power acquired through the marriage of his son is all we can offer him. Unfortunately my only sister, Toka, is eleven years of age and trapped under siege at Mortmane. Lord Veluron?"

"I have only my brother, Taikon."

"Then there is but one option," said Lady Snowsnake. "Lady Miura's daughter, Messura. But Miura will not countenance it, I know this. In her eyes the night-flower and the spiral may never be conjoined."

"All the same," said Gomon. "Lady Miura may be regent of the Mizuno, but as a member of the Starfire Council the authority is yours. This is war."

"If Lord Kyo accepts such a proposal, he must do one thing in return – turn his death-ships against the Kurotako fleet when they least expect it," said Jukon. "And at the same time, we must drive the Vigilants from our city."

"There is yet another possibility," said Veluron. "The Storm mavens pledged us their support, did they not? Why not appeal to them to raise a land army, as they have in times before? That would allow us to storm the Hakamanko without deploying the bulk of our own forces. You must excuse my reluctance to trust Lord Kyodokuron – he's already murdered my parents and brother once, or so he thought."

"We'll do both," said Jukon. "Send word to Lord Kyo and the Storm Shrine at once; Lord Gomon, you should personally beseech Lord Kyo, and fetch his answer. Lady Miura mentions the Corpse Moon in her letter – it rises in just five days. Now; where is the rider who delivered this box? Bring him before the council."

Guards escorted the man into the chamber; he was pinched of face and form, and his filthy tunic was sewn with the emblem of a skeletal serpent.

"Your reply, greatlord?"

"A question. You knew of the box's content?"

"I... no, greatlord," the rider insisted. "I know nothing."

"You know nothing? I see." Jukon stepped closer. "And does nothing know you?"

"Greatlord?"

"So you cannot deny it. You know nothing, and nothing knows you; you are a creature of the void. And so you shall return to it. Gomi vengeance starts here – send him to the Rascal, with full prejudice."

Jukon knew that killing an envoy was considered a severe breach of honour, yet his rage at Hebon's violations could not be assuaged by such rigours; blood was now his only currency. *And I will be paid in full.*

# THE SKINNED SWINE

"Eleven in all," said Dorion. "Five on the right, six on the left. The monks called me Dorion Six-Toes. How did you know?"

"An informed surmising," said Kuron Kirizono, examining the grave-robber's exposed feet. "You can put your boots back on now."

Dorion looked up at Kirizono with trepidation. Although he was well-built for his age and had trained at sword, this brute towered over him and looked as if he could cut him in half with one blow. What exactly did they want with him?

"Did your mother tell you much about your father before she sent you to temple?" Kirizono continued.

"Just the usual nonsense, that he was someone rich and important; so important that she couldn't say who, as if that makes any sense. Morgomox, my master, said my mother was a whore and that whores fucked so many men they could never know who seeded them. I suppose that's true."

"There are different kinds of whores," said Kuron. "Now; tell me why the Celestial Horde expelled you. And don't lie, because I'll know."

Dorion hesitated; should he tell the truth? They already suspected him to be a despoiler of the dead, after all, and nothing was worse than that. "If you must know, I was caught stealing a brace of pig's trotters from the butcher. Twice."

Kirizono laughed at that, and the ones standing behind him laughed as well. "Safe to say that your vocation is theft, then," he said. "Except you've gone from dead animals to dead people."

"I'm not proud of it," said Dorion, "but that's what the maven asks of me, so how can I refuse? What he does with the corpses I don't know, and I don't ask. Some kind of alchemy, I suppose."

"Some kind," said Kuron. "In any case, you'll not be going back to the Ossuary;

from now on you'll train as one of us."

"But Morgomox–"

"Fuck Morgomox. I am Kuron Kirizono, Black Reaper to Emperor Raikon, and these are men of the Blue Dragon Hand, defenders of the Shadow Castle. Ride with us, and embrace your true destiny as scion of Clan Akutenshi."

"Scion?"

Kirizono looked at Nezumon Nano; Nano gave a curt nod.

"It means your father was the emperor; and now you will be emperor too."

Dorion said nothing. Was this a mockery? *I am a bastard whoreson, a thief, a grave-robber; such a man cannot be emperor.* He knew the tales of the Akutenshi bloodline and their congenital deformity, but had always just thought it an amusing coincidence; the monks even used to tease him about it. *Dorion Six-Toes,* they would say, *emperor of the midden-heap.* After a while, he said: "My mother told you this? Is she still alive?"

"She is; and you will see her again soon. Your mother was Mordassa, concubine to Emperor Raikon; it is known that she was with child when she escaped the Imperial Forest and took to sea. Only the Three Sorrows themselves could have wrought such a miracle, for no others hunted by the emperor are ever said to have lived. Raikon was known as Deathstar; why do you think Mordassa named you Killstar?"

And then, slowly, Dorion began to believe; and in the believing, his mind was flooded with possibilities. "Then if this is all true, when will I take power? How will it happen; when will I arise as the Emperor Dorion?"

"The road ahead is long," warned Kuron. "And make no mistake, there will be those who seek to kill you. Nor will you be known as Dorion; as your father's bastard, you will be enthroned as Emperor Raikon the Second. This is the law of the Triad."

Night had long fallen when Mekuron Taka returned from Metal Town. Yuron Fuki was with him, but Zokon Buta was not. They were carrying a large sack, and Dorion knew from its outline that a corpse was in it.

"It did not go well," said Taka. "At first there was no problem; we paid for the woman Spitkiss as before, and this time she showed us her arse, as the mavens requested. It was as they said. But when we asked her to come with us, she refused."

"You told her that her son was waiting?" said Kirizono.

"We did; but she said she'd told us everything and wanted nothing more to do with the matter. When we insisted, she screamed for the brothel guard. Unfortunately there were also a number of soldiers from the Ossuary in the house, and we had to fight our way out. Buta was killed, and the woman–" he glanced at Dorion "–sorry, boy, but the woman also died when she slipped on a stair and fell; her neck was snapped.”

“This is her?” said Kirizono.

“It is.”

“Are you ready to see your mother’s body?” he said to Dorion.

“It will hardly be the first,” Dorion replied.

Kirizono opened the neck of the sack and pulled out the nude corpse. Its head flopped to one side, and blood was running from the blue-tinged lips.

“Turn her over,” he said to Taka. The woman’s buttocks were flaccid and smeared with excrement, but the branding, whitened with age, was clear enough; two thunderbolts in a V, seared deep into the flesh, marking Mordassa as sex-slave and chattel of the Deathstar.

“I suppose we need one more coffin for the wain,” said Taka.

# THE OSSUARY

"An intriguing proposal," said Kyo the Killer. "You offer my son Kyowashon the hand in marriage of Lady Messura, with mastery of Castle Bloodflower and all its lands, as well as all mineral rights long disputed by the Taiyo; and all I must do is cross the Kurotako? Surely you know I have already sworn to drive their fleet from Sunstorm?"

"Of course, Lord Kyo," said Gomon. "We wish merely to compound the transaction." *He knows we know, and yet we have to play this game.*

"Well; it is an offer I would normally be inclined to accept, I confess it. And yet, there is one obstacle – my son is but recently betrothed. Step forward, my dear."

The girl emerged from the shadows behind the high back of Lord Kyodokuron's throne of power, an oppressive chair carved in ebony and decorated with a hundred leering deathsheads. Her hair was piled high upon her head and ringed with brazen circlets, her gown of matching hue and sewn with stars. Around her neck was an amulet embossed with a black sea-beast.

"May I present my son's future wife, Lady Soma Kurotako."

Gomon bowed, trying to conceal his dismay. Why – how – was Soma Kurotako in the claws of the Seikyo? She was supposed to plight troth to his brother, last he had heard. This marriage would surely draw Kyo into the war as an ally of the Octopus, and signal the end of Sunstorm.

"However," Kyo continued, "perhaps we should let my son speak for himself; he is now of age, after all."

"Thank you, father." Kyowashon Seikyo arose and stepped closer to the throne. He was yet a boy, Gomon noted, with his father's vulturine eyes but somewhat lighter of complexion and hair. "It seems I now have a choice," he said. "Marry the Lady Soma and inherit a rock in the Bay of Bones, or wed the Lady Messura and stand master of a haunted ruins."

*He has his own voice, at least.* Gomon found himself anticipating the boy's next words, as were Lord Kyo and Lady Soma, judging by their faces.

"It strikes me that as long as Lady Soma is our guest, her father Lord Sado will be amenable to our wishes; why risk death-ships driving his fleet away when we could merely order him to withdraw? And by the same token, is marriage really necessary? I dare say that Castle Bloodflower could be restored to glory in a year or two. I am perhaps inclined to favour Lady Messura; I hear she is a great beauty."

Gomon noticed him glance at Soma, with a distinct glimmer of cruelty. *His father's son.* Could either of them ever truly be trusted?

"May I speak?" said Lady Soma. "The choice my father faces is not so simple as seems. Do not forget, my younger sister Suna is married to the Hakamanko hunchback; therefore you would ask him to choose between us. As much as I might come to harm if he refuses to withdraw the fleet, so might my sister suffer if he does."

"It sounds as if you are recommending a third action," said Lord Kyo. "A strike against your own father's ships. That would indeed absolve him of responsibility, but at what cost?"

"My mother died in a mysterious mishap at sea. My father wed my sister to a mad cripple, and sent me on an errand of death. I truly believe his fealty to Lord Hebon outweighs his love for any of us. After all, he already has his two male heirs – my brothers Croton and Kuchon."

"I have news in that regard," said Gomon. "Regretfully your brother Croton was slain at the battle of Mortmane, by the hand of my brother Chikon, once your intended. I am sorry." He yet wondered what she meant by an errand of death, and how it led her to the Ossuary.

Before Soma could react, Lord Kyo said to her: "Sad tidings. But you don't seem so sorry about my son choosing another."

The girl trembled. Her face was drained of blood, and a single tear stained her cheek. "Please... may I retire to my chamber?"

Kyo smiled thinly, waving her away. "Very well," he said. "Lord Gomon, it seems we may accept your offer after all. Lord Nikon Tabu, commander of our death-ships, has spent the last two weeks fitting his dromon with a new war engine, one which he assures me has the power to sling a burning horse halfway up a mountain; it would be a shame to waste his endeavours. The Kurotako girl will continue to enjoy our hospitality, as a measure of insurance in these troubled times."

"As you say, Lord Kyo," said Gomon. "We are deeply obliged."

"And you might like to know that agents of the Akutenshi are abroad," Kyo added. "To what end I could not say, but it seems they did not all perish with their emperor. Now, if you will excuse me, my maven is plaguing me to find him a new apprentice; it seems his last one has vanished into the ether."

Alone in her quarters in the castle's rearmost tower, Soma Kurotako sat by an open window. *Men are like spiders ever weaving webs,* she thought, *in which wives and daughters are merely trapped flies waiting to be devoured.* In the bailey below, the Big Chopper, Lord Kyo's carnifex, was mopping a welter of blood from the execution block.

The morning's first snowflake swirled in and settled on her hand, beautiful for a moment then quickly melting into a droplet devoid of form or meaning. She closed her eyes, and sobbed.

# THE BONESTAR LABYRINTH

The Battle of the Bonestar was fought in near darkness, with only sputtering firebrands and swinging lanterns for light. The underground passageways were narrow, so that only two men could stand abreast, and where they opened into alcoves and chambers death loomed in many forms.

Jukon Gomi and the maven Valadian Goldenbones had located the hidden hellgate to the labyrinth once used by its creator, the emperor Hentaikon, by imprinting a map of Kobutsuden with a star chart delineating the constellation of the Fire Scorpion during the apex of the Killing Moon. This configuration placed the scorpion's eye directly above the Winter Palace, with its claws at either wing; it also showed the heartstar Chelicor above Skullhaven cemetery and the sting of the scorpion's tail at the extreme west of the city, above the house of lunatics; what lay deeper below they could not say with certainty, but Valadian suggested that every star correlated with an axis chamber of the subterranean maze.

The scorpion's eye led them to the palace's imperial gallery, where the flooring was a mosaic of square marble slabs engraved with the personal seal of every emperor since Hentaikon. There, beneath the seal-stone of Hentaikon's younger brother and successor Katakaikon, they found a hinged trap-door of solid metal more than twelve inches thick, which when prised and levered open revealed a set of steps spiralling down and down into a baleful and noxious unknown. The door had been engraved on both sides with complex signatures of runes, which Valadian identified as ancient codes to bind demons deep inside the earth.

The Takasha agent Flamon Neko, at his own insistence, led the underground invasion force tasked with penetrating the Bonestar and exterminating the cult of the Holy Eye; the capture of its leader Slavos Sek and of Moshino, murderer and mutilator of women, was the mission's utmost priority. *I want Moshino alive if possible,* Jukon told him, *but dead will serve.* Either way Moshino's head would be spiked on the walls of the citadel, but Jukon knew that the rabble would prefer to watch him tortured and disembowelled first. Sek was a creature of the shadows; it would suffice to bury him in quicklime, still breathing or not.

It took Flamon thirty minutes to complete the descent, fiery torch thrusting into the gloom, followed by hundred after hundred of soldiers from the city defence, each armed with flame and sword. The steps ended in an entrance tunnel; as the Cave Cat edged forwards with upheld torch and poised blade, he could see the walls on each side carved with lurid, feculent effigies; giant centipedes encircling and penetrating nude women, spiders with human skulls hanging from their webs, vampire bats ejaculating scorpions into the screaming mouths of the impaled.

The first attack came as a blur of sound in the darkness, a hooded face rearing briefly in the firebrand's flare, a dagger thrust that skewed off Flamon's ringmail with a spark-flash. He slashed ahead of him with his sword but found only air, heard only soft retreating footsteps. Soldiers poured into the chamber behind him, massing their torches; the Vigilant was gone, but they could see that the chamber was constructed as a pentagon, with four more tunnels branching away in different directions. As his fighters emerged from the entranceway, Flamon pointed groups of them into each of the openings; realising that each passageway would most likely emerge into another pentagonal chamber with another four passageways, and that this would repeat as the labyrinth spread itself across the length and breadth of the city's subterrain, he wondered if he had enough men to even reach its terminus; but it was too late to summon reinforcements now. At some point the Bonestar would reach its maximal width, and then start to narrow in on itself until it resolved in another single chamber – or so he assumed. To visualise its entire structure in his mind was impossible.

In reality, the labyrinth was asymmetrical and fraught with perils. Some tunnels were bricked off at the opening or led into stone walls, others ended in steep stairways which ascended into the cellars of city buildings, others opened into four-doored dungeons filled with corpses and skeletons. When men were forced to redouble their steps they fell prey to vermillion-robed Vigilant assassins armed with butcher-knives who lurched from the shadows; others took false turns into recesses and plunged into sunken vats of flesh-dissolving acid or ran into walls fixed with protruding metal spikes that punctured them from eyeball to groin. Elsewhere sections of tunnel-wall were perforated with holes from which spears shot out to run men through, triggered by a footfall, while naphtha spilled from murder-holes in the ceiling, igniting and engulfing others in white fire. Some stepped into animal-traps of serrated metal and were left with shredded limbs, or slashed their veins open as they felt their way along wallways embedded with glass shards; everywhere pale scorpions and cockroaches crunched underfoot, the stink of their innards mingling with acrid torch smoke and the pervasive reek of human excrement and rotten meat to turn tunnels into choking tombs.

Wherever the city defenders were able to engage the Vigilants one-on-one they found many armed only with daggers and easily slain, but others were sword-wielding clan fighters with tattooed faces beneath their cowls, more than able to dismember and decapitate. Flamon could only guess at the outcome of the invasion as he directed the last of his soldiers into the tunnels, but if it were measured by the death-screams that echoed through the maze, he feared a bloody picture.

He took the left-hand tunnel that opened before him, planning to next bear right, then left again, then right, hoping that such a course might eventually lead him to the end of the labyrinth, far beneath the Fire Scorpion's sting. But after the third dead end and reversal of direction, he realised he had already lost his bearings. The tunnels and chambers were littered with heads, limbs and piles of maimed and scorched corpses, both of Vigilants and city soldiers, with more of the latter than the former. A few of the dead cultists wore purple robes, identifying them as coven masters, but he was looking for one garbed in pink, the colour said to be worn by Slavos Sek as Primal Optic of the cult. The killer Moshino was only known to be marked by his skin, said to be squamous like the hide of a snake, although some had even speculated that Moshino and Sek were one and the same.

Flamon pressed forward, ever mindful of ambush; it came inside a tunnel, when one of the robed bodies sprang to life behind him, screaming *"Triad cunt!"* and plunging a dagger into his back. The blade pierced his ringmail, but only the tip entered his flesh. He slashed backwards with his sword, pivoting as he did so, and felt it cut through bone with a splatter of blood on brick. He peered ahead of him by torchlight and saw the Vigilant on his knees, the bottom half of his face hacked off; the severed jawbone hung by a twist of tendon, the man's tongue still stuck between its teeth, bathed in a cataract of gore. Flamon left him to die slowly.

After threading the remaining stretch of tunnel, where several of his men had been speared or burnt alive, Flamon entered the largest chamber he had yet encountered; its walls were decorated with cultic fetishes and, like every other surface in the maze, scrawled with pictographs of vermin. At centre was what appeared to be a sarcophagus, on which someone had once daubed the name of Hentaikon in blood. He guessed that this was the Scorpion's Nest, where the mad emperor's heart was entombed, which by Jukon's map meant that Skullhaven lay directly above. He would have searched for an egress to the graveyard, but there was no time; he could see that the fighting had been at its fiercest here, and could detect distant shouts and ringing steel ahead. The stench of rotting flesh was now at it most intense, emanating from what appeared to be a collapsed sculpture made from dead infants; amongst the other corpses and body parts scattered across the burial chamber Flamon noticed a freshly severed forearm which appeared to be a woman's, with silver-banded fingers. He picked it up, and by the light of his torch he saw that its skin was covered with tattoos of interlinked roses and scorpions. He quickly threw it back and followed the noise of the fighting, wondering what other horrors awaited in the Bonestar's lightless embrace.

It took Neko another three hours to navigate the labyrinth to its crisis; three hours of false turns and dead ends, wading through blood and bodies, fending off attackers, straining his eyes in the gloom until he was almost blind. In the end there were just four of them left, out of hundreds. The Bonestar had been reduced to a final chamber, a final doorway into abject blackness, barred by a shrieking one-armed witch. She clung to its frame with her remaining hand, the other just an elbow-stump which twitched and spurted blood in their eyes. Two of them attacked her at once, chopping and thrusting at her tattoo-covered body as she raved at them with death-curses and obscenities, refusing to relinquish her grip and let them pass. Finally Flamon joined in the assault, finding a broken spear on the floor and jabbing it into her eyeball. Even so it took them a full two minutes to hack Silversoil away, bit by bit, scattering her in thirteen pieces; by the time all four men burst into the chamber and filled it with firelight, Moshino was gone.

They were still vainly probing the walls to locate the concealed portal and stairway up to the Black Cage when Moshino finished raping and strangling Sister Lycosa. He seized the master key from her cincture and unlocked every cell in the mansion, urging the inmates to rise up and join him. "*Snakes in the night!*" he screamed, "*snakes in the skull!*" First to his side was Drok, the cannibal Vigilant, followed by a dozen more both male and female. Among them were Cat-A-Bodkins the flayer, Sugary Meg the baby-broiler, an axeman known as the Knave of Stumps, Captain Kisscrawl the mad hangman, the girl-child Baby Brimstone who set ablaze both her parents, Rumpcluster who nailed a whore to a bell tower, Brother Bone the pig-licking priest, and Lord Shuffleskin who claimed each night to turn into a wolf, a bat, or a caterpillar.

By the time Flamon Neko retraced his steps to the entrance of the Bonestar – an ordeal which took almost half a day – and raised a desperate alarum in the Winter Palace, Moshino and his lunatic cohorts were far away, lost in the night and halfway to the sanctuary of Hellhaven.

# GOLDENGATE

Each day the tear tattoos faded more and more, until after a week the Night Weepers no longer wept.

"So who are you really?" Hekon would ask every morning, and was finally answered when Nox told him: "I am Noxon Taiyo, also called Night Sun, brother of Nakasendaron; and my friends here are Flame Riders, warrior horsemen of the Fireball Dead. "

"Night Sun? You are the one who slew the cannibal giant in trial by combat?"

"The same. Shok Skull Hog stood accused of killing, cooking and eating more than fifty women from our villages, and claimed the right to fight for his freedom. Not surprising, since he stood eight feet tall and wielded a solid iron braining hammer that could shiver rocks to dust."

"Yet you killed him. How?"

Nox laughed. "If I tell you my secrets you might use them against me, hunchback. After all, one day you may face me yourself. Remember; the Taiyo are descended from the Yamayaga clan, whose regent was Bankairon Demon-Slayer."

Suna saw Hekon's face sour at the mention of Bankairon and the prospect of summary justice, and secretly smiled. During these daily exchanges she had tried to keep silent, fearing to speak against her husband in case, by some vile trickery, he managed to elude their captors. She knew that he would like as not feed her to the würms if she had not shown loyalty, albeit feigned, and she prayed the Taiyo would finally free her from him when they reached their destination. Suna was looking forward to the day when Hekon Hakamanko was made to answer for his atrocities; she was witness to many of them, and would speak to condemn him without hesitation if it meant her liberation.

A few days later they crossed into Goldengate, following the coastal path which wound its way to the Sunstorm Castle. Here the cliffs were less steep, and easier to scale from below. When the castle's pink spires finally appeared in the distance, the vision was marred by a dark stain; a flotilla of uninvited ships was anchored out to sea, masts adorned in fluttering black and silver.

"Do you see the flags? Those are Kurotako ships," crowed the hunchback. "Release me and my wife, or your precious Sunstorm will be razed to rubble."

"That's one way to look at it," said Nox. "This is another: if those ships are not gone by next moonrise, your head will be separated from your twisted body. Let's see whose view prevails, shall we?"

Hekon learned that the Sunstorm Castle was much like a painted courtesan with a cancerous womb; radiant on the outside but rotten at its core, which is where he languished in a rat-filthed cage for three full days and nights as the Corpse Moon entered its primary phase. He was attended by Sawtooth, the Taiyo carnifex, a cadaverous club-foot with shaven head and hollowed eyes, who each evening brought him a metal bowl filled with raw salted cabbage and a pitcher of tepid water dashed with dead flies. The carnifex never spoke, and Hekon was glad of it; he had seen some of Sawtooth's handiwork, briefly, when the cell facing his was torchlit at feeding time. Now he understood the ceaseless, morbid groans that emanated from the dark. The prisoner within was strapped into a leather harness, and was hanging by it from the wall; he was otherwise naked, and Hekon could see that all four of his arms and legs had been cut down to crudely sutured stumps. The man's horror-filled eyes fixed his, just for a second, before Sawtooth snuffed out the light.

On the third morning came a reprieve; the carnifex led the hunchback back up into the castle's main gatehouse, where Noxon Taiyo and his nephew Taikon awaited.

"The hour of truth has arrived," said Nox. "The fleet, or your head; one will be gone before noon."

"My wife," said Hekon. "Where is she?"

"Lady Suna is quartered in the Saturn Tower," said Taikon. "Under guard, but unharmed. Her fate much depends on what transpires this morn."

"Then why not use her to bargain with?" said the hunchback. "She is a Kurotako, after all."

"Ignoble of mind as well as body," said Nox. "I told you so."

"So you did, nuncle. I just have one question: shall we hang him from the battlements, or dip him in the sea? Perhaps a salt-wash would be best, since he's evidently soiled himself more than once."

Nox smiled. "Either way I fear the ships are too far away to recognize him," he said. "We'll have to push out and let them have a good look."

Uragon Mono, captain of the *Eight-Eyed Squid* and flotilla commander, was scanning the western horizon for a first sign of the Taiyo death-ships when a Shell Crush crewman diverted his attention to shore. A catboat was being rowed towards them flying the crossed flag of truce, with a crooked figure lashed to its foremast. The craft stopped halfway out; three other men stood behind the captive. There they waited, until Mono and a pair of Shark White rippers were lowered into the water and came within range. One of them was Crogor, clan chieftain, who swam out to the *Squid* under cover of darkness two nights before with a dozen of his crew.

"I am Taikon Taiyo," said Taikon.

"I am Uragon Mono," said the Kurotako captain, both men bowing their heads. Hekon Hakamanko also spoke, but the gag in his mouth made his words unintelligible.

"What are you thinking now?" Taikon asked the captain.

Uragon Mono studied the hunchback for some moments, and Taikon could see that he understood the situation. Eventually Mono said: "A sudden night fog; bones blaze in the jaws of death, fading to ashes."

Both men bowed again, and both boats turned back to their point of origin. Within an hour the Kurotako ships had raised sail and anchor; a light breeze helped stir them into motion, and the shadow of siege was lifted from Sunstorm's coral spires.

As they watched the fleet grow ever more distant and finally vanish, Lord Nakasendaron Taiyo gave thanks to his brother and the maven Vorgovanian, whose prosthetic arts had rendered Nox and his Flame Riders in the likeness of Night Weepers, allowing them to infiltrate the Hakamanko horde. Then a raucous shout went up. "Ships to the south!"

Far out to sea, the goliath dromon *Hellfire Scream* was emerging into view, spearheading a formation of five pure white Taiyo death-ships at the tip of a thirty-strong pack of smaller destroyers. Commander Nikon Tabu, feared and revered along the coast as Lord Fleshstripper, stood on deck in full battle uniform of black body-costume embroidered with the bones of a silver wolf skeleton and half-mask of grinning lupine fangs covering the lower part of his face, his figure framed by a cloak of titanium mesh. Blood-red Seikyo banners blazoned with a flower of death flew from both masts, and the dromon's two blood-red sails were each blazoned with a single giant wolf skull. The vessel's bow was fitted with a bronze underwater ram, its prow mounted with piston-driven fire-throwing machines; at the newly extended stern a massive catapult had been bolted to the deck, its armature and sling as formidable as any seen on land.

Propelled by five hundred oarsmen, the *Hellfire Scream* was surely the fastest and most lethal warship ever built.

The other Skeleton Sealords each commanded an unmodified, three hundred-oar dromon: the *Corpse Pyre*, under Sudon Nyo; the *Black Inferno*, under Aon Baka; the *Cinder Bride* under Kiron Kuto; and the *Red Death* under Momon Jaga, also called The Lobster. Each lord wore the same battle uniform as their fleet commander, and each was equally set in their mission to cripple and disperse the Kurotako fleet.

Except that the Kurotako fleet was gone.

# THE TEMPLEDARK

"I'm not stupid, you know," said Darkon. He couldn't hold back any longer. "That sword… I'm no maven but I do know about swords, and I know volcanic steel when I see it."

"Forgive me," said Quexarian. "It is regarded as a matter only for the mavens. In times of anarchy, the deathswords are coveted as a manifestation of both imperial and religious power. The swords are the Thirteen Angels of Fire, venerated as sacred instruments in the *Elemental Testament*."

"Really? I always thought that the Angels of Fire were… angels."

"Some read the scripture in this literal way," said Quex, "it's true. But amongst templar scholars, the consensus holds that the Thirteen Angels are the thirteen deathswords, forged in the fiery Ark at Mount Komonyama."

Darkon stared into the night. There was word of war in the west of the Templedark where Castle Mortmane was under siege, so they had avoided the Cackmire Causeway and taken a more circuitous route to the Crow River, crossing directly north of the Storm Shrine. Someone had burnt down the bridge, but the river narrowed there and had frozen over as winter reared, allowing them to traverse a solid crust of ice. They would reach the shrine within two days, and finally be rid of the sack of skulls.

"You'll truly tell them that those are the lost heads of the White Light Brotherhood?" he asked Quexarian.

"Why, is it a lie? Who can say. It is known that the twelve skulls of the Brotherhood were kept in the wolf temple. These are twelve skulls from the wolf temple. It's not as if we just dug them up from some graveyard along the way. Soon they will be enshrined at the Temple of Tears, an inspiration to the people of Kobutsuden."

"If you say. And after that?"

"That will be at the discretion of the Storm mavens. Until our own temple is rebuilt, we answer to them. And it won't be rebuilt until this war is done. Now, get some sleep."

At the temple of Arashon they were hailed by the high maven Cassavion, who listened intently as Quexarian detailed their exploits atop Mount Mooncry.

"You are evidently a great warrior, Brother Darkon," he said afterwards. "And you, maven Quexarian, have achieved what dozens before could not, at no small personal hazard. The Triad owes you a great debt."

"I ask for little, save a few days rest and a new mission," said Quexarian.

That night Quex and Darkon slept soundly for the first time in two weeks, without fear of throat-slitters emerging from the dark. In the morning, the maven Tardassion invited them to partake of bread and temple wine.

"You have a reputation as a fearless binder and banisher of demons, maven Quexarian," he said. "But if I'm not mistaken, an exorcist must also deal with other manifestations of evil, such as hauntings and blasphemies; is it not so?"

"It is so," said Quex.

"Good. Because a matter is at hand which involves both. You are aware of the legend of Castle Bloodflower?"

"Castle Bloodflower lies in ruins," Darkon interjected. "It was sacked during the Serpent Wars, marking the fall of the Satogawa."

"Correct," said Tardassion. "You may also know the legend of Lady Koma Satogawa, Lord Skyon's widow, who opened her own belly rather than be taken, tortured and raped. Lady Koma left a death-poem, daubed in her lifesblood, before she expired; it was also a malediction upon the castle's attackers and their descendants. *I spit on your graves, I curse your sons and daughters; my ghost will return and grind your bones into dust, drown you in rivers of blood.*"

"Brave woman," said Darkon.

"Indeed," said Quex. "Even so, it is recorded that more than a hundred soldiers spent their seed inside her corpse before it grew cold."

"Which only adds weight to the reports we have received from nearby villages of late," said Tardassion. "Reports of a woman's vengeful ghost stalking the ruins by night."

"The Decimation," muttered Darkon. "Don't they say that such events awaken ghosts?"

"They do. And the blasphemies?" asked Quex.

"During the sacking of Bloodflower the Satogawa maven, Shattonax, was burnt as a warlock. This was for good reason; Shattonax had been dancing with demons. He devised a depraved working with the aim of creating a homunculus, or moonchild – an inhuman night-fiend with the power to suck out men's souls by the hundred, without remission. Yet the dangerous diaries and grimoires used by Shattonax for this black magic were never recovered; it is said that his laboratory lies deep underground, where the commonfolk fear to tread. Your mission, maven Quexarian, is to retrieve these blasphemous documents, whilst seeming to exorcise Bloodflower of its phantoms."

"More subterfuge," said Quexarian. "Well, at least this time you know everything, Brother Darkon. So will you join me on this quest?"

"Looks like I already have," said Darkon Domo.

# THE WINTER PALACE

Flamon Neko placed the head on the council table. Although he had washed it of blood, the damage was evident; one eye was missing, and the other side of the face had been split apart from scalp to chin, exposing the bone beneath.

"This is the witch who was guarding the final chamber," he said.

Jukon Gomi picked it up by the hair, examining the tattoos that marked every inch of skin. "Lady Silversoil," he said. "The one they called the mother of bloody roses. This confirms that it was Moshino, her precious bastard, who escaped and ravaged the Black Cage."

"I failed," said Neko.

Jukon gestured with an upraised palm. "No. The cult of the Holy Eye was exterminated, Silversoil was killed; Moshino will be next. The Bonestar and its dead will be cleansed with fire, and every chamber, entrance and egress sealed for all eternity. The heart of Hentaikon is to be removed from its tomb and secured in the winter crypt, its resting-place unmarked."

"And Slavos Sek?" asked Neko. "Lord Hikidashon ordered me to hasten his death, and yet he still lives."

"Perhaps," said Gomon Takasha. "But my father now has more pressing concerns. Mortmane is besieged; return to the castle if you can, to aid our cause. I will give you a letter to pass on."

"No-one has ever seen Slavos Sek," added Jukon. "Let's not waste any more time on a phantom."

"What news from the Taiyo?" said Lady Snowsnake. "The Corpse Moon is risen. If Lord Kyo keeps his word, the Seikyo death-ships should already be breathing fire on the Kurotako."

"We still await word from my father," said Veluron Taiyo. "All is in the balance.

But if success is confirmed, rest assured he will send reinforcements at once. Then, with the city now secure, we can plan offensives against snake and octopus."

At the next day's meeting, Jukon presented two scrolls received during the night and early dawn. "The first comes from Sunstorm," he announced. "Victory is ours; the Kurotako fleet is dispersed. Lord Veluron's uncle, Night Sun, marches to the city with a force of three thousand fighters. A thousand more have been dispatched to fortify the Nightmare Castle. And there is more – Hebon Hakamanko's son, Hekon the hunchback, is held hostage at Sunstorm along with his wife, Lady Suna Kurotako."

"The Triad is with us," said Gomon.

"And so the Ossuary will soon host a wedding," said Lady Snowsnake. "I wonder how Lady Miura will take this news."

"As kindly as the plague, if it's anything like the Feast of Demons," said Veluron wrily.

"Small matter compared to the rest," Gomon insisted. "Not only are we to be reinforced, we also hold leverage over both the Hakamanko and the Kurotako. The tide turns."

"Even so," said Jukon, "strange events elsewhere darken our moment of triumph." He held up the second scroll. "This letter is from the Storm and Sun temples, signed by the high mavens. They decline our request for a land army, but that is not all. The letter declares that Emperor Raikon had a son, who now stands rightful heir to the winter throne; the mavens are satisfied by this boy's claim, and believe him to be of Akutenshi blood. They ask that our league cede power, and instead serve as council to the new emperor."

"And who is this pretender?" asked Gomon. "Where did he come from? Raikon was a sodomite who never took wife."

"He is named as Dorion Killstar," said Jukon. "The letter gives no more detail, save that we are to present the Key of Bones and the Akutenshi deathsword as symbols of relinquishing power. The boy is now ensconced at the Sepulchre, ancestral castle of the Hassha, and awaits our homage before the waning of the Ice Moon."

"Raikon may have favoured his concubines' arses," said Lady Snowsnake, "but it only takes one misstep to plant seed elsewhere. How can we prove otherwise?"

Jukon put down the scroll. "Raikon was destroyed by the Three Sorrows themselves for his sins. Sodomy, murder, torture, demonolatry, black magic – if this boy is truly his son, how we can know he will be any different? The Starfire Order was formed to end the age of emperors, to mark the extinguishment of the tainted line of the Akutenshi. But if we refute this claim, it will not be proof that denies it – it will be bloodshed."

"May I speak?" said the maven Valadian Goldenbones. "It seems to me that while peace is under threat from the Hakamanko – who, I believe, serve an ancient evil which craves resurrection – it might be wisest to fall behind this Killstar, thereby consolidating imperial and templar power against a common enemy. A three-way war will only tear our lands asunder."

"And yet," said Jukon, "it appears to be our destiny."

# THE MIRROR CASTLE

"Arise, Gorn, Lord of Mirrors."

The ceremony was conducted in the castle's sanctum, a circular conceit lined with a single, continuous looking glass in which reflections were distorted and multiplied over and over until they disappeared into infinity. Gorn looked at his thousandfold image and felt his head start to spin. *I came for a ringfort and ended up with a castle; how the fuck did that happen?*

Lord Hebon Hakamanko stood before him holding the deathsword Kurosatsu, the black slaughter; its touch had anointed Gorn, conferring lordship and mastery of a realm far beyond his expectations.

"You stand worthy of the accolade," assured Hebon. "It was your berserker attack which turned the battle in our favour, your men who slaughtered Kamosukon Gomi, your cry which signalled victory. Mastery of the Mirror Castle was a prize sought by my son, but where is he now? Back in the shadows of Skull Castle, trying to control his wife. I am sure you will make a more than adequate replacement."

Magmatharion, maven to Clan Gomi, handed Gorn a silvered metal ring hung with more than fifty keys of differing sizes. Like most of the Gomi household, he had elected servitude to a new master over decapitation. "The keys to the castle, Lord Gorn," he said. "This one–" he lifted a three-toothed spindle from the bunch "–unlocks the scrying dome."

Gorn wondered what that meant, but said nothing. He was waiting for Lord Hebon to either say something else, or leave; the Snake Lord, with his sibilant tones and icy eyes, unnerved him more than any berserker. *At least when some cunt's trying to gut you you know where you are, but this one makes your fucking skin crawl. And what the fuck is in that velvet bag?*

It was a messenger who ended Gorn's discomfort; a rider had arrived from

Skull Castle, he said, and a scroll awaited Lord Hebon's attention. As Magmatharion showed the usurper the way to the council chamber, Gorn was escorted to his own quarters in the North Tower. The candlelit rooms were draped in velvets, with cushioned couches and a huge bed piled with furs. *So this is how the Shinojin live,* he thought.

Later, as he idly examined the keys and tried to recall which one the maven had singled out, he heard a commotion in the courtyard below. Lord Hebon was leaving, flanked by his war general Hellhawk and followed by the surviving members of his lifesguard, the Tongues of the Basilisk.

That evening at dinner, Gorn asked Magmatharion why the Snake Lord had left in such haste.

"Ill news," said the maven. "It seems that Lord Hebon's son did not return to Skull Castle; he is presumed captured or dead. Lord Hebon is withdrawing to Lizard's Den."

"Shame. Now, what's this key you showed me?"

"The scrying dome sits atop the South Tower," said Magmatharion. "It is where Lord Kamosukon was wont to contemplate the expanse of the demesne, the heavens, and beyond."

"Beyond?"

"Beyond... the scope of the naked eye, shall we say. Lord Kamo believed that by gazing long into the dome's orbs of fluxing quicksilver, he could divine glimpses of his own future within his mind."

Gorn laughed. "I wonder if he saw himself slung over a horse with a turnip up his arse. Anyway, I don't need a dome to see my future," he said. "Three serving-girls and a cask of wine, that's all the future I need for tonight."

"I'll have Crabpenny see to it at once," said Magmatharion. His rueful tone suggested a certain disdain for Gorn's simple ways, but the sword-shifter was unmindful; he was Gorn, Lord of Mirrors, and no bastard was going to piss on that.

By moon's wane, Gorn realised that playing lord of the castle had its drears as well; in demanding fealty of the commonfolk Lord Hebon had also assumed responsibility for their protection, and it was Gorn who was left to deal with it. Each afternoon he was forced to sit through a parade of disgruntled peasants with complaints ranging from wife-beating to witchcraft, and dispense summary justice. One man rode all the way from Mount Rottenstag with his sister's frozen corpse, claiming she'd been buggered to death by a snow-creature and demanding compensation; another warned of Crimson Curse pirates raiding coastal villages south of the Port of Shrikes, and snatching away moon-cursed daughters by night. Gorn found himself as indifferent to one as the other.

At night he took to feasting and carousing with Urstinx and the other Blood Eagle clansmen of his castle guard, and the more they drank the more they sang and boasted of battles and blood, while Magmatharion and others of the Gomi household kept ever greater distance. One evening Cagominx, burliest of the berserkers and the one who had opened Lord Kamosukon's skull, downed a whole flagon of ale in one gulp, stood up, and vomited the contents of his stomach in a continuous stream from both mouth and nose with such violence that it seemed he might suffocate; then his skin turned corpse-green, his eyes glazed over and he slumped backwards, toppling from the dais and smashing his brow against the stone floor. Liquid sewage had exploded from his anus and was dripping down the back of his thighs. Gorn backed away in horror; the vomit was full of writhing black worms and globules of gore, and its stench made others void their guts until the whole table was awash in red bile, beer and chunks of undigested suckling.

The next morning Cagominx was confirmed dead, the black worms bursting from his eyeballs. Gorn had the maven and the bane virago, Lady Vixenvane, brought before him, but both denied all knowledge of the cause.

"Tainted rabbit, perhaps?" offered Magmatharian. "What do you say, our lady?"

Vixenvane stared at Gorn with a defiance he found perversely arousing; her slender form was encased in a gown of raven silk that matched her hair, sashed in scarlet, and she exuded the scent of a rare, night-blooming flower. But when she spoke Gorn saw images in his head, strange cruel scenes of diseased genitals and predatory birds ripping apart their own young. "The spiral hole," she said, "where dead men dig their dark graves deep; a priest cracks flies with teeth of gold."

He could only watch in silence, beguiled, as she turned and walked away.

# CASTLE BLOODFLOWER

"So if we do find these grimoires, what do we do with them?" asked Darkon.

"Were you ever shown the Forbidden Chamber at the Temple of Dreams in Kyukiden? It's lost now, of course, but the mavens of the Triad have plans to create another, in Kobutsuden. The grimoires of Shattonax, should we find them, would be among the primary exhibits."

"We were taken there, once," said Darkon. "Part of training, to know the kind of evils that exist in this world. Bit boring, really – except for the mummified witch. What was her name again?"

"Metaluna," said Quexarian. "Metaluna, the Centipede Priestess. She was condemned for butchering children and bathing in their blood, supposedly a ritual to capture eternal youth. They called her the Centipede Priestess after hundreds of tiny limbs were found piled in her cellars."

"I remember now. I often wondered why she wasn't burnt – I thought they always burnt witches?"

"But Metaluna was high-born; she was the Lady Metaluna Mishima, of Castle Nightfog. And so they walled her up in a room atop the Tower of Shades for the rest of her days, which were short. More than a century later the room was unsealed and they found her body, which had been near perfectly preserved due to lack of air."

"So it worked, then – she did get eternal youth. She just wasn't alive to enjoy it." Darkon laughed at the thought, but the memory of the witch's desiccated face, her blood-veined yellow eyes open and staring, still unnerved him more than he cared to admit.

The next day they gazed for the first time upon the ruins of Castle Bloodflower. High up on a summit, the castle's broken walls and buttresses had been ravaged first by fire, and then by time. A single tower stood intact, steepling at the sun. In the surrounding villages only women, the very young, and the very old remained; all the able-bodied men of the Viles had either joined the Kurotako forces under Tazon Ando or, in fewer cases, migrated to the city and sworn allegiance to the cult of Vigilism, becoming henchmen of the Holy Eye. Mizuno rangers no longer patrolled the western hills, having withdrawn to the Nightmare Castle or joined the Starfire forces stationed at Kobutsuden.

All the villagefolk they spoke to told a similar tale; *she comes from the ruins by night, Lady Koma the White Widow, wailing and holding her bowels in her hands.*

"And what does she want, this widow?" Quex asked one crone.

"Vengeance," said the woman. "She comes to eat our bones and drink our blood. Last night she took a girl-child and carried her away to the castle; the girl is nowhere to be found."

"Show me," said Quex.

The crone led them to a hovel where another old woman sat raving in a chair, half-bald, her left cheek overwhelmed by wen clusters as dark and shiny as goat dung. "My son's child is gone, gone with the Widow, gone to the land of ghosts."

In a corner of the hovel, the girl's straw pallet was stained with a smear of blood. Quex examined it briefly.

"Fresh," he said to Darkon. To the old women he said: "I am here to exorcise your village, and the castle, in the name of the Triad. The White Widow will be driven back to whatever hell she came from. If we can save your children, we will."

Before leaving Quex used brush and ink to inscribe the door of the hovel with runes. "To ward off the dead who walk by night," he explained.

Later, Darkon said: "So what is she, if not ghost or vampire?"

"A creature that seeks the first moontide of the young," said Quex, "but not to drink. This is merely a mummery; I believe these lands are plagued by slavers who trade in breeding stock, selling captives to the ebon races who dwell beyond the southern seas."

"Slavers? Why would slavers need a haunting to cow these villages, when they could just take what they want... old men, women and children are no match for armed pirates."

"I would say that the abductors are merely agents, who transport their prey to ships along the coast... perhaps two or more females, using a plot of fear and persuasion. Nothing you cannot deal with, Darkon – I remember how you tamed the She-Dogs."

"Aye, and I still can't wash the stink away. But if such is the task, I'll undertake it as duty compels. To Bloodflower."

# THE SEPULCHRE

"So Morgomox never told you the purpose of his experiments?"

Kuron Kirizono was watching Dorion intently, looking for any signs of dissembling. If the stories he had heard were true, the alchemist's work was an abomination punishable by death; and once the Akutenshi retook the winter throne, he intended to enforce all remedies to the fullest extent.

"Not exactly. But there were rumours in the castle... they say that Lord Kyo was tired of feeding his mine workers and dealing with their complaints, and wanted a more docile work force. One with little need of food, medicine or coin."

"I have heard of such before," said the Black Reaper, "but never employing such methods. Centuries ago the Gomi are said to have stripped their goldmines bare by using workers poisoned with brainscratch, a potion which rendered them as senseless as walking corpses, yet still able to dig without remission until their hearts finally stopped. But this..."

"Reaper!"

The shout came from the courtyard of the Sepulchre, where agents of the Blue Dragon Hand were engaged in combat training. Nezumon Nano, known as Devil Bat, was motioning at Dorion Killstar to join them. "Time for today's lesson."

The Blue Dragon Hand were adepts in the way of the scarab supplicant, a martial mime of insect kinetics which afforded fighters the power to decapitate foemen with a single, two-handed forceps blow. One-handed strikes could also cut off limbs or snatch a heart, still beating, from a chest. These lethal vitiations were delivered with such speed that the eye could no longer follow. But Dorion was yet to be convinced. Although they seemed to work on practice scarecrows, a human body was surely a different proposition.

"Let's find out, shall we?" said Nano, as if reading his mind. It was then that

Dorion realised that the scarecrow had been replaced with a real man – one of the Blind Brotherhood, the ascetic order which had inhabited the Sepulchre since it was appropriated by the Sun mavens following the fall of the Hassha. The Blind Brothers took vows of sensory introversion, sewing their eyelids shut to better live in a state of contemplation.

"Don't worry, he died in his sleep last night – and what the brothers can't see won't harm them. Their service to the emperor doesn't end with death, you know. In any case, you're used to playing with dead things, or so I've heard."

That much was true. In acquiring materials for the maven Morgomox, Dorion must have cut down, dug up or otherwise salvaged more than a hundred corpses. But to use the body of a recently deceased holy man for martial training... that was another matter.

It was the Black Reaper who saved him. "Wait, Nano," he said. "I believe I have a better use for the dead brother. A trial by cruentation. It is said that when a blasphemer touches the corpse of a monk, the corpse will bleed and reveal his sins. What do you say, Killstar?"

"And if it bleeds?"

"Purgation. Your father had certain... tastes, which did not endear him to the people and may have hastened his downfall in the eyes of the Triad. Our task is to prepare you for the imperial throne, and that must include cleansing your soul of past and inherited sins."

"Very well," said Dorion. "I am no blasphemer, and took no joy in my night-work."

"Then place your hands upon the dead man's chest. If his eyes shed tears of blood, you must be purged; if not, you stand redeemed."

The Blind Brother's lid-stitches had been snipped, leaving the eyes, occluded by years of closure, agape for the grave in a reversal of customary rites. *Sightless in life, all-seeing in death*, was the axiom of their sect. Dorion stepped forward and pressed his palms against cold flesh, watching the monk's face with trepidation. For a second he thought he saw blood welling in the corner of one eye-socket, but it was just the head of a burrowing maggot; he was vindicated!

Nezumon Nano smiled to himself. Just as his trick with the Blind Brother was a test of character, so he understood that Kirizono's intervention was staged to give Dorion self-belief, a sense of his divine right to become emperor. *Corpses don't weep,* he thought. *But many men may bleed before the throne is returned to us.*

They spent the rest of the daylight hours with weapons and tools of chaos;

ceramic grenades that exploded in blinding white fire, silver stars with razor edges to open a man's throat, caltrops to cripple horses, iron darts tipped with paroxysmic poisons, wall-gouges for scaling castles as swiftly as a burning rat.

When darkness fell the Blind Brothers congregated in the castle chapel for chanting and prayers to the night, just as they had for the past three hundred years; their massed voices reverberated through the Sepulchre and burst into the sky, a black liturgy for a black and brooding world.

# PART FOUR
# THE THREE LEAGUE WAR

# MAIDENSTONE

*The moon is the eye of the serpent, an eye that weeps blood. The blood-eye is the Holy Eye.*
The words cascade through Moshino's brain, his mother's words, a blossom of bloody
roses on a midnight grave. Nothing stirs in the village save a she-cat with a pregnant
vole squeaking faintly in its jaws, winged beetles boring into dung, a dance of spider
and moth. Captain Kisscrawl slings his hanging-noose over a twisted branch, Lord
Shuffleskin flaps his arms like a bat. Baby Brimstone stamps on a dung-heap and recoils
with a giggle as insects take flight, whirring and glittering in the moonlight; white-
smocked Sugary Meg peers through windows searching for her cooked babies while
Brother Bone, swine-hunter, sniffs the frosty air.

*"Cock-a-doodle-doo!"*

Maidenstone's new rooster, Cat-A-Bodkins, starts to crow; candlelight shines,
a dog barks, then two more, Lord Shuffleskin howls, a cart-horse snickers. An old man
in soiled nightshirt emerges, holding a scythe.

"Father Death, the shit-stained reaper," says Moshino. "King of the valley of
bones."

*"Father Death, Father Death,"* they sing. *"Father Death, Father Death, bless us
with your bony breath."*

Rumpcluster raises his smock and pisses at him, Sugary Meg bares her breasts
and sticks out her tongue. More faces appear at windows, with the sound of slotted
door-bolts. The old man turns back; Moshino is faster.

"Night's a-cold, Old Father. Grant us your filthy embers."

Inside the hovel a woman and her daughter huddle in hiding, shaking as the
phantoms titter and croon. Drok seizes an ankle, pulls them from beneath the table.
The girl tries to run away, the woman cries out. Baby Brimstone holds the girl's hand.
"Let's play suck-the-centipede."

Drok tears open the woman's shift, exposing her haunch.

"Chop chop chop?" asks the Knave of Stumps.

"I only eats the round bits," drools Drok. "Eyes, teats, arsehole." And the woman starts to weep.

*Bloody tears for each coil of the great red snake, for the soft dolls behind the vampire veil, for the unborn and the undead.* Moshino sees his mother's face, wreathed in stings and thorns. *Never forget who you are.*

Kisscrawl drags the old man to the tree while Rumpcluster skips and pokes him with a stick; white faces watch, none venture forth. The noose tightens as they hoist him up, feet kicking, eyes bulging, flesh purpling, corpse swinging.

*"Father Death, Father Death, burn us with your bony breath."*

"Bankairon is dead," Moshino shouts, "his Night Angels are dead. Behold the angel-slayers, the Night Demons, the black Hounds of Hellhaven."

They bark, and they bay, and they howl, whipping the dogs into a frenzy, wolves in the woods amplifying the tumult until it drowns in its own reverberation. Baby Brimstone sets the first fire, shrieking in delight as it flares and feeds. Squeals and cackles peal from the pigsty, Cat-A-Bodkins prances in a mask of freshly-flayed skin, the Knave of Stumps screams *"Chop chop chop!"*

Moshino stares north to Hellhaven's towering plague-angel, then east to the würm-infested marshes beyond. *I am seeded from the snake; and to the snake I will return.* A shooting star explodes, trailing a gash of scintillant spectres.

# THE WINTER PALACE

"Let us call this a conflict between three leagues," said Jukon. "Starfire, Angels, and Vermin. A dangerous game of many possibilities and unknown consequences we can only guess at."

A large cloth map of Novalis was spread across the council table, with three types of dyed wooden discs piled upon it; yellow, white, and black. The white were positioned at the Sepulchre in Goldengate, at the shrines of Sun and Storms, and at the Shadow Castle on the northernmost coast. The yellow, at Castle Mortmane, the Nightmare Castle, the Sunstorm Castle, and the city of Kobutsuden. The black discs were mostly scattered north of the Crow River, and seemed to outnumber the others; they were positioned in the Mirror Castle, by a series of ringforts along the Stone Brides, surrounding Castle Mortmane, at Skull Castle, and at the Slaughterhouse. Only one part of the map, Wolf's Jaw, was devoid of markers.

"If we, the Starfire, choose to remain in Kobutsuden and defend key and sword, the Angels would like as not raise a land army around the Celestial Horde, a force which could invade the city and storm the Winter Palace. If we take the battle to the pretender and lay siege to the Sepulchre, they could again raise an army to repel us. This threat from the League of Angels means that once again we are unable to march against the Vermin who infest the north. And while Lord Hebon holds my sister, if indeed she lives, our capture of the hunchback is countered. What do you suggest?"

"I see only one option," said Gomon Takasha. "The Angels and Vermin must be incited to engage each other; we wait, and move when both sides are weakened. But how?"

"A provocation," said Lady Snowsnake. "A provocation so egregious that the white put aside thoughts of the throne and turn all attention to the black. Meanwhile the wedding of Kyowashon Seikyo and Messura Mizuno must be consummated with all haste. Once Lord Kyowashon is installed here–" she reached over and pushed a yellow disc onto Castle Bloodflower "–we may find ourselves with a new ally, whether Kyo the Killer likes it or not."

"Agreed," said Jukon. "What is the news?"

"Although the Kurotako fleet was dispersed, and Lord Kyo sent his death-ships as pledged, it was the Taiyo themselves who ended the siege by threatening the life of Hekon, son of Lord Sado's ally and husband of Lord Sado's daughter; Lady Miura used this default to persuade Lord Kyo that the wedding is best hosted at the Nightmare Castle. The ceremony will be held when the Carrion Moon is full; Miura casts it as the Masque of the Black Phoenix."

"A matter of weeks," said Jukon. "The mavens await our answer by the waning of the Ice Moon; perhaps this masque presents opportunity?"

"I have a notion in that respect," said Veluron Taiyo. "And once again, the hunchback may hold the key. When Hectoclarion the High attended the palace, his arrival was confirmed by messenger bird?"

"It was," said Jukon. "An albino pigeon, pink of eye and beak, as used by all the Triad temples. We still have the creature caged – I imagine every castle has at least one."

"Perfect," said Veluron. "Maven Valadian; I should like to visit the teratorium, if you would, before I depart for Sunstorm."

# CASTLE BLOODFLOWER

"Last time I'm walking around with these pig guts," said Xexara. "They makes my fucking tits stink."

"Just one more moonling and the cage'll be full," urged the witch. "Then we'll get our coiny gold from Captain Scarebones."

"If you say. Only one village left anyways."

The girl's ankle-long white gown was smeared with phosphor and gore, her face and hands whitened with chalk, and she cradled the entrails in front of her like a sickly new-born. Five others, younger than her, were locked in a cell of the dungeon beneath Castle Bloodflower's one remaining tower, some silent, some sobbing, one wailing. At the end of the underground corridor a great circle of wrought iron was set into the wall, its surface ridged with a wreath of interlocking insect pincers, the emblem of Clan Satogawa. The edges of the circle were indented here and there, where some had vainly tried to pry it open over the centuries.

"You little shitbirds stop skirling now," said the witch. "On the morrow we're all going down to the sea-shore."

Quexarian and Darkon watched as the ghost-girl and the harridan emerged from the ruins and started down the steep incline, glowing in the moon's septic rays.

"Only two," whispered Darkon, "but there may be more inside."

"Let's find out," said Quex.

Bloodflower was a sprawling lop-sided square of broken walls at varying height, all buried in ivy, the ground in-between thick with discoloured grass and a patchwork of moss-covered flagstones. A gaoler's wain, fixed with a barred cage, stood next to the tree where an old horse was tethered. Three of the castle's corner towers had long since toppled into rubble, so the exorcist and the warrior-priest headed straight for the fourth. Once inside they immediately heard distressed voices from the subterrain.

Darkon Domo descended first, blade drawn. A torch still burned by the gateway, revealing the five captive girls. They were all garbed in night attire, and there was nothing else in the cell save for straw, two brimming waste buckets and a pile of torn-up rags. The rest of the dungeon was empty.

"I'm a monk," said Darkon. "Where are the keys?"

Quexarian was already examining the iron wall-disc, running his fingertips over its battered surface. "Those who came before us had the right of it," he muttered. "This is most certainly a doorway – probably leading to a catacombs, perfect for all sorts of clandestine doings. Now, if only…"

"Perhaps it's a magic door," joked Darkon, "and you need to say a spell."

"Or spell a saying. Do you see the four raised dials, at each cardinal point of the door? The sixteen ideograms engraved upon them each conveys a spoken sound, in the ancient runic script. If four runes are correctly aligned, one on each dial, the four locks will open, I'm sure of it. Now; reading the runes is the hard part – the key word should be something simple."

"SA-TO-GA-WA?"

Quex turned the dials accordingly; first clockwise, which did nothing, then anti-clockwise. On completing the second sequence they heard four heavy bolts snap back simultaneously, and the rim of the door detached slightly from the wall. Darkon grasped it and pulled, and the iron circle swung open on two moaning hinges.

"You surprise me again," said Quex. "I thought it too obvious."

"A simple guess from a simple man. You all stay here," said Darkon to the liberated girls, "and if you see the Widow coming back, start yelling."

The passageways of the catacombs were high and narrow, and every ten yards or so inset with a cruciform opening. Through these spy-slots they could see the tombs of the Satogawa bloodline. Every chamber was filled with forgotten riches – full-length life portraits of the deceased and their battle exploits in gilded frames, coffers overflowing with gold and silver medallions, swords, decorative shields, and other ornaments, as well as the skeletons of wolves walled up alive to guard the corpses that lay within arching marble coffins.

At the very centre of the catacombs was a laboratorium, part equipped for alchemical processes and part for the pursuit of the occult.

"This is doubtless where Shattonax attempted to raise the moonchild," said Quex, "an underworld surrounded by the dead where none might disturb him or punish his blasphemies."

"Until they did," said Darkon. "But how did they discover him?"

"It is said that Shattonax became a haunter of graveyards, and many suspected him of necrolatry. In fact, his working involved midnight orgies during which he attempted to conduct the seeding of whores by priapic ghosts... but enough of that. We should take what we came for, and leave."

"These books and manuscripts?"

"All of them."

Even as Quex relocked the iron door by setting its dials aspin, one of the girls appeared at the foot of the dungeon steps. "She's coming!"

"What do you advise, maven?" Darkon asked. "If we let them go they'll just do the same thing elsewhere."

Quexarian paused for a second, then replied: "I promised the villagefolk an exorcism. So should it be. Whatever's in them, drive it out."

"Understood," said Darkon.

He motioned the girls back down and into the cell, then waited behind the gate. The girl and the witch entered, dragging a new young victim by the hair, and went to lock her up with the others.

"It's already open," said Xexara, a half second before Darkon's godsword Shirometsu, the white destroyer, plunged into one side of her head and out the other with a spew of blood and bone that flew into the witch's eyes. The old hag started shrieking and then cursing while Darkon wrenched the sword free, his boot on the dead girl's face.

"*Fucking shitbones!*" the witch screamed, "*fucking blackheart dog bastard—*"

The remainder of her rant was curtailed when Darkon delivered a sweeping and venomous death-strike. Shirometsu cut into the side of the harridan's belly just beneath the ribs with such velocity that it scythed clean across, shearing through the spine and completely separating the thorax from the lower half of her body. Her foul-smelling intestines slopped out onto the dungeon floor as her trunk fell away in a torrent of blood, filth and worms.

Girls screamed, Quexarian raised a sleeve to his mouth, retching; a wad of half-chewed cockroach slipped from the witch's dead lips.

"Moon justice," said Darkon Domo.

# THE MIRROR CASTLE

Gorn gazed at the quicksilver orbs until his eyes hurt, but all he saw in his mind was the curve of Lady Vixenvane's rump as she walked away from him. *Fucking witch has hexed me,* he thought. Ever since Cagominx's death he'd made Crabpenny, his elderly attendant, taste his food before eating it, but he was sure Vixenvane had other means of bewitching her victims. *That perfume she spreads around, like a corpse baked in almonds.* He soon realised that dark was falling; through the convex lens of the scrying dome the world turned upside down, as if a giant had picked it up and was shaking new-born stars from the peaks of the Brides. Gorn felt dizzy; he cursed and lurched away in search of ale.

"What found fettle, Lord of Mirrors?" Urstinx was chewing on a lamb-bone, his mouth smeared with grease. Gorn sat.

"Shit fettle," he said. He looked at Urstinx; the scar-latticed berserker was seemingly content with his daily meat and drink, unmindful of his surroundings. How could Gorn explain that he felt buried alive, that for him the Mirror Castle was an opulent tomb filled with terrors? He didn't trust Magmatharion, the old maven, any more than the bane virago; even Crabpenny had a facial tic which made him appear part mocking, part malevolent. And then there was the dwarf; Ragus, his name was, a beastly scoundrel who chuntered and skittered in the shadows making signs with his stubby fingers. *Lord Kamo kept him for good luck,* the serving-girls had told him. *He found him in a cave, eating snakes.* Gorn had seen how Kamosukon Gomi ended up; that was luck he could do without.

"No wonder these high lords go mad," he said to Urstinx. "The more power and coin you've got, the more some cunt wants to take it all away from you." Urstinx shrugged; they both kept drinking. Remembering his simple days as a guard at the Winter Palace, Gorn found himself wishing the two could change places. *Man the walls by day, drink by night, and fuck the rest.*

At one point Magmatharion appeared, but soon scurried away when Gorn hurled an empty ale-cup in his direction. It chipped some wall-tile away, revealing a nest of tiny green ants.

"Is that wise, brother?" said Urstinx. "These old bastards know curses and such."

Gorn spat on the floor. "I'm not scared of some pus-eyed pigeon-licker," he sneered. "I've killed his like before. One of them attended my poor sister, when she were dying of the canker. He said she had worms in her tits and started waving raw meat around, saying that the worms'd come out to eat it. And then he tried to get coin from us."

"You didn't pay him then?"

"I paid him, but the coin were wrapped in the meat, and I made him swallow the lot until he choked to death. Bastard."

As midnight approached Gorn was sliding into a state of collapse; Urstinx and another helped him to his quarters and threw him onto his bed, where he immediately lost consciousness and plunged into a bottomless roiling sleep.

As he peered into the mirror it cracked and exploded into a million tiny shards that threatened to shred his eyeballs; when he looked again Kesh was staring back, his face split in half by a deep diagonal sword-slash. Red hornets crawled from the ragged wound, their heads changing to human skulls. Kesh was speaking, but the words were beyond his hearing. Then his visage dissolved into Cagominx's, a mask of screeching black worms, and the room suddenly grew icy cold. Lady Vixenvane was standing behind him, nude, with five-pointed stars painted over her nipples in blood. She held out her hand and he was giving her his own teeth as they loosened and fell from his gums, until she held them all like a pile of gore-crusted pearls. One by one she slipped the teeth inside her vagina, which began to foam and gnash like the jaws of a rabid wolf. Just as he thought she would eat him alive her head was gripped by the pincer of a gigantic insect, and torn into mangled chunks; as her exposed brain became a nest of dead rats he saw that the insect was Tazon Ando. *Skin the snake,* Ando was saying, *skin the snake and burn the world...*

And then Gorn of Mirrors woke up, and finally saw his future.

The next day he summoned Vakko, Kill-Claw chieftain, and Urstinx, leader of the Blood Eagle berserkers, to a meet.

"Vakko; you'll stand for me while I'm gone. Deal with the village complaints, and keep an eye on that poison bitch. And try not to kill anyone. Urstinx; you'll come with me. Put together a war party of all your fighters by tomorrow."

"To what end?"

"War, of course. With any cunt that wants it. But first, we ride to Mortmane."

That night, after drinking a copious farewell, Gorn retired for the final time as lord of the Mirror Castle. Vakko didn't know it, but the sword-shifter had no intention of returning to the faceted keep with its refractions and malignant geometries. As he neared the upper landing, something scuttled in the shadows. His sword was half-drawn before he realised it was just the dwarf, Ragus. With a quick look to see who was watching, Gorn spun around and launched an almighty kick at the dwarf's backside. With a yelp Ragus was pitched headfirst down the stairway, somersaulting as he gathered momentum; then his brow banged against the wall and his body went limp. The next roll landed the dwarf on his neck; Gorn heard a soft crunch, followed by a splatter from the miscreant's voiding bowels.

"Dirty little bastard," he spat.

# THE SLAUGHTERHOUSE

Lord Sadogashon Kurotako sat at the head of the sculpted porphyry table, attended by the remnants of his council: Lady Nightstorm, bane virago, to his left and Unon Octo, treasurer, to his right. His elder son Croton was dead, killed at the Battle of Mortmane, head spiked, bones lost; his daughters Soma and Suna were both missing, presumed captured or dead; his maven Chromocrax had deserted him and vanished in the night; half of his fleet had been destroyed at Gluttonport Bay, the other half routed from Sunstorm. From sea-captain Uragon Mono's account, which told of Hekon Hakamanko being held captive by the Taiyo, he could only assume that they held Suna too, if she lived. Moreover, Crimson Curse pirates had taken advantage of his depleted and diverted fleet by staging raids on the Isle of Gaunts, unearthing and breaking into two tomb-ships and stealing the gold and artefacts buried within. To add insult they had also taken the remains of the tombs' occupants – Takashimon Kurotako, his direct ancestor, and Makon Kurotako, fabled as Lord Stingray, hero of the ancient Twenty-Island War – and now held them for ransom. *And all this because of one bad alliance.*

"There is just one question we must answer today," he said. "Do we renew our support for the Hakamanko, or sue for peace with the Starfire Order?"

"Lady Suna is no longer in Hebon's clutches," said Lady Nightstorm, "so what binds us to him now? I say we prevent further ruin by proclaiming ourselves unjoined, like the Seikyo. I do not believe the Order will pursue retribution; destroying Hebon is surely their main objective."

"But if she is held with the hunchback... he might still bring her harm," said Octo.

"Then those are the terms," said Sadogashon. "Our withdrawal in exchange for amnesty and the promise that my daughter will be safe from the hunchback's embrace while this war lasts. One dead child is enough."

"I will send riders to the Winter Palace and Sunstorm at once, Lord Sado," said Octo. "But there is also the matter of the Crimson Curse; they demand golden coin by the apex of the Ice Moon, or the mummies of Takashimon and Lord Stingray will be hurled into the deep and lost forever."

"How were these demands sent?" asked Sadogashon. "I've yet to meet a pirate who could read or write."

"It's true, the Crimson Curse have always envoyed by word of mouth. But this time we received a written scroll, instructing us to send a single ship north of Scaleport; it was signed *Captain Bloodspike*."

"Bloodspike? I thought their leader was that bastard Scarebones… well, no matter; they all die the same. Send for Mushon Yowa – he will be given a chance to redeem the ignominy of defeat at Gluttonport. Nightstorm; please accompany me to Chromocrax's vault. I have my eye on one of the agents he bequeathed us before his vanishing, a cold beauty with fire-red tresses and a full round belly. I believe I shall name her Lady Catcurse."

# THE SUNSTORM CASTLE

"A bold plan, brother," said Taikon Taiyo. "And a blasphemy punishable by the cruellest death."

"This is war," said Veluron, "and in war the rules change; am I not right, father?"

Lord Nakasendaron pondered for a while, then said: "When sides are chosen, consequences must be accepted – by all. But if your plan succeeds in every respect, it will not be us who pay the price. I say proceed. Taikon?"

"We have the bird, the bones, and the ring; so long as Vorgovanian and Lady Feverclaw can play their parts, I suppose there is every chance of success. Shall we begin?"

Save for the carnifex Sawtooth, the two brothers and the maven were Hekon Hakamanko's first visitors in more than a month. Their torches, which they mounted in sconces on the walls outside his cell, illuminated that whole part of the dungeon; Hekon saw that the limbless horror opposite him was now dangling lifelessly in its harness, explaining the recent absence of groans.

"What day is this?" he asked. "What hour?"

"Morning, on the most fortunate day of your life," said Taikon.

"How so?"

"Because we've decided not to kill you, hunchback. In fact, we intend to negotiate terms with your father; his surrender, in return for your release."

Hekon's eyes seemed to light up, momentarily, then dim once more. "Sweet words, but you do not know my father. He will never surrender under any terms. Better ask him to spare your stinking lives, once he crushes your lands underfoot to ensure my liberation. Do you know what it feels like, the kiss of a marsh dragon?"

Taikon smiled. "Perhaps you'd like to hear some other news. The Kurotako have put down arms; your beloved father is without allies. And you will never see your wife again."

To this, Hekon said nothing. Veluron said: "And now, we're going to make a mask of your pretty face to send to Lord Hebon, just so he knows we have you."

"A mask?" hissed the hunchback. "Did you not send him my signet?"

"We thought of it, but a ring could merely have been stolen. Seeing your face is much more... *dramatic*, don't you think? In fact, you can have that ring back tomorrow. Maven."

Vorgovanian stepped forward carrying a vat of molten white wax, and Sawtooth unlocked the hunchback's cage. "Don't worry," said the maven, "it won't burn."

Hekon scrambled backwards, upturning a pail of his own sewage. "This is murder!" he cried. "How will I breathe?"

"Nose-holes," said Veluron. "Either we make the mask, or Sawtooth cuts off your true face. Now; which will it be?"

Peering up at the carnifex and his huge serrated blade, and seeing the four-stumped corpse hanging beyond, Hekon made his choice.

"Very wise," said Taikon. "And if you keep behaving well, we may even let you attend a wedding."

# THE NIGHTMARE CASTLE

Beneath the gargoyles' gaze they filed into the castle, the lowered drawbridge manned on each side by black-cloaked honour guards of the Vertigo Watch, the ramparts overhung with cascading primrose banners bearing the black whorl of Clan Mizuno, alternating with blood-red counterpoints blazoned with the circle of eight white skulls that signalled Clan Seikyo. Each guest was afforded lavish quarters in the Dream Tower, save for Lady Snowsnake, white-haired Mizuno war-witch, who took to her old chamber in the Terror Tower overlooking Gluttonport Bay. A sole figure could be seen in a lofty window of the castle's third main structure, the Fever Tower, occasionally raising and lowering an arm in salutation; other than that the figure did not move. Although the window was too remote to allow close scrutiny of the waving man, many swore that it was Lord Akumuron.

At darkfall the castle bell chimed thrice, summoning all to the great torchlit hall where banquet tables were arranged in rows and a stage raised in readiness for the Masque of the Black Phoenix. Every table was ready piled with platters of unhinged bay oysters, blue onions mashed with butter, and pig trotters glazed in garlic honey; dark rice wine and frothing beer began to flow as soon as the guests were seated. Among those gathered were Lord Kyodokuron Seikyo, accompanied by the sealord Nikon Tabu and several other generals with their wives; Lord Gomon Takasha of Mortmane; the Mizuno general Batsuron Boko and his wife, Vona; the maven Chironax and the maven Chromocrax; Corvon Natto, castellan of Castle Nightfog, and his wife, Zira; and more than two dozen other officials from among the Shinojin of southern Novalis. Young Lord Kyowashon and his promised bride, Lady Messura, were being kept apart until the following day's ceremony. At the very back of the hall sat Lady Snowsnake with the Taiyo brothers, Taikon and Veluron, and between them an unexpected – and for many unwelcome – presence, the hunchback Hekon Hakamanko; the masque's host, Lady

Miura, had yet to appear, and none had yet seen her since arriving.

"By what right do they bring the hunchback here?" said a voice among the growing babble. "I've heard he makes his own wife bathe in a vat of cockroaches, and wears swaddling stitched from a baby's skin."

"Aye, and when the moon's full he dances with corpses in the swamp, nude, his cock tied with a silver bell."

"And where's Lady Miura?" asked another.

"Busy elsewhere, perhaps," another replied. "They say her lusts are so fierce that she oft-times leaves the castle by night, in disguise, and carries on a whore's work at the Gluttonport brothel. She wears an eye-mask to deceive her unsuspecting customers, and goes by name of Lady Suckshaft."

After an hour of more feasting and idle chatter, a group of seven musicians appeared at the side of the stage; a cymbal crash and the repetitive, one-note scratch of a viol announced the beginning of the opening antimasque. First on stage was a capering dwarf dressed and snouted in hogskins, a string of raw sausages trailing from his ample backside. *Shitting here, shitting there, shitting shitting everywhere,* sang the dwarf, spinning in circles, until another figure emerged from the shadows, a monster with the head of a wolf. *Stinking swine, stinking swine, I will use thy guts for twine,* growled the wolf-man, and with that he brought down a huge hammer on the dwarf's head, squashing him completely flat – an illusion facilitated by trap-door – as the cymbal crashed again and the onlookers erupted in a gale of brutal laughter.

The masque proper began against a painted backdrop of the volcano Mount Komonyama and Kyukiden, city in the snow. A contorted figure emerged onto the stage, garbed in a black tunic blazoned with silver thunderbolts in a V, masked in ivory, and flanked by a pair of living skeletons. The musicians now started up a dark fugue, marked by a slowly pounding field-drum offset by tabor and cymbal, a repetitive pattern played by two lutes with dissonant tuning, and over that a cascade of jarring viol shrieks and the continuous, morbid droning of a psalterium. The mood in the great hall became more solemn and silent, as the guests realised they were watching a garish travesty of the crimes and divine punishment of the emperor Raikon Akutenshi.

Horror after horror unfurled on stage, simulations of torture, murder, impaling, anal rape and demon worship, until the boards were coated with the animal blood and entrails used in the illusions and the music rose to a pitch bordering on cacophony; then, finally, the backdrop began to shake and a hail of painted, mashed-paper rocks engulfed the figure of Raikon, the music descended into pure noise, and a crashing curtain marked the hour of the Decimation.

"Hellfire," said Corvon Natto, "that was a bit grim."

Most in the hall shared Natto's sentiment, with one notable exception – Hekon Hakamanko, who cackled aloud at every act of carnage, much to the annoyance of those sitting near him.

"You're as welcome here as a whore with cunt-worm, hunchback," said one, "so keep your greasy mouth shut."

After another antimasque – featuring two dwarfs, a weasel and a wishing-well – briefly lightened the evening's tone, the Masque of the Black Phoenix resumed for its apotheosis. Against a backdrop of night sky three nude female figures appeared – Moon Sorrow Sukion, masked in silver; Storm Sorrow Arashon, masked in bronze; and Sun Sorrow Hoshon, masked in gold. Each one's entire body was painted to match their visages. Accompanied by just a mournful viol signature and sporadic drumbeat, the Three Sorrows bitterly lamented the destruction of Thundervoid, each weeping glittery black tears which soon appeared to flood the stage, until, with an abrupt clashing of cymbal and tabor, Black Phoenix herself erupted from below; it was Lady Miura, arms outstretched and raised, arrayed in a jet velvet gown with neckline slashed so low and wide that both her heavy breasts were fully exposed, the nipples darkened with rouge, and from wrist to waist great wings of raven feathers that gleamed blue-black in the torchlight. Her mask was carved from onyx, with the vicious beak of a raptor, and embellished with licks of flame. *From the black lake,* said four voices in unison, *the phoenix rises, born of fire; sun, moon and storms in one fell form. Death stalks the world with cruel claws and burning eye, engulfing the age of shadows.*

All seven musicians joined in now, recapitulating the masque's theme with a rapid and mounting discord, as the four female figures lined up at the front of the stage to bow, once, before the curtain dropped to bring an end to the proceedings. By now the revellers were drunk to a one, their appreciation for the half-naked performers both raucous and prolonged. But when the curtain lifted once again, Lady Miura Mizuno was nowhere to be seen.

# THE SEPULCHRE

Dorion Killstar was exhausted.

"Come on, boy," said Kuron Kirizono. "You're only just out of your bed."

"If you call me boy when I'm emperor..." Dorion began, but thought better of it. The Black Reaper was not to be crossed and, if and when he did become emperor, he would need him at his side more than any other. He picked up the blunted sword again.

"Now," said Kuron, "pretend I'm the bastard that threw your dam downstairs and broke her neck."

"I thought she tripped..."

"All right then, pretend I'm the one who buggered her so hard she couldn't walk straight."

That seemed to work. "You speak of the emperor's mother!" Dorion yelled, and tried to skewer the Reaper with a two-handed upthrust.

"Better," said Kuron as he side-stepped the attack. "Now–"

A shout rang out from the ramparts.

"Runner!"

Nezumon Nano quickly scaled three sets of steps and joined Yonakon Chimori atop the stone walkway. A lone figure had burst from the Shrouded Woods and was charging full pelt towards the Sepulchre gates; about a hundred yards behind they could see a pack of screaming Skull Hog man-eaters in pursuit, waving axes and evidently eyeing the runner as a rich repast.

"Arrows!" Nano shouted, and within seconds six bowmen of the Blue Dragon Hand were in place and ready. As the first man drew ever closer Nano realised that it was Tsunamon Shinga, the Terror Tempest, an agent sent to spy on the Winter Palace; they could ill afford to lose whatever information he carried. "Fire!"

A fan of arrows sprayed from the castle bulwark, over Shinga's head, and struck the first wave of his pursuers; some were pierced through the eye or mouth, some the throat, while others deflected the shafts with spiked targes. A dozen of them were still in pursuit when the next flurry hit, felling another five, but the rest kept coming. As Shinga neared the gate, it remained shut. Nano threw down a rope secured to a crenellation; the chaos agent caught it and, barely slowing, used it to run straight up the wall of the castle, leaving the Skull Hogs baying below. The savages' bloodlust had overwhelmed their caution; before they could retreat Nano yelled: "Pit!"

Levers cranked beside the gate and the ground abruptly fell away from beneath the Skull Hogs' feet as two great wooden trapdoors, concealed by a layer of grass and soil, opened downwards into the earth. The pit was over forty feet deep, and it took the man-eaters almost a full two seconds to hit the sharpened stakes. Most were still vertical when they were impaled, the wooden points penetrating the area around their genital parts and lodging deep inside their torsos. Nearly all died instantly; the others were left to perish in total darkness when the wooden doors crashed shut again. No trace of them remained.

Shinga made his report that afternoon. He had spent almost a month inside the Kobutsuden citadel, and infiltrated the Winter Palace by posing as an artisan. "The Order do not intend to pay homage," he said. "A great vault of iron has been constructed within the palace, and the key and sword are now locked within it. It is guarded both outside and from within; two armed soldiers remain inside at all times. Here is a map."

Shinga pulled a scroll from his tunic, unrolled it and weighted it open on the table. "To reach the vault you must first breach the citadel, which is now closed to all unauthorised persons; the only gate is permanently barred, and to enter it is necessary to present papers to the watchmen. After that, the Winter Palace, which is also under heavy guard. Once inside the palace, you must reach here–" he pointed to a circle on the map "–to access the chambers where the vault sits. Every corridor of approach is mined with traps."

"What else?" asked Nezumon Nano.

"Troops," said Shinga. "Noxon Taiyo, the Night Sun, has brought three thousand fighters to the capital. They are everywhere."

Nano was silent for several minutes, studying the map and calculating stratagems. Then he said: "It is not impossible. If guards are stationed within the vault, it must have air-holes. Things with holes can be entered. We will assemble a mission force; I will lead, and Shinga will be our guide. I need five more."

Many came forward – including Dorion, who was quickly but gently rebuffed – and Nano completed the force with some of his most experienced night-prowlers:

Jagon Ketsu, the Demon Blood; Kagon Shura, the Slaughter Shadow; Ishon Ushi, the Stone Ox; Yuron Fuki, the Ghost Blizzard; and Sasora Sato, the Hand's only female agent, known as Lady Sugarsting.

"The waning of the Ice Moon heralds the darkest pall of the year," said Nano. "A perfect time for corpses that walk by night."

"Then we are the Living Dead," said Sugarsting, "the seven who swallowed the stars."

# THE NIGHTMARE CASTLE

One by one they entered the castle chapel and were seated, many with heads still pounding from the previous night's revels, minds still imprinted with the image of the Black Phoenix rising at the end of Lady Miura's masque. On the chapel's dais was an altar piled high with wedding gifts; cosmetic boxes ingrained with powdered gold, ornate mirrors and stands, playing cards, musical instruments, dolls, calligraphy tools, incense boxes and candles, silken cushions and pillows, gowns, silver tableware, ceremonial chests, combs, books, and painted screens. Pride of place went to an expansive painting, a rare folding triptych by Taison III showing an erotic scene of three nude figures in demonic masks – two male, one female – entwined in copulation while an impertinent peasant peeped through a window blind; entitled *The Night Spy*, this was Lord Kyodokuron's endowment to the bride.

Hectoclarion, high maven of the Sun Shrine, stood ready to conduct the ceremony. His robes were of shimmering golden cloth, embroidered with a veritable galaxy of red suns radiant, and upon his head was a stiffened golden cowl cut from the same material. Lord Kyo presented his young son, Kyowashon, while Lady Miura offered up her daughter Messura. The bride was garbed in a gown of snow-white silk, with a like robe overlaid, and her auburn hair was affixed with volute silver pins.

After exchanging secret binding poems, inscribed in ink upon strips of vellum made from the penis-skin of goats to endue fertility, Kyowashon and Messura shared a goblet of rice wine proffered by the high maven; then Messura's outer robe was shed, and in its place she donned another garment in red, gold, silver and black, decorated with ivory deathsheads, given by Kyowashon. The union of flower and spiral was now sealed according to ritual, and required only physical consummation to be forever law.

The guests arose as Kyowashon and his bride turned from the altar, followed by Hectoclarion the High; the dagger slipped from Hekon Hakamanko's sleeve and into his hand, its steel stained with violet bane. With a shout of "For Hakamankon!" the hunchback lunged forwards. Kyowashon bravely leapt in front of Messura to shield her, but they were not Hekon's target; his strike was aimed at Hectoclarion, who raised up both hands to protect his face. The dagger slashed him across the left palm, drawing blood. Before the hunchback could thrust again, Taikon Taiyo grasped him around his throat and pulled him backwards, and then two Vertigo Watchmen seized his arms and the three of them dragged the gibbering attacker away from the chapel and out of sight.

Within thirty minutes, Hectoclarion's hand was completely without sensation. He could feel the numbness spreading up his arm, across his chest, could see the skin starting to discolour. He prayed to the Triad for deliverance while Lady Snowsnake, unsure how to save him, covered his body with leeches and tried to bleed out the hunchback's poison. After an hour the high maven fell silent; his entire body had turned black, the skin drying and cracking, and wormy sores began to erupt from beneath. Cataracts filmed his eyes, his teeth slid from parched grey gums, and finally steam began to leak from the fissures in his flesh as his blood boiled and evaporated, cooking his brain and viscera.

Even as Hectoclarion the High expired, a majestic white messenger bird flew into the temple of the Sun. The maven Katavarian took the rolled parchment from its leg, and studied the words scrawled across it. KILL DEATH WAR HAKAMANKON, the message read, and it was stamped in crimson ink with a ring-sigil of the skeletal, self-devouring snake; Katavarian showed it to his fellow mavens with great perturbation.

Four days later, the meaning of the message became hideously clear when an entourage arrived from the Nightmare Castle, headed by Taikon Taiyo and bearing two burial caskets, one of rough wood and the other cast in gold.

"Hectoclarion the High was murdered with poison by the hunchback, Hekon Hakamanko," said Taikon. "As he attacked, he cried out *For Hakamankon*; he was immediately arrested and, under inquisition, confessed that the killing was ordered by his father, Lord Hebon, in the name of the Vermin League. Sadly the hunchback's twisted body was weak, and he died before facing the hangman. His foul corpse was burnt; I bring you his bones, as proof of justice done." He gestured at the wooden coffin, which was lidless. Katavarian and the other Sun mavens peered at its contents, and saw a fire-scorched skeleton with femurs evidently shattered by torture screws; the spine was wildly deformed and bent in a great crooked arch, depressing the neck and skull.

The corpse in the golden casket was clothed in the solar raiment of the temple, its visage veiled. The shrivelled, coal-black, worm-eaten thing that they found beneath the covering inspired both fear and holy rage. Within the hour a decision was declared, a reply inscribed in blood. At the coop-tower Katavarian selected a bottle labelled *Skull Castle*, removed its stopper, and let several drops of the clear scent splash over the message, which he then affixed to the pink leg of his hardiest albino carrier. The bird took to the air, circled the temple twice, then arrowed at the distant Hakamanko fortress on pure white wings of war.

# THUNDERVOID

Fifty leagues past Scaleport the sea turned white, infused with a sulphurous fog which swirled over the desolate coast of Thundervoid. From the prow of the *Hexbound Heart* Mushon Yowa caught glimpses of a blighted terrain scattered with bleached, gnarled trees and cracks in the glassy ground which sporadically erupted with black geysers of putrid, liquefied corpse meat. Then a horn sounded, thrice, from the waters beyond.

Yowa signalled to his two escort destroyers, the *Fear Fathom* and the *Sea Vampire*, to drop anchor; according to the terms demanded by Captain Bloodspike, only one ship could proceed to the zone designated for paying ransom. *The Hexbound Heart* drifted further into the fog, through a coastal wash clotted with dead fish and seabirds, until two Crimson Curse bloodships came into view. The ships, named the *Sewer Slut* and the *Lazy Leper*, were already at anchor; Yowa ordered his own vessel to halt, and waited. Next to him, pale hands fixed to the foredeck rail, stood Lady Catcurse.

A man appeared on the *Sewer Slut*'s bow, wild-haired and salt-stained; whether it was Bloodspike or not, Yowa had no way of knowing. The pirate leaned forwards over his ship's figurehead – the wood-carved head and torso of a nude prostitute – and yelled out.

"Put the gold in a catboat and row it over," he said. "And no filthy tricks, eight-arms. In fact," he added, "why don't you bring the lovely lady with you? Don't worry, you'll get her back in one piece."

"Not possible," said Yowa. "She's with child, can't you see?"

"I see plenty," the pirate replied, motioning with his hand. A dozen more men appeared behind him, carrying spears and grapnels. "I see two ships to one and two men to one, all in our favour. So let's keep it simple, shall we? The bitch and the coin, in a boat – now."

"And what you stole?"

"Them that we *borrowed*, will be in another boat. Once we've got the gold, they're all yours. Captain Bloodspike is a fair man, you'll see."

Yowa took Lady Catcurse by the waist and guided her away from the rail. "Load the gold," he said to his crewmen. When the two chests were aboard, he sat Catcurse down at the stern and climbed in beside her. "Lower away."

There was little more than two hundred yards between the *Hexbound Heart* and the *Sewer Slut*. Masking his nose and mouth from the noxious fumes Yowa sculled across the short expanse, wary of bubbles breaking the milky surface, while the pirate came towards him. He'd heard tales of strange monsters infesting Thundervoid's turbid sound, hybrids spawned in the comet's fury. When the two vessels drew abreast of each other, the man said: "Change boats; just you."

Yowa found the mouldering mummies of Takashimon and Makon Kurotako in the pirate's boat, seemingly undamaged. He watched as the pirate opened both chests, scooped up handfuls of golden coins, and then closed them. Lady Catcurse was silent and motionless, her face hidden behind a kerchief and swirling tendrils of fog.

"Don't say much, do she?" sneered the pirate. "No matter; once the gold's on board and counted, we'll send her back down."

Both men returned to their motherships and the boats were hoisted aboard. Yowa stood and waited for the commotion while the anchor was slowly and silently weighed, oars dropped in readiness.

It didn't take long. The wild-haired pirate appeared at the *Sewer Slut*'s prow, raging, and hurled a fistful of lead jettons towards the *Hexbound Heart*.

"You think you can cheat Captain Bloodspike?" he screamed. "Your bitch is good as dead, you eight-arms cunt! I'll cut her fucking whelp out and feed it to the sharks!"

Yowa said nothing; the *Hexbound Heart* began to move steadily in reverse, away from the Crimson Curse bloodships. Before they could stir into motion, Lady Catcurse's clockwork tripped a set of internal levers, opening a metal compartment and spilling its contents into a receptacle below it. The pirates prodding her face in puzzlement were the first to die, reduced to burnt bone and ashes when her belly exploded into a towering white fireball that rained instant destruction upon the *Sewer Slut* and all aboard; within seconds the ship's blazing mast and sails crashed onto the deck of the *Lazy Leper* alongside, spreading the inferno, and as the *Sewer Slut* cracked into two pieces and sank into the scalding sea the *Lazy Leper*'s crew jumped after it, bodies ablaze, their vessel flaring up like an incandescent torch.

The noise and brilliance of the destruction were so intense that Captain

Bloodspike heard and saw it from the deck of the *Red Wraith*, even though his ship was anchored half a league up the coast off the ruins of Creeper's Cove. He grimaced, guessing that the Kurotako had somehow won the day, and rubbed at the stump of his missing ring-finger. Bloodspike was a ghost figure, a man left to die who rose up from his watery grave and seized power through fear of the dead that walk. While Captain Scarebones, former chieftain of the Crimson Curse, now plied a slaver's trade off the western Viles, Bloodspike had sworn to terrorize the east; the Hakamanko, the Kurotako, and above all the Smash-Bones savages who infested the Jackdaws, were each his deep-avowed foe.

His ship's crew were creatures of nightmare, cruelly disfigured No-Face clansmen who fled from the würms which destroyed their flesh, migrating north after the Decimation and settling in the newly formed wasteland. He found them in the fractured shadows of a dead coastal village which he renamed Creeper's Cove after their talisman, the Creeper, a moaning human beast that staggered aimlessly at the end of a twenty-foot chain; the Creeper had only half a face – the other was just exposed skull – but in the village of the No-Faces, that raised him to the rank of idiot deity.

Whatever the fate of the *Sewer Slut* and the *Lazy Leper*, the Curse still had another half-dozen bloodships anchored off the cove, even though a similar number had sailed west with Captain Scarebones. Bloodspike knew that the Kurotako fleet was now returned to the Red Rock, making it once again impregnable; it was time to make a new war-plan – one that would make him feared and famed throughout Novalis.

# THE OSSUARY

"What's all that noise?' asked Soma sleepily. "It can't be morning already."

Lady Hexheart slipped from the bed and felt her way along the wall to the chamber window. She pried apart the heavy velvet curtains just enough to peer down at the courtyard; a shaft of dawn sun splashed the floor and lit up her naked figure, bringing to life the blue and red tattoo of a tiger-demon which covered her back and upper arms. Soma saw a bite-mark on her right buttock, not far from the anus.

"They're leaving for Bloodflower today," Hexheart said. "Five hundred soldiers, and five hundred artisans and labourers to restore the castle for Kyowashon and his bride. Ships will transport them to the coast; from there it's less than a day's march."

She closed the curtains again, snuffing out the light, and hurried back to bed. At first the young virago had befriended her out of pity, Soma believed; the lonely girl in the tower, far from home. They would sometimes dine and drink wine together, and Hexheart would tell her tales of her mother, Hexheart the Elder, and her potions. Soma's favourite was nightbleed, which was used to infect a Spider Hook village when it rose up. After chaos agents of the Skull Creed introduced this poison into the village well, the clansfolk began falling prey to vivid, bloody nightmares of murdering their own families. Soon the nightmares grew into sleep-walking trances, during which they acted out these atrocities with unchecked ferocity and violence. Within a week the whole village was a charnel piled with butchered corpses; just one man remained, too frightened to fall asleep. None could ever blame the Seikyo, and it was accepted that the village had turned upon itself in a frenzy of deadly moon rage.

One evening Hexheart brought one of her own confections, a philtre she called dreamfinger which they added to their wine; the result was a delirium that ended with the girls in bed together, naked and entwined. After that Hexheart visited with dreamfinger more often until, while Lord Kyo was away at his son's wedding rites, she stayed there every night.

Two days later, Lord Kyo returned.

Soma was instructed to join him at dinner the next evening; she was seated next to him at head of table, with the maven Morgomox opposite.

"Your sister is alive and well," Kyo told her, "and under the protection of the Taiyo. I was assured this by Lord Taikon Taiyo himself. And she is also free of her husband, the hunchback – he was killed in the Mizuno dungeons after murdering the high maven of the Sun Temple. Moreover, your father has agreed to put down arms. Of course, your sister must remain a guest of the Taiyo to ensure his continued compliance, at least until the war is at an end. As you must remain ours – I assured Lady Miura Mizuno, my new sister-by-law, as much."

All in all, it was welcome news; the death of Hekon the hunchback most especially. Surely it would not now be long before the Hakamanko revolt was quashed, by one agency or another.

"And Lord Kyowashon?" she asked, showing polite interest.

"On the way to Castle Bloodflower, with his bride and three hundred troops."

That night Lady Soma Kurotako dreamt of her childhood by the sea, where she and her sister would winkle hermit crabs from their pirated shells and skewer them on sticks. She saw the ocean turn deep red, the sky yellow, and then the crabs became human babes, mewling and puking blood.

When she awoke Lady Hexheart was gone; a black orchid lay in her place, its labella dusted with lice.

# CASTLE MORTMANE

In the guise of a one-eyed beggar, Flamon Neko slipped through the siege ring on a night when driving rain blotted out the moon and stars, watchfires no sooner lit than extinguished. In near blackness he approached the castle's postern gate, announcing his presence by emitting the piercing cry of a screech owl. After a minute a bucket was lowered on a rusted chain; Neko pulled a wooden cylinder from the tatters of his pauper's tunic and placed it inside. Five more minutes and the outer gate was raised, just enough for a man to stoop beneath. As it closed behind him Neko found himself within the castle wall; the inner gate was ahead, plated in thick metal with spear-slits, and above him the stonework was inset with murder holes that bristled with wicked down-thrusting spikes. The tunnel was just high and wide enough for a single horseman to pass through.

"Name."

"Flamon Neko, of the Iron Pentagram."

"Your words?"

"*Death wears five faces.*"

The gate ahead opened outwards, and the chaos agent entered Mortmane. Chikon Takasha, bearded and emaciated, greeted him and handed him back the cylinder. "Let's take this to my father," he said.

Lord Hikidashon Takasha sat in his quarters atop the Joker's Keep; like his son, he had lost a great amount of weight since Flamon last saw him. A grim man at best, he now resembled a starving lammergeyer, his eyes like pellets of lead. On his writing table sat the boiled skull of Croton Kurotako.

Flamon handed him the cylinder, and Hikidashon retrieved the sealed scroll which his younger son, Gomon, had entrusted to the spy. By candlelight he read the letter, then handed it to Chikon.

"Well, let us hope that Noxon Taiyo is able to march north soon," he said. "Another moon's turn and we'll be reduced to eating our own boots and saddles, or rats if we can catch any. And after that... we dine on the dead."

"The gate?" asked Neko.

"One man might leave and return unseen, perhaps; but what can one man carry? We tried to dig tunnels, but that bastard Ando has sunk a trench around the castle at least forty feet deep; when our men broke earth they were trapped inside it, and speared like swine in a shithouse."

"I would put their number at two thousand," said Neko. "When I mingled with the camp followers, I heard some voices of dissent."

"It's true that some have deserted," said Chikon. "And when news came of Lord Sadogashon's amnesty, most of the Kurotako fighters struck out for Bloodtooth. But Tazon Ando's followers are loyal; those who still remain will support him to the end, I'm sure of it. Our men are weak from hunger, some are sick. Perhaps two hundred are fit for battle, no more than that. You saw Ando's siege engine?"

"A mangonel, the size of a barn."

"Aye. He calls it Boiler's Bane, and each day finds some new filth to sling at us. Rotten pigs, buckets of human shit, a burning donkey, sharpened rocks, a rain of skulls filled with tapeworms, even a nude whore dead from the pox. It destroys the men's morale."

"Each day I pray he'll sling himself," said Hikidashon, stroking his deathsword Kyami, master of darkness. "Then there'd be a bloody reckoning."

The clangour and clamour began at dawn, as they did every day, one thousand besiegers smashing sword against shield and shouting a repeated refrain. "Wife-boiler!" they yelled, "Horse-fucker! Wife-boiler! Horse-fucker! All fall down! *Wife-boiler! Horse-fucker! All fall down!*" The racket continued through the day, taken up by the next thousand and then by the first again, while every hour on the hour Boiler's Bane hurled contemptuous offerings over the castle walls; as Flamon Neko watched from the battlements he was almost decapitated by the latest, a live goat which bleated piteously as it flew past him. He looked back and saw it smash against the courtyard flagstones, exploding and showering a group of Hell-Claw clansmen with hot blood and entrails. He knew that some would eat parts of the goat, hunger overtaking reason, and die slowly, painfully from the poison in which Tazon Ando had doubtless steeped its meat and very bones.

At noon Neko met with three other agents of the Iron Pentagram, the Takasha band of assassins – Yakyon Shoko, the Night Terror; Himitson Kitsu, the Mystery Fox;

and Yuron Shindo, the Temple Ghost.

"Pavo and Wana never returned from the Valley of Flies; Tobu was killed here," Shoko told him. "A suicide mission; he left by the gate and circumvented the siege ring, trying to attack from the rear and put an end to Tazon Ando. But Ando is protected by a double ring of steel; Tobu cut through the first, but his wounds weakened him. The next day Ando slung his mutilated corpse back over the parapet, his head sewn inside his belly with snail-shells for eyes."

"Since his downfall Ando is without honour," said Neko. "He used to teach us the way of the sword; now he follows the way of the serpent." He reached into his belt pouch and pulled out a small phial of foul-coloured liquid. "Flace, from the hag Gorgongrone. If Ando drinks this, he won't need a catapult to fly. But how?"

# SKULL CASTLE

Hebon Hakamanko twisted the bird's head slowly until it tore away from the neck with a spurt of bright blood and a flurry of tiny white feathers, then hurled its lifeless body against the wall in a fury. The unrolled message said HOLY WAR in letters of dried coagulate, crafted in the script of the mavens. *First the treacherous cowardice of the Kurotako, and now this.*

Next day one of Hebon's scouts returned from the Viles and relayed the rumours of the hour: his son, Hekon, had murdered the high maven of the Sun Temple, and was in turn tortured, killed and burnt; and he, Hebon, had declared war upon the Triad. Now the Celestial Horde was preparing for battle, with warrior-priests of the Sun and Storms at the head of a massing land army. Their mission: destroy Skull Castle.

Whatever the truth of his son's involvement and death, and whoever had sent the false declaration, mattered not to Hebon; the hour of war was at hand, the hour when the Vermin League must rise again to assert dominion over Novalis, just as it had in the old country more than one thousand years before. He knew that to launch an assault on Lizard's Den, the Horde would have to first gather at the Storm Shrine; that gave him a full week to make preparations. Every last living würm would be flushed from the Mad Marshes, chained and bridled, every last able-bodied clansman in the dark demesne armed and pressed into service.

At midnight a council of war was held atop the castle's tallest and most convoluted tower, the Black Bone, attended by the maven Borborax, the würm-rider Vexion, General Hakon Hora the Hellhawk, and several other commanders; the seat usually occupied by Lady Vulvomane, Hakamanko bane virago, stood empty. The chamber was banded by an ancient frieze, secretly crafted during the castle's creation, depicting the final days of the emperor Jaikon. It showed Jaikon assailed by the forces of Zenmarion, King of Hell – demons riding centipedes, lychworms, spiders, scorpions and bats while seven giant skeletons and seven shit-monsters strode beside them, and at the head the black magus Hakamankon and his witch bride Komaja, sat astride the great red death-snake Hebochi. The frieze was ordered by Haxokokon, first overlord of Clan Hakamanko, whispered by some to be Hakamankon's only son.

"The Shines are ours," said Lord Hebon, "and when Mortmane falls, we will master all lands north of the Crow River. The Kurotako have served their purpose. Let the Celestial Horde crash against us; our würms will burn the meat from their bones, holy or not. How many are in harness, Vexion?"

"More than thirty, including those of the moat," said the lizard-rider. "And we may glean twice as many again from the swamps."

"And fighters?"

"Five thousand encamped, and thousands more to be enjoined," said Hellhawk. "The templar warriors number only six hundred sixty-six; they will no doubt raise many thousands from among the commonfolk, but those are not true fighters. Any one of our trained men could kill ten of them."

"And Skull Castle is supplied for a full year of siege, if need be," added Borborax.

"You will bring all warlocks to the castle," said Hebon to Hellhawk. "A great working will be at the heart of our machine. And find me a new war-witch, with all haste."

"There is a girl of the Blind Cat–" Hellhawk began, but was cut off by an urgent clattering and clanging from below; the bronze carillon in the Belfry of Beasts was sounding an alarum with a distinct message: *strangers approaching*.

It started as a flaring of firelight in the gloom, out beyond the castle perimeter; then, of a sudden, the flare became an inferno. A skewbald mare screamed and then careened into view at a mad gallop, tail on fire, pulling a driverless cart filled with burning scarecrows and heading straight for the outer gates. The drawbridge was up; the beast plunged headfirst into the castle's deep-sunk moat, dragging the blazing cart behind it, and crashed with a sickening impact followed by the stench of dead horse and dead lizard sizzling on a bonefyre.

Then from the darkness voices emerged, chanting softly, slowly rising in volume as they grew ever nearer. *Red snake, red snake, in the night,* they sang, *we will set your skulls alight, all the dead men burning bright, red snake, red snake, in the night.* A group of skipping, whirling figures could now be seen by the flickering flames which rose from the moat, seemingly unmindful of the hundred arrows trained on them from the battlements above.

"They killed a dragon," said Vexion bitterly. "I say feather the bastards, whoever they are. General?"

Hellhawk looked at his overlord for a signal.

"Hold," said Lord Hebon. "Bring them to me alive."

An hour later he received them down in Skull Castle's ante-dungeon, where a raised iron chair faced the entrance allowing prisoners to be inspected and judged before incarceration in the system of vaults beyond. His carnifex, Mad Dog, stood next to him, nursing a chipped and rusty war-hammer. One by one the night-callers were dragged in by Tongues of the Basilisk and lined up before the dais.

They were a filthy, stinking crew, most dressed in torn hospice shifts deep-stained with blood, piss and ordure. Some tittered, others muttered to themselves beneath their breath. There were both males and females among them; one was a girl-child no more than seven or eight years of age, necklaced in defleshed finger-bones. At the fore stood a youth with black hair and red-flecked eyes, his skin dried and scaled like a reptile. He stared at Lord Hebon with mute insolence, then made a sudden step forward; a trident shaft struck him hard in the face, dropping him onto one knee.

He spat out a bloody tooth, followed by a single word.

"Father."

# THE SUNSTORM CASTLE

"Is it really true?" she asked Taikon. "He's really dead?"

"Who told you? That handmaiden of yours, no doubt."

"So you confirm it?"

"Trust me," said Taikon. "You can be sure that the hunchback will never trouble you again."

Finally, the words that Suna Kurotako had yearned to hear. And yet even now, her joy was darkened by the shadow of captivity. The confines of this strange castle would surely grow as cruel as the hunchback's clutches, one merely replaced by the other.

"Then I am free," she said. "Except I'm not, am I? When will you permit me to leave this place?"

"You know my father's edict," Taikon replied. "You must remain here to deter any renewed aggression by Lord Sadogashon."

Suna shook her head grimly. "My father cares nothing for me," she said. "He sold me to Hekon, to that monstrous cripple, just to pay a debt. Do you really think my welfare counts for anything with him? Or that of my sister? He has Kuchon, his future heir, and he has his red rock and his iron castle; ransom me and you'd be lucky to get a rotten fish in return. And I will swear an oath on the *Elemental Testament* never to return to Bloodtooth."

Taikon looked pensive. Then he said: "I could speak to my father again. But if not here, where would you go? To join your sister in Wolf's Jaw? These are dangerous times."

"Perhaps," said Suna. "When you were a child, did you read *Wake Of The She-Sword*?"

"The exploits of Red Girl? Not much... it wasn't really a boy's book, if I remember rightly."

"Perhaps not. But it was my favourite, by far. I wished I could be just like her, an outcast wandering Novalis and striking down evil in the name of the Triad."

"A noble ambition, to be sure... but Red Girl was a templar assassin, a killer born and bred, versed in the arts of war from childhood... and I think you'll find that in reality she was a killer-for-coin."

"Yes, but I prefer the romantic version," said Suna. "And I'm no swordswoman, it's true. But there are other ways to kill. Oh... you look shocked."

"I admit, it's hard to imagine one so gentle, and fair of form and face, as an assassin," said Taikon. It was true; none could deny her beauty.

"You are kind to say so," Suna replied. "But those years while I suffered at the hunchback's hands, his cruelty and his torment... you don't know how feverishly I burned with the desire to drive a knife through his gloating face. And those feelings, I've discovered, never really go away. You should know, too, that our marriage was never consummated; as far as I know, Hekon prefers – preferred – dead things. My point is this: Red Girl, as you may recall, was a temple virgin; she was only killed in battle after she was seduced by a warrior chieftain later in life. When she lost her maidenhead, she lost her power. Mine are both intact."

Taikon smiled. *I'm truly glad to hear that.* "So if not the sword...?"

"Poisons," said Suna. "I ask that you make me apprentice to Lady Feverclaw, that she might teach me of her secret arts. In her honour, and that of Red Girl, I pray you may soon know me as Suna Crimsonclaw, bane virago."

She smiled, drawing Taikon's eye to the gap between her front teeth, lips pasted with cochineal. Two hundred feet below, in Sunstorm's foulest dungeon, the hunchback wept in darkness.

# THE SEPULCHRE

They came by the thousand; farmers, craftsmen, monks, merchants, bearing tools and rudimentary weapons, answering the call from the temple of the Sun. Watching them swarm over the land surrounding the Sepulchre as far as the eye could see, Dorion could understand why they were called the Hive.

"When the Horde moves out, the Hive moves in," explained Kuron Kirizono. "So it has always been when the Triad becomes involved in conflict. You have followers – loyal followers. And so it begins."

"So the Horde are actually going to war?"

"First they march to the Storm Shrine, and along the way will gather thousands more to join the Hive. This holy war against the Hakamanko might yet work to our advantage; if Jukon Gomi and his cohorts see the Horde so engaged they may be emboldened to march north, hoping to break the siege at Mortmane. Less troops in the citadel can only make our task easier."

"And so we wait?"

"We wait. Sasora Sato will report back from the city as soon as she has news; she can be very persuasive, or so Nano tells me. Now; haven't you training to attend to?"

He had. Kagon Shura, the Slaughter Shadow, was teaching him the ways of the night attack, illuminated by some examples from history. One of the most famous night attacks, he told him, was that carried out during the Serpent Wars by Hakamanko chaos agents the Lizard Crux against Castle Nightfog, fortress of Clan Mishima. The clan's overlord, Usagon, had been slain in battle but his younger brother Anagon refused to surrender; the Crux's mission was to infiltrate the castle and assassinate Anagon, thereby ending the clan's male line. Thirteen agents, dressed in black from head to toe, attacked in the dead of night. Six sacrificed their lives in order to divert the castle's sentries, while the other seven used ropes to scale the walls and penetrate the interior. Anagon was surrounded as he slept; when he awoke he was urged to kill himself with honour, but was too craven, and so his head was sliced off, slowly, with a dagger. Clan Mishima was extinguished and Castle Nightfog passed to the Takasha, rulers of the Templedark.

"I remember that story," said Dorion. "Isn't it called the Night of the Dragon?"

"In popular legend," said Kagon, "the six who died dressed as three marsh dragons – two men in each costume – to distract the würms which roamed the inner moat, and were killed during an attempt at mating. But I can assure you this was not the case."

"But shouldn't Castle Nightfog have passed to the Hakamanko, if they carried out the night attack?"

"This lies at the root of the Hakamanko dissent. After the wars ended, a pact was made between the surviving eight clans to hunt würms to extinction throughout Novalis; but Fekon Fork-Tongue, bitter over the loss of Nightfog, reneged on this agreement. He secretly kept a last colony of dragons deep in the Mad Marshes, and continued to breed them. And that is why the Hakamanko, as sole keepers of the deadly lizards, are so dangerous to this day."

*It sounds as if würm eggs are worth more than keys and swords*, thought Dorion, but said nothing. When he was emperor, he would order the swamps to be drained; and if the Hakamanko resisted, he would impale them on metal spikes, just as his father would have. *If this is to be the last war, then only fear will make it so. Those who kneel shall know mercy; those who do not...*

And then Dorion Killstar found himself in the grip of a vivid reverie, his mind aflame with a panorama of blood, fire and destruction in which the bodies of his enemies were gutted and cut into pieces, boiled, pierced with arrows and spears, incinerated on pyres, immersed in vats of acid, hung from gallows and ramparts, dragged over blazing coals, crucified, bled dry, pulled apart by foaming stallions, hurled against stone bulwarks or into ravines by catapults, tied to rocks and thrown into the sea, fed to rabid wolves, skinned, blinded, castrated...

It was only when Jagon Shura shook him that the visions faded away, and he found himself standing in the Sepulchre's inner bailey, dusk falling, the night-song of the Blind Brothers starting to rise.

Just five days later, Lady Sugarsting returned from Kobutsuden with her report: Noxon Taiyo, the Night Sun, was leaving for Mortmane with two thousand troops within the week.

# HOOK HARBOUR

Captain Scarebones was sucking at his black lover's teat when the shout went up.

"Death-ships!"

With a curse he rolled away and lurched to the seaward window of his quarters atop the *Mermaid* inn, squinting through his hair braids with wine-soaked eyes.

Bathed in yellow dawn light, the pirate's nest of Hook Harbour was yet asleep as Lord Fleshstripper's goliath dromon the *Hellfire Scream* skirred from the melting mists, followed by its four deadly cohorts. While the fighting men of the Viles had been called to war, leaving the Mizuno unable to patrol and protect their western lands, the Crimson Curse had used the coastal settlement as a base to launch raids into the demesne and transport captured females across the southern seas to sell as livestock. But Scarebones was unaware that Castle Bloodflower and its environs – a rich source of human cattle – had recently passed by marriage into the hands of Clan Seikyo. Until now.

Eleven of the pirates' thirteen bloodships were at anchor when the Seikyo struck, with just two in transit. While the *Hellfire Scream* used its stern-bolted catapult to fling immense balls of flaming resin at the harbour's buildings, the *Corpse Pyre*, the *Black Inferno*, the *Cinder Bride* and the *Red Death* directly attacked the stationary fleet, ramming into them at angles and incinerating the sinking wreckage with fire-throwing machines. Those pirates still aboard had no chance of retaliation or escape; they were drowned or burnt to ashes by the dozen, and those that skirted the fire were hacked to pieces as the Skeleton Sealords and their skull-masked marauders overran them.

Dressed and buckled, Captain Scarebones dropped into the *Mermaid*'s warren of hidden tunnels just before a fireball crashed through its roof, roasting alive Nvora, his nude and abandoned paramour. The first time he saw the women of the distant firelands, their skin so black that it shone like liquid diamond, Scarebones took them for dark goddesses fallen to earth. And there were many more to replace Nvora, once he escaped from Hook Harbour.

Wending through the underground maze the captain gathered up a scattered handful of his fleeing comrades, enough to crew the *Sick Dog* and make good their flight. He kept the small ship hidden from plain sight, away from the other vessels in an inlet beyond the promontory where the tunnels spilled out onto the beach.

But Nikon Tabu, the feared Lord Fleshstripper, was not easily deceived. While the other commanders, led by Momon Jaga – called the Lobster for the clattering metal pincers that were screwed into the bones of his wrist-stumps – stormed through the fire-ravaged harbour on a rampage of merciless butchery, Tabu held fast his position offshore.

Two hours after the assault began, most of Hook Harbour was a smouldering ruin strewn with corpses. Parts of burning ships drifted along the waterfront, where more dead bodies floated among the debris; the four Seikyo dromons commanded by Sudon Nyo, Aon Baka, Kiron Kuta and Momon Jaga remained unscathed. And then the *Sick Dog* broke cover.

"Pursuit!" yelled Lord Fleshstripper, and then: "*Death speed!*"

The *Hellfire Scream*'s time-beater pounded on his drum, raising the pace rapidly until the oarsmen were straining at the limits of endurance. Although Captain Scarebones had the wind in his sails and a head start, Tabu knew that the dromon would overtake him within the hour. He stood at the ship's prow in full battle-costume of black and silver, a skeletal reaper poised to harvest souls. The Kurotako fleet had escaped his wrath, and the Crimson Curse would pay the price.

When the *Sick Dog* came within range, Tabu ordered his catapult crew to unleash the night orb, one of many weapon loads originally designed by Lady Hexheart for an attack on the Sunstorm Castle. That attack had been aborted, but the night orb remained ready for purpose. "Make it count," he said.

The war engine's twisted rope, woven from human hair, was released and the wooden arm flew forwards launching its missile in a soaring arc, clearing the dromon's own sails and then descending rapidly towards the *Sick Dog* some three hundred yards ahead. The wooden sphere smashed against the ship's mast, releasing a shower of five hundred papery bat skulls which exploded as they struck the deck below. A turgid brown ichor splattered over the pirates manning the sails, and where it clung to their skin it started to crackle and smoke, quickly burning through to the bone. Brineballs, the bosun, was hit in the right eye and leapt overboard in an attempt to douse his agony, while others simply collapsed as their internal organs dissolved.

Captain Scarebones was backed against the starboard rail, falchion drawn. As his men screamed and clutched at their wounds the *Hellfire Scream* drew ever closer, the *Sick Dog* listing out of control, until the dromon's bronze beak ploughed into its stern with a wood-splintering impact that ended the pursuit.

"Take the captain alive," said Lord Fleshstripper. "Skin the rest."

The fight was a short one. Scarebones inflicted two grievous wounds, but was eventually overpowered by the Seikyo sea-fighters and dragged onto the *Hellfire Scream*; the *Sick Dog* drifted away, smoking from stern to bow and taking on water, nothing left of its crew but raw bloody meat cratered with coruscating lesions.

Lord Fleshstripper pulled down his half-mask of grinning silver skull-teeth and raised a damning finger at his captive. "Captain Scarebones," he said, "you stand accused of invasion, rape, theft, pillage and abduction against Clan Seikyo, Castle Bloodflower and the people of the Viles. Moreover, you stand accused of selling those same people into slavery, and profiting thereby. What say you?"

The pirate sneered. "I say fuck Clan Seikyo, fuck you and fuck every cunt, in the name of liberty. No quarter, no surrender." Scarebones punctuated his defiance with a spew of rank mucus, besmirching the ship's white deck.

"Guilty," pronounced Nikon Tabu. "In the name of Lord Kyodokuron Seikyo, I sentence you to death by execution. Anoint him."

Captain Scarebones was tied to the sling of the dromon's war engine and a bucket of resin was tipped over his head. Just before they launched him the resin was ignited, turning him into a human torch. He flew out across the ocean like a blazing comet trailing fire for several seconds before plummeting into the cerulean waters with a single salty splash and a wisp of smoke, and then was gone forever.

# SKULL CASTLE

Hebon Hakamanko, Lord of Skulls, sat back in his clan throne of twining brazen snakes and beckoned the witch towards him.

"You are the one called Blind Cat Bex?"

"The same, blacklord."

"And if I wish to sleep the sleep of the dead?"

"Sweetdive, blacklord. Made from the honey of bees that feed on nectar of the carrion flower."

"Bring it at once; for I would commune with ancient souls."

Without waiting for reply Hebon turned to the black-haired youth beside him. "Moshino."

"Yes, father."

"As my son reborn, you will reign over Skull Castle while I sojourn in the darklands. Guide the maven Borborax in the ways of our great working; General Hora will deal with our military deployment. And your Hellhaven madhounds – be sure to keep them well to heel."

Lord Hebon took repose in the castle crypt, where the tombs of the first Hakamanko were sculpted from bronze coated with centuries of chaotic verdigris; the lid of each sarcophagus twisted up into the huge head of a striking cobra, hood flaring, fangs bared. One thousand candles were lit, and Hebon's burial chamber was filled with purple flowers which exuded a scent akin to rotting corpses. After ingesting the witch's sweetdive, the lizard lord lay back upon his velveted bier and was slowly overtaken by a profound narcotic stupor, his breath shallow, heart barely beating. Hebon had descended into the realm of the dead only once before, for it had nearly claimed him; but now he craved wisdom which he believed only Haxokokon, first of his line, could impart. He slept for three whole days and three whole nights.

Far above, in the fat tower known as the Dragon's Neck, Moshino presided over a coven of five warlocks gathered from the lower clans: the Frog-Eater, from the Iron Talons; Sim Sourtooth, from the Cut-Bellies; Mik Maggot-Dancer, from the Scorpion Blacks; Crowface Crak, from the Tower Bats; and Wetweasel, from the Night Weepers. Borborax listened to their conjectures, but heard nothing of science; this was a world of superstition, delusion, and madness.

"I am Moshino, bastard of Hellhaven," Moshino told them, "a killer in the name of the Holy Eye, and son of your overlord Hebon, the Red Snake Risen. My dam Silversoil, the poison witch, the lady of bloody roses, bade me butcher bitches in the night, and from their bellies I gouged three and twenty dolls and stitched them in a hex. This was the Silversoil working, the first of the Holy Eye, the blood eye, the moon that weeps red tears; and the moon that weeps is the eye of the snake, the serpent that devours its own bones. You are summoned here for a great new working, one which will strike at the heart of our enemies. Who among you sees with the serpent eye?"

"Frog eye," said the Frog-Eater.

"Maggot eye," said Mik Maggot-Dancer.

"Bird eye," said Crowface Crak from behind his metal beak.

"Stoat eye," said Wetweasel.

Sim Sourtooth shuffled forwards, making circles with thumb and forefinger and raising them up to his face. "Sim Sourtooth sees all," he croaked. "Frog eats maggot, bird eats frog, stoat eats bird. When stoat shits, snake slithers."

"Brother Sourtooth has the right of it," said Moshino. "Borborax; prepare the tower's privy shafts. Our working will go beyond the raising of the homunculus; no dwarf shall we conjure from a mare's womb, but a giant from the sewage pits of Skull Castle. This is the hour of the Shit Man who walks tall as the titan moon."

On the morning of his waking, Lord Hebon held council with Moshino, Borborax, Hellhawk and Blind Cat Bex. "When I fell," he told them, "I fell full one thousand years and more through the darkness. I was at Kago when Metakaikon, the emperor Jaikon's young son, led a train of survivors from the imperial court to a fleet of one thousand waiting war-ships on the coast, bound for Novalis as the old country sank beneath a torrent of blood. And I was on one of those ships, an infant nursed by an unwitting mother of the Nobunaga clan whose own child had been snatched from the cradle by agents of Hakamankon, leaving me in its stead. Like a hidden plague they bore me with them to the new land, to the bosom of ancient Kyukiden. Through the eyes of our forebear Haxokokon I beheld the death of Bankairon, arch persecutor of our league. And more – it was my own hand which held the bloody dagger when it slit the demon-slayer's throat. We sank his corpse in the bowels of Mount Komonyama, also called the Devil's Arsehole, where it might be reduced to true nothingness; but by some agency the volcano was extinguished."

"Then the legend is true," said Hellhawk. "The Vermin League followed Bankairon to Novalis, and struck with the hand of vengeance. Yet even now his bones lie beneath the mountain, protected by the Triad."

"Aye," said Borborax, "and legend also tells that whosoever retrieves the bones may wield them as a talisman against the night."

"Or may destroy them once and for all," added Lord Hebon. "In any case, my excursion beyond the tombs of time confirms that Haxokokon was indeed the secret son of Hakamankon and Komaja."

He turned to Bex. "Your witchways serve us well. Are you willing to succour Skull Castle again, even unto death?"

"I am, blacklord."

"Then kneel; and rise, Lady Catamane of Skulls."

# THE WINTER PALACE

Seven agents of chaos moved in silent masked procession through the moonless night, four shouldering a coffin, but Jukon Gomi could see nothing beyond the city gates save the vague outline of trees as they swayed in the frosted wind.

Somewhere Noxon Taiyo was heading to the Templedark with his army, somewhere the Celestial Horde and Hive were advancing to the southern plain of the Crow River, starfire and angels railing at an infestation of pestilent vermin in the northlands. *And when it's done we'll turn upon each other, like rabid dogs fighting over a bone.* Was there truly no other way? The blood, and the pain, and the endless death… yet in the eyes of the Triad, those who held Kobutsuden were now rebels, their amnesty expiring when the Ice Moon waned into a lightless demise. Jukon wondered whether Dorion Killstar, this young pretender, bastard son of a whore and a madman, could somehow prove to be the saviour of Novalis; but how could they take a chance? Tainted blood could not be leeched, any more than a turd could be transmuted into gold. And then there was Kuron Kirizono, Raikon's hulking enforcer, renowned for the Reaper's Roast and other atrocities throughout Thundervoid; with such a man as his right hand, Killstar's aura was already one of violence and intimidation. Jukon's only choice was to stand firm, to keep faith with the judgement already levied in fire by the Three Sorrows.

He saw nothing as the black-clad agents of the Blue Dragon Hand gathered in the shadow of the citadel, resting their load against its outer wall. Kagon Shura, the Slaughter Shadow, and Jagon Ketsu, the Demon Blood, removed the coffin lid; Lady Burnbolt lay within, already stripped naked, waxen breasts jutting outward above her rounded belly, eyes open and fixed like frozen splashes of luminous jade. Nezumon Nano, the Devil Bat, inserted a key into her navel and turned it clockwise, just once. Beneath his breath he said: "Sixty minutes."

One by one they scaled the stout oak which rose beside the wall; Ishon Ushi, the Stone Ox, removed the bolt thrower that was strapped to his colossal shoulders and passed it up to Nano. One end of a thick rope was tied around the tree's trunk, the other to the metal eye of a heavy bolt; then Nano unleashed the projectile, firing partly into the wind. It shot across the space between the citadel wall and the nearest turret of the Winter Palace, punching a hole through the stonework and anchoring itself with a ring of sturdy metal barbs; the cold streets below were near empty, and the shower of displaced granite fell unnoticed. After tightening and tying off the rope, the chaos agents shinned along it one after the after, high above the citadel rooftops, swinging down and into an embrasure in the tower. The silence was cracked once, by a glass eyeball clattering along the cobbles pursued by a half-blind beggar, then resumed.

"It's a privy," hissed Yuron Fuki, the Ghost Blizzard, pressing his mask tight against his mouth and nose to block the sharp reek of ammonia and stale faeces; a vase of dead flowers lay spilled by his feet, and two small pink lizards clung to the ceiling. The latrine's door opened onto a deserted circular landing.

"Which way?" asked Nano.

"Down," said Tsunamon Shinga, the Terror Tempest, clutching his hand-drawn map of the palace interior and indicating a descending stairway. "We have to go around the quadrangle and enter the main enclave."

A single guard stood at the tower entrance watching out for intruders, never dreaming that death would strike from within. Jagon Ketsu's hand clamped over his mouth as the dagger opened the front of his throat, and they pulled his corpse inside before too much blood could spray across the walkway which they followed around, clinging to the dense shadows, until they reached a palace side-door and slipped inside.

The iron vault which held the imperial key and sword was positioned at the rear of the building, behind guarded doors; three dim unmanned corridors led to it from the vestibule but all, according to Shinga, were set with concealed death-traps – doors in the floor which opened into spike-filled pits or underground cells which quickly flooded to the brim with suffocating sand, triggered by the weight of a human footfall. There was time to traverse but one of these passageways; Sasora Sato, known as Lady Sugarsting, chose the central of the three. Nano secured a length of rope to a pillar and handed her the slack.

Ishon Ushi lifted her up on his shoulders as if she were a child, placing her within reach of the wooden ceiling; she drove an expanding bolt into the timber, anchoring it, then another, threading the rope through each eye-hole as she went, and so progressed along the long corridor in suspension, before sliding down the ulterior wall where a locked door presented itself. Sato could see the faint edge of the final trap-door in the floor, and estimated there was just enough room for all seven to assemble in the tiny end-space. She pulled down hard on the rope.

Five climbed and descended safely, but as Ishon Ushi approached the last stretch of rope the wood above him fractured with a sharp report, the ceiling section starting to collapse under his weight; he released the rope and tried to leap across the final expanse of floor, but his trailing foot kicked against a trap. The panels flew inward and, before Nezumon Nano could grab his arm, Ushi slipped and fell backwards into the pit. Even as they heard the sound of the spikes puncturing his bulky frame and saw the first eruption of blood from below, the door in front of them flew open, almost sending Yuron Fuki pitching after his dead comrade.

The first palace guard through the door was killed by the Slaughter Shadow with a scarab supplicant forceps blow that entered at the eye and punched a hole clear through his skull before retracting with a fistful of brain. There were another nineteen crowded behind him; as the Blue Dragon agents engaged them with razor-stars, poisoned darts and vein-shredding daggers, Lady Sugarsting sprang up the wall and into the hole that now gaped in the corridor's ceiling. Crawling through the space between floors along rat-gnawed beams, she stopped above the iron vault's ante-chamber and softly pulled up another ceiling panel, finding herself above and slightly behind the palace defenders as they tried to cram into the doorway. A wire noose dropped and silently looped around the neck of the rearmost guard, tautening instantly and cutting off his airways. As the noose grew tighter and tighter it cut deep into his throat; blood started running in a river and then, finally, the man's head was completely severed and dropped to the floor with a wet thud.

Feeling hot blood splash over his face the next guard turned, but before he could look up Lady Sugarsting's second noose was around his neck and beginning its lethal constriction. By the time his head came off there were only two of his fellow defenders left standing; one was killed when Yuron Fuki drove a wall-spike through his temple, the other tried to surrender but was shown no mercy by Kagon Shura who slashed a silver star across his eyes, slicing them open, and then back across his throat. Jagon Ketsu and Tsunamon Shinga also lay among the dead, but there was no time to mourn their loss. The iron vault stood before them, seemingly impregnable and bolted from within.

Nezumon Nano was already primed for the final assault; he quickly located the vault's air-holes, its one weakness, and used a blow-pipe to fire through a succession of ceramic pellets which exploded inside, releasing choking clouds of toxic yellow gas. After two minutes the guards within, unable to breathe, were forced to unbolt the great vault door in order to escape; Nano's final gamble – that the sentries would put their own survival ahead of duty – had born fruit. The men were half-dead by the time they emerged, blinded and coughing blood, but Nano and Shura cut their throats anyway. Raising his mask to leave the merest eye-slit, Nano took a gulp of air and plunged into the bilious iron chamber.

When he emerged clutching the Key of Bones and the deathsword Tekizan, only a downstretched hand – Shura's – was visible in the ante-chamber; Nano grasped it and was hauled into the ceiling space a moment before Jukon Gomi and a dozen palace guards poured into the room from a concealed entrance. They were still searching amongst the carnage when the four Blue Dragon agents smashed through the ceiling beyond the far end of the corridor, dropped down and left by the same way they came in nearly an hour before.

"Stop them!" yelled Jukon. The vault was still too thick with gas to see what was missing, but in his heart he already knew. He had been so preoccupied with fomenting a war and diverting the Celestial Horde northwards that he never considered an attack of this nature as an imminent threat.

As Jukon rushed from the palace's main portal the darkness erupted with a devastating explosion of fire and dazzling light which blew away a vast section of the citadel wall and set ablaze a whole row of buildings, along with those trapped inside. Screams pierced the air already thick with smoke, fragmented debris and globules of molten wax. A man's blown-off head came spinning through the night, hair alight, and landed on the ground by Jukon's boot. A clockwork key, half-melted, was embedded in its brow like a vampire butterfly from the metal hells.

Every guard ran to the source of the inferno, allowing the four surviving raiders to slip through a deserted postern gate and disperse through the city, shedding their black cloth masks and vanishing into the teeming rabble.

# CASTLE MORTMANE

"Do you recall the story behind the painting?" asked Hikidashon, indicating *The Night Hag.*

Chikon studied the ominous diptych; what he recalled most was how it used to terrify him as a child. "It's the cannibal Yashroki, is it not? A servant of Baragasha who dwelt on Rajo moor... according to legend she would lure gravid travellers in order to cut out their unborn and eat them. Why do you ask?"

"A scene of horror, yet for the artist it also presents elements of the erotic – the way the victim is stripped nude, tied and hung upside down... it shows us how some revel in cruelty to the point of ecstasy. I believe Tazon Ando is such a man."

"Father... I know well the crimes Ando committed against us. And he will be punished for them."

"And if not? If he takes Mortmane... what might he do to your sister, if we can no longer protect her? The fact that she is but a child inflames him even more. We dare not wait for the Winter Palace to deliver us, we must act now." He turned to Flamon Neko, the Cave Cat. "Your plan?"

"As you say, Lord Hiki, Ando is driven by his lusts above all; lust for vengeance, and lust for the Lady Toka. This is his weakness. Perhaps both lust could be satisfied by one victory... if Lady Toka was offered to him as bride–"

"Never!" shouted Chikon, hand going to the hilt of his battlesword Membaku. "How could you suggest such an obscenity?"

"Please, Lord Chikon, let me explain," said Neko. "Ando has not seen Lady Toka for several years, since she was but five years of age; and there is a kitchen girl who bears enough resemblance to perhaps fool him. Not forever, but enough to cede us more time. We must trust that Noxon Taiyo is advancing with all speed."

"All well and good," said Hikidashon, "but not enough; Ando has to die."

"Then there is one final play," said Neko, "if the girl can carry it through – poison, from Lady Blastofane. An unguent, smeared inside the private parts, that would infect Ando in the bridal bed – death by depucelation."

"Then the girl dies too," said Chikon.

"She dies as soon as he accepts her, one way or another," said Hikidashon, "or she starves with the rest of us. Neko, your plan has poetic beauty – the traitor deceived and slain by his own foul desires, screaming as worms devour his cock. Chikon; let us ready this kitchen girl, and set up a parley under flag of truce."

Chikon reported back the following morning. "Ando agrees to meet. The girl has been told she is being rescued, and will be the wife of a great general; and that the unguent, secretly applied, will quicken her seeding with child and secure her future. She need merely assume the guise of another."

"Then go," said Hikidashon, "and may the Three Sorrows aid our cause."

Beyond the walls the daily chorus was as loud as ever. *Wife-boiler! Horse-fucker! All fall down!* Then, as Chikon emerged from the castle on horseback, the fields fell quiet. Hikidashon watched from atop the Joker's Keep as Tazon Ando rode out to face him, a meeting in the empty terrain between opposing forces. They talked for a long while, then Ando appeared to hand something to Chikon – a letter, which he read and then passed back. Then both parties turned and rode away to their respective ranks. The taunting shouts and clattering of shields began again almost immediately, and within minutes Boiler's Bane had delivered its second offering of the day, a giant scarecrow stuffed with horse dung and manticoras.

"What was all that about?" asked Gorn. Since his arrival two days earlier he had been expecting to help storm the castle, but now the way forward seemed less clear. "Are we taking Mortmane, or not?"

"Yes and no," said Tazon Ando. "I have no quarrel with Chikon Takasha or his sister, or with any other within Mortmane save for one – Hikidashon, the man who wronged me. Now, by allowing Chikon to meet with me, he has sown the seeds of his own destruction."

"Really? Because he looks quite safe up there in his Joker's tower – even if he's not laughing."

"You've obviously never played darkthrone – or you would know that the Joker is Death."

"Not much for cards, me; I'm more of a bone-rattler."

"Darkthrone uses both cards and dice – one to initiate killing, the other to determine the number of dead. I'll teach you how to play, one day."

"Not sure I'll be around long enough. After this I've made a deal with Urstinx and his boys – we're calling ourselves the Beasts of Blood, for hire to the highest bidder. A hundred berserkers can turn the tide of any battle, if applied at the right point. We'll set ourselves up at Hellhaven, that old madhouse just across the river; I've had enough of castles, they give me the shits. So is there a plan, or not?"

Ando smiled. "By this time tomorrow, all with be resolved. And you won't even need to get your sword wet."

# THE TEMPLE OF TEARS

It was almost noon when Quex and Darkon arrived at the foot of Kobutsuden's Hill of Angels. The whole citadel appeared to be in an uproar; smoke was still curling from the wreckage of a demolished wall and a row of burnt-out buildings, and a pair of monks were kneeling on the steps of the Temple of Tears furiously scrubbing at a large expanse of congealed blood.

"Looks like war," said Darkon. "I thought all the fighting was going to be up north."

Inside the temple they found the high maven, Namidarian, engaged in conversation with a man of around fifty, with greying hair, and a younger, plumper man who appeared to be his subordinate. When the two men eventually left, Namidarian said: "Greetings, brothers. You find us at a grim time."

The maven went on to relate recent events at the Winter Palace, when the imperial key and deathsword were stolen by audacious raiders, and then an equally shocking discovery that very morning.

"When Brother Braxion opened the temple doors, he found a dead man lying on the steps, pooled in blood. As I was just explaining to Questor Vordulax, prefect of the Starfire Watch, we found something most extraordinary – although not unprecedented – upon examining the corpse. The killer had cut out a deep rectangle of flesh from his victim's torso, and replaced it with a small wooden drawer."

"Fascinating," said Quexarian. "Did this drawer contain anything?"

"Most certainly – inside we found a severed finger, toad bones, a pearl embedded in a ball of dung, and a long white centipede studded with glass stars. The finger was not the victim's, I might add. This is the second time a corpse mutilated in such a way has been found outside the temple."

"And the earlier body – do you recall its contents?"

"Only some kind of venomous creature, which stung and killed the watchman who discovered it."

Quexarian fell silent then, as if searching his memory for some long-forgotten fact. Darkon stepped forward, held up his carry-sack and said: "We bring you a gift for the new Forbidden Chamber: the blasphemous grimoires of Shattonax, from the catacombs at Castle Bloodflower."

"Most welcome," said Namidarian. "It was long feared these were lost or, worse, fallen into wrong hands. We already have a number of other exhibits, which may interest you... come, let me show you."

The chamber was located at the rear of the temple, behind a door of blackened wrought iron embellished with demon-binding runes. Namidarian unlocked the door and waved his guests ahead. Wall-torches emitted a low, guttering light in which Darkon thought he could see the movement of mammoth hawk moths.

"This–" the maven pointed to a human skull which had been painted puce and decorated with white hexagonal jewels "–is the sole remnant of Lord Krobon Inoshi, ancient overlord of Skin Castle, whose corpse was stolen from its tomb by rebel priests and used in profane rituals designed to summon forth ice monsters from the frozen hells. And this–" he motioned towards a large, soot-stained cauldron "–is the very crucible in which Lord Pelluron Taiyo and his wife were cooked by Skull Hog savages during the Hundred-Finger Revolt. The cannibals believed that by eating and digesting their victims, they could forever incarcerate their souls in prisons of excrement."

"A most infamous incident," said Quexarian. "But going back to this morning's events, if I may; I believe that a very dangerous individual is at large in the city – an individual begging for our help, who is in mortal need of exorcism."

"But first we have to catch him," said Darkon. "And something tells me that's going to be my job."

"Actually that reminds me," said Namidarian, reaching into his robes and producing a loosely rolled letter. "I almost forgot – this came by white wing last evening." He handed it to Darkon. "Seems like your exploits have made quite an impression at the Storm Shrine," he added. "You've been conscripted."

# CASTLE MORTMANE

"By this time tomorrow, all with be resolved," said Chikon. "Ando accepts Toka's hand, and in the morning we will deliver the girl."

"And the letter he gave you – what was in it, exactly?" asked Lord Hikidashon.

"Terms of surrender – I rejected them in light of our new agreement, which will be drawn up for signature on the morrow."

"Then victory is ours, for he signs his own order of death."

That evening, Chikon met with the Iron Pentagram in the sequestered subterrain where he kept skulls of the vanquished lined upon racks. The four chaos agents looked drawn, no more than pallid haunts in the fire-gloom.

"Tazon Ando is a wronged man," he told them, "just as my mother was wrongfully executed. She was killed for one thing, and one thing only – love. Hear me out, brothers, for I ask your loyalty and trust."

"We were all raised in Mortmane together," said Flamon Neko. "We know your word to be true."

"Today I indeed learned a cruel truth," said Chikon, "and that truth is this: my father is a violent man, great in battle, but when drunk he turned his rage upon my mother. After years of assaults she turned to another – to Tazon Ando – for love. When my father found out he took vengeance by concealing the affair and accusing Ando, falsely, of lusting after my infant sister; when Ando escaped, my father sated his thirst for revenge by punishing my mother with death, claiming she pandered to an obscene defilement – one which never took place. I now know all this to be true, for today Tazon Ando showed me my mother's locket – gifted to him – and a declaration of love, written in her own hand. But this love was never consummated, there was no adultery committed; Ando swears it, the letter confirms it.

"There will be no wedding, false or not, no end to the siege until Ando savours justice. Should Mortmane fall and be put to the torch, should we all die, because of my father's crimes? As much as it pains me, I say that on the morrow our Lord Hikidashon must answer to the man he wronged. And so tonight, before dawn, we must open the castle gates."

"But there will be slaughter," said Yakyon Shoto.

"No. Ando alone will enter the Joker's Keep, and only he or my father will emerge. Either way, the siege will be ended."

"And if your father is victorious?"

"Then we face death, or a life of exile – much as now. So; are you with me?"

"Both men stand accused by the other; let us consider it a trial by combat," said Flamon Neko. "Under those terms, we will not bar the way."

At the hour of the hangman, directly before dawn, Lord Hikidashon Takasha was awoken by a relentless hammering on the door of his keep, followed by the shouting of a lone voice.

"Horse-fucker! Step forward to meet your doom!"

*Ando. The traitor is within the walls. Why do they not butcher him?*

It took the overlord several minutes to fully regain his senses, dress and arm himself, and peer down through the twilight from his chamber window. Tazon Ando stood at the portal, sword drawn, yet none moved to arrest him. And then Hikidashon recognized Chikon, standing passively behind the intruder.

"Betrayed by my own son!" he thundered.

Chikon looked up with a sudden, uncontrollable surge of rage and disgust. "Betrayed? You boiled my fucking mother!" With that, he turned away; despite everything, he would not watch his father die. Then the keep door shattered under Ando's boot, and the avenger bounded up its spiralling steps.

By the time he reached the high level, Hikidashon had emerged and was standing on the roofed walkway that joined the Joker's Keep to the Tower of Tombs, both hands gripping his war-hammer Yabuhaikin, smasher of spines. Halfway between the two men a spider was dangling on a web strand, its bulbous olive abdomen grained with red whorls.

"I shall not soil my keep with your blood, traitor," spat the Takasha overlord. "You die out here, like a dog."

"Better fangs than horns."

The jibe stirred Hikidashon into action; he strode at Ando with grim purpose, golden hammer raised above one shoulder. When the blow came, it was ferocious enough to crush bone to flinders; a lesser blade would have shattered beneath it, but the deathsword Akafuku deflected the hammer's arc just enough that its spiked iron head buried itself in the wooden planks of the bridge.

Hikidashon wrenched his weapon free just in time to avoid Ando's counterthrust, tearing up a whole section of the flooring. Then the hammer swung again, straight at Ando's head; as he stepped back to avoid it, his foot plunged straight through the hole in the walkway, trapping him fast. As Hikidashon raised Yabuhaikin for the death-strike, Ando made a desperate swing with Akafuku, the volcanic steel cutting clean through his attacker's leg at mid-shin. Hikidashon collapsed with a gurgling cry, releasing his grip on the war-hammer as the stump of his leg began to leak blood in bright waves. Ando struggled to free his own leg from the woodwork; Hikidashon pulled himself to his one remaining foot and limped away, his breath shallow, body convulsing, back to the Joker's Keep.

When Ando found him Hikidashon was slumped against a wall in his chamber, white-faced, *The Night Hag* above him, a pool of blood spreading from his ruined limb. His death-poem was written on the panelling beside him, scrawled by a shaking finger dipped in gore. *Black snow is falling, the full moon is dripping blood; I saw my own ghost trapped in a broken mirror, raising up my severed head.*

"You've fucked your last horse," Ando said, and with a swing of the deathsword he beheaded the man who had wronged him.

Chikon Takasha climbed the steps of the keep in dread of what he might find. As he reached the level of the walkway he saw a heavy spoor of lifesblood, leading from the single severed foot and lower leg which still stood there. The trail continued into the keep's interior; minutes later, Chikon was gazing down ruefully at his father's maimed corpse. His mother was avenged, and yet he felt only the absolute desolation of being alone in the world.

"He composed the poem the night I was born," Chikon said. "I suppose that tells you something."

"Only that some men fear to have children, that for them it represents a loss of purity, a draining of their life-force into another," Tazon Ando replied. "No fault lies with you, for who among us asks to be given life?"

"And yet, his dark vision was true; for by my actions I have killed him."

And then Chikon snatched up his father's bloody head from the floor, wedging it under one arm as he unsheathed Membaku and braced it against the chamber wall, hilt-first. Before Ando could stop him Chikon fell forwards onto the blade's point; it drove clean through his throat and burst from the back of his neck, sending him staggering sideways towards the tower window, lifesblood rushing in torrents from his lips, and even as he died he launched himself with his final expiration of breath, plunging from the keep with Hikidashon's head still tight in his grasp, down and down, smashing onto the flagstones below like one of the corpses fired from Boiler's Bane. The head rolled a little way, then came to rest staring up blindly at the rising sun.

# THE WINTER PALACE

"Welcome back to council, Prefect Vordulax," said Jukon Gomi. "As I mentioned, Lord Gomon is already on march to Mortmane, his clan castle, to accept control from Noxon Taiyo and the Takasha general Tazon Ando. Once in place, he faces the sad duty of burying his father and elder brother. When the Night Sun returns, he will take permanent place at this table."

"Until then I am at your service," said Zan Vordulax.

"And do you have matters to report?"

"Nothing of sufficient import to trouble us at this time of war." *Save the return of a killer I thought dead, and whom the temple mavens believe is possessed by demons.*

"Snowsnake?"

"The Nightmare Castle is secure; Lord Kyodokuron abstains from the war, but has provided Lady Miura with a thousand-strong castle guard armoured in iceshield, who now fly the banner of the Black Phoenix."

"And you, Veluron; what news from Sunstorm?"

"None of consequence. Mortmane concerns me more; are you sure that the castle will be secure?"

"The siege forces are dispersed. Many returned home to their smallforts and villages; some marched north to join the Hakamanko, but Hebon will need all his might to resist the Celestial Horde. And Noxon will leave half of his troops with Gomon when he comes back. Our main threat comes from Dorian Killstar and his rebels; who can predict what they will do next?"

"The dead night attackers had the thunderbolts of Clan Akutenshi tattooed on the soles of their feet," added Lady Snowsnake, "marking them as the emperor's chaos agents. So we may be sure that Killstar now has the key and sword."

It was the old maven Valadian Goldenbones who spoke next. "There is reason to believe that the Key of Bones has value beyond the merely symbolic. The forbidden library in House of Antiquaries holds a crude and illicit copy, made covertly by the renegade priest Cthaon, of a tome entitled *The Volcanic Codex*. Written by the Shadow mavens of ancient Kyukiden, this volume documents artefacts and weapons forged in the Ark, the mountain furnace of Komonyama, one thousand years ago. It speaks of the Seven Deadly Archangels, a force who will rise when the Age of Shadows falls upon the world. And the Seven Keys of Death are the power behind this force."

"But the other keys are lost, buried in the ice tombs of Kyukiden," said Jukon.

"Are they? Or do they repose at the Shadow Castle, waiting for their circle of power to be completed?"

"The Shadow Castle is a myth," hissed Lady Snowsnake. "An invisible fortress at the end of the world – surely none have seen it for good reason..."

"And yet, the Black Reaper and the Blue Dragon Hand were not killed in the Decimation," observed Jukon. "Does that not speak to a sanctuary beyond the city in the snow?"

"Impossible to say with certainty," said Valadian. "But if the Shadow Castle does exist, we can safely assume one thing – Dorion Killstar is bound for it even as we speak."

# GHOSTFINGER

The merchantman *Silver Sorrow* – one of many belonging to traders recruited for the Celestial Hive – lay at anchor in the shadow of Ghostfinger, tallest of the light-towers which lined the coastal stretch of the Stump, that truncated limb of the Viles which separated the ocean from Goldengate and, on its eastern border, was pocked by the stone warren known as the Eidolon Caves.

Two weeks earlier a night force had marched from the Sepulchre to the Sun Shrine, and from there split itself into two entities – Dorian Killstar and his entourage, bound for the coast, and the seven agents of chaos whose daring raid on the Winter Palace in Kobutsuden would be celebrated by future generations as the Night of the Living Dead. Now, the two would meet again aboard the *Silver Sorrow*, bound for the Port of Shrikes; from there it was a short haul by catboat to where the Akutenshi spy-ship *Thunderwing* lay ready to spirit them north to the Shadow Castle.

When the four agents of the Blue Dragon Hand reached Ghostfinger the Wolf Moon was already at its zenith, sowing the midnight tide with an undertow of shimmering luminescence. The derelict watchtower loomed above as they descended the near-vertical cliff-face to the beach and pushed a waiting rowboat out to sea, where the merchantman awaited them in total darkness. The Black Reaper was already aboard.

"News of your success precedes you," he said to Nezumon Nano. "All the south is ablaze with it, or so it seems. May I see the artefacts?"

Nano handed Kuron Kirizono the wrap of black velvet from his shoulder-sack. Tekizan, decapitator of foemen, glittered in the moonlight as Kirizono held it up by its hilt. "This is yours," he said to Dorion. "And this–" he picked up the Key of Bones "– belongs to the maven Glitterax."

"Three fell," said Nano. "Ketsu, Ushi, and Shinga."

"And they will be honoured at the Shadow Castle," Kirizono promised. "But now we must set sail – at once."

The *Silver Sorrow*'s captain, Sparkon Nimbo – called Paperskull by his crewmen for the many drawings of sea-monsters tattooed on his hairless pate – barked a series of commands. Within minutes the ship's anchor was raised and its hull began to creak with motion.

Not long after dawn they passed by the ruins of Hook Harbour, where the shore was still littered with the skeletal remains of cremated bloodships and drowned corsairs, the latter stripped clean by butcherbirds. Dorion Killstar stood on the forecastle, marvelling at the lightness and sharpness of his deathsword and its blade of volcanic steel. Soon he and Nano found a new game to play, involving bilge vermin dredged up by Lord Saltshanks, the ship's polydactyl ratter. "Six toes, just like me. Must be an omen," said Dorion. Nano would throw one of the live rats into the air, and Dorion's challenge was to slice it in half with Tekizan before it fell to deck. At first a few landed unscathed and scampered away, but by the second day not a single rat remained in one piece, boy and blade bonded in blood.

And then, on the third day, the Port of Shrikes came into view. As the *Silver Sorrow* edged towards dock the Akutenshi stowed themselves in the merchantman's hold, merging with its cargo of salted squid, bear pelts and rice liquor. Portside a Hakamanko officer boarded the vessel, accompanied by two enforcers. "Documents," he said, and then: "Your business?"

"Trade, pure and simple," said Sparkon Nimbo. "We'll be gone by sunrise."

"Once we've inspected the hold. Lord Hebon demands war tax on all goods entering Lizard's Den and the Shines."

Nimbo said nothing; to protest would only engender more suspicion. He watched as the two armed men disappeared below deck.

They were met by Lady Sugarsting, who engaged them in a discourse which grew ever more intense as she slowly dissuaded them from inspecting the depths of the ship's interior. Dorion peered from behind a rack of spread skins, watching as the agent punctuated her words with circular movements of an open-palmed hand; the men's eyes seemed to follow, as if her words and gestures were exerting some form of magnetic attraction. Then, their expressions visibly softened, the men turned and retraced their steps.

"How did you do that?" Dorion asked her that night, as the Akutenshi were lowered over the seaward side of the vessel in a pair of lamplit catboats.

"Poison kisses, sugar stings," she replied, with a smile as mysterious as the secret blossoming of a rare carnivorous flower. And suddenly, Dorion Killstar was spellbound.

# STICKLEBACK BIGHT

It took most of the remaining dark hours to drift along the coast to Stickleback Bight, and when they got there *Thunderwing* was gone.

"The Hakamanko soldiers… they commandeered the ship, there was nothing we could do," said the sea-village elder. "They said it was a smuggling vessel, because of the black sails. Now they use it for patrols, returning every three days. They do this with all the ships they can seize."

"And when are they due to return?" asked Kuron Kirizono.

"This very morning," the man replied.

"And then?"

"And then they come ashore to drink and to rape our wives and daughters for a day and a night. Any who intervene are slaughtered." With that the man motioned towards the harbour wall. Three heads were spiked there, gull-pecked and green.

The Black Reaper turned to Dorion Killstar. "Today the rats will be the human kind," he said.

They waited in the sea-village chapel, where icons and statues of the Three Sorrows had all been smashed and pissed on by Hakamanko patrols, the altar desecrated with crude etchings of snakes and scorpions with exaggerated human genitals. The more Dorion thought about what was to come, the more his hands shook and his stomach churned. He was used to handling dead bodies, but he'd never had to kill one first.

"Let the deathsword guide your hand," Kirizono told him. "The vampire steel feeds not just on the blood of your enemies, but also on your own rage. You must let it flow…"

He never finished his speech, for just then a horn sounded to signal a ship approaching. From the chapel dark they watched as *Thunderwing* washed in from sea, anchoring in the shallows. More than a dozen Hakamanko fighters disembarked and waded ashore, tunics sewn with a snake-bone motif; they were heading straight for the Fat Egg, the only tavern in Stickleback Bight. As they went they hammered on doors, shouting. *Women! Now!*

What they got was something different.

Kuron Kirizono stood in the tavern doorway, filling it. None of the soldiers moved or spoke.

"You are guilty of stealing an imperial ship," said Kirizono. "The penalty is death."

One of them laughed, nervously. Then another, evidently their captain, stood up and drew his sword. "Kill him!" he yelled.

As they poured towards him Kirizono stepped forward crying "For Raikon!" and landed a hacking blow on the first of them, severing his arm at the shoulder. Without pausing he swung his blade back, up, and across the next, carving off his face. Then the fight became a red gavotte, a whirlwind of steel, exploding bone chips and ribboning meat, and in that moment the Black Reaper became as one with his greatsword Oshi, the king of death made flesh, and his song was as beautiful and terrible as the feasting of a thousand blood-crazed wolves in the crystal chasm of night.

After the death-dance two soldiers still stirred beneath the pile of heads, limbs and entrails left by the Reaper's butchery. One was the captain, his right ear shorn off by a blow which should have opened his skull; the other was a blond-haired man curled by a wall, weeping and clutching at the stumps of his legs.

"Finish him," Kirizono said to Dorion.

"But he can't fight back... is it right?"

"Call it mercy," said Jagon Shura.

Dorion approached the maimed soldier and raised Tekizan above his right shoulder, gripping it with both hands. Suddenly he saw an image of the death-strike in his mind's eye, and all hesitation drained away. The deathsword came scything down, effortlessly, and its edge removed the man's head so cleanly that Dorion scarcely felt it. A great jet of lifesblood went up, then splashed him all over like hot rain. Elated, he turned to the one-eared captain.

"I demand a fair trial," the man said, hand raised to defend his neck. "Even in war, there must be justice."

Dorion drove his blade into the captain's belly and then twisted it clockways as hard as he could. When he pulled it free the man's intestines followed, uncoiling like steaming snakes cut free from a sack. Just before his heart stopped he saw the blood-splattered youth leaning over him, eyes burning with a lust for unbridled havoc.

"I *am* justice," said Dorion Killstar.

# THE SHADOW CASTLE

"So you are the one," said Glitterax. "Our future emperor, Raikon the Second. Welcome to the Shadow Castle."

"Please, call me Dorion," said Dorion Killstar. "I am no emperor until all Novalis kneels before me."

"Wise words," said Kuron Kirizono. "Glitterax will continue your education in alchemical matters – and don't worry, he won't be asking you to fetch any corpses."

"I am obliged," said Dorion.

"Tekizan has tasted fresh blood," Kirizono said to the maven. "And so it begins. What news of the Holy War?"

"The Celestial Horde advances on two fronts, Sun and Storm, each backed by ten thousand drone fighters. The Snake Lord sends his lizard-riders and banner-bearers; our spies also report rumours that he has recognised a second son, a witch's bastard devoted to conjurings."

Dorion spent his first day at the castle exploring its different levels and structures. He found that its sea-facing walls were seamed here and there with ragged openings, no more than cracks in the rock-face, through which he could squint out at what lay beyond. It was a frigid, watery void without colour, without visible end, gravid with latent terrors. *This truly is the edge of the world,* he thought.

Everywhere he went, the shadow-men watched him; the dark form of each Akutenshi emperor, seared into the natural rock. One day his silhouette would be imprinted there too, Glitterax told him, marking the rise of a new dynasty. But he would not see the maven again that day.

As soon as the Black Reaper passed him the Key of Bones, Glitterax had taken it in both hands like a long-lost child and hurried away to the chancel, bolting the doors behind him. The seven female bodies were still reposed upon their biers, the fragrant candles still burning, the nude gemstone statues still frozen in heroic pose. But now he held the seventh and final instrument of power, forged by the Shadow mavens in the white hot core of the volcano.

Of the seven sleeping seraphim only Lady Morella, gowned in white, lay devoid of her metal nucleus. Glitterax poised above her, key in hand, then gently pushed the circular disc into the aperture between her exposed breasts. When he rotated it clockways, once, he was sure he felt a surge of energy through his fingers, heard the crackle of orgones in the metacarrion. One by one he stooped over each supine form, reaching down to twist the heart-keys, until all seven seemed to spark with the pulse of life – Morvenna, Valessa, Carnella, Tyranna, Sybella, Samara and Morella, Akutenshi warcraft incarnate.

Glitterax stood back and exulted over his working. The Seven Deadly Archangels were risen and Dorion Killstar wielded the deathsword Tekizan, Black Reaper at his side. And now all of Novalis would learn the meaning of divine terror – from the western wastelands to the decadent south, and back to the black haunts of Skull Castle in the east. Haunts where even now Moshino, bastard of Hellhaven, and his pack of madhounds gurgled and grimaced as they conducted their own rites of war, straining to breathe life into the prone form of Baron Feculax, a thirty-foot giant made entirely of human filth.

# PART FIVE
# THE AGE OF SHADOWS

# SKULL CASTLE

"Moshino! *Moshino!*"

Lord Hebon's shout rang through the corridors of Skull Castle, but he got no response. *He must be beyond the walls again,* Hebon told himself, *or else agaze in the gallery.* He had noticed how his son was drawn unerringly, time and time again, to one particular portrait of the many that hung in the castle's ancestral hall; it was a likeness of Hojexon Hakamanko, only son of Haxokokon. While Haxokoken had built the clan's redoubt at the edge of the Mad Marshes, it was Hojexon – known as Deathwürm by posterity – who first mastered the venom-spraying lizards that roamed within the swampland depths. Astride a massive, green-scaled creature named Vorko, Hojexon led a cohort of seven würm-riders in rampages across the demesne, subjugating the feral clans that dwelt there; men called them the Bone-Raiders, for they left nothing in their wake save a swathe of smoking skeletons.

Moshino would look upon Deathwürm's image for hours on end, as one hexed by his own reflection; and it was as if one twin were mirrored by the other, so alike were their red-eyed visages.

Since starting to mould the homunculus – or shit giant, as the boy called it – Moshino had grown ever more impulsive and harder to control. Just the day before, his gang of lunatics had run riot in the search for bones; luckily they were unable to breach the black crypts of Hebon's ancestors, but graveyards guarding generations of deceased castle mavens and viragos were upturned. One of the madmen was seen prancing with a thighbone to his lips like a flute, while another crashed two skulls together and howled in a shower of corpse-worms.

Hebon knew that Moshino saw the world through the eyes of a puzzled and vicious child, nurtured on shapes, japes and sing-song. Growing up in Hellhaven his only family were the madfolk; from homicidal butchers who hopped in circles with their heads wrapped in sausages to one-eyed leper fire-starters, Moshino had seen them all and thought each one as normal as the next. And then there was his mother, Lady Silversoil, self-proclaimed mother of scorpions, who fed him sour milk from the teat and psychosis from the tongue. Little wonder, then, that this bastard beast-boy felt no remorse at the slaughtering of women and unborn babes, and now had no doubt that Baron Feculax would soon stride out across the marshes, roaring and spitting fiery turds, and mash the holy forces of Storms and Sun into red gruel underfoot.

Most days Hebon's time was consumed by reports from the battlefront. The Celestial Horde had now advanced to the fringes of the Mad Marshes, where hundred upon hundred of their foot soldiers threatened to overwhelm the first defensive line of Hakamanko würm-riders. Bolgo, one of Hebon's most prized marsh dragons, had been captured and put through a meat-grinder. Each night the warrior-priests hanged any prisoners taken during the day; Vexion, Bolgo's rider and Hebon's champion, was among those who perished naked and jerking at rope's end while feral dogs circled below, hungry to gobble up each body's final evacuation.

Each night the Snake Lord brooded over these vexations, cursing his dead son for the act of madness which had brought war upon them. *I should never have let him out of the castle, I should have locked him away with his dead playthings and his whining bride. Moshino was the warrior, not Hekon; but I never knew he was even born. Now it falls to Heba, flesh of my flesh, to shatter Starfire from within.* And so Hebon Hakamanko would sit ashadow, sleepless and silent, stroking a lock of his sister's bone-white hair.

While his father received messengers and conspired with council, Moshino toiled to breathe fire of life into his latrine-spawned leviathan, Baron Feculax. They had now raised up the thirty-foot effigy with hempen hawsers; it stood before the castle drawbridge like an ancient sentinel, its iron skeletal core caked in sun-dried excrement and an inch-thick veneer of dead flies, maggots and intestinal parasites. Its eyes were ragged holes lined with shattered fox-skulls, where burning candles gave the flickering illusion of sentience. According to the *Black Psalter*, an immolation of consecrated human remains was essential to complete the working, and Moshino's Hellhaven madhounds were out on the charnel trail.

It was near sunwane when a tuneless chanting heralded the return of the bone-foragers. *Scorpion claw and scorpion eye, spider-belly in the sky, kiss the king and watch him die, scorpion claw and scorpion eye.* The words were sung in two jarring voices, the piping tones of Baby Brimstone and the phlegm-soaked croak of Wormcrackle, one of the old candlemen scooped up from Hellhaven during the night-trek from the Black Cage to Skull Castle. The other madhounds were giggling and whooping as they pulled along a cart laden with corpses. Some of the bodies had been newly unearthed, others not.

"This 'un's fresh from gallows," drooled the Knave of Stumps. "There's enough bones here to build a tattle-tower, once we scrape off meat."

Moshino turned to the warlocks Crowface Crak and Mik Maggot-Dancer. "Get scraping," he said.

By gloaming some two dozen bodies had been defleshed, the rotting meat and guts fed to the moat-würms apart from a few lengths of intestine which Cat-A-Bodkins kept for skipping rope. The skeletal remains were disarticulated and placed in piles – skulls, thigh-bones, shoulder-blades, hip-bones, ribs, spines, all separated into discrete arrays so that come morning Moshino could sift through and pick the finest specimens of each. These would be fused into a master skeleton, a kingly composite fit for sacrificial cremation.

The chill of encroaching night saw a yellowy fog rise up from the swamps below, thick with particles of scorched human skin. The stench took Moshino's mind back to his childhood in Hellhaven, when the Sun mavens would fire up a row of cast-iron ovens to dispose of human remains, the butchered cadavers of lunatics subjected to vivisection in the pursuit of anatomical science. As the bodies smoked and sizzled Lady Silversoil would soothe Moshino with the same lullabies that he had now passed on to his cackling crew, who recited them as they gathered around a blaze of bloody shrouds and coffin wood. *A spider and a sparrow, a monster made of marrow, the king of knives chopped up his wives and burnt them in a barrow* they sang, and *maggots in the mirror, a shadowful of shivers, the king of swords chopped up his whore and threw her in the river.*

"When brother death the bony man turns to ash, the brown baron's hour is upon us," said Moshino as he poked the fire with a stick. "Who brought supper?"

"Me!" cried Captain Kisscrawl, pulling out a red-stained cloth bundle.

"And me!" added Baby Brimstone, producing a stone jar.

Inside the cloth was a dead hare, a pregnant female with its back snapped in two, eyes missing. Brimstone put a hand into her container and pulled out a fistful of fat pink beetles.

"Cook 'em in the jar," said the Knave of Stumps, "and skewer t'other from tooth to arse."

As the madhounds prepared their evening feast, Crowface Crak and the Maggot-Dancer slipped away. Like most of the lower clans they abhorred the company of lunatics, yet they knew that their lives depended on appeasing Moshino; any dissent and Lord Hebon would have them skinned and salted, then burn alive their families and villagefolk.

In the shelter of Crak's fur-draped tent, Crak said: "Come dawn they'll set bonefyres, nought will happen, and we'll be back paring corpses. I'd rather be down below fighting the crusaders."

"Aye," said Mik. "Better a sword through the heart than a slow death up here with the mad cunts."

Just then they heard a terrible scream. As they peered out from the tent a woman's severed head plummeted from the sky and smashed into the grass outside. Gouts of blood exploded from its mouth upon impact, and there were white worms swimming in the blood. Where the head came from, or whose it once was, neither man could say.

# THE SHADOW CASTLE

"But if I am your emperor, and you serve me, should you not obey my every command?" demanded Dorion.

Kuron Kirizono smiled. Raikon's young bastard was becoming more assertive as each day of training and tuition passed, an unfettering of the hellfire heritage simmering in his blood. "In the course of time; but now I serve you by keeping you alive until you may claim the imperial throne, and to keep you alive I must control you. Have faith, Dorion. The time draws ever nearer."

Dorion paused, then said: "And what about the Blue Dragon Hand? Lady Sugarsting, for one – is she not subject to my will?"

"Like me, the Hand are sworn to protect their emperor. But you are not yet that. I've seen you watching Sasora, Dorion, but chaos agents are not concubines. For her sex is a weapon, not a duty."

"A weapon?"

"How do you think Noxon Taiyo was persuaded to march north with his army, leaving the Winter Palace exposed to our night-raid? Once Sasora traps a man's cock inside her, he is powerless to resist. Take care, Dorion – she's a scorpion, and I'm sure you know what happens when scorpions mate."

Dorion had heard. *The female kills and devours the male. Not quite how I see my future. And yet...*

In truth, Dorion Killstar was ill-versed in matters carnal. Although born and raised in a brothel, he was sent to train at the Sun Shrine before puberty, taking a monastic vow of celibacy. His first time with a girl came later, while serving at the Ossuary. She was a beauty who haunted his dreams; full-lipped, blonde-haired... and dead. Seeing her nude corpse on its mortuary slab next to the murdered butcher whose arms he was sent to steal, Dorion was unable to control his lust. Soon after that the nightmares began, frightful sojourns during which his soul was tormented in a realm beyond the tomb.

Sasora Sato had seen Dorion watching, too. A boyish infatuation, perhaps, but one day that boy would be emperor. And when the Wolf Moon rose and fell without bringing its tidings of blood, a seed of ambition was planted deep within her mind. In an ornately framed looking-glass she studied her naked belly, tautly curved above an arrow-head of straight black hair. Her breasts, each nipple circled by a foreclaw of the indigo dragon tattoo adorning her upper torso, back and buttocks, were already ripening. When this happened once before she quickly sought remedy from Lady Slaxonslit, the emperor's bane virago; but Slaxonslit and her nightside apothecary were long buried in the rubble of Kyukiden. If the comet strike which destroyed the city was willed by the Triad, then Sato would let the Triad guide her now.

The Fever Moon was little more than a lucent rind when Glitterax made his first war report. In the Shadow Castle's lower levels, lapped by the waters of a phosphorescent underground lake, the maven unfurled a map of Novalis in front of Killstar, Devil Bat and Black Reaper, last council of the Akutenshi bloodline. It was now several weeks since the Seven Archangels had left the castle, each accompanied by two agents of chaos; only two Blue Dragons remained behind to help tutor the emperor-to-be in ways of warfare and wisdom.

"As you know," said Glitterax, "*Thunderwing* sailed west to the Port of Shrikes, and from there our angels of death entered the world of men. And so the blood crusade begins."

"So who will they kill first?" asked Dorion impatiently. "This Jukon Gomi, who persists with his Starfire rebels, or the sorcerer Hakamanko?"

"Neither. For now, the Celestial Horde lead our offensive; and already they are cutting a path to Skull Castle. And the clans of Starfire, despite their resistance, are not our true enemy – yet. The Archangels have a different mission – to reunite the thirteen deathswords forged by our first emperor."

"We already hold Tekizan, the imperial sword," said Kirizono. "What of the others?"

"Kinzokami, Jigobanmon, Seppunryu and Kyami are held by clans of the Starfire Order. Yahana lies lost in the swamps of Lizard's Den. Kaijuken and Honekiri are both held by the Seikyo; Akafuku was stolen by a Takasha rebel, named Tazon Ando. Kurosatsu, and probably Obochi, are held by the Hakamanko, while Yomuji sits in its ancestral hall at Bloodtooth. Only Sensoni, held at the Storm Shrine, is within our orbit; a temple rider bears it to the Sepulchre as I speak. There the Blind Brotherhood will secure every recovered sword in the castle's underground armoury."

"And if we take them all back?" asked Dorion.

"Death-power," said Glitterax, and his eyes were flaming mirrors.

# THE WINTER PALACE

The messenger was a Flame Rider of the Fireball Dead, fiercely loyal to Sunstorm, and he said: "Our troops will reach the city by nightfall on the morrow, led by General Gentetsu. Lord Noxon flies in pursuit of the Takasha rebel and murderer Tazon Ando, last reported bound for the Valley of Flies."

"What?"

This was not news Jukon Gomi wished to hear; Noxon Taiyo was supposed to make swift return from Mortmane and take his seat on the Starfire Council, not risk his life charging across the heartlands after some fugitive. Hebon Hakamanko and the pretender Dorion Killstar were the threat they should be most concerned with, surely that was self-evident.

"Tell me he did not go alone."

"He did not," said the messenger. "A battalion of my fellow Flame Riders accompanies him. They are sworn to spike the rebel's head upon the gates of Kobutsuden by moon's end."

"Very noble," said Jukon, waving the man away. He looked at Veluron Taiyo and shook his head. "Is your uncle always so impulsive, so reckless?"

"Night Sun is the most fearless of us all," said Veluron. "And hunting is his favourite sport."

Jukon said nothing more to him. He knew that Noxon Taiyo was the shining hero of Goldengate, the sun-blessed warrior who slew the cannibal giant, who tracked and captured the evil hunchback; this also made him a symbol of the Starfire cause whom they could ill afford to lose. Instead he turned to Lady Snowsnake, and asked: "What news of your Black Phoenix?"

The white-haired war-witch scowled, baring metal-clad teeth. "Little to nothing. After the assassination of Hectoclarion she retreated to the Terror Tower, where she is guarded night and day by the Vertigo Watch. In his last letter Chironax complained that these days she ignores his counsel, and prefers to consort with the Kurotako maven Chromocrax, a maker of dolls."

"I see," said Jukon. *Then she can clearly be of no help in the matter. Night Sun is a man alone. Unless...*

And in that moment Jukon Gomi cast aside the burden that had weighed upon him since the moment he discovered the smoking skull, sword and key of Raikon Akutenshi in the ashes of Thundervoid, a burden of office that threatened to crush young shoulders more used to swinging the bloody sword of battle. He surrendered to the spectres that ruptured his sleep each and every night, spectres of vengeance railing for retribution against the man who killed his father and sister, and against all those who threatened to plunge Novalis into chaos and negation.

"Then I will go Noxon's aid myself," he announced. "No use sitting here and waiting any longer; the time for action is at hand. From this moment on, the Starfire Order takes war to its enemies."

Snowsnake and Veluron looked at each other, taken aback by this sudden change of heart. Valadian Goldenbones asked: "But our plan? To wait until the outcome of the Horde's assault upon the Hakamanko is clear?"

"The plan is good," said Jukon. "But I won't be waiting here with you. A rock-ranger needs to range, and that's what I intend to do."

The maven blew a breath, but seemed to accept Jukon's decision. "And the council?"

"Keep Vordulax in place for now, and I'll find someone to hold my seat. You will assume the role of arbiter until I return."

That evening Jukon called together fifty loyal and seasoned men, Gomi rock-rangers with whom he had long patrolled the northern and southern foothills of the Stone Brides. Most had fought beside him in the rice revolt, harvesting heads of Spectre Moth renegades who rose up over taxation and launched raids on a chain of ringforts from Mount Snowblaze to Mount Rottenstag. He elected the oldest, Andon Kato, to be his proxy at council; the rest were told to make ready to ride out at dawn.

The Fever Moon was nearing its zenith, bathing Jukon's face with addled rays as he lay abed. He was thinking of his sister Juka, his twin, and their childhood games in the angular alcoves of the Mirror Castle. Above all she favoured a charade they called *pistacat*, in which they would covertly spy upon their father, Lord Kamosukon, as he sat adream within his scrying dome. Juka would copy the swirling quicksilver shapes in his orbs onto parchment, and gave them the names of demons; Baron Pistacat, she said, was the demon king of the castle, and the shapes were his minions. Their mother, Jetta, was still alive then, but when the ulceration sickness rotted her bones to black soup Juka changed; although it made no sense, she blamed herself for their mother's death, insisting that the disease was inflicted by the scrying-demons.

Jukon knew in his heart that Juka was also dead, but he vowed not to rest until her body or bones were returned to him and buried in the palace crypt far beneath him. Until her killer, the Snake Lord, was drained of every drop of blood. First he would join with Night Sun to destroy Tazon Ando for his crimes against Starfire; then the real battle would begin.

# CASTLE MORTMANE

She came on silver horseback, doom in a deep purple gown. On one side rode Kagon Shura, the Slaughter Shadow, and on the other Yonakon Chimori, the Bloody Midnight. Hidden beneath a high velvet collar, the Key of Venoms throbbed, silently, in Lady Valessa's breast.

Deep within Mortmane, Gomon Takasha sat in shadow. Behind him hung Flayon I's *Night Hag*, the painting favoured by the father he had but recently interred far below, in the crypt where he and his brother Chikon, also dead and buried, once comported. Above the sinister diptych hung the clan deathsword Kyami, master of darkness. Gomon now carried Chikon's blade, Membaku, and had sworn to one day bury it in the heart of Tazon Ando, his father's killer. Ando had already vanished when Gomon arrived from Kobutsuden; Noxon Taiyo – whose forces came too late to avert tragedy – had set out for the Winter Palace soon after the double funeral. And so Gomon sat, and brooded on the future of his clan.

Shortly past noon a cry rang out from atop the castle spy-tower.

"Riders!"

Fearing a new assault by Hebon Hakamanko, who now controlled most of the Shines to the north, Mortmane was in a permanent state of alert; but the approaching figures numbered just three, and flew a banner of truce. And one of them, Gomon saw, was a woman.

He received them in the castle library, a circular room which spanned the lower rung of the Joker's Keep, where the woman announced: "I am Lady Valessa of the Shadow Castle, and these are my lifesguard. I come as peace envoy in the name of Dorion Killstar, the one and true emperor of Novalis."

Her voice was deeper than Gomon might have expected, and seemed to carry its own faint echo. And she had larger eyes than any woman he had ever met, as rich in purple promise as the dress which tightly encased the curves of her body. "The Shadow Castle is real?" he asked. "I had always thought it from myth. But tell me of this peace you mention."

"I speak of uniting the Akutenshi and the Starfire Order against a common foe," said Valessa. "But we have travelled long and far; might we avail of your hospitality, and discuss the matter at dinner?"

"Very well," said Gomon. He doubted that the Akutenshi had anything worthwhile to offer short of withdrawing their audacious claim to power, but the allure of this dark-haired, statue-like visitor was undeniably compelling. He would hear her proposition and then, perhaps, suggest some terms of his own.

As night palled Mortmane's siege-scarred walls, Gomon sat across from Lady Valessa at the castle's high table; her two guardsmen, relieved of weaponry, were seated on the lower level. The envoy scarcely seemed to eat or drink, and fixed him intently with her gaze as she spoke.

"My proposal is simple," she said. "We ask only for your deathsword, Kyami; in return, the emperor offers his protection against the Hakamanko."

Gomon frowned for a second, then laughed softly. "Forgive me, but I thought you were here to propose an alliance; that sounds more like pledging fealty to an unproven pretender. I can tell you that the Starfire Council would never accede to such a request. Surely you know this?"

"Which is why I am asking you directly," said Valessa, her voice seeming to resound upon itself as if two spoke from one throat. "Let me assure you of this: once the Akutenshi hold all thirteen deathswords, no power in Novalis will be able to resist us. This is your chance to align with that power."

"Or prevent it," said Gomon. "If Kyami remains at Mortmane, your ambitions are still-born, are they not? Even if you could somehow obtain the other swords."

Lady Valessa's head tilted almost imperceptibly. For a second, Gomon thought he saw a glow beneath her gown; at the same time, from the corner of his eye, he was aware of Morla, his servant-girl, glaring up with unmasked jealousy from the gallery. *That will cost her tits another stripe of the lash*, he thought, just as Valessa began coughing violently. "Water!" Gomon demanded, but then the coughing stopped and Valessa leaned forward over the table. Something emerged from the painted purple bow of her lips, slowly, and dropped onto her plate. It looked like an egg woven from coarse black hair, matted with slime, and it stank of rancid bile.

"The lady has taken ill," said Gomon. "Accompany her to her chamber at once. And remove this filth from the hall."

Finding his appetite lost along with any thoughts of seducing the voluptuous stranger, Gomon retired to his own quarters. The woman's cold arrogance troubled him; *why would she so nakedly reveal her clan's intentions?* It was as if she spoke of an inevitable outcome, a course of events which Gomon had, in truth, no hope of averting. He looked up at Kyami, the blade once wielded by his father and their forebears stretching back to the rule of Metakaikon. If the legend of Shadow Castle was real, then why not the volcanic power of the deathswords, sibling blades which fed off each other's dark energy in a vampire hex? This, after all, was the Age of Shadows – a time when all prophecies were said to become manifest.

Gomon snuffed out his candles and took to bed. *In the morning she'll be gone,* he told himself. And he would send warning word to Jukon Gomi on the hooves of Mortmane's swiftest stallion.

# THE VELVET CASTLE

"These masques are always the same," sighed Viron Voraxo as the curtain fell. "The dwarf fucks the slattern, then the dwarf is hanged by the avenging husband, then the husband is poisoned by the slattern. If the dwarf-hangings weren't real, it would be all too tedious."

"Well, we shan't go short of rope-fodder," said Glamgaxion. "Rumour has it that a whole tribe of dissident dwarfs are rampaging through the northside foothills of the Brides – it seems that some have infested the ruins of Skin Castle, where they hold nightly orgies and sacrifices to sybaritic idols. Their leader, a powdered rogue by name of Silko Smallbones, once served as catamite to the Moon mavens of Sukion. Now they follow the Idiot King, a renegade berserker who took the Night Ride before the battle of Slaughtershriek – they say his body returned, but his mind did not."

"No surprise," said Voraxo. "Lord Hebon speaks of a new order, but in truth the whole of the Shines is now reduced to chaos. We must act quickly, before Lizard's Den is over-run by the Celestial Horde."

"Our spies are seldom wrong," the wall-eyed maven assured him. "The Beasts of Blood have already proven their worth; in the paid service of Kyowashon Seikyo they wiped an army of marauding Corpse-Riders from the Stump, despite being outnumbered two to one. Nothing remained of the Corpse-Riders save a gore-rimed lake of crushed and powdered bone. And we are offering twice as much as Lord Kyowashon."

"And the Kurotako?"

"Lord Sadogashon has already signed our blood charter, and accepted coin; three of his ships stand ready to sail north from the Bay of Bones."

Voraxo seemed satisfied by this. He waved Glamgaxion about his business and sat back in the dark of the small, windowless hall which served as a theatre for his entertainment. Tapestries covered every expanse of wall, woven with images of fornication. Tonight he would send word to Baron Kravox that their plan was underway; before the Fire Moon rose, he was sure, they would possess the mortal remains of Bankairon Demon-Slayer.

*Eyeballs of shit and a skeleton of roses.* Viron Voraxo never forgot those words, the first uttered to him by Kravox during his sole, yet momentous, séance at the Velvet Castle. Bald, emaciated and taloned, the Baron had resembled some ancient gargoyle come to life as his attenuated frame unfurled in stiff, jerking increments from the litter which had borne him from Skullhaven in the south. Black hollows ringed his eye-sockets, matched by thick, mica-dusted swatches of charcoal on the lids. And when he spoke, the sound evoked nothing so much as a plague of insects on the wing.

That night they had pored over an original binding of the *Black Psalter* until, just before cock-crow, Kravox's servants hurried him away to the pitch-dark, ice-cooled room especially prepared for him according to his prior demands.

"It is written in these pages that when the Age of Shadows falls upon us, a scion of Hell will rise to rule Novalis," Kravox had begun. "As you must know, Lord Hebon believes himself to be this scion, by way of direct descent from Hakamanton, founder of the Vermin League, whose master was the infernal king Zenmarion. He believes that the first overlord of Clan Hakamanko, his ancestor Haxokokon, was no less than Hakamanton's own offspring. Be this true or not, the *Black Psalter* is clear – the role of the league is not to elect, but to create."

Kravox had pointed to an out-folding sequence of pages, hand-painted by the necroxicon's nameless authors. It showed all the elements of a black magic working; scorpions, flowers, human embryos arranged in geometric patterns, hooked crosses of excrement squeezed from the bowels of dissected corpses, and chains of flesh-eating myriapods. On the final page was an illustration of the working's climax: the birthing of a towering homunculus, housed in a skin of spiky, chitinous plate. Next to it human bones were piled, burning with blue flame.

"A blasphemous combustion of sacred bones bestows life," Kravox had explained. "The master of the homunculus is master of Novalis. But Hebon is a snake, boned on the inside; his flesh will burn in the furnace of creation."

The baron's words had rung true with Viron. *Hebon has often spoken of his birthright; for him, the homunculus is merely a symbol. Yet it was here, in this very castle one thousand years ago, that Haxokokon and my own forefather the maven Vikozakoton first raised a colossal beast to sodomise the brides of Hell.*

"This fundamental schism of serpent and scorpion is at the crux of our dilemma," Kravox concluded. "To uphold the *Psalter* is to rebel against our overlord; but to do nothing is a desecration that would surely see the imperial clans prevail against a false prophet."

Voraxo remembered falling silent at the baron's revelations, and realising that the annihilation of Emperor Raikon, just a moon's turn before, had left a vacuum which could only be filled by the most ruthless and tenacious among them.

"Tell me what to do," he said finally. "With your wealth and my position in Hebon's hierarchy, we are uniquely placed to change the course of history."

Baron Kravox said nothing. His long forefinger hovered over the illustration of the working, then tapped the burning bones with a discoloured talon, twice. Voraxo shivered, the candles dimmed and flared.

A freezing wind swept in from the glassy wastes of Thundervoid, gravid with invisible organisms; they splashed against the northern walls of the Velvet Castle, intractably taking root.

# THE SUNSTORM CASTLE

After three months of intensive training in the preparation and administering of poisons, Lady Suna Kurotako – thenceforth to be known as Crimsonclaw, the bloody hand of death – was set free from Sunstorm, with an armed escort to Kobutsuden and sufficient coin for a month's lodging and board.

"I trust you will find a position suited to your talents," Taikon Taiyo told her on the morning of her departure. "Lady Feverclaw tells me that you have a natural gift for banecraft which goes beyond mere science and into the realm of art."

"The good lady flatters me," said Suna. "But it's true that I was able to create my own signature – a toxic perfume which, when absorbed through the skin, will paralyse the human heart within thirty minutes. I call it hekonite, in deference to the former husband whose cruelties so often froze my own heart with dread. I only wish he were alive to sample it."

Taikon said nothing; Suna leaned forward, kissed him once on the lips, and was gone.

*Her beauty masks a shredded soul*, thought Taikon that night. *I fear for any who cross her*. And yet, he already felt her absence more keenly than he ever imagined. On the morrow he would turn his attention to matters of war, he decided; though Goldengate was as yet unscathed by the horrors unfolding in the north, rumour had it that the Takasha rebel Tazon Ando had crossed the lawless heartlands south of the Crow River and was returning to haunt the Valley of Flies, rekindling the threat of invasion by a barbarian horde. Perhaps the time had come to wipe out this Ando once and for all.

Hundreds of feet below Taikon's chambers, in a place where there was no night and no day, the carnifex Sawtooth was feeding the castle's prisoners. He had gladly provided two moribund specimens for the deadly experiments carried out in recent weeks by Lady Feverclaw and her young pupil; not only did it free two cells for new inmates, but their corpses – butchered and put through the mincer along with a clutch of dead rats – had provided fodder for the rest of his wretched charges for a fortnight.

As was his custom, Sawtooth saved Sunstorm's most nefarious denizen until last. The hunchback was slumped in a corner of the subterrain's most remote dungeon, glazed in a filth of his own faeces and retchings. The cell was covered in a layer of rat droppings in which yellow tooth shards and bird-bones were scattered.

"You stink like a corpse embalmed in piss," the carnifex hissed. "Here, I brought you a treat to suck on."

It was a rotten human pubis on the bone, with putrid sweetmeats still attached. The hunchback fell upon it with surprising speed, at first mewling like an animal and then, as the flesh parted between his reeking gums, moaning with a stark and terrifying cannibal ecstasy.

*Fuck knows why they even want to keep the bastard alive,* thought Sawtooth. *The world thinks him dead already. But if he ever gets out, they'll wish they'd let me quarter 'im.*

He clanged shut the barred outer gate, locked it twice, and left Hekon Hakamanko to his feast.

It was just one day later when an elegant woman and her two guards reined up at the Sunstorm gates, seeking audience with Lord Nakasendaron. The weather had turned overnight, wind whipping in from the sea with remorseless salt-bitter stabs. Never one to turn away a lady in a tempest, the overlord duly received her in the upper storey of the Starburst Tower, beneath its crowning golden triskelion of the broken sun set in black stone which stared out across Novalis like a cosmic eye. His wife, Yuta, sat beside him.

The woman had dried her rain-drenched hair, but still wore the same black velvet gown. It clung to her breasts, belly and hips like a second skin; beneath the fabric Nakasendaron could see the outline of wide nipples, and between them what looked like the shape of an amulet.

"I am Lady Morvenna of the Shadow Castle," she said. "I come as peace envoy in the name of Dorion Killstar, the one and true emperor of Novalis."

Her voice seemed to reverberate, as if her shadow whispered with her as she spoke. Nakasendaron turned up his palms. "Go on."

"Our army, the Celestial Horde and Hive, are sworn to drive Hebon Hakamanko and his Vermin League from the north and crush them in their nest. Once the snake is skinned, Starfire and Akutenshi will be left with a mutual interest – the prosperity of Novalis. But Hakamanko is an elusive foe; in order to ensure his demise, we must wield the power of the thirteen imperial deathswords. And so, for the greater good of our land, I ask you to return to us Kinzokami, the metal wolf."

"Return?"

It was Lady Yuta who spat the word. "The deathswords were bestowed upon the thirteen clans by Emperor Metakaikon to seal the union of Novalis; no upstart can break that ancient covenant."

"My wife speaks wisely," added Nakasendaron. "You are surely aware that our league refutes this Killstar's claim; you cannot expect sacred instruments to be handed over to some lackluck butcher's boy, or whatever he was before you dragged him up – especially after the brazen raid on the Winter Palace."

Lady Morvenna's eyes widened; they seemed to be nearly all black, edged in pure white slivers. "Many of the swords are already scattered, even lost," she continued. "By reuniting them we seek to strengthen and renew Metakaikon's design. As I said, it is for the greater good of Novalis."

Yuta shook her head; Nakasendaron leaned forwards, and said: "We have no fear of Hakamanko and his minions; do not forget, the Taiyo are descended from the Yamayaga, the clan of Bankairon Demon-Slayer. You and your men are welcome to wait out the storm beneath our roof; but do not ask this again."

To that Lady Morvenna merely gave a short, angled bow of the head; then she turned abruptly and began the ever-circling descent to the courtyard where two agents of the Blue Dragon Hand awaited.

The rain doubled in its icy fury, the sky a web of seething electric mayhem as the three rode out, slowly, in single file; at the head was Chikushon Gekka, the Moon Beast, while Kagizumon Toka, the Lizard Claw, took the rear. As the gates of Sunstorm closed behind them Lady Morvenna, Archangel of Voids, raised her face to the darkness and screamed.

# THE SHADOW CASTLE

The nightmare began as ever, two purple moons spinning slowly through a star-riven sky, ever an inch from collision; a red sea of magma boiled below, and Dorion was a torn shadow on its shore. Beneath his feet the coils of a colossal sea-snake churned in mud, paralysing him with fear; the vampire castle loomed beyond, its silhouette hacked from black ore. Then he was trapped inside its walls, pursued by a phantom predator; but as he tried to run his feet sank into the flagstones, limbs in seizure. A heavy shape pinned him to the ground, crushing his lungs, its hot breath and drool scorching his mouth. He was naked, claws raking his body, and then he knew that the beast was a she-wolf; but it stank like a crucified mollusc, and spider-corpses floated in the crimson jelly of its eyes. He felt rank loins pressing down on him, a soaking heat threatening to burn away his genitals. "Dorion," whispered the she-wolf. "*Dorion...*"

He awoke, but at once he realised he must yet be dreaming. The beast was still heavy on his chest, its breath on his face, its nethers gripping his cock like molten steel. Then candlelight flooded his eyes and he saw a woman's face, swollen breasts pressed against him, etched with the claws and scales of a blue dragon. *This is no illusion,* thought Dorion at last, and his mind convulsed with perverse ecstasy as he realised Lady Sugarsting was raping him in his bed.

She left as quietly as she must have entered, finger to lips, slipping from his chamber with a final look that promised *I'll be here again.* Dorion lay motionless, his body drained of energy. He wondered why she hadn't woken him from the beginning, even considered that it might be part of his training. If so, he'd clearly failed miserably. An enemy agent might have infected him with some terrible pox, if not simply slit his throat. *The dreams,* he thought. *The dreams are so deep and real that they fuse with the waking world.*

After a sparse morning meal Dorion spent time alone in the Tomb of

Phantoms, an archive on the castle's fourth level which seemed to him half temple, half museum. It housed over three hundred tattooed skins removed from deceased members of the Blue Dragon Hand stretching back to the days of the emperor Mirokulaikon. Indeliby inscribed with intricate and ornate decorations from neck to ankle, these relics had been pared from the dead agents in one piece and then scraped and salt-cured; some even included the penis skin, as beautifully inked as the rest. Each memento was hung on its own wire frame. Dragons naturally predominated the designs, which were augmented by other mythical creatures, demons, flowers and ideograms. Some were based on popular paintings of their day, including battle scenes by the artist Flayon II or pornographic couplings by Taison III.

Dorion was most drawn to a skin that had once been attached to Ankokon Hakamono, the Dark Destroyer, a legendary agent from century seven who, Kuron Kirizono told him, had assassinated Lord Sakulon Satogawa using just a raven feather. Hakamono's back was covered by a tattoo showing a temple boy being sodomised by a creature half man and half dragon; in the dragon's eye was a flaming ideogram representing a concept unique to the Blue Dragon Hand which, Kirizono explained, could be expressed most succinctly as *sex is violence, violence is sex.*

At training that afternoon Dorion tried to catch Sasora Sato's eye, but each glance cost him a blow to the temple from Nezumon Nano's battle-stick. The Black Reaper watched on in silence; neither of them seemed to know what had transpired during the night. And he wasn't about to tell them.

*Once Sasora traps a man's cock inside her, he is powerless to resist.* Kirizono's words came back to haunt Dorion later that evening. *No,* he told himself. *I am no ordinary man, I am the son of an emperor; no woman will control me.* Even so he lay awake for most of the night, half from worry about Lady Sugarsting's powers, half from fear she might not come again. And when she didn't, Dorion Killstar grew even more tightly ensnarled in her web of wiles.

# THE MAD MARSHES

First, the dead marsh dragons were decapitated with band-saws wielded by two teams of butchers; once the venom sacs were carefully removed from the throat, the head and body were skinned and fed into one of two industrial lizard-grinders which templar engineers had constructed on the far rise facing the swamps. These Triad war machines reared starkly against a skyline which was forever the colour of acid-scarred tin, next to row upon row of gallows hung with crow-clustered Hakamanko corpses in varying stages of decay and devourment. The minced lizard meat and bones had already formed a small lake of putrescent slurry; hogs fed from it, gluttonously, until it was their turn to be dismembered.

"I'm getting fucking sick of pork. Can't we hunt down a few deer?" said Darkon Domo. His night-blue armour, forged from iceshield and dented from battle, weighed heavy on a frame more accustomed to the freedom of mail and mantle.

"There are none," replied Moton Hanzo. "The dragons ate them all decades ago; now they feed on human meat alone."

Hanzo was a warrior-priest of the Sun Shrine, golden-armoured and golden-haired. He owed Darkon Domo his life, for when an Iron Talon fighter was about thrust a sword up into his groin from behind and castrate him it was Darkon who severed the man's arms, both at once, with a fearsome swipe of his godsword Shirometsu, the white destroyer.

For more than a moon's passing the Celestial Horde and Hive had besieged the marshlands that ringed Skull Castle, a doom-infested quagmire that had to be conquered in order to storm Lord Hebon's stronghold. The only other approach to the castle was by sea, but the cliffs which rose up along the Lizard's Den coast were as sheer and slippery as glass, and more than a quarter mile high.

The ferocity of the Hakamanko ground forces – Iron Talons, bat-eating

Nightshaders, Blind Cats, Cut-Bellies, Scorpion Blacks, blood-drinking Tower Bats, and Night Weepers – was more than equalled by the marsh dragons, whose discharges of smoking black venom burned through anything not protected by iceshield, including the legs of horses. The warrior-priests of the Horde all wore the protective armour, but not so the swarming soldiers of the Hive; iceshield was a rare and expensive commodity, its value assiduously manipulated by the Seikyo.

The Hakamanko were an enemy at home in the wastes of the Mad Marshes, where life-sucking quicksands and an array of poisonous predators posed a new prism of mortal danger. Even more deadly were the man-traps devised by Hebon's son, Hekon the hunchback; Darkon had witnessed men plunge into underwater cages lined with needles, seen their legs shorn off by razor-bladed snares, bowels blasted out by hellfire grenades launched from foot-triggered waist-high slingshots, breastbones shattered by down-swinging hammers bolted with iron plate.

Deeper within the marshes they had discovered a hidden breeding ground where defleshed human skulls with sawn-off bone-caps were arranged in spirals to serve as repositories for lizard eggs, and the beasts that spawned there had evidently been fed with the carcasses of women. Darkon and his comrades put that whole place to the torch, and when a number of the eggs cracked open from the heat and embryonic reptiles emerged, they squashed them beneath their bootheels in a burst of boiling blood.

Even in camp, there was danger from silent invaders. One man was afflicted by a swamp hornet which laid eggs in his eyeball as he slept; a day later the eye exploded as a thousand tiny insects burst out and took wing. Another Hive recruit perished when centipedes burrowed into his arteries and devoured his heart, and a number of others lost limbs turned to brown mush by snake-bites.

Now, in one of the infrequent lulls in the conflict, Darkon found himself reflecting on this season of carnage. Hanzo had also had fallen silent. Death and its stench were everywhere. They were an infinity away from the comforts of Kobutsuden, where Darkon's former companion Quexarian was no doubt ensconced at the House of Antiquaries, researching relics and unfogging mysteries. Would he ever see the old Moon maven again? Only one thing seemed certain – Hebon Hakamanko had to die before any resolution could come to bear upon the Age of Shadows.

Overhead two raptors tore apart a dove on the wing, showering the ground with hot viscera. Hanzo stirred the mess with his finger.

"Bloody rain, hangman's gain," he pronounced, and Darkon dared not doubt him.

# THE VILES

"Hikidashon falsely accused me and killed his wife for loving me, and so I killed *him*," said Tazon Ando to Crow River Crosh. "And now someone – a Taiyo, judging by those banners – is trying to kill *me*. Revenge truly is a cycle which never ends... it just goes on until no-one even remembers why it even started."

The two men squinted across the expanse of rock-cluttered terrain which lay between them and the distant border. Their pursuers were encamped on the other side, tiny ciphers emerging into the glare of dawn.

"They're still half a day behind us," said Crosh. "If we can get to the caves by nightfall, we can end this. And Starfire might never even know what happened."

But Starfire knew already. Fifty miles to the east, Jukon Gomi and his rangers emerged from the night and rode without surcease, devouring the road from the city to the Valley of Flies. Jukon's sword Noretsu, splitter of brains, had already tasted blood; the head of a Kill-Claw rapist swung from his saddle, crusted in egg-laying flies. Like Noxon Taiyo and his Flame Riders, the Gomi rangers were bent on dogging Ando and his lifesguard of river clansmen to extinction point.

On the cliffs above the Jackdaws Lady Tyranna, Archangel of Shadows, was helped from her horse by Yorunon Hachi, the Night Wasp.

"The Bloodtooth Islands lie to the north," said the Blue Dragon chaos agent. "There Lady Sybella seeks the deathsword Yomuji. Tazon Ando's redoubt lies some miles to the west."

"And here?"

"Pirates. Smash-Bones clansmen haunt the caves and rocks below, preying on passing ships and the storm-broken."

Tyranna peered down at the grey beach; she could see a few tide-tossed smallboats, rocks smattered with salt-bleached human bones, a lone man pissing into the sea. The Key of Shadows was a hot metal stigma pulsing between her breasts.

"What of it?" she asked.

"They once stole the deathsword Akafuku," replied Rakuron Choko, the Vengeance Bolt. "That is blasphemy."

"Death to them," decreed the Night Wasp.

It was late afternoon when the Gomi rangers were forced to halt their charge. Sakon Tano's horse buckled beneath him, pitching Tano into the mud, and Jukon knew that the beast was at its limit. Others would soon follow unless they were rested at once.

"No doubt Ando will soon be in range of the valley," said Kuron Soga. "By all accounts he is a creature of the night, and to follow him into the growing darkness would be suicide. Who knows how many fighters are still encamped there, how many traps are set?"

"Our spies have reported only a scattering of women and children," said Jukon, "but you have the right of it. Ando knows the valley and its hiding-places like no other; let's just hope that Noxon Taiyo shows caution for once."

An hour later Andon Bara, wiliest of the Gomi scouts, returned from his expedition with welcome news. "Noxon Taiyo is holding ground two miles to the north," he said. "He awaits our arrival at first light."

As dusk doused the Jackdaws Feric Smash-Bones still stood gazing out at the ocean, and his body was just as hard and lifeless as the rock beneath his feet. A seagull with a beakful of bloody fish was perched on the pirate's large stone cock, from which an arc of stone piss was frozen in mid-flow. The torchlit caves behind him were filled with similar statues, Smash-Bones savages petrified where they stood or sat or lay. One was caught mid-rape, along with his screaming prisoner; another was crouched over the sand-midden, a stone stool poking from his stone anus. Some had crab claws or octopus pulp half-chewed between stone teeth.

And not one of them cast a shadow.

# CASTLE MORTMANE

Futohoko – that was the swift stallion's name – never left its stable. In fact, the wretched beast never even saw the light of dawn.

The serving-girl who cleared away the ball of hair and slime sicked up by Lady Valessa had left it in one of the animal troughs, along with the waste from the night's meal; like Futohoko, she never woke up.

Nor did her fellow kitchen workers, nor did those who had been seated in Lady Valessa's proximity; and nor did Gomon Takasha.

Morla found him on her early morning visit, just before sunrise. As soon as she stripped naked and crawled onto the bed, she felt something was awry. Gomon never moved, and she could detect an unfamilar odour which reminded her of a baby's faeces infused with oleander. She tugged at his shoulder. It was icy, and when his body rolled over into the candlelight, Morla started to scream.

Every vein in Gomon's body had turned black and was visible through his skin, which was so white and papery that sheets of it sloughed away at her touch. Worst of all were his eyes, which had popped out amid slicks of dark gore. His tongue, purple-black and half-severed, extruded from his mouth and his splintered teeth lay scattered across the bloody bolster. For a moment Morla thought she saw some kind of insect poke its antlered head from a nostril; then it was gone.

Every corpse was the same.

By mid-morning Flamon Neko, the Cave Cat, spearhead of the Iron Pentagram, found himself in the position of acting clan regent. The only Takasha left alive now was Lady Toka, who at age twelve was three years away from assuming control of Mortmane.

Gomon had been murdered, Neko was sure of it; yet how? The only possible explanation was poisoning, and the only plausible suspects were the three visitors who arrived the day before. This Lady Valessa came under flag of truce, but had proved herself an assassin of the most deadly and treacherous kind.

"Bring her to me," said Neko.

But when Himitson Kitsu, the Mystery Fox, and his cohort of Hell-Claw clansmen entered the Joker's Keep, they found only more corpses. Every guard stationed there had perished during the night, stricken by the same dread affliction. And Lady Valessa had vanished, along with her two companions.

Flamon Neko knew that pursuit was futile; who could say where the Akutenshi killers had gone? By now they could already be halfway to Thundervoid in the north, or on some ship bound for Wolf's Jaw in the south. Gomon, his friend since boyhood, was dead; and nothing would ever change that.

Sentangarion and Lady Blastofane, gloved and heavily masked, both examined Gomon's body. Neither could identify the cause of his death.

"This is no poison I have ever seen," said Blastofane. "What can turn veins black, skin white and cold as ice in the turn of one night?"

"Indeed," mused the maven. "And what can cause such pressure inside the skull that the eyeballs are ejected and the teeth grind themselves to gravel? If I didn't know better, I would say that our mysterious visitor was a witch. We are looking at a disruption or perversion of the metacarrion itself."

"It is said that Raikon Akutenshi danced with demons," said Flamon. "No doubt his acolytes are like-minded. The Shadow Castle must be razed."

"If you can find it," said Blastofane.

"First, let us bury our dead," said Sentangarion. "We must burn them all in a plague-pit beyond the walls – save for Lord Gomon, of course. He may be interred in the crypt with his family, provided his casket is tightly sealed. Eviscerating the body might be unwise; suffice to push his eyes back in and sew tight the lids."

And so, less than a month after the funeral of Lord Hikidashon Takasha the Wife-Boiler and his elder son Chikon, Gomon Takasha joined them and his mother's hound-harried remnants in the recesses far beneath Mortmane's Tower of Tombs.

It was only three days later, when Toka asked him "Where's Kyami?", that Flamon Neko realised the deathsword was missing.

# MOUNT KOMONYAMA

"Remember – there's nothing here but rocks, ash and bones," urged Captain Bloodspike as he led his men into the deepening dark of the Devil's Arsehole. He'd picked those No-Face pirates who still had at least one eye to see, but they were terrified to a man by the silent wastes of Thundervoid, which was now whispered to be the domain of vengeful ghouls.

They'd sailed the *Red Wraith* as far upriver as they could, but some seven miles from the volcano the waterway was completely blocked by a dam of part-skeletonized corpses and carcasses. The ship had drifted into that dense tangle of remains and come to a shuddering halt. This far north the air was near freezing, and as they set out on foot Bloodspike doubted that all would survive the march.

He was right. But it was not the cold that killed Nak No-Ears.

Beneath the vitreous surface of the Black Lake, thousands of slowly rotting bodies had turned into a noxious slurry of liquid meat that slowly churned and shifted for mile after mile, alive with strange insects and aquatic life-forms never before glimpsed in Novalis. Gas from this charnel morass continually formed fissures in the obsidian, which from time to time would erupt with geysers of putrefaction. Bloodspike had noted this phenomenon before, but never considered it a danger. Until now.

The surface blew out directly beneath Nak No-Ears, driving daggers of fragmented rock-glass up into his groin and guts and sending one leg flying across the lake. Nak was blown into the air and dropped several yards away in a lifeless, ruined heap. Bloodspike could see white, crab-like creatures crawling from the newly-formed crevice, bearded with fluorescent cilia, some bigger than a ship's cat. And then the pirates started to run.

As he glanced back, Bloodspike saw the pallid crustaceans pulling Nak's fresh corpse back down below the surface as the geyser began to subside. The stench of months-old death pursued the disfigured mariners, provoking some to vomit as they ran; only those without noses were immune to its choking horror.

Within a mile of Komonyama the jet-black lake suddenly ceded to the pure white glamour of the ice-covered rock upon which Kyukiden once stood, forming a stark borderline over which they poured in ragged file, thankful to evade the threat of imminent dismemberment from below.

Less than one hour later the pirates were clambering over the wreckage of Devil's Ring, the garrison which had once fortified Komonyama against marauders. The volcano's guardians were now nothing but irradiated bone which cracked and crunched underfoot.

From the edge of the crater they could see the ruins of Kyukiden away to the east, the tips of its broken spires poking from the snow like parasites burrowing through virgin skin.

"The volcano has slept for centuries," Captain Bloodspike told his men. "Its secrets are now ours for the plunder."

And with that, the descent into Komonyama's deep had begun.

The assault on Creeper's Cove unfolded at around the same time. Spying at least five Crimson Curse ships anchored in the bay half a league ahead, Mushon Yowa realised that Lord Voraxo's fears were well-founded – the Beasts of Blood were not the only freebooters trailing the holy relics of Komonyama.

"Time to earn your coin," he said to Gorn of Gluttonport. The three Kurotako ships were crewed by Shell Crush sailors, but the fighting men on board were all from Gorn's band of berserker mercenaries. And so the *Hexbound Heart*, the *Fear Fathom* and the *Sea Vampire* had dropped anchor just offshore. The Blood Eagle clansmen struck out for land in catboats, a hundred of them assembling on the beach's fused periphery. Milky white waters lapped at their feet, pregnant wth virulent life.

"A cursed place of ghosts, shit and monsters," said Urstinx. "Even the air's filled with death."

"The black gas," said Gorn. "That's what they call it – all the gas from the decomposing meat. It seeps through the fucking cracks. And fuck knows what else is down there."

"Let's get it done with then. First the village, then the volcano."

"Aye. Fuck 'em all," said Gorn.

And then the Beasts of Blood uncorked their skins of shapestrong, gulping down the brew of mushrooms and gore, smearing it over faces, arms and chests, seeking the strength and savagery of the wolves and bears they were named for. Swords beat against shields, metal claws clashed and sparked. The drug gripped their brains and hearts ever tighter as they marched on Creeper's Cove, convulsing their bodies with vomiting and voiding of bowels, eyes thick with blood, howling and roaring, all caution cast aside with animal abandon.

The rapture of their advance alerted the Crimson Curse and gave them time to man defences, but it made little difference. They were used to ship-to-ship fighting, they were used to over-running defenceless homesteads; nothing could have prepared them for the feral onlaught of the Beasts of Blood.

The berserkers were like some organic mincing-machine into which their victims were sucked whole and then discarded in a wake of bloody morsels. Their swords thrust and swiped and hacked with remorseless ferocity, and even when a pirate falchion bit into flesh it seemed to only inflame their collective rage; one No-Face fighter cut off a berserker's arm, then found himself dying as the attacker, unslowed, bit out his throat in a lupine frenzy. Another was still alive as a Beast devoured his ripped-out liver.

The pirates fell back but there was nowhere to run. Bear-claws sheared through faces and bellies in a hailstorm of eyeballs, teeth and vital organs, a hurricane of shit and blood.

When it was over, not a single Crimson Curse clansman still stood. The Blood Eagles were drenched in red from head to foot, some draped in entrails and sinew, some holding severed heads, some chewing chunks of raw flesh. Only a handful had fallen.

For a second, complete silence fell on the village of Creeper's Cove. Then the moans and screams of the dying, the splash of blood sluicing from blades, and the exaltations of the berserkers swelled up in symphony. But Gorn could hear something else; the dull, regular thumping of a fist against wood. It punctuated the after-battle noise with ever-increasing volume, and seemed to be coming from a shack at the far end of the settlement. "Come on," he said to Urstinx.

They used the points of their swords to lift up the wooden strut which barred the shack's door, and it swung outward with a shriek of rusted iron. All they could see was gloom. Then, with a sudden lunge which startled even Gorn, a monster loomed into the twilight. It had a horrific face half flesh and half exposed bone, with one empty eye socket and straggles of filthy silver hair on what remained of its scalp; yellow spittle foamed on gnashing, gumless teeth. It clutched at the two invaders with its grave-cold hands, and might have clawed Gorn's throat away had not the chain around its ankle abruptly halted its advance.

The sword-shifter cursed, raised Gut-Fucker above his right shoulder, and with an almighty downstroke chopped off Hozon Ama's head.

# THE SUNSTORM CASTLE

Nakasendaron Taiyo stood on the Sunstorm battlements, watching as Lady Morvenna of the Shadow Castle and her two guards rode away through the deluge. He wondered why she'd given up so easily; why come all the way from Thundervoid and then leave again with barely so much as a protest? On the hill facing the castle, some half mile away, was a single leafless oak. The three riders stopped beneath it, dismounted, and tethered their horses. *Not much shelter there,* thought Lord Naka, *but I suppose it's better than nothing.*

Two hours later the rain-storm had abated, but the distant figures were still beneath the tree. The two Blue Dragon Hand agents were sitting cross-legged, but Lady Morvenna was standing in exactly the same position, arms slightly raised, her gaze fixed upon the castle. Taikon Taiyo had taken his father's place on watch, and was intent on waiting until the Akutenshi finally turned and left; their presence seemed increasingly malevolent and made him uneasy, as if they were hatching a hex.

Hours passed. Lady Morvenna did not move.

*She must be stark nude beneath that gown,* Taikon said to himself, *and pissing where she stands. No-one can hold it that long.* For a second he had a vision of his face beneath the gown's soaking black hem, mouth agape, but quickly pushed it aside.

"Soldier! Take over."

That night, Taikon had a dream just before dawn. He dreamt that a gigantic black vulture swooped down and took him in its talons, carrying him over a pure white sea to a temple carved from stone. Bird-masked priests bound him to an altar and caressed his naked body with delicate, swine-hair brushes. Dead skin swirled like a snow-storm. *Boil a seed before it dries,* sang the priests in unison, *cut a stalk and watch it rise, in the flowers of your eyes, something cold and rotten lies.* A vulture-priestess loomed over his face, unrobed, her soft breasts brushing his forehead. Her nipples were scarred and pierced with silver rings and she wore a necklace of coiled human bowel that slithered like a snake. Then she took up a sacrificial dagger, its blade dripping green bile, and plunged it at Taikon's heart.

The first thing that flashed across his mind when he bolted awake was a silhouette of the woman on the hill. He knew before he looked from the tower window that she would still be standing there. Her two chaos agents were away to one side of the oak, stretching and striking combat feints in the morning's pink rays, but Lady Morvenna had moved not a single inch. Taikon called out for the castle watch. He would send a patrol to either drive the Akutenshi away or, if necessary, cut them down where they stood. Then he heard a girl's scream, quickly followed by his father crying out in horror.

He rushed to his parents' night chamber. One of the maids had evidently fainted, and lay slumped across the floor tapestry; Lady Yuta was sitting up in bed and Nakasendaron was gripping her by the shoulders and shaking her, as if to wake her from sleep.

When Taikon saw his mother's face, he understood why.

One side of it had collapsed during the night, stiff downturned lips releasing a string of bloody drool that flowed over her chin, throat and shift; but the true terror was her eyes. Both were wide open but completely filmed over with cataracts of glistening, bright red membrane. She sat there like a kind of living corpse, motionless save for shallow breathing. A noise came from her throat as if she was trying to speak, but her teeth and jaw were so tightly clenched that nothing escaped but a moribund murmur. The bed was a reeking soil of expelled fluids and waste.

"Some night-demon has snatched her soul," cried Nakasendaron. "Now it rots in the vale of spectres, and we are left with only a shell."

"Vorgovanian," said Taikon. "Surely he will remedy this."

But when the old maven saw Yuta, his expression darkened. "The apoplexy," he pronounced. "Our lady has been struck down. I fear that her mind has been erased."

"But her eyes?'

"The eyes are unusual, it is true," said Vorgovanian. "They speak to a soul that bleeds in purgatory, I have no doubt of it."

Nakasendaron raised his hands to cover his face, and his body trembled.

"That woman," said Taikon. "That Lady Morvenna... this is witch's work. She must be brought back and tried. And if guilty, burned alive."

The maven said nothing; Nakasendaron nodded assent, willing to grasp anything which might make sense of this catastrophic turn.

It was nigh on mid-morning when Bubon Tanko, chief of the Sunstorm watch, rode out with a dozen of his men. On the distant hill they could see three figures outlined against the sun, standing abreast, unmoving. It was said that the woman had been standing like that for nigh on a day now, but Tanko was sure that a slash of his steel-hooked whip across the arse would soon shift her. As for the other two, Lord Taikon had said to hang them there and then; that old oak had been used for executing rebels and traiters since the Serpent Wars, and the crows were always hungry for more cooling flesh.

Kon Zakko's horse stiffened first, as if suddenly frozen in mid-canter; it crashed to ground with a snapping of bones, sending Zakko flying over its neck. Both beast and rider lay still as others fell around them. Zakko's face was hideously contorted, as if the hands of an invisible giant had twisted and stretched it like clay. His eyes were occluded by bloody membranes, his mouth twitched and spat mindlessly. Every other watchman was the same, and so was every horse. Their bodies lay strewn across the field like meat on a butcher's slab.

Looking down from the hilltop, Chikashon Gekka and Kagizumon Toka knew that this was just the beginning. Gekka, who was pulling the guts from a skinned rabbit, said: "Best make another fire."

Lady Morvenna said nothing; she continued to stand and stare ahead with her black unblinking eyes, black hair flicking in the wind. The Key of Voids was hot, and sang with blue light.

For the first time in three centuries, the Sunstorm Castle was besieged.

# THE VILES

His armour was hard black leather over mail, a golden sun triskelion stitched into breast and back. He rode a white, heavy-boned horse and at his side hung Seppunryu, the dragon kiss, once deathsword to Clan Mishima of Castle Nightfog, long banished to the land of the dead.

Behind him were fifty Flame Riders, most ferocious of the Taiyo vassals, with braided locks, shaven jaws and eyelids tattooed red. Atop the sun-bloodied rise they stood in line, spears in hand, poised to swoop like exterminating angels through the Valley of Flies.

"Noxon!" shouted Jukon Gomi. Approaching from the south-west, Jukon's rangers were equal in number, and he felt assured that when combined the two forces could finally quell Tazon Ando and his remnants, however treacherous the terrain. Noxon Taiyo, the giant-slayer, also known as Night Sun, wheeled his mount towards the Starfire commander.

"I'm honoured," he said. "I thought you too busy with council matters to worry about the likes of me."

"Novalis needs its heroes," replied Jukon. "I'd not have you die chasing some outlaw when there are far greater battles to come. Besides, I've made a decision – from now on, my place is in the field."

"Here's to heroes, then," said Noxon. "Now; time to wreak justice. Ando is wanted for the murder of Lord Hikidashon, a capital crime against Starfire. His head is duly forfeit."

"And after that?"

"Perhaps a visit to the Red Rock, what do you say? To my mind, the Octopus holds the key – Scaleport can only be reached from Bloodtooth, and only the Kurotako have the ships to do it. From Scaleport we could assault Skull Castle from the north, even as its southern defences are ravaged by the templar crusaders."

"But our strategy is already decided," said Jukon. "We wait until both the Horde and the Hakamanko are reduced by mutual destruction. By engaging Lord Hebon now, would we not be helping those who support the pretender? Surely better to work on our city's defences? Sooner or later, the chaos that reigns in the north will cross the Crow River, depend upon it."

"Only chaos kills chaos," replied Noxon. "Come; let's attend to matters at hand, and speak more of it in the course of time."

Jukon signalled his men to join ranks with the Flame Riders. He could see that Night Sun was a force who burned as brightly and fiercely as the star he was named for; a man of many virtues, no doubt, but patience was not among them. *Such a man may win a war, but lose an empire,* he thought. He was reminded of a story that his sister Juka used to tell him, the legend of a bandit named The Eye Shaking King who, long ago, demanded a kiss from Lady Brista, wife of a Hassha overlord. When she scorned him he ambushed their entourage on the open road and cut off her head. *It is said,* Juka would tell him with deliberate relish, *that The Eye Shaking King slept with that head every night until the flesh rotted from the bone, and every night he kissed the lips of the Lady Brista.* And that, he felt, was also the nature of Noxon Taiyo – once his mind was set he could not, would not be denied.

"We cannot run forever," Tazon Ando had said just a few hours earlier, after he and his Crow River fighters found their former valley refuge deserted save for starvelings, midnight moths and a littering of horse skulls. "True, we could hide in the caves for months and they might never find us – but since we have food and water for but a few days, that's not much of an option either. Flamon Neko respected the truce we made at first, but then unleashed his Taiyo hunting-hound, and he is seemingly not one to give up. Here–" he handed Crosh one of two freshly unearthed coin-sacks "–half the gold is yours, you've earned it. Go back to your villages, stay close to your womenfolk."

"And you?" asked Crosh.

"They won't advance until dawn. I'll double back under darkness and head for the city, start a new life. I've done what I needed to do. You'd best take this, as well – I can't be seen with it. If you can sell it without getting hanged, it'll fetch a good price. Give me yours."

Passing Crosh the stolen deathsword Akafuku, Ando took his horse by the reins and started back on foot along the narrow valley pathway, heading west by the watery light of the Fire Scorpion.

Lady Tyranna watched his progress intently from her vantage point above, her huge brown eyes sucking in every scintilla, willing him to cast a shadow.

# THE MAD MARSHES

After the passing of two moons, the Triad forces had cleared little more than a half mile of swamplands. Killing every living creature and burning whatever would burn, they pushed back the Hakamanko inch by blood-soaked inch. Hundreds of Hive foot soldiers had already been skeletonized by the caustic venom vomited out by the marsh dragons, their smoking remains slowly claimed by the quicksands and sucking mud. Whenever a lizard fell, which was rare, warrior-priests of the Celestial Horde would charge through on horseback, cutting down as many of the Snake Lord's vassal clansmen as they were able. But this strategy was not without risk; many horses became bogged down, leaving their riders open to attack. Darkon Domo saw one stranded Sun warrior hacked to pieces by a dozen Night Weepers, who then stamped on the dead man's terrified mount until it was trampled into the swamp and drowned.

Spies clad in würm skins were sent deep into the wilderness; few ever returned, and those that did were seemingly addled by swamp poisons, babbling of brown giants and burning bone mountains. Every night the Triad generals conducted mass prayers, beseeching the Three Sorrows for strength and guidance. As the last survivor of the Horde's Moon division, Darkon was called upon to complete the trinity with Storms and Sun.

Afterwards, as he chewed on pork and parsnips, the warrior-priest often found himself doubting the wisdom of the crusade.

"Hebon's castle is surrounded by the marshes; we could be here a year and not reach the other side. And how many will die in that time?"

"Aye," said Moton Hanzo, "but the mavens have made their decree. For the murder of Hectoclarion, every Hakamanko must die – whether it takes one year or a hundred. Look on the positive – you'll almost certainly be dead before the end."

"Very fucking comforting."

Hanzo chuckled. "And if you weren't doing this? Where would you be?"

"I'd be safe in the city, helping an old man find relics and drinking ale. And there'd be no dragons trying to burn my bloody arse off."

"Well. From what you've told me, you're no stranger to sticking your head in places you probably shouldn't. Mount Mooncry, Bloodflower – those sound like dangerous missions."

"More so Mooncry; but aye," agreed Darkon. "What of it?"

"Strikes me there's only one way to end this quickly. Someone has to assassinate Lord Hebon."

"That's already clear; but how to do it, less so. We don't have girl assassins any more, as far as I know. And Hebon might be twisted, but he's not known for buggering young men."

"No," ceded the Sun priest, "seduction is not an option. Neither is breeching the castle by stealth or force. Which leaves only one possibility."

"Which is?"

Darkon had racked his brains many a night, but no way of getting to Lord Hebon had ever come to him. Had he missed something obvious?

Moton leaned closer.

"Betrayal," he smiled.

"Go on."

"Hebon's alchemist, Borborax, is the one who sends and receives all messages by wing. He's the only one inside Skull Castle we could engage directly. We need to find an offer he can't refuse, and persuade him to let us in. The castle is riddled with secret catacombs and tunnels, and one of them must be accessible from outside the walls. It's said that Hekon the hunchback built such a tunnel to the nearby woods, so he might frolic with boy-corpses by moonlight."

"What kind of offer? Gold?"

"His kind shit gold. No, we need something more frightening than that; something to convince him his life is forfeit unless he turns on Hebon."

"But his life would be forfeit if he did," said Darkon. "I've heard tales of Hebon feeding traitors alive to the würms, piece by carved-off piece."

"Then we must offer him something more," said Moton. "Glory, lands, or power that money cannot buy."

"Or all three," said Darkon, spitting out a twist of gristle. "Let me know when you've found the answer."

As he rose to his feet and headed to the piss-trench, Domo wondered where this might end. Even if they managed to penetrate Skull Castle, could they truly kill Hebon Hakamanko in his own chambers? *I'm a sword-fighter, not a chaos agent who can blend into the bloody shadows. And fuck knows what horrors go on in that place.*

Far above, green and purple shooting stars seared the sky. That night Darkon Domo barely slept, and when he did he dreamt of dragons.

# THUNDERVOID

During the battle the Crimson Curse defender had been half gutted by a beserker's sword which thrust in straight and sliced out sideways, opening his belly with a deluge of intestine and half-digested fish; now he was dying, slowly and in agony, and Gorn was quickly drawn to his fearful cries. He placed the tip of his sword against the man's throat, promising a quick death in exchange for words.

After the transaction was completed, Gorn turned to Urstinx and said: "Looks like their captain, some cunt called Bloodspike, is already up the Devil's Arsehole. It's perfect."

"How so?"

"Saves us the fucking trouble. There's only one way out; all we have to do is anchor at the river's mouth, and wait."

"And if he's not got the bones?"

"Let's just hope he does," said Gorn. "But if not, we kill him anyway and go up there ourselves. One way or another, we're finishing this and getting paid."

Inside the volcano, the roughly-hewn steps seemed to spiral down and down endlessly; but after an hour, they ended at an enormous iron door set into the rock. The stagnant air stank of sulphur, making it difficult to breathe. Captain Bloodspike and Skash No-Lips pushed at the door, which was more than double their height. At first, it would not move. Then Jik No-Nose joined in, the three straining against the barrier until, with a dull scraping sound, it slowly inched inward.

The pirates poured into the ancient underground vault, illuminating every recess with their massing torches. It appeared to be a cavernous complex of cathedral and foundry, where industrial machinery and religious icons were seamlessly meshed in a metal phantasium.

"The Ark," breathed Captain Bloodspike. "This is where the Shadow mavens of Kyukiden forged the indices and instruments of the Triad."

"Dolls of death and blades of vampire steel," muttered Skash, once a Cut-Belly warlord before würm-venom burned away most of his face and one hand. "Or so the legends say."

The back wall of the vault was adorned with a massive three-dimensional pictograph wrought in bronze, a sun and moon in semi-eclipse each divided diagonally by a jagged lightning strike, the bolts converging in a V. Combining the three elemental symbols of the Triad with the thunderous sigil of the Akutenshi, this device overhung three dynamic statues representing the Sorrows in mortal form – Hoshon, mistress of the fiery hells; Sukion, mistress of the frozen hells; and Arashon, mistress of the liquid hells. They were shown as naked warriors, each wielding a huge sword of stone, and their faces bore an expression of infinite love honed to the point of murder.

The Ark's floor was dominated by a coffin-shaped copper crucible at its centre, around which were ranged a manifold of athanors, moulds and matrices. Industrial tools hung on racks, once used in the creation of miracles.

"All this ended when the volcano was extinguished," said Bloodspike. "Without its fire, the forges fell silent; within a generation, the Shadow mavens were no more."

"What happened to the volcano?" asked Jik.

"They say that the murder of Bankairon Yamayaga, the demon-hunter, quenched its wrath. And that's exactly why we're here."

"But the treasure... there's treasure, you said."

Bloodspike smiled thinly. "Take what you will," he said. "Any golden icons, relics, antiquities you can carry. But the real riches, if legend tells true, lie within that crucible."

It took two of the No-Face pirates to set the time-weathered cog wheels in motion; as they turned so a ramp gradually emerged from the furnace. Upon it was a human skeleton, picked clean by centuries of decay.

"These are the sainted bones of the Demon-Slayer," said Bloodspike, "and they are worth an emperor's ransom. His killers stowed his body here, thinking it would be incinerated in a blasphemous inferno. But the flames never returned. Here, on the shoulder-blade; do you see the tooth-marks? That is where Bankairon was bitten by the spider-vampire. And this fracture across the thigh is no doubt where the demon king Arkestron struck a blow with his maul. But here, above all, is the certain proof." He held up the skeleton's left hand, showing a signet ring still clinking on its smallest finger. "The seal of the Yamayaga, a night-moth set in jade."

They left Komonyama at first light, hoping to reach the *Red Wraith* before noon and the open sea by third nightfall. Bankairon's bones clicked and rattled in their burlap, as if sending some secret code to the horrors beneath the Black Lake.

Two more pirates perished in explosions of corpse-meat, shredded bodies hooked into the underglass by white claws, before the crew clambered aboard Bloodspike's flagship. Freezing wind filled the sails, oars churned through poisoned water, and they slowly disengaged from the dam of the dead.

Thirty leagues downriver, the Beasts of Blood were waiting.

# THE VALLEY OF FLIES

After they'd tracked Ando for an hour, Lady Tyranna said: "He does not bear the deathsword; I feel it in my heart, which grows colder by the minute."

"Then where is it?" asked Yorunon Hachi. "Ando is condemned to die for his theft, but retrieving Akafuku is paramount."

"This is nigh impossible," said Rakuron Choko. "When the swords are held behind castle walls, locating them is simple; but when they are abroad, forever moving in all directions..."

"Do not despair," said Tyranna. "The keys and the deathswords are as sister and brother, both forged in the same volcanic fire; one purrs when the other is near. My heart will be our guide. Let this Ando go for now; we must retrace our steps."

But when they returned to the incline above the caves, Akafuku felt no closer.

"Perhaps he buried it," said Choko.

"Perhaps," said Tyranna. "A sword is still within our grasp, I am sure of it. Let us bide until morning, when shadows once more rise from the grave of night."

Two hours after sunrise, the Akutenshi's wait was rewarded. A soft throbbing in the Key of Shadows told Lady Tyranna that its metal kin was nigh. Away to the west, a war party of one hundred Starfire head-hunters was slowly encroaching along the ravine, two riders out in front.

"The one in black and gold is Night Sun," said Hachi, "a warrior of great renown. Some say he is descended from the Yamayaga – perhaps from Bankairon himself."

"He wields Seppunryu, the dragon kiss," added Choko. "It was stolen by the Hakamanko during the Serpent Wars, but Night Sun has seen its liberation. As a mere custodian, he may acquiesce without need for conflict."

"Even great warriors are dogged by their shadow," said Lady Tyranna. "And if he has a shadow, he is mine. Take me to him."

By the time they had descended into the valley, flag of truce affixed to saddles, the Starfire battalion had come to a halt outside the cave system once infested by Ando's rebels. Noxon Taiyo and his fellow front-rider were already inside one of the entranceways, searching for signs of recent life. Two Gomi rock-rangers, Flamon Kuno and Pukon Sota, eased their mounts forwards to confront the elegantly attired woman and her two companions.

"Your business?" asked Sota.

"I am Lady Tyranna of the Shadow Castle, and these are my lifesguard. I come as peace envoy in the name of Dorion Killstar, the one and true emperor of Novalis. I seek your leader, the Night Sun."

"Jukon Gomi is our leader. We are rangers of the Stone Brides. And it is Jukon Gomi who presides over the empire of Novalis, in the name of Starfire."

"And yet, I would speak with the Night Sun."

Her white face was impassive, but her words resounded in a way which reminded Sota of two voices speaking in unison, one a fraction deeper than the other.

For a second, Sota made no reply. Yorunon Hachi, the Night Wasp, shifted in his saddle. They were semi-circled by head-hunters, some cradling primed crossbows. Then another voice, a man's, called out from one of the caverns.

"You there!"

Lady Tyranna peered into the darkness of the cave, her eyes widening like liquid moons. She could see pale faces, but the morning's rays offered no illumination. "Won't you step into the light?" she asked.

Noxon started forwards, but felt a hand grasp his wrist.

"Wait," said Jukon, "there may be archers in the rocks."

"I think I prefer the gloom," said Noxon to Tyranna. "After all, my name is not Day Sun. Now; how may I please you?"

"Return the deathsword Seppunryu; that is all. Then we may part ways."

Noxon smiled, then looked down at the sword. It was not his, admittedly, but to hand over such a weapon... he gave Jukon a questioning look. Jukon responded directly to Lady Tyranna.

"The sword must remain in the custody of Starfire, until the matter of imperial–"

He stopped speaking when one of the Fireball Dead – whether by accident or design, none would never know – loosed a steel-barbed crossbow bolt which tore into the side of the woman's left breast and exited from the right with a spray of clear, gelatinous fluid and shredded nipple tissue.

She did not scream; she did not fall from her horse; and neither, it seemed, did she bleed. High overhead, a vulture screeched. Then the Flame Rider's mount reared upwards and back as if some invisible force had slammed into it, and at the apex of its rise it suddenly went rigid, lips peeled back from rotting teeth, as if turned to granite. The crossbowman was also frozen, his skin turned grey and etched with hairline cracks, eyes like calcified pebbles.

As Tyranna spun her own gelding about to face the Starfire battalion, more and more of them were stricken. Many flew backwards towards the sun as if violently shoved by unseen hands, stony bodies fragmenting when they landed on the hard-baked ground. Some loosed bolts before they fell, and one punctured Rakuron Choko's throat. Yorunon Hachi reached out as if to grab his lady's bridle, spinning a razor-edged star towards Flamon Kuno's face with his other hand.

Then a rain of stone birds pelted down from the sky and smashed into the figures below, cracking skull-bones and fracturing limbs. One struck and impaled Tyranna's horse on the rump, causing it to bolt forwards with a shriek towards the cave-mouth where Noxon, Jukon and a dozen others were safe in the shadowless dark.

As it galloped past Noxon he reached up and grabbed what felt like an arm, jerking Lady Tyranna from her saddle. The horse rushed on into blackness, gripped by blind panic, then plunged into a pit. After falling for several seconds it landed on the basalt shore of a boiling subterranean lake, exploding in a savage plume of blood, bones and viscera. The beast's mangled head was sent spinning through the air before splashing into the steam-shrouded tarn, followed by its blown-out eyeballs.

"No light!" shouted Jukon. "Did you not see? Our men were killed by their own shadows, which leapt inside them... surely you saw it?"

"Whatever happened, it was not natural," ceded Noxon. Lady Tyranna squirmed silently in his grip, the Key of Shadows burning between her bolt-torn breasts.

"And neither is she," said Jukon.

# SKULL CASTLE

It was a tale so often told to Moshino by his mother that he was able to repeat it word by word. *For days I drifted on the ship of ashes, about to perish from thirst when pirates took me up and used me for their filthy lusts, day upon day, until my legs were bathed in blood. After one moon passed the pirate ship was sunk by defenders of the Octopus, who plucked me from the deep. The blind bargeman set me ashore, where I wandered like a stricken beast, used by many more men before Sun priests found me, ripe with child, and took me to the house of the holy iron angel.*

"What compelled me to make that choice?" asked Lord Hebon. "Why cast out Silversoil alive when I could have had her butchered in her bed? There can only be one answer – Moshino was destined to be born."

"Indeed," said Borborax. "Yet the boy's nature, his aberrations – adulation of ordures, love for the madfolk – are troublesome to me. Forgive me, Lord Hebon, but I fear he may bring calamity upon our clan."

"How so? You have heard his mother's tale – she was raped a thousand times, yet Moshino clung to life within her womb. He would not be denied."

The maven clasped his hands together. "My very fear. The calumnies against the Hakamanko, long-whispered down the years but never proven... Moshino is those horrors made flesh. Unchecked, his very existence may provide justification for those who would not just enslave but exterminate us."

"That hour has already passed," said Hebon. "My other son Hekon's murder of the high Sun maven has already condemned us to death, there should be no doubt. No; Moshino will not be constrained, but unleashed. Send for Lady Catamane, at once."

Alone, Hebon gazed long upon *The Phantom Of Slaughtershriek*, Flayon II's garish evocation of the Firebrand Nyctalope. Like the Nyctalope, who died in battle rather than surrender to the Gomi, the Snake Lord had sworn to lead the Vermin League to either glory or annihilation; under his watch no Hakamanko would ever live in servitude, or suffer the chains of imprisonment. Moshino had been saved and delivered to him by Zenmarion, King of Hell, he was sure of it. And now he would repay that debt in full.

As usual, Moshino was nowhere to be seen within the walls of Skull Castle. He had taken to collecting the heads of the war prisoners executed each day at noon by Mad Dog's pole axe; while their decapitated bodies were fed to the würms which still prowled the castle moat, Moshino would plunge the bloody trophies into a cauldron of boiling water, stirring them round and round until the flesh turned to grey pulp and melted away.

Each day he arranged the steaming skulls in circles on the ground, surrounding Baron Feculax with ring upon white ring. The Hellhaven madhounds wreathed the deathsheads in nettles and used them for skipping games. Old Sucklestench took to polishing each one, and even gave them names. "This 'un's Captain Seesaw," he would say to Sugary Meg, holding up a newly-gleaming specimen, "and that 'un there, by your foot, that's the Queen of Strawberries."

With each dawn Baby Brimstone set fire to a new pile of pilfered bones. The lunatics danced widdershins around each blaze, hand in hand, singing and chanting, but to no avail; Baron Feculax would not stir. *Baron, Baron, hear our plea, see the fire we set for thee* they sang, over and over, but the shit giant heeded them not.

Hebon had tasked Moshino with the birthing of the homunculus as a distraction; now, he had conceived a far more urgent mission for his snake-eyed bastard. He was to take command of a special force, comprising würm-riders, warlocks and agents of the Reptile Crux, and head north to the Sperm Weald. From there Moshino's raiders were to cross into the Shines and mass an army from any loyal clansmen willing to fight, then cross the border into the Templedark and descend upon Castle Nightfog. If Nightfog could be taken, it would serve as staging-post for attacks against the Triad crusaders from the rear. *And if Moshino could learn the ways of war, none might resist his onslaught.*

As soon as Lady Catamane came to his chamber, Hebon bid her strip nude. "You were able to draft the vermix?" he asked her.

"I have it here," she said, showing him the dark pink paste in her open hand. "I used the pale violet flower, moontide from a red-haired serving wench, and the seed of a virgin boy."

"Then drink."

Catamane let the paste slide into the proffered wine and swilled it around until it dissolved. "Snakes in the night, snakes in the skull."

"Snakes in the night, snakes in the skull. Remember; we must summon the red serpent for my son Moshino, to empower and protect him in the future days."

"Moshino," she repeated, and then her eyes rolled back as the vermix fired its tendrils through every vein. Hebon studied her as she began to writhe; unlike his former viragos, Catamane was of low birth, her body scarred and crudely tattooed with tribal markings. Her breasts, though full and heavy, hung low and were purpled where the skin had stretched. Drool now hung from her ring-pierced lips.

Then she fell forwards with a moan, buttocks raised and spread, and he knew that she was shitting forth the snake.

Even as Lady Catamane laboured, Moshino's frustration with Baron Feculax reached its breaking-point. "Give me that!" he yelled, snatching a hatchet from the Knave of Stumps and violently hacking through one of the two hawsers anchoring Feculax to the battlements of Skull Castle. The shit giant's left side swung forwards, threatening to tilt over; chunks of its wormy, black-brown flesh fell away, raining over the ground below. Then, with a garbled scream, Moshino severed the remaining hawser.

Lunatics and warlocks scattered in terror as the thirty-foot figure came free and, finally, moved forwards under its own weight. It slowly toppled face-first into the ground, the iron endo-skeleton twisting on impact and sloughing off huge sheets of dried excrement. The legs and arms buckled, and the head broke clean off from the neck. Brother Bone, the pig-licking priest, was squashed beneath the Baron's chest and reduced to a bloody mash; poor old Sucklestench, too aged to jump aside, was impaled by a broken-off finger which disembowelled him where he stood.

The survivors watched as the Baron's huge head began to roll away down the slope that descended from the castle's perch. It quickly gathered momentum, shedding rock-hard clags of insect-riddled filth, and plunged into the Mad Marshes where it disappeared behind a yellowy veil of swamp-fog. Seconds later a scream rang out, and then a templar spy in lizard skin crawled into view; everything below his waist had been torn off by the hurtling head, and his innards were trailing behind him.

"Victory," said Moshino.

# THE HOUSE OF SILVER SPECTRES

After what seemed an age, she heard footsteps enter the room; then the blindfold was finally removed.

"Put this on," said the blonde-haired girl, handing her a white shift. It was the same one who, some thirty minutes earlier, had bid her strip naked and then slipped an oiled finger into her most intimate orifices. *Can't be too careful,* the girl had said. *Two years back we were infiltrated by a chaos agent who pulled a hidden spike out of her arsehole and stabbed one of us in the eye.*

She welcomed the garment. The chill air in the manse had stiffened her nipples, and they had begun to ache. As her eyes coped with the candlelight, she saw that the House of Silver Spectres was very different, at least on the inside, to most of the drab, dilapidated buildings in Swilly Town. *Judging by the number of stairs they made me climb, this must be the upper storey,* she told herself. Each corner of the room was furnished with divans, patterned drapes and candelabra. The windows, if there ever were any, had been completely boarded over with the same polished teak that lined every wall. Underfoot she could feel a luxurious weave, and the ceiling was high and vaulted. A cornice ran around the entire room, decorated with grinning plaster skulls.

The blonde girl stood next to two others; one had brown hair, the other black, and the black-haired girl wore a jewelled eyepatch to the left. They all wore robes of black velvet, low-cut and silver-sashed.

"So," said the blonde, "tell us all your name."

"They call me Lady Crimsonclaw."

The girl appeared to stifle a laugh, then said: "There are no ladies in this house. And no clan names, either. First names only."

"Soma," said Suna.

"Soma? Perfect. I'm Zoya. This is Fera, and this one-eyed beauty is Seka. Our way is the way of cruelty; for us, death must always be a punishment, and we only sanction those who truly deserve to die. For centuries, the Silver Spectres have used only wire, needles, blades and banes. Our last poisoner was caught and burnt as a witch by the Seikyo, which is why we seek another – and how you heard about us in the dark places, no doubt.”

“Just so. I wish to serve justice upon all men who enslave, rape, torment and abuse womankind. This is my mission.”

“Very good,” said Fera. “But you should know that this life has many dangers – agents from all the clans seek our destruction. And again, cruelty is our creed – my last kill was a dog-raper, and before he died his cock was pierced and cooked by fifty burning needles. Zoya likes to saw off her victims’ hands and feet with wire loops – slowly. And Seka uses her cat-claw to slice apart men’s bodies with hundreds of bone-deep cuts. Now; tell us of your slowest, most excruciating banes.”

For a second, Suna hesitated. In truth, she had never actually used banes to kill a real person, and she questioned her appetite to inflict the kind of suffering of which the Spectres spoke. But this was a chance to fulfil her driving urge, to protect others from monsters like Hekon Hakamanko; had she not come to Kobutsuden for precisely this reason?

“Blackboil,” she said. “It makes the body cook itself, by degree. And creepvein, which paralyses the victim yet allows them to experience the most profound and prolonged agonies.”

“I know of blackboil,” said Seka. “But not creepvein. Perhaps a demonstration...”

“Use it in your test,” said Zoya. “Fulfil this sanction to our satisfaction, and this house may become your new home.”

With that she handed Suna a black envelope, sealed with silver wax.

“We’ll be watching; you have seven days.”

Once more she was blindfolded, then allowed to dress; they led her out and into the stinking streets, turning left, then right, then left again until she knew not north from south. “Seven days,” said Zoya’s voice in her ear; and then she was alone.

Suna spent the next morning at Skullhaven, mourning-veiled, upturning stones to reveal what lay hidden beneath. By noon her jar was filled with wriggling centipedes; green, red-brown, but mostly black. As she watched them writhe she kept reliving, to her surprise, the sensation of Zoya’s probing finger.

Back in her rooms she set to distilling the creepvein ichor, following the formula so often boastfully detailed by Hekon the hunchback. As she toiled she couldn’t help but remember the shack in the forest where Hozon Ama, the warrior-priest who once swore to champion her, had ended up hanging in chains, immobilized by the poison, half his face burnt down to the bone.

Suna knew that such savagery was also the signature of the Silver Spectres, said to have been founded in ancient Kyukiden by Red Girl, the spurned templar assassin. Among the sisterhood's first victims were the Sun mavens who renounced her; the highest of them, Kleptoklovian, was found hanging upside down, naked, his right eyeball cut out and embedded in his rectum, his severed penis hanging from the bloody eye-socket. Now she was about to join the very same sect, and would be expected to be equally merciless.

*I must remember my new name,* she said to herself, and as she did so she thought of her sister, the real Soma, safe but effectively imprisoned in Kyo the Killer's Ossuary. One day she would cross to Wolf's Jaw and liberate her. *One day...*

Before retiring for the night Suna picked up the black envelope, took out the note and read it one more time.

*Namidarian.*

*Molester of children.*

*The Temple of Tears.*

It repeated in her mind, like a parasitic prayer, until she slid into the void of sleep.

# THE SUNSTORM CASTLE

"If thirteen failed, send a hundred," said Lord Nakasendaron. "If they fail, send a thousand."

Taikon Taiyo could see his father's pain. But he knew that it was not as simple as overwhelming numbers; through his spyglass he had seen the rictus of the dead upon man and beast, red-filmed eyes wide in hideously upscrewed faces, lips crusted with pink foam. "It is hard to say that Tanko failed, father. He never even had a chance; he and his men were felled by an invisible assassin, and died in apoplexy before they ever reached the hill. What say you, maven?"

Vorgovanian exhaled sourly. "As you say, Lord Taikon; I would be averse to sending more horses and riders until we better understand this woman's powers. Whether virago or witch, she has cast a veil of death around Sunstorm. And something tells me that she could stand there for another year if she wished, and never move an inch."

"There is another option," said Taikon. "She asks for Kinzokami – why not give it to her, and be done? We will snatch it back in times to come, when we purge Novalis of the Akutenshi revenants and spike her craven head on the Saturn Tower."

Nakasendaron paused for a long while, then said: "Kinzokami was the deathsword of Clan Hexo, forged by the Shadow mavens under Emperor Metakaikon, founder of Novalis. Like this castle, it became ours when Lady Tera, the last living Hexo, married Dankairon Mino, direct descendent of the Yamayaga. But let us not forget that Metakaikon was also progenitor of the Akutenshi bloodline, and the thirteen deathswords were his gift to the founding clans. Perhaps Yuta was wrong; whether or not we credit the claim of the young pretender, this Killstar, does the sword not truly belong to those that created it?"

"You surprise me, Lord Naka," said Vorgovanian. "But I have to agree;

Kinzokami has symbolic power, but does that matter more than the life or death of our people? Sometimes a sword is nothing more than a sword."

"Then it's settled," said Taikon. "Kinzokami will serve the Taiyo one last time, by ridding us of the witch's curse. And when this is over, when a new order rises, we will be reunited in blood."

It was the hottest hour of the day when Taikon Taiyo rode out alone from the gates of Sunstorm under the crossed flag of truce. In his right hand he held aloft Kinzokami, the metal wolf; its blade of volcanic steel flashed and refracted like a silvered lens in the light. As he steered his mount around the caravan of fallen corpses, he could see the hangman's hill ahead. Beneath the bare boughs of its centuried oak stood Lady Morvenna of the Shadow Castle, unmoving, defiant. To her left her two Blue Dragon Hand agents were both crouched, seemingly at ease. As he drew nearer they stood, hands hovering over weapon-belts.

Taikon reined up at the foot of the hill, its slope verdant from blood-rich soil. *If plague were abroad I'd be stricken or dead already, like the others. But if not plague – what?*

"Hundreds have died where you stand," he called up to Lady Morvenna. "That tree is haunted to its roots."

She made no reply.

"Tell us," said the Moon Beast.

"Very well then. You asked for the deathsword – will you take it and leave?"

"As we always said."

Taikon dismounted. He was irked that the woman did not speak.

"First tell me one thing – what killed our guardsmen, and our lady?"

"Greed," said Lady Morvenna finally. Her voice resonated with a strange undercurrent, like the mating sound of wasps.

Taikon felt his anger rise anew at this retort, but knew that either the apoplexy or the two chaos agents would strike him down before he could drive Kinzokami through her throat. Instead he plunged it into the ground with both hands, leaving it swaying there as he turned away.

Taikon never looked back until he reached the castle gates, but when he did the sword, the agents and the woman had gone. Something black was hanging from the oak tree.

His spyglass revealed that it was Lady Morvenna's gown. A naked witch was riding through Goldengate, armed with the deathsword of Clan Taiyo.

*This truly is the Age of Shadows,* he thought. *And none can say how long its terrors and dark wonders will persist.*

That night Lord Nakasendaron sat staring at the empty niche where Kinzokami once reposed. In the space of just one day he had lost his wife, his sword, his honour. Only one thing now remained to him – *vengeance.*

Bold, black, and bloody.

# THUNDERVOID

"The Skull of Swords," grinned Gorn, flipping over the wrinkled card. "Hand me them dice."

Urstinx looked at him blankly.

"I've told you, the Skull of Swords is the bastard death-card of them all – six throws. Get ready to lose your night army."

Urstinx pushed the carved-bone cubes towards Gorn, then scattered his cards face down on the table. "I'm done," he said, swilling the lees of his rye mash.

In truth, Gorn knew only the bare rudiments of darkthrone himself, picked up from Tazon Ando during the siege of Mortmane. The worn set of twenty-three cards was Ando's parting gift. He idly studied the hand-painted design that decorated each one, a snow-covered graveyard and a skeletal hand emerging from a crypt. If Gorn could read letters, he would have known that the name on the crypt door was SEK.

Both men were huddled in leather and furs, freezing ocean air from above seeping into the cabin and chilling their flesh despite the glowing brazier by their feet.

"How much longer?" said Urstinx.

After a pause, Gorn replied: "We'll give him one more day. After that, we go looking." He knew that the trail to Komonyama was treacherous, and that the pirate Bloodspike might never even make it back. There were stories not only of monsters in the sea and rivers, but of sudden white death lurking beneath the decimated demesne's glassy surface. And who knew what other dangers awaited in the guts of the volcano itself? *Sorrows willing, we'll never need find out.*

Just before dusk, his prayers were answered when Mushon Yowa appeared below deck.

"Pirates," he said.

Within minutes the three Kurotako ships were manoeuvring into the river's mouth in an arrowhead formation, with Yowa's *Hexbound Heart* at the tip. Captain Bloodspike's vessel, the *Red Wraith*, was approaching at speed with wind-filled sails.

"He'll have to stop," said Gorn, standing at the prow with hands on hips. "A direct collision will sink him before us; we've twice his bulk."

"Let's hope *he* knows that," said Urstinx.

As the *Red Wraith* grew ever closer, Gorn was starting to wonder. If the ship did go down and its cargo was lost, so was their chance of getting paid by Viron Voraxo. The waters were cold enough to freeze blood, and so murky with poisons that no living man could survive them; salvage would be impossible.

"Get the men ready to board ship," he told Urstinx. "If that madman hits us we'll need to sweep through before the whole lot goes under."

As the pirate ship drew closer, Gorn could see a figure planted on its foredeck, staring back at him across the ever-diminishing expanse of river that separated them. *Bloodspike, no doubt.* The man was tall but clearly not young; age had begun to stoop his shoulders, and his tangled grey mane circled a bald pate. Another minute, and the two men would be face to face.

Then Bloodspike's arm went up, the sails dropped down, and Gorn saw an enormous anchor launching from astern. Still the *Red Wraith* plowed on towards the *Hexbound Heart*; only when the two ships' prows were yards apart did the anchor chain pull taut, sending a shuddering wave of curtailed momentum through the pirate vessel. Captain Bloodspike lurched forwards, steadied himself on the wooden rail.

"Make way, eight-arms!" he shouted at Gorn. "Now!"

"Not me," replied Gorn, showing his two hands. "Your strife with the Octopus is none of my concern; I work for me. Now; give us what you took from the volcano, and we'll gladly move aside."

Bloodspike motioned with his arm, and Jik No-Nose stepped forward. He was carrying a burlap bundle, which he dangled over the side of the ship. "I'd sooner send it to the deep," said Bloodspike.

Gorn said nothing, trying to assess whether his adversary was bluffing. This wasn't working out as he'd planned; they probably should've chained the river, he realised, and launched an ambush when the pirate ship crashed to a halt. He'd given Bloodspike too much warning.

"How much?" he said eventually. "Name your price, and let's keep things friendly."

Bloodspike raised a hand to his beard, and seemed to be weighing Gorn's proposal. Gorn noticed that his ring finger was just a stump, and an image of Akumuron

Mizuno's blackened, rotting digit floated up, unbidden, at the back of his mind.

And then he realised.

"Fuck's blood!" he exclaimed. "It's you, isn't it? You're Akumuron, Lord of Nightmares... you're supposed to be fucking dead, last I heard."

The pirate made no response, but the more Gorn looked at him, the more certain he was.

"You hired me to shift sword more than two years back... me and Kesh. It was you that bought him from the Grinding Pits... Mastiff, they used to call him, after he took too much firefinger and bit off another fighter's cock."

At that, Captain Bloodspike seemed to relent. "And if you're right... how does that solve our problem?" he asked. "You must know I want more than coin."

Gorn's mind was already racing. *No, dead men don't just want coin. They want revenge, revenge on the world of the living. Kill him now and the bones are lost... the only choice is to play this out.*

"Show me," Gorn said. "Show me what's in the sack."

Bloodspike turned his head, nodded once at Jik. The mutilated mariner reached into the burlap, rummaged for a second, then held up a jawless skull. Voraxo had spoken of an alchemical test to prove the bones authentic, but Gorn knew nothing of that. He'd have to rely on the word of a dead Mizuno overlord turned resurrected pirate.

"Come aboard, and tell me what you want," he said.

Bloodspike gave a cold smile. "So you can ransom me for the bones? I've already lost one finger, and I plan to keep the rest. We can talk here just fine. Now; tell me who's paying you, and why."

"Some perfumed cunt called Voraxo, from the Velvet Castle. All I know is, he wants to break away from the Hakamanko... but what the bones've got to do with it, I couldn't tell you."

"I think I already know," said Bloodspike. His tone seemed to have further softened at mention of Voraxo, and Gorn sensed for the first time that they might resolve this without the spilling of blood.

"Pray tell," he said.

# THE NIGHTMARE CASTLE

"There *are* diseases which turn the body to solid bone," said Chironax, "but each takes a good number of years to progress. A man becoming a statue in seconds – that is not something science could allow me to believe."

Noxon Taiyo sighed and reached into his carry-sack. "Believe this."

He dropped Pukon Sota's head onto the maven's desk with a crash which threatened to splinter the polished rosewood. Chironax recoiled, eyes blinking. The dead ranger's skin had the texture of cracked grey leather, the flesh visible within the neck of similar hue and as tough and dry as long-boiled meat. Even the spinal bone was grey, its granular marrow set like mortar. The jaw was hinged open, rigid, and the wide-staring eyes were shiny, blood-veined stones.

"This," said Jukon Gomi, "is what happens when a man's shadow hides inside his body. I saw it with my own eyes – we both did."

Chironax looked at one and then the other, and knew that the pair were in deadly earnest. "Leave the head with me," he said. "Allow me to perform some tests, a dissection."

"You'll need a hammer and spike," Noxon replied.

Jukon said: "Very well. But this is not the only wonder brought back from the Valley of Flies."

He unfolded a velvet cloth, showing Chironax the star-shaped silver disc wrapped within. "You see the ideogram? This is the Key of Shadows, one of the seven imperial instruments. It was held in a metal receptacle buried in a woman's chest, and only when we removed it did the light in her eyes go out. I ask you – what sort of woman is that?"

Again, Chironax paused for thought. Then he said: "I believe that is a question for brother Chromocrax."

The doll-maven was tinkering with his new replica of Lady Kollabia, the Bloodtooth Virgin once sacrificed in a demonstration of explosive force to Miura Mizuno, when he heard a rapping at the laboratory door.

"Kargon? Is that you?"

He hardly ever saw the boy these days, ever since Lady Miura – or Black Phoenix, as she now called herself – had seemingly taken a shine to him. Once he'd glimpsed him in a tower window, stark naked, before the drapes were abruptly pulled across by a red-nailed hand. But Kargon had his own key, he remembered; this must be someone else.

"Coming!"

It was Seron Kako, white-armoured captain of the Vertigo Watch. Next to him stood a young, black-haired man of equal stature whose own breastplate, black inset with a coral spiral, was Kako's wrought in negative.

"Lord Jukon Gomi, overlord of the Starfire Order," Kako announced.

Chromocrax bowed. "A rare honour. Have you come to inspect my death-doll?"

Jukon shook his head wrily. "Actually, I'd like you to inspect mine."

It took them a full twenty minutes to descend into the lower levels of the Terror Tower, where Jukon Gomi's mysterious prisoner was hidden away in near total gloom. She was spread out on a torture-table, hooded, motionless and stripped naked, an empty, circular metal aperture set between what remained of her breasts.

"Her guards were Blue Dragon Hand," said Jukon. "One died, one escaped. She is Akutenshi, of the Shadow Castle."

"And her name?" asked Chromocrax, his excitement mounting. "Did she tell you her name?"

"Tyranna."

The maven closed his eyes. It was a beautiful, fabled name he had known all his life, since first reading Gammabarion's *War Of The Dolls* as a child.

"My dear Lord Jukon," he breathed, "this is a miracle indeed… you have captured nothing less than one of the Seven Deadly Archangels."

*And so the pendulum swings,* thought Jukon as the midnight hour approached. The Key of Bones was lost, but now he held something even more precious. Their decision to bring Lady Tyranna here, away from the million eyes of the city, had proven wise; more so since this old maven, Chromocrax, was evidently more learned in such matters than most of his peers. Yet his orders to the doll-maker were clear; there would be no invasion or destruction of Tyranna's body, for she was not dead but merely dormant, and a priceless prize in the power game with the Akutenshi. And so she would remain as long as Jukon held her in his grasp.

# THE SLAUGHTERHOUSE

"It would indeed be a great honour to return Yomuji to its creators, Lady Sybella," said Sadogashon Kutotako, balancing the sword on the palms of his hands and eyeing his compressed reflection in the vampire steel. The bane virago Lady Nightstorm stood behind him, one hand resting on his clan chair of chiselled crimson seastone. "Or then again, perhaps I'll just fuck you with it."

As if on cue, two Arms of the Octopus stepped forward and took hold of Sybella, one on each side. Her lifesguards, Yuron Fuki and Shibiton Vogo, had protested vehemently, but vainly, when she acceded to the demands of Blind Baragon. The ferryman would only allow her to cross from Blood Crag to the Red Rock if unaccompanied and under armed guard; now she was alone in the Slaughterhouse at the mercy of Lord Bloodtooth, his courtiers and his watchmen.

"I remind you once again," she said to Sadogashon, "I am the envoy of Dorion Killstar, true emperor of Novalis, and come under flag of truce."

"I see no flag," replied the Octopus, "just an Akutenshi whore. We want no part of your empire, or your wars. You should have gone begging elsewhere; there is nothing but death here for you and your kind."

He turned to Lady Nightstorm. "What do you think?" he asked. "Should we feed her to Crogor?"

Lady Sybella never struggled. But her eyes, the same midnight blue as her tightly contoured gown, seemed to grow larger by the second as if drinking all light from the vestibule. *If those eyes could weep,* Nightstorm found herself thinking, *they might drown the world in blood.*

And then Sybella wept.

Across the Bay of Bones, the two Blue Dragon agents fretted on their lady's return.

"The black barge is not coming back," said Fuki, the Ghost Blizzard. "Have we delivered the Archangel into a death-trap?"

"The Kurotako are devolved," replied Vogo, the Corpse Whisper, pushing back a loose lock of hair. "They support neither Starfire nor Snake. So why should they risk war with the Shadow Castle over a sword?"

"Perhaps because we number but twenty?" suggested Fuki. "This Lord Sado is known for violence and lust; they say he drowned his own wife when she complained about his concubines, and fed her to the sharks."

"We may be twenty, but the Celestial Hive are twenty thousand. They could form a human bridge across this bay, and smash the iron castle to flinders."

"Aye, but human beasts like Sado live within the moment; caution is not in their nature. Think only of our own late emperor... Wait; did you hear that?"

It started as the dull groan of sheet metal under torture. Then the groaning turned to a series of sharp retorts as fractures appeared across the black surface of the Slaughterhouse and bolts were blasted outwards with projectile force. Finally a great section of lower wall peeled away to one side, and the foaming torrent of salt water burst out as if a great dam had been ruptured. Drowned corpses were floating in the water as it sluiced over the porphyry rocks and into the ocean like a raging cataract; one of them was Lord Sadogashon Kurotako's, snagged on a slimy pinnacle.

For a second it seeemed that the Slaughterhouse itself might tear apart and topple, but then the water began to subside, leaving a single ragged hole agape in the castle cladding. Lifeless bodies were strewn over the Red Rock in the flood's wake, as Shark White and Shell Crush clansmen on surrounding islands took to their catboats and servitors emerged, panic-stricken, from the upper levels of the deluged edifice. The pale face of a boy-child could be seen in one window, peering down at his father's mortal remains.

Then came a grinding of chains, as the black barge was once more set in motion. The guards who had crossed on it were nowhere to be seen. Blind Baragon was at the vessel's prow, as ever, but his hands did not move. One of the iron bolts exploding from the castle wall had shot through his forehead, right between his lidless, white-filmed eyes. A small hole, trickling blood, marked its entry. But when it emerged at the back of his head the bolt had blown out the entire skull and brains, leaving only a gaping shell.

Lady Sybella stood behind the dead ferryman. Her hair and gown were saturated, as if she had just emerged from the sea; in her right hand, thrust into the air, she held the deathsword Yomuji, the maggot bride.

Before any realised what was happening amidst the chaos, the barge reached its destination. It scraped along the rocky edge of Blood Crag before coming to a halt, and Yuron Fuki quickly pulled Sybella up and onto the stone jetty where their horses were tied.

For a short while the three Akutenshi stood and watched as the Red Rock was consumed by frantic Kurotako retainers and vassals, swarming around their dead overlord like ants mourning a cannibalised queen. A few seemed to point in their direction, but they were too distant to pose any threat.

As they rode away from the crag heading south-west towards the Sepulchre, Shibiton Vogo reflected that this day would soon become legend, and that children as yet unborn would one day marvel at the tale of the Archangel and the Octopus.

# THE SHADOW CASTLE

Every morning Sasora studied the curvature of her belly in the looking-glass, praying to Sorrow Sukion that the swelling would hold at bay until the Killing Moon spun away from its zenith. When that time finally arrived, she would be ready to reveal her secret; but to whom? She believed that the Black Reaper would welcome an addition to the resurgent Akutenshi bloodline, but he was unpredictable; he might just as easily kill her and burn her body without the young emperor-to-be even knowing.

One the other hand, she knew that Dorion was in her sway. She had visited him twice again since their first nocturnal encounter, each time lingering a little longer, pressing a little closer, nurturing within him a feverish obsession with the scent and wet heat of her cunt. Even if the thought of her gravid belly scared him, she was sure that the burning lust which the young inevitably mistake for love would over-ride his apprehension. And once he believed that Night Sun's child was his, none could ever dare gainsay it. *Dorion, then. And just a few more weeks to wait.*

By noon, the sea beyond the walls was as grey and flat as hammer-beaten iron. An albino bird swooped down from the cold dead sky and fluttered onto its perch. Around its pink leg was a scroll from the Sun Shrine, and Glitterax hurriedly relayed it to Kuron Kirizono.

"The message is from Hachi," he announced, "and ill-met. *The Lady Tyranna is lost, held hostage by the lords of Starfire. Choko is dead. I await your direction.*"

Kirizono threw the scroll onto the council table, his face darkening.

"Dire news," said Glitterax. "But let us not despair. The remaining Archangels are yet abroad, and will seek out their sister as unerringly as a hound tracks its prey. They are connected through the metacarrion, and that bond cannot be shattered. And let us not forget that two more deathswords have already been retrieved, and are securely held at the Sepulchre."

"But if Lady Tyranna is held in a place of no shadows, powerless? What if she is destroyed?"

"Jukon Gomi is not that stupid," Glitterax assured the Reaper. "As Hachi says, he will hold her to ransom. The question is, where?"

"From the Valley of Flies there are few safe havens," said Kirizono. "To the west, Smash-Bone pirates control the coast. To the north, only wastelands held by rebel clans – it's said that impaling spikes line the Burnt Cat Bridge, and not one is shy a Starfire corpse. Their nearest refuge lies in either Kobutsuden to the east, or at the Nightmare Castle in the south where the Mizuno bitch cowers behind a Taiyo army. Since the deathsword Seppunryu that Tyranna hunted is held by Noxon Taiyo, my bet is on the castle."

"And what of the Night Wasp?"

"Send reply by whitest wing; tell him to cross to the Sepulchre, and form a spear with Shura, Chimori, Gekka and Toka. Lady Samara is already bound for the Nightmare Castle; let them join her lifesguard. Miura Mizuno harbours the deathsword Jigobanmon and, it seems, Seppunryu and Lady Tyranna both. Soon all three will be once more ours. Nano; fetch Dorion."

"There is one more thing," said Glitterax as the Devil Bat turned away. "I have heard that my brother, Chromocrax, now resides at Nightmare; and, by all accounts, he has the ear of Lady Miura. Let me add a note for Brother Katavarian, and ask him in turn to send word to Chromo. What better than a spy in our opponent's very bosom?"

# THE REDWRAITH

In the end, Gorn had decided to board the pirate ship, alone, to parlay with its captain. He was hoping that Bloodspike, once Akumuron, was still more lord than corsair so far as honour went; besides, he had nothing to gain by Gorn's death. Nor would holding him ransom hold any sway with the berserkers, who would never let something as meaningless as a man's life stand between them and their chance of gold, friend or not.

Bloodspike's cabin was sparsely appointed, but its wall sported one conspicuous trophy – the mummified head of its previous occupant.

"That's old Captain Crowspit," said the pirate as he splashed rye mash into two tarnished pewter cups. "Once second-in-command under Captain Scarebones until I seized the *Red Wraith*, and half the Curse chose to follow me. Scarebones had a slaver's life in mind, but I offered them more blood and booty."

"Then I'd best tell you this now," said Gorn. "Blood was all they got; my boys killed every last one of them five days back."

Bloodspike shrugged. "What I'd expect. They were small men with small minds, no better than the scum who took my finger. Of course I indulged their petty lust for coin, but that was never more than a sop to keep them loyal. When I reap my vengeance it will be measured in souls, not gold. The future of Novalis is at stake."

Gorn took a sip from his cup, wincing at the liquor's sour heat. "How so?"

"Some call it history, some legend," said the pirate, "but either way it's happening again now. The Vermin League is real, and it's led by a madman who wants–"

"Lord Hebon," Gorn interrupted. "I know; I've met him."

"Then you also know I'm not lying. Unless you want Novalis ruled by demon-worshippers, you'll listen to what I have to say."

"Go on."

"When Bankairon Yamayaga was murdered by the Hakamanko, the Akutenshi hid the truth. The tales of him sailing back to Shinowana to save Emperor Jaikon are nothing but myth woven by Metakaikon and the Shadow mavens. But secretly, they responded by creating the imperial instruments; so began the Age of Lightning. Now the Age of Shadows is upon us, and Bankairon's bones are worth far more than coin. They stand as a symbol of light against darkness, and within the Vermin League their desecration and immolation is revered as a black magic working that can raise the powers of Hell."

Gorn set his cup down. "A friend of mine once said there's no magic in this world, just drugs that make you think there is. I'm with him."

"And yet thinking is believing, and belief is a weapon more powerful than steel. My plan for the bones was to use them as a pyre for Lord Hebon, to burn him alive in a cleansing inferno. And after that... well, it matters not; I'm now alone, save for these few faceless wretches, and those dreams are turned to dust. This Viron Voraxo seeks to usurp the Snake Lord, by what you say; then let us help him start a conflict that will rip the Hakamanko apart from within. All I ask of you is safe escort; otherwise the Kurotako sea-swine will hang me at first opportunity."

Gorn paused for a moment. *He's lost his mind, let alone his fucking finger. But if we can keep him happy and still get paid, that's good enough for me.* "Right then," he said. "Sounds like we've got a deal. Just make sure that ugly cunt doesn't drop the bones overboard."

During the short sail down the coast Gorn thought of Hebon Hakamanko, his black robe patterned with twining red snakes, his heavily ringed hand ever clutching a bag that stank of rotten meat. *Whatever he is, it's not good. If Voraxo can get rid of him, so much the better.* But Gorn had also heard whispers about the Velvet Castle, about orgies of depravity and refineries where Tower Bat clansmen bottled blood to be stored like fine wine. He drew his fur cloak more tightly around his shoulders and watched his breath as it steamed in swirls like mist above a graveyard.

Captain Bloodspike was right; belief was a powerful weapon. But fear was more deadly yet.

# CASTLE NIGHTFOG

Corvon Natto stood atop the Tower of Shades, highest vantage-point of Castle Nightfog. Far to the south-east he could see black smoke rising from Lizard's Den, and knew that the Hakamanko were under prolonged assault. Natto prayed that the fighting would not spread any further north; Nightfog, the ancient seat of Clan Mishima, was ill-manned to engage in ground warfare. The Takasha guard who manned its walls were thinly deployed, and even hunting for food brought its own dangers when rebel clansmen in the Viles were free to make cross-border raids at will. Nightfog had never been successfully stormed, but these were truly trying times.

Yet what concerned Natto most was the scroll which had arrived by Starfire rider that very morning, bearing the solar seal of Clan Taiyo. The message was a dire warning from Lord Taikon, and had been relayed to all Starfire overlords and castellans.

*Beware witch envoys from the Shadow Castle,* it read. *They seek our swords of power and bring only death; do not suffer them to enter your strongholds, else all will be lost. The one named Lady Morvenna killed my mother. Burn them all.*

Castle Nightfog held no deathsword – Seppunryu, the dragon kiss, was lost during the Serpent Wars – but it was the name of Lady Morvenna which caught Corvon Natto's eye and set his mind afire. That night at dinner he found himself gazing upon the hall's great mural, *Doll-Hunter's Night Attack,* the only one of its kind ever painted by the fabled portrait artist Chixon I. Commissioned by Lord Usagon Mishima in the year 687, the vast painting covered an entire wall from floor to ceiling and took Chixon seven months to complete. It showed Usagon's ancestor, Lord Tekaton Mishima, on horseback impaling three nude female dolls with his lance. The dolls were transfixed through their throats, one behind the other, and Lord Tekaton was lifting them high into the air as his legendary white stallion Kurochinko reared up on its massive hind legs. Kurochinko's dark-sheathed penis, carefully delineated by the artist, hung down to the ground in a great curving arc as if to reinforce the domination of male over female. Across the bottom of the image, inches above the hall's flagstones, was an ornate inscription. *Flowers bloom in the night-land. Inside each, a conspiracy of scars.*

"What troubles you?" asked Lady Zira.

Natto turned his eyes back to his wife. Three times she had let slip a child before it was fully formed, spoiling her womb and leaving him devoid of issue; yet he had never strayed to another's bed, and nor would he deceive her now.

"History," he said. "Or myth. My forefather, Kirron Natto, was chosen as first castellan of Nightfog by the Takasha for a specific reason – he was directly descended from Nubon Natto, one of those who, legend tells, first rose up to persecute a holocaust against the unnatural creations of Emperor Metakaikon and his Shadow mavens. Nubon Natto and Tekaton Mishima were both founders of the Knights of Slithammer, the secret society of doll-hunters who purged the Templedark from point to point during the stormlit end years of century one."

"Then you are also descended from Nubon," observed Zira. "But this *is* just myth, is it not? Why do you mention it now?"

"The dolls," said Corvon. "They're back."

# APPENDIX ONE
# THE EBON WEIRD

"It was an epoch of bloodthirsty devils. The emperor Jaikon was old and frail, his realm decaying beneath a death hex cast by the demon king, Arkestron, and his cannibal concubine, Baragasha. They feasted on the corpses of babies, infants, victims procured by their roaming black coven, the Vermin League. Jaikon sought salvation by summoning his protector Bankairon, regent of the Yamayaga clan, and his four guardian reavers, the Night Angels – Ogon Kayo, Bayon Teppa, Semon Ginza, and Nankon Dojo. This was the time of the Hell Crusade.

"It is said that the magician Hakamankon, master of serpents, lay at the putrid heart of the Vermin League. Hakamankon, who commanded the rape of Tamagaisho, the Hell-prostitute, by the giant snake Hebochi, a bestial union that engendered equally bestial offspring – a witch-child named Komaja, and her twin brother, the devil-child Arkestron.

"When Komaja was nine years old, she found a dead body and kept it as a companion until it crumbled. When she was eleven, she acquired a taste for corpse-meat. When she was thirteen, she killed and devoured the guardian monks who had raised her.

"Cast into the wilderness, Komaja was adopted by Hikarion, a toad immortal, who taught her secret arts of necromancy and the resurrection of the dead. When Komaja was fully-grown, Hikarion returned her to Hakamankon, who took her for his bride at a clandestine orgy, the masque of the red snake.

"Komaja's twin, the devil-child, was also banished. No temple would accept him, and so he was nailed inside a binding box of lizard-bones and hurled into icy waters. But the devil-child did not die; it is said that he dined upon the bones until the box was rotted away.

"He walked through winter wastes to the mountain of Jigo, where he fed on corpses and grew into a demon of death. Men called him Arkestron. With his bare hands, Arkestron forged a castle of twisted metal. Inside the castle he built a chamber of human bones, and inside this chamber he performed nightly sacrifices, rites and atrocities, until he was able to raise Zenmarion, the King of Hell.

"Zenmarion gave Arkestron command of five torture-demons from his deepest circles of damnation – Kumakara, Torakuma, Hoshikuma, Kanaguma, and Baragasha. The cruel depredations of these evil angels struck fear and despair throughout the land, *which Arkestron swore to destroy by annihilating all human progeny. His malediction burned in a cataclysm of still-birth and cradle-death, and the bones of children rose up in gleaming white mountains...*

*"...Rajo, the great gate of Haigo city, lay in ruins, desecrated by a death cult of infant sacrifices to the she-demon Baragasha. These obscene rites were presided over by the cannibal hag Yashroki, high priestess of ordures and filth.*

*"Bankairon ordered Bayon Teppa, most battle-hardened of his Night Angels, to Rajo without delay. His mission was to exorcise all evil from the gate and its beleaguered surrounds.*

*"Three weeks later, through woodlands blasted by lightning and driving rain, Teppa invaded the hovel of the hag Yashroki and took away her head as she slept, tying it tight in a leather sack. At Rajo, he confronted Baragasha. Her face twisted and palpitated, her eyeballs boiled; gouts of venomous saliva rained across Teppa's armour, scorching the metal. The she-demon was angry, and hungry.*

*"Teppa's blade swung in a great blow; Baragasha's left arm was severed above the elbow. With a profane ululation, the she-demon ebbed away and vanished into spirals of the night. Her arm, oozing foetid pus, convulsed on the ground; Teppa seized the limb and locked it away in his spell box, a wooden conundrum inscribed with binding symbols by ancient Szuchin monks. He would return with two trophies of war, and a glorious tale to tell. But the demon limb banged ceaselessly against the box's inner lid all the way back to the city.*

*"That night in a Haigo inn, Teppa was hailed as a hero. A new dancer, Akiko, begged to hear the story of his conquest of Baragasha, and to see the monster's severed arm. After six bottles of rice wine, Teppa was unable to refuse.*

*"After showing off the twisted and bloody limb, Teppa fell asleep with the one-armed girl naked in his bed. When he awoke, in deepest night, she was no longer next to him; and she was no longer human. Before he could grasp his sword, Baragasha flew from the inn, her severed limb still clamped between foul fangs, and coiled away into the forest far beyond. She lived – but never again would she or her cannibal hag haunt the great arch of Rajo...*

*"...Soon after Baragasha was banished from Rajo, Bankairon received word from his most powerful Night Angel, Ogon Kayo, who was fighting demons in Renko province, near the city of Kago. Kayo told of a gigantic flying skull that burned a nocturnal fire-trail of terror; he urged Bankairon to join him in Renko with all haste.*

*"Pursuing the skull a few nights later, Bankairon and his loyal reaver discovered a huge, derelict palace high in the mountains, a ruin haunted by evil ghosts. On the very next day Bankairon fell sick, and was laid low in one of the palace's vast, web-strewn bed chambers. At midnight, he was visited by a beautiful woman who brought him medicine; she said she was a spinstress, the last surviving servant of the palace.*

*"For two more nights, the pale lady attended to Bankairon. But his fever only worsened. At the fourth midnight, Bankairon captured her true image in his amulet, the Mirror of Souls; he then knew at once that his nurse was a spider-vampire – a shape-changing assassin from the Vermin League.*

*"Bankairon was weak; the vampire shrank back to avoid his sword-strike, and as she fled into the night she spat a mesh of rank, viscous webbing over the delirious demon-hunter. But Bankairon's blade had bitten its victim's breast. A trail of black blood led Kayo and his men along a vertiginous mountain path until, at dawn, they discovered the entrance to a subterranean lair. And there they saw the spider-vampire in all its true eight-legged horror, surrounded by webs which were hung with human skeletons.*

*"Metal spikes, axes, spears and swords plunged into the creature's swollen belly, releasing the tortured souls of its victims as its life bled into the dirt. Each soul was in the form of a tiny spider with a screaming man's head, and there were hundreds of them.*

*"With the destruction of the vampire, Bankairon's sickness left him. And from that day on, his sword which caused the trail of blood was known as Kumokiri, the spider-slasher...*

*"...High in his castle of burnished metal atop the goblin-haunted mountain of Jigo, the demon king Arkestron railed for revenge against those who had maimed his concubine, Baragasha. His supplications were duly heard by Zenmarion, King of Hell, and soon Zenmarion's cruellest demon, a monster with blue skin and red hair by name of Astaron, was regurgitated from the underworld.*

*"In Hell, Astaron's daily task was the dismembering of sinners who were chained to a great rock; on earth, he was given an equally singular purpose – the extermination of Bankairon and his valiant Night Angels.*

*"The blue demon set forth to Soko, where he slaughtered twenty warriors of the Yamayaga clan. Hearing of this murderous rampage, Bankairon and his reavers made haste to the afflicted countryside. A week later, as they emerged from dense forest onto the field of Soko, they found nothing but death. The rotted corpses of men were mingled with those of cattle; most had been stripped clean of flesh. Even for a demon from Hell, killing was hungry work.*

"Suddenly, one of the bestial carcasses burst into life. Concealed beneath its pestilent hide, Astaron sprang his heinous death-trap. Unfortunately for the Hell-creature, Bankairon's sword Kumokiri had an unquenchable thirst for demon blood, an insatiable hunger for demon flesh. As did Ogon Kayo's axe, which cleaved Astaron's head from his shoulders even as Kumokiri pinned him to the ground.

"Legend tells that Astaron's head, though completely severed, continued to scream foul blasphemies for several days during the ride back to Kago. And that his headless body, still swinging its sword, careened blindly about the field of Soko until the sun set deep in the west...

"...At the emperor's palace in Kago, Bankairon presented the head of Astaron, a trophy to mark a great victory in the Hell Crusade. But Jaikon wanted more; he ordered Bankairon to storm the metal castle of Arkestron on Mount Jigo, and to return with the monster's head. Bankairon and his Night Angels were joined by the knight Kimitaka, whose daughter was abducted by the demon Kumakara for his shackle of naked girl-slaves. The six warriors made vengeance vows at the shrine of Sensorion, god of war.

"Disguised as priests, the six pursued the blighted road that led to the slopes of Mount Jigo. Shadowed by thick forest, fearful of attack by cannibal goblins, they forged upward amid glacial sheets of black granite, across chasms whose distant depths dimly gleamed with the bones of the fallen, along paths of pulverised teeth and tunnels hewn from pure avalanche, to Kinzonamida – the demon's castle of metal tears.

"Guardian demons ushered the wanderers through the twisted iron gates, through great concentric hallways daubed with eyeballs and crimson fur, and into the demon king's pleasure chamber. There sprawled Arkestron, surrounded by devils and naked slaves. Next to him sat Baragasha, her arm stump fitted with a spiked metal fist. Arkestron welcomed his new guests; the soft flesh of six priests would make a fine dinner.

"Leering at them, Arkestron extended all hospitality. It was part of his cruelty, his perverse pleasure, to pamper his victims before butchering them. Food, wine and women were proffered; the monster's guests partook. Fearful of being recognised, Bayon Teppa, the maimer of Baragasha, remained hooded and disguised.

"When the first cups were drained, Bankairon offered his host a special devotion – monastic wine, the rarest vintage. Each man pulled a bottle from his travel-bag, and poured a cup for their demonic drinking companions. But for Arkestron and Baragasha, only an entire bottle would suffice.

"The wine was poisoned. One by one, the demons slipped into a death-like slumber. First, they had to be bound. Then, they had to be dismembered. Finally

*Bankairon's sword, Kumokiri, sheared through the neck of Arkestron in a sweep of savage death.*

*"But death did not come. The monster's eyes opened and the grievous head flew up into the air, hovering, expanding in size, vomiting curses, flames and plagues of insects, and invoking the forces of Hell...*

*"...The ruins of the Aken palace, in the forest of Simo, was a house of snakes, a house of scorpions, a house of spiders. It was a house of the dead, a black mausoleum where the magician Hakamankon sat upon a gigantic, venomous toad, while his witch-bride Komaja rode the neck of Hebochi, the red nightmare serpent. Their servants were goblins, gargoyles, and vagina-faced ghosts. By night they summoned forth the dwellers of a thousand graveyards – rotting meat, skin and bones for the Vermin League.*

*"The emperor Jaikon now faced the hordes of Zenmarion, King of Hell. Even as Bankairon and his Night Angels battled the demon king Arkestron on Mount Jigo, a corpse army heralded by Hebochi and led by seven towering skeletons, each made of a thousand dead men's bones fused by rage, and seven giants made from human waste, was advancing to the very gates of Kago. This was the beginning of endless carnage, a war which drove the emperor Jaikon's son, Metakaikon, to abandon his homeland in search of a new empire across the fathomless sea."*

# APPENDIX TWO
# THE CLANS OF NOVALIS

## CLAN AKUTENSHI

The Imperial Clan

Founded in Shinowana before historical records began. The last Akutenshi emperor of Shinowana was Jaikon. His son, Metakaikon, founded Clan Akutenshi of Novalis in the year zero. The clan's demesne is Thundervoid. The clan's ancestral homes are the Camellia Keep in the northern capital Kyukiden, and the Shadow Castle. They also built the Winter Palace, in the southern capital Kobutsuden. The clan's banner shows two silver thunderbolts convergent upon black. Their deathsword is Tekizan, decapitator of foemen.

RAIKON AKUTENSHI, known as DEATHSTAR – The Emperor.

THE BLUE DRAGON HAND – A secret sect of twenty-three chaos agents.

KURON KIRIZONO, known as BLACK REAPER – Clan general.

GLITTERAX – Clan maven.

LADY SLAXONSLIT – Clan bane virago.

THE RASCAL – Clan carnifex (Kobutsuden).

GORN OF GLUTTONPORT – A former palace guard (Kobutsuden).

VASSAL CLANS OF THE DEMESNE

The Ice Cock clan.

The Root Skin clan.

**CLAN GOMI**

Founded by Shishukon Gomi in the year one. The clan's demesne is the Shines. The clan's ancestral home is the Mirror Castle; they are also wardens of Skin Castle. The clan's banner shows a flesh-hued vortex upon black. Their deathsword is Obochi, the graveyard king.

LORD KAMOSUKON GOMI – Clan overlord.

LORD VAKON GOMI – His elder son.

LORD JUKON GOMI – His son.

LADY JUKA GOMI – His daughter, a twin to Jukon.

MAGMATHARION – Clan maven.

GRAVEDIGGER – Clan carnifex.

LADY VIXENVANE – Clan bane virago.

THE DUST DEMONS – The clan horseguard.

VASSAL CLANS OF THE DEMESNE

The Rape Chain clan.

The Wormheart clan.

The Golden Maggot clan.

The Spectre Moth clan.

The Hag Bleeder clan.

The Split-Tongue Raven clan.

The Crookback Cur clan.

## CLAN HAKAMANKO

Founded by Haxokokon Hakamanko (originally known as Kaiton Nobunaga) in the year seventeen. The clan's demesne is Lizard's Den. The clan's ancestral home is Skull Castle; they are also wardens of the Velvet Castle. The clan's banner shows a white self-devouring snake skeleton upon crimson. Their deathsword is Kurosatsu, the black slaughter.

LORD HEBON HAKAMANKO – Clan overlord.
LORD HEKON HAKAMANKO – His son, a hunchback.
LADY SUNA HAKAMANKO – Hekon's wife, of Clan Kurotako.
HAKON HORA, known as HELLHAWK – Clan general.
BORBORAX – Clan maven.
MAD DOG – Clan carnifex.
LADY VULVOMANE – Clan bane virago.
THE TONGUES OF THE BASILISK – Lord Hebon's lifesguard.
THE REPTILE CRUX – A secret sect of chaos agents.

VASSAL CLANS OF THE DEMESNE
The Iron Talon clan.
The Nightshade clan.
The Blind Cat clan.
The Cut-Belly clan.
The Scorpion Black clan.
The Tower Bat clan.
The Night Weeper clan.
The No-Face clan.

**CLAN TAKASHA**

Founded by Hoshimakon Takasha in the year three. The clan's demesne is the Templedark. The clan's ancestral home is Castle Mortmane; they are also wardens of Castle Nightfog. The clan's banner shows a five-pointed sapphire star upon gold. Their deathsword is Kyami, master of darkness.

LORD HIKIDASHON TAKASHA – Clan overlord.

LORD CHIKON TAKASHA – His elder son.

LORD GOMON TAKASHA – His son.

TOKA TAKASHA – His daughter, aged eleven.

TAZON ANDO – Clan general, a rebel.

SENTANGARION – Clan maven.

BONEHEAD – Clan carnifex.

LADY BLASTOFANE – Clan bane virago.

THE IRON PENTAGRAM – A secret sect of chaos agents.

VASSAL CLANS OF THE DEMESNE

The Hell-Claw clan.

The Demon Red clan.

The Rat Rock clan.

The Crow River clan.

## CLAN KUROTAKO

Founded by Kusokagon Kurotako in the year zero. The clan's demesne is the Bloodtooth Islands. The clan's ancestral home is the Slaughterhouse. The clan's banner shows a black cephalopod upon silver. Their deathsword is Yomuji, the maggot bride.

LORD SADOGASHON KUROTAKO – Clan overlord.

LORD CROTON KUROTAKO – His elder son.

KUCHON KUROTAKO – His son, aged eleven.

LADY SOMA KUROTAKO – His elder daughter.

LADY SUNA KUROTAKO – His daughter.

THE BRIDES OF THE OCTOPUS – His concubines.

KON INUSAME – Fleet commander.

CHROMOCRAX – Clan maven.

KARGON – Apprentice to Chromocrax.

THE CUTTER – Clan carnifex.

LADY NIGHTSTORM – Clan bane virago.

LADY BURNBOLT – A chaos agent.

THE BLOODTOOTH VIRGINS – A secret sect of thirteen chaos agents.

VASSAL CLANS OF THE DEMESNE

The Shark White clan (cannibals).

The Shell Crush clan.

The Crimson Curse clan (pirates, in revolt).

**CLAN MIZUNO**

Founded by Amon Mizuno in the year thirteen. The clan's demesne is the Viles. The clan's ancestral home is the Nightmare Castle. The clan's banner shows a black vortex upon primrose yellow. Their deathsword is Akafuku, the red vengeance.

LORD AKUMURON MIZUNO – Clan overlord.

LADY MIURA MIZUNO – His wife, descended from Clan Hassha.

KICHIGON MIZUNO – His brother, sent to the madhouse.

LADY MESSURA MIZUNO – His daughter.

BATSURON BOKO – Clan general.

CHIRONAX – Clan maven.

THE SCAR FAERY – Clan carnifex.

LADY SNOWSNAKE – Clan bane virago.

THE VERTIGO WATCH – The castle guard.

VASSAL CLANS OF THE DEMESNE

The Maw Fetter clan.

The Grey Ghost clan.

The Whip Flay clan.

The Devil-Dog clan.

The Blood Eagle clan.

The Kill-Claw clan.

The Sickle Wasp Clan.

The Smash-Bones clan (pirates, in revolt).

## CLAN TAIYO

Founded by Dankairon Taiyo (born Mino) in the year three hundred and thirteen. The clan's demesne is Goldengate. The clan's ancestral home is the Sunstorm Castle, built on the ruins of the Six-Star Castle. The clan's banner shows a golden triskelion of the broken sun upon black. Their deathsword is Kinzokami, the metal wolf, originally of Clan Hexo.

LORD NAKASENDARON TAIYO – Clan overlord.
LADY YUTA TAIYO – His wife, of Clan Gomi (a cousin to Kamosukon).
NOXON TAIYO, known as NIGHT SUN – His brother.
LORD TAIKON TAIYO – His elder son.
LORD VELURON TAIYO – His son.
VORGOVANIAN – Clan maven.
SAWTOOTH – Clan carnifex.
LADY FEVERCLAW – Clan bane virago.
THE SOLAR FLAME – A secret sect of chaos agents.

VASSAL CLANS OF THE DEMESNE
The Skull Hog clan (cannibals).
The Diamond Fang clan.
The Fireball Dead clan.
The Iron Dream clan.
The Slit-Civet clan.

**CLAN SEIKYO**

Founded by Kyonon Seikyo in the year seven. The clan's demesne is Wolf's Jaw. The clan's ancestral home is the Ossuary. The clan's banner shows a black death-flower upon blood red. Their deathsword is Honekiri, the bone-cleaver.

LORD KYODOKURON SEIKYO – Clan overlord.

LORD KYOWASHON SEIKYO – His son.

LORD NIKON TABU, known as FLESHSTRIPPER – His fleet commander.

MORGOMOX – Clan maven.

DORION KILLSTAR – Apprentice to Morgomox, and corpse-thief.

THE BIG CHOPPER – Clan carnifex.

LADY HEXHEART – Clan bane virago.

THE SKULL CREED – A secret sect of chaos agents.

VASSAL CLANS OF THE DEMESNE

The Quicksilver clan.

The Phantom Fox clan.

The Spider Hook clan.

The Corpse-Rider clan.

The Blood Jackal clan.

# THE EXTINGUISHED CLANS

**CLAN AKAICHI**

Founded by Atakaton Akaichi in the year seven. Extinguished in the year seven hundred and twenty-three. The clan's ancestral home was the Velvet Castle, in Lizard's Den. The clan's banner showed a row of three scarlet bats upon saffron. Their deathsword was Yahana, the midnight flower.

**CLAN HEXO**

Founded by Jaxojomon Hexo in the year three. Extinguished in the year seven hundred and twenty-two. The clan's ancestral home was the Six-Star Castle, in Goldengate. The clan's banner showed a white wolf's skull upon gravesoil brown. Their deathsword was Kinzokami, the metal wolf.

**CLAN SATOGAWA**

Founded by Satokrokon Satogawa in the year twelve. Extinguished in the year seven hundred and twenty. The clan's ancestral home was Castle Bloodflower, in the Viles. The clan's banner showed a white wreath of insect pincers upon midnight blue. Their deathsword was Jigomonban, Hell's gatekeeper.

**CLAN MISHIMA**

Founded by Tekaton Mishima in the year one. Extinguished in the year seven hundred and twenty-three. The clan's ancestral home was Castle Nightfog, in the Templedark. The clan's banner showed a row of seven black swords upon rose pink. Their deathsword was Seppunryu, the dragon kiss.

**CLAN HASSHA**

Founded by Hidemon Hassha in the year nine. Extinguished in the year seven hundred and twenty-one. The clan's ancestral home was the Sepulchre, in Goldengate. The clan's banner showed a black spaded spearhead upon white. Their deathsword was Kaijuken, the monster blade.

**CLAN INOSHI**

Founded by Himanton Inoshi in the year eight. Extinguished in the year seven hundred and twenty-two. The clan's ancestral home was Skin Castle, in the Shines. The clan's banner showed a triskelion of golden tusks upon purple. Their deathsword was Sensoni, the war demon.